Once, she touch
in a kille

Now, she wil

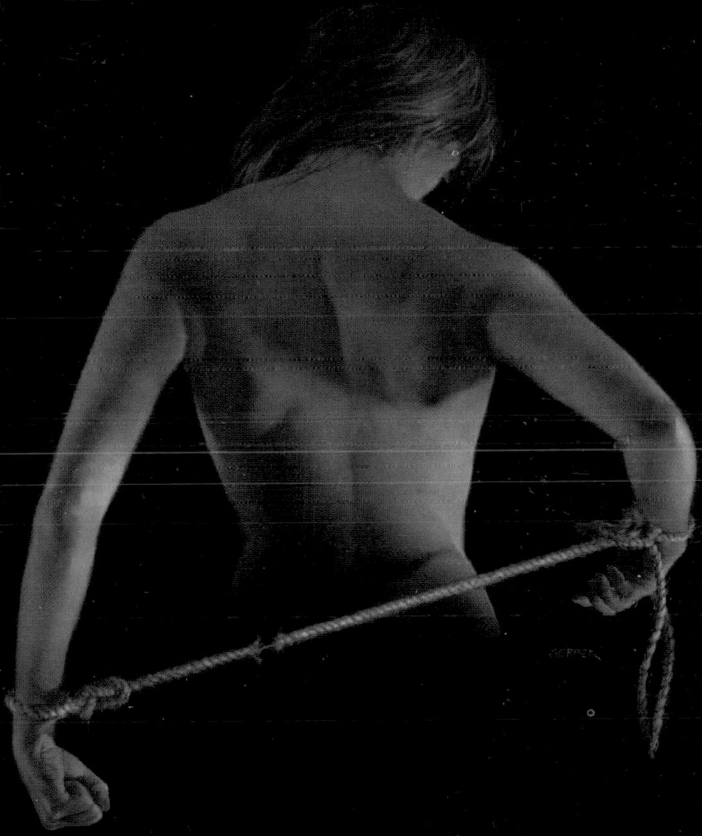

Other titles by Robert W. Walker

PURE INSTINCT

ROBERT W. WALKER

JOVE BOOKS, NEW YORK

PURE INSTINCT

A Jove Book / published by arrangement with
the author

PRINTING HISTORY
Jove edition / October 1995

ISBN: 0-515-11755-2

A JOVE BOOK®
Jove Books are published by The Berkley Publishing Group,
200 Madison Avenue, New York, New York 10016.
JOVE and the "J" design are trademarks
belonging to Jove Publications, Inc.

PRINTED IN THE UNITED STATES OF AMERICA

10 9 8 7 6 5 4 3 2 1

For my parents, Janie Elizabeth MacEachern Walker and Richard Herman Walker, to whom, of course, I owe the greatest debt of all . . . and for my pure storytelling instinct which they might well have squelched at an early age but did not, allowing my imagination to explore and soar instead . . . God bless them both.

Acknowledgments

In creating "authenticated" fiction, the author relied on nonfiction accounts and therefore owes a debt of thanks to innumerable FBI bulletins, as well as Arthur R. Lyons and Marcello Truzzi, Ph.D., for their wonderful work on psychic detection and detectives, *The Blue Sense—Psychic Detectives and Crimes.* I would also like to thank John Dillmann for *The French Quarter Killers,* and Samuel Yochelson, Ph.D., M.D., and Stanton E. Samenow for *The Criminal Personality, Vol. 1: A Profile for Change.* Also consulted was *Birnbaum's New Orleans* guidebook. My thanks also to novelists D.J. Donaldson for *Cajun Nights* and James Lee Burke for *A Stained White Radiance.*

As for The Root Mon's Credo and poetic voice, I have only the Root Mon himself to thank; he came to me in a waking dream . . .

— 1 —

My heart is like fire in a close vessel:
I am ready to burst for want of vent.

—John Wesley

Quantico, Virginia

Jessica Coran was not one to believe in the supernatural or visions, quests or even overzealous dream characters who bartered for attention, but there seemed no way to elude the faceless, nameless entity that now nightly climbed into her bed and invaded her mind with its presence. Was it a he, a she, corporeal or cloud, a disguised human image larger than life with a heavily made-up mask? Or was it truly nonhuman, some god of the night, immortal? Too dark, too nebulous in its contours, a shifting outline, detail lacking . . . too unreal to pinpoint . . . just out of mental reach, yet threatening . . . ever threatening. Person, place or thing? She could not know, not for certain.

All she felt was an overwhelming sense of pressure and bulk. The thing took up space, and usually that meant on her chest as she slept. It insisted on being listened to, but the damned thing never spoke a word. Excruciatingly painful, extraordinarily frustrating, it was a mindful creature without a mouth or words to convey its thoughts to her, like a wounded animal unable even to whine, its limbs working as if on strings controlled by a puppeteer.

Was it some sort of supernormal yet real visitor which moved about her room and increased her weight against the bed when it straddled her? Or was it, as her shrink, Donna Lemonte, no doubt would say, some dark portion of herself that had clawed its way from out of her own psyche to the surface?

No telling . . . at least not from what was known; informa-

1

tion sadly lacking . . . evidence inconclusive . . . no basis for discovery . . .

At one moment she thought it the ghost—or at least the vestibuled memory—of Otto Boutine, her first love, who'd died while saving her from a killer's grasp. Then she thought it her father's spirit, or that part of him which lived on in her, come with a warning, a foreboding. But in either case, she ought to be able to make out the features, to reinvent them fully and distinctly, even happily, but this she could not do.

Now, even as she slept and pondered these questions, she believed that a resolution was possible, and that perhaps—just perhaps—the phantom was a conglomerate of faceless victims from the many and various serial-killer cases she'd worked over the years, all come to finally collect. . . .

Hardly scientific or logical, she knew, but dream disturbances weren't exactly something she could pop under her microscope or slice into with her scalpel and examine more closely. Behind her closed eyelids she could only stare at the dark, inky mass which blotted out all light and made the air in her lungs stale with heat and fear.

Her visitor spoke out of a blank hole, the face a wall, but only slight, meandering gibberish surfaced, as if the words had too far to travel to live once they found her. The words came out as a meaningless hum like that of a refrigerator, mindless and mechanical; still, it all felt like an ominous, rational warning, something to protect her or send her flying over a cliff, the topmost precipice of which she only narrowly engaged on bare toes.

The idea of flight—any flight—was soothing, inviting, despite the consequences. So she stood, as it were, on the verge of plummeting down into the Grand Canyon of her soul, but what or who waited at the bottom for her? A comforting father? Otto? Love everlasting in Hawaii with Jim Parry? Or would Mad Matthew Matisak be there at the bottom, the vulture's patience rewarded, his talons sunk deep into her throat?

Jessica started from the dream just as her body hurled over the side of both the dream precipice and the bed. She'd once again been earnestly mindful of the blocked and retarded warnings, but that forceful, *steady-like-a-tuning-fork* message had kept right on, emanating from the deaf and dumb night image that she somehow knew was there to help her, despite the Grim Reaper costume it chose to appear in.

The warm yet fetid feeling emanating from the silent shadow was similar to the one she'd felt not long ago at a mountaintop shrine in Hawaii where a shaman, a psychic of sorts, had foretold her unappetizing future, which had, to a certain strange degree, already come true. The aged shaman had predicted that she would corner her prey in a land of red paths where the glinting sun would bathe all in the hue of blood orange. And then James Parry and she had in fact located Lopaka Kowona, the worst serial killer in Honolulu's history—or what was left of him—after his own people had finished with him, resorting to a primal instinct that had turned her stomach.

Now the old shaman's words rang anew in her ears during every silent moment, as if he had not been speaking of Hawaii at all, but of Oklahoma, U.S.A., where the red earth mingled with a bloody sun and an even bloodier new manhunt for the escaped madman, Matthew Matisak. The manhunt had come to a dead end after the initial find of an assortment of bloodless bodies in Oklahoma, Matisak having drained his victims of their precious heart's milk.

Using an ordinary surge machine found in a nearby barn, the monster had only become more hideous and resourceful since his original captivity two and a half years before.

"Alone with the Devil," she mourned aloud. "At three in the morning anyone's allowed a little madness," she continued aloud, as if speaking were an antidote, an autonomous reaction like a shiver to cold. Maybe she could find the timbre in her voice to chase off the demons.

She'd been reading before bed from a volume of Mark Twain's writings still on the table just above her head. Maybe she'd try to go back to Samuel Clemens's witticisms for respite. Three in the morning and she couldn't sleep. Was it the Prozac? Some people had a marked increase in insomnia as a side effect. Or was it the disturbing, unseeable, untouchable visitor now nightly in bed with her?

"Fuck this," she shouted to the room, still sitting on the floor beside her bed. She drew up her knees and rocked back and forth, tears freely coming even as her father's faraway words whispered in her ear: "Be strong, Jess . . . be brave, but don't ignore informed fear."

Outside, both at her door and below in the lobby, armed and ready, special agents of the FBI guarded her as if she were the First Lady. This annoyed her no end. It was a condition placed on her by Bureau Chief Paul Zanek, and she was damned sick of it altogether after the first week, much less now after six agonizing months—the length of time Matisak had remained at large.

She was sick of playing the victim; sick of being the hunted instead of the hunter; sick of Matisak's having turned her life inside out; sick of the games and the psychological toying he performed with each murder, leaving word at each slaughter-house that it was all done for her, so that he would be strong, healthy and in control when he came for her. Sick of other agents thinking she had somehow been responsible for the fiend's latest kill spree.

What was worse yet was the fact that her once-pleasant, protective apartment had now become her compound, her cage. Working sporadically on cases at the lab with body-guards over each shoulder hadn't helped the situation.

She snatched at the bedside table, foolishly grabbing a hand-ful of wires and turning over her clock and telephone, sending up a cacophony of metallic noise and crying out, "Dammit! I want out of this bloody Hell!"

Instantly her bedroom was invaded by two armed men in neatly attired suits and ties, prepared to blow away all evil, but quite literally unable to do so, their steady eyes and guns searching for the invisible intruder that never was, save in her mind.

"Take it easy, Sims, damnit all!" Her arms waving, she told Loydd Sims, shift commander this watch, "Just a bad night."

"Sorry, ma'am, but when we heard you shout—"

"Please, just get the hell out of my place. Go back to Zanek and tell him for me that I've given you notice. You're relieved of command. Go find a movie, sports or rock star to protect, or a goddamned thoroughbred or show dog insured by Lloyds of London to cover. Go on, do it!"

"I have my orders, Dr. Coran," replied Sims with an unbecoming frown. He was a tall, strong young man, and his arms far more than his guns might have comforted her, but his and his partner's gung-ho presence did little to help her disposition.

"Your orders, huh? Your *orders* are my fucking life, Sims! Do you and Zanek know that?"

"You'll have to take that up with the Chief, Dr. Coran." He jerked his head toward the door, an indication to his partner that they'd best leave.

She threw a shoe at the door as it closed. Then she cried in great, heaving sobs. "I'm a goddamned prisoner here. In my own goddamned apartment, I'm a prisoner."

She determined to go over Zanek's head, take her argument to the new division commander, Santiva, to see what a higher authority could do for her. She didn't particularly want to piss Zanek off, however, so she'd have to do what was necessary in the discreetest of political fashion. Once she convinced the new guy to look at things from her point of view, she'd ask him to give it to Zanek in such a way as to provide Zanek with an out, and at the same time perhaps make Zanek think that it was his idea in the first place. Santiva could manipulate Paul Zanck to recognize that it was in the best interest of all involved that Dr. Jessica Coran be returned to field-assignment duties immediately. She even had a case in mind, something that'd been brewing for some time now in New Orleans.

She wouldn't dwell on the fact that no matter where she was assigned, she'd be standing bait for the menacing, escaped madman who was stalking her. It was the only way left to draw the bastard out, she believed, to bait him into the open and to face him down once and for all and for good. Either way, an end, a closure to this nightmare was required if she were ever to enjoy sanity and peace in her life again.

She grabbed the brown clasp envelope J.T. had pushed on her, telling her it was given him by the police commissioner of New Orleans. She poured its contents over her bed and began to read the news clippings on what reporters in the Crescent City were calling the "Have-a-Heart" murders, which were largely centered around the French Quarter, gay and cross-dressing men being the victims. She began to read

in earnest, the information making her heart race far more than
Mark Twain had.

Good friend and lab partner, J.T., and he was so very right.
At least someone understood. He'd told her that she should
get back to doing what she did best, that she was right to be
upset, and that she should take on the New Orleans case. Her
analytical mind told her she was ready, even if the right side
of her brain and her emotions were screaming, tolling warning
bells that must be keeping up all of Quantico, Virginia.

Richard Stephens, police commissioner in New Orleans, Louisiana, had done the sights and had taken the tours and was
about fed up with the arm's-length treatment he'd received
from FBI Bureau Chief Paul Zanek here at Quantico. At three
in the morning, he was still restless and unable to sleep, so he
returned to the files that littered the table in Quantico's only
inn, a bed-and-breakfast called the Debonshire. It seemed that
lately manila file folders had become a large part of his life,
and the longer he stayed in Quantico, Virginia, the more wor-
risome his mission had become.

Meanwhile, back in New Orleans, party-goers were behaving in as strange and twisted a manner as many L.A. residents
during the O.J. Simpson cut-and-run debacle of '94. He knew
the diehard New Orleans revelers, and could imagine them
singing the Bonnie Raitt song "Have a Heart" and toasting
the latest serial killing of a gay man in the Big Easy—four
known and linked now. Meanwhile gay activists and human
rights groups were calling for a complete overhaul of city government and the NOPD for *perceived* wrongs and a *perceived*
callousness and indifference on the part of elected officials and
city employees such as himself. The heat was enough to have
both the mayor and the governor of the state on the phone,
chewing out Stephens's ass for circumstances beyond his control. But with Lew Meade's direction, he'd wound himself
through and around the FBI bureaucracy from Meade's Louisiana branch office to here, just outside D.C.

The news from Landry at the NOPD was neither forthcoming nor useful when it finally arrived here, and Stephens was
feeling like a man who'd crawled out on the limb of a twig
blowing in a gale and about to snap. Some damned thing had

to be done, and it had to be done soon, tomorrow, and if Zanek couldn't give him satisfaction, he'd take it to a higher level. He had one more chain he might yank.

He nervously fidgeted about the material he'd already read, information about this psychic detective Zanek had been pushing on him, Dr. Kim Desinor, something of an FBI secret, as her files indicated, since the agency did not wish her identity and the fact she was a psychic to be generally known. Her credentials were impressive, if they could be believed, but he wasn't so sure he did believe that the cases in question wouldn't have been solved without her intervention.

He pushed Desinor's file aside and again stared through the case files of Dr. Jessica Coran. He'd read her impressive record with great interest. She'd be a perfect foil and possible temporary replacement for that drunken scoundrel Frank Wardlaw back in New Orleans. Her experience with serial killers far exceeded anything Wardlaw or anyone else on the "Hearts" murder investigation had ever fucking seen. Stephens read of her experience with Mad Matthew Matisak in Chicago, the complex Claw case in New York City, and the equally puzzling Kowona case in Hawaii, in which all she'd had to go on was a single limb from one of the victims!

No doubt about it, Coran was something of a miracle worker when it came to laboratory work and minutiae—from fibers to blood samples taken at the scene. Of the two, scientific sleuth or psychic detective, Stephens clearly had his own preference. He would continue to argue for Dr. Coran's help tomorrow morning in Zanek's office.

He went to the window and looked out over the green and manicured villagelike Quantico, Virginia. It was an extremely small town with a population of a mere 690—with a nearby air force base and FBI Headquarters, both of them with many thousands of people who otherwise had minimal contact or ties with the town. What few high-rise buildings there were in the area had cropped up as government-subsidized housing for base and FBI personnel who preferred to live on the other side of the fences but very near the compounds and the action. Dr. Coran lived in one of these nearby residences, and he'd made some minimal contact with her through a secondary, not Zanek.

Stephens cranked open the small French window and filled his lungs with the clear Virginia night air. The place was in stark contrast to his city of jazz and nightlife; Quantico was by comparison the quietest place on earth, but in the distance he could see the lighted towers of the newest buildings on the FBI grounds where men and women worked around the clock at the largest crime lab in the world. Stark contrasts seemed the order of the day.

The town, the military base and the FBI compound, which looked for all outward appearances like a large, red-bricked private college, were all nestled together in an idyllic Virginia hills setting where the greatest depravity seemed to be crimes of fashion, or the occasional grammatical infraction, parking violation or unpaid ticket—and even these were rare.

Still, Washington was twenty minutes away via the turnpike, and the nearby FBI Headquarters with its compound and gates remained a constant reminder that crime in all its guises was a nationwide problem in America, a problem so out of proportion that the president, in his last speech, had called it the greatest civil war fought on the continent since the War Between the States.

New Orleans was having it out with crime on the streets, like any other major American city, and always had. But recently, the statistics had been rising to the point that no breathing space was left for the drowning citizenry—or the authorities, for that matter. In one tavern window in the French Quarter, where thousands of tourists passed by in any given afternoon, a sign had been put up by the bar owner which read:

> A Tale of Two Cities . . .
> Total murders to date this year:
> New Orleans, pop. 475,000—184
> Boston Mass., pop. 565,000—34
> January 1, 1995, thru May 28, 1995
> (150 days)

The wire services had picked up the story and run photos of the freaking sign, and the soaring murder rate had placed Stephens's city into the dubious race for the "Nation's Murder

Capital,'' replacing the ''Nation's Mardi Gras Capital'' in the minds of many. Tourism and industry and the city's economy were at jeopardy. Mardi Gras, Jazz Fest and boozy Bourbon Street aside, there was an important billion-dollar deal in the works with the prospect of a government contract being offered to the city.

''Christ,'' Stephens said aloud. Zen and the art of politics. The Big Easy was now being called the Big Uneasy and entire neighborhoods were arming themselves, hiring private guard patrols; men and women alike were purchasing the new handbags and carryalls which allowed them to hold firmly to the trigger of a gun inside the bag at all times. It was a gun dealer's delight, and alarm companies were thriving as well.

A recent classified ad in the *Times-Picayune* had offered a New Orleans Murder Map, a tricolored, eleven-by-seventeen deal showing areas with highest crime rates, noting the most widely publicized and sensational cases—as with the Japanese exchange student who was blown away by a frightened home owner a few years back. Stephens had purchased copies of the damnable ugly map himself, had taken them down to each of his precinct captains, had blown it out their asses and had the bloody things posted in every freaking squad room in the city as a constant reminder of what every foot soldier and every sergeant, lieutenant and captain in this war had to remember. The battle lines were drawn and there was more than one front.

It was a national disgrace for New Orleans and its police force when people in New Jersey and Chicago were saying, ''Everyone's heard that you can't raise children in New Orleans, that you all are murdering one another at top speed there.''

Stephens nervously stepped away from the window and paced the room. He'd been told in no uncertain terms by the governor himself that if the ''Have-a-Heart'' killer was not located and behind bars soon, then P.C. Stephens might as well turn in his shield, that he had no future in New Orleans. The city needed a show; the city needed a scapegoat, a diversion, even a three-ringed circus if it took that. He had to make the right choices from here on out, and to hell with what the detectives and the captains back home wanted.

He found the booze that had traveled with him all the way from New Orleans. He imagined himself in a new line of work, maybe that of a smuggler, getting the best from Bourbon Street, say, into Mexico or Canada, where they'd pay top dollar for the stuff. He laughed at the notion, but he had been thinking about going into another line of work when this was over, pulling up stakes, maybe retiring, who knows? Hell, he was nearing fifty-seven, a fine record up until recently.... What did he have to lose? What did he have to gain? Maybe keep what hair he had left and hold back the wrinkles a bit longer, settle that bleeding ulcer....

He poured himself a half-tumbler of the bourbon over ice—a potion he had to have, despite doctor's orders. He stared momentarily into the deep, brown liquid as he swirled it around. It was difficult these days to take pleasure even in the simplest indulgence. God, how long had it been since he'd been with a woman? he silently asked himself.

New Orleans had had 389 homicides the past year, a fifty-eight-percent increase over the 246 in 1989. On a per-capita basis—and damn per-capita statistics anyway, he thought—that placed his city ahead of Washington, D.C., and goddamned Detroit! As of May 28th, Washington had reported 146 homicides, while New Orleans had had 184.

Stephens was sick of hearing excuses from his captains, as when Carl Landry, defending his department and detectives, had said that the crime rate climbs significantly in the oppressive heat of a New Orleans summer. The year before thirty-one people were slain in June, forty-seven in July and forty-three in August. All Stephens knew was that, at the present rate, the city was headed for an all-time record in the neighborhood of five hundred homicides this year, and that averaged out at over one hundred victims per 100,000 citizens. Little wonder the higher-ups were concerned and skittish about their vital tourism and convention business, for although attacks on tourists were rare, and the French Quarter maintained the greatest concentration of police and boasted one of the lowest crime rates, soaring kill ratios and sensationalized stories—particularly about the "Heartthrob" killer who had killed in the French Quarter—had garnered nationwide attention.

"Jesus H. Christ," Stephens uttered between sips of his bourbon, taking a seat. Was it his fault or the fault of the police or the system when some 235 of those 389 people slain last year had been dispatched by someone they knew, mostly family members, and 131 of the killings had involved arguments, usually over trivial and stupid items? As of now 110 remained unsolved, the victim-killer relationship as yet unknown, but only forty-nine of the victims were known to have been killed by strangers. And 174 of the victims were kids between fifteen and twenty-four. Kids killing kids. Kids without any values or sense of morality or sense of life's sanctity.

He lifted Jessica Coran's folder off the coffee table before him, and he again stared at her photo. She was a strikingly beautiful woman with eyes as hard as steel. He toyed with the idea of contacting her directly, perhaps to set up a breakfast meeting, get his wishes out in the open, see how she might respond, but he immediately thought better of the notion. After all, the FBI functioned as a paramilitary operation, and if Zanek got wind of his meeting alone with his agent, it could blow the whole deal.

Still, he had it on good authority that she had gotten the materials he'd forwarded, a thorough set of clippings and files that recounted the list of victims in New Orleans, and anything new was E-mailed to him on an hourly basis. He had worked through a fellow he'd met at the FBI laboratory only the day before, a Dr. John T. Thorpe, who had assured him that Jessica Coran would get the information. The younger man had even said that it was the kind of case Dr. Coran could get excited about.

"Dear God, I hope so," he said to the empty room, tossing Jessica's file back onto the table and going back to the disarray that was his bed, praying now he might get some sleep. Beside his bed, a second bottle of bourbon awaited his grasp. He poured a final nightcap, shut off the light and lay still, hopeful and anxious.

Her heart is like an ordered house
Good fairies harbor in.

—Christina Rossetti

Quantico, Virginia, FBI Headquarters

Young Tom Benton watched in awe while Dr. Kimberly Faith Desinor placed her thumb and index finger onto the ransom note as it was lifted from its cellophane sheath between tweezers held by Special Agent Neil Parlen of Georgia. Dr. Faith, as she was sometimes called by those who knew her well enough to joke, was now the only person to make human contact with the document since it had been handled by the kidnapper or kidnappers. She must touch the note, feel its weight, bond and weave, its every fiber. It was her job to manhandle the evidence.

Unlike most law-enforcement officials trained to keep their grubby, enzyme-secreting hands off, she was uniquely qualified for a hands-on experience with the incriminating evidence—once all traditional avenues of detection had failed. And failed they had, miserably.

They stood in a semi-darkened room, much preferred by Dr. Desinor whenever she went into trance. She'd known absolutely nothing of the case in Georgia save what she'd read in the papers, which was very little, and even the application Parlen had made to Dr. Desinor's psychic detection unit of the FBI had had to travel through a paper labyrinth the size of a botanical maze in order for Parlen to gain paranormal assistance for his investigation. The application itself was intentionally sketchy, seeming just a routine application for Headquarters assistance, no one wanting to draw undue attention to the fact the FBI was in any way involved in paranormal studies or psychic detection.

Even before touching the note, which she'd never seen before this moment, Desinor knew the perpetrator was an amateur. The note was a patchwork of large and small words, cutout block letters from slick magazines, tabloids and the *Ladies Home Journal*, telltale signs of a poor education and weak grammar showing through nonetheless, such as the use of a double negative in the third sentence, and a subject-verb-agreement error in the last sentence. Of course, the errors might well have been put in on purpose, to throw the police off. A linguist would be looking for a poorly educated man, possibly an unskilled laborer, possibly of Southern origin and a low socioeconomic background. Hardly facts which would nail a suspect.

The bad guy or guys had foolishly used Scotch tape, which left a variety of prints from several fingers and thumbs, but none of these had found a match in the world's largest fingerprint bank here at Quantico, further proof of the cherry quality of the culprits.

Now that all the usual FBI measures had failed, Parlen had come to Kim Desinor. And why not? What did he have to lose? No one would even know, so there was no chance for embarrassment. The ransom notes had stopped. Leads were now gone as dry as Sahara soil. The prints remained useless without a match. The ransom note itself was now only an annoying reminder to Parlen that his field office in Georgia had failed miserably in Decatur.

A last-resort, last-ditch effort that Parlen had little belief in was what it had all come down to, in the person of Dr. Desinor, a Ph.D. in psychology and sociology who also juggled psychic powers here in the Behavioral Science Division of the FBI. Psychic powers were ostensibly not part of her working repertoire, however, or so the public was to be made to believe. For the past ten years, use of psi powers under any FBI umbrella had been not only downplayed but denied outright. There didn't appear to be any change in this policy on the horizon, so funding continued by the grace of the budgetary gods above, and lately, they weren't looking too kindly on Dr. Faith and her small office.

"Back away from me, both of you," she instructed the two men in the room with her—Benton, her aide and student, and Parlen, the skeptical agent. Benton was studying under her, while Parlen was following orders, transporting the goods from Decatur, Georgia, where the manhunt for the missing bank executive, Harold Michael Sendak, continued under a cloud of criticism and hopelessness. The abductors had been so frightened off, it appeared, that Sendak must be dead by now, the case now eleven weeks old.

Kim Desinor felt the ransom note speak to her immediately. There was something about the weave and fiber that was quite alive with energy, although it was simple copier paper with no special qualities about it. Still, it sent out an image, sharp and piercing, into her mind. A life force had left an indelible mark on the paper, and it was desperately but haltingly attempting to speak to her.

Dr. Desinor took in a deep gasp of air, breathing in the life force, taking it inside her, filling her mind with its resolute images while the more amorphous, peripheral images floated off like flotsam on a river. She forced herself to ignore the smoke and unfocused mirror images for the main event.

The room, with its stark white walls, was sealed to prevent any undue noise or disturbance while she worked, although there remained one thick glass window looking into Dr. Desinor's crowded office, where the shelves were overflowing with volumes dealing with psychiatry and psychology and psychic powers. The room was soundproof and a camera was mounted near the ceiling which recorded every session, including today's. Here there were no phones, no buzzing intercoms or other office disturbances. There wouldn't even be any other people, save Benton, if Parlen hadn't insisted on being here. His damned negative thoughts rose like heat off a Texas-Louisiana highway during a drought, further obscuring her grasp of the images fighting for dominance in her psyche.

When she felt a breakthrough, all other sensory paths were completely shut down, sometimes for only a moment, sometimes for minutes at a time. She felt no other bodies or heat sources in the room, and she could not hear anyone's whisper and she saw no faces. Nor did she see the camera or the walls or the window or the light flashing on her phone in the office next door.

Suddenly, she was no longer truly in the little cubicle; she was several hundred miles away, in Decatur.

She first heard the whispering of voices, not from Benton or Parlen, but from Georgia. Meaningless back-scatter, jabbering gibberish, the mumblings, grumblings and ravings of maniacs—ghost voices, some psychics insisted. She believed them to be the emanations of the past, imprinted on the object, in this case the ransom note, now being replayed in her head via the antennae of her fingertips. Nothing mystical or supernatural about it, so far as she was concerned. Simply a heightened sixth sense of higher awareness, like the higher memory of a computer.

The voices sounded at first like a foreign tongue, but they just needed to be adjusted, tuned into, so to speak.

She believed her "power" an inborn instinct that gave its owner the ability to increase or heighten all the normal senses into one forcefully focused laserlike sense, a gift or a curse, however one chose to look at it, however one chose to use it, or be used by it.

The voices sounded like tolling bells without harmony, clanging into one another, disjointed and chaotic at first; the images welling up from the paper made no direct sense either. Usually, if anything formed, it was symbolic, which in and of itself would remain pointless, like the cradle she now saw. . . . What was the cradle, and why was it so still and flat and unable to rock?

"Cradle . . . I see a cradle. . . . " she said aloud.

Parlen's eyes widened and he muttered, "Cradle? What kind of cradle?"

"Strange cradle . . . cradle of death, not life . . ."

"What do you mean, cradle of death?"

"Stone cradle . . . stones and cradle . . ."

Parlen's eyes widened and he said in a near-whisper, "You mean Craddle . . . Craddle Storage? What about it?"

Benton shushed the agent.

Kim Desinor was coming clear on two salient points: Sendak had been buried alive but aboveground, possibly in a crypt, and the ransom note had been handled by more than one person before she herself had touched it. Whether an eager investigator or an accomplice, she could not yet say. Even so, the number *1* kept insinuating itself like a brand across her brain. It was so persistent that she decided there must only be one criminal mind at work. But then, who else had handled the document?

Was the picture cluttered by an overzealous officer of the law, perhaps Parlen himself? Everyone at the FBI had been extremely careful to provide an unbreakable chain of custody for the Georgia document.

Still, she sensed the ransom note had been handled by a large man with evil intentions and someone smaller, milder, someone leaning toward the color green, a person with a rainbow aura around . . . her. She had something to do with the number *1*. It was definitely a female, and she held a deep-seated remorse, powerful frustrations and guilt capped tightly in a bottle, her heart trapped in a bottle, a vessel of some sort. The bottle was her body.

Then it came to Dr. Desinor.

It came like a candle being lit; not in a word, not in a single image, but in a wide, encompassing hunch that gave her a warm feeling of closure. It was an all-encompassing instinct, an intuitive, educated guess based on a raggedy-looking toy doll with a dirty face and ill-fitting clothes, the image of the second perpetrator.

"Well?" said Parlen, impatient now.

"It's the daughter."

"The daughter? What daughter? There is no—"

"Sendak's daughter."

"Goddamned waste of time." Parlen tweezered the ransom note, uselessly returning it to its protective bed of polyethylene. "Sendak doesn't have any daughters. Two sons, no daughters, sorry, and thanks for your time. We'll check at Craddle's Storage out on Highway 1 just the same." For all the good it'll do, she read his unspoken thought.

"Beside Craddle's Storage out there, there's a company where they make pre-stressed concrete," Parlen added as he prepared to leave. "You said something about stones and cradles. . . . But I rather doubt there's any connection whatsoever. . . . I won't hold out much hope."

Parlen was about to leave when she said, "Oh, but he did have a daughter, and she played a role in his death. He wasn't meant to suffocate, but he did, and she is his only daughter, and she works at a place that has something to do with the number one. Maybe even works for this Craddle Storage place?''

"And those places look like mausoleums, don't they," added young Benton excitedly before Dr. Desinor put up a hand to stop him.

Unimpressed, Parlen continued in the same vein. "I'm telling you, Doctor, the man has no daughters. We talked to everyone involved and—''

"Illegitimate . . . other side of the tracks . . . didn't want any part of the kidnapping . . . tried to stop her boyfriend or a possible husband who'd found out about the family connection . . .''

"No one like that has surfaced in our investigation in Decatur.''

"Not necessarily in Decatur. Elsewhere, perhaps. Have you talked to Mrs. Sendak about—''

"Of course! She's been repeatedly grilled!''

"—about the other woman? Mr. Sendak's activities outside the home?''

"Well, no . . . not exactly, not so far as I know . . .''

She took in a great breath of air, trying to regain her fix on the here and now. "I suggest you return to Decatur and do so, Mr. Parlen.''

Young Tom Benton's impudent, full lips curled into a smile. Kim Desinor looked past him and through the glass partition to the blinking light on her phone. She rushed from the darkened room into the office where the noise of marching cadets on the Quantico drill grounds beat out a rhythm with foot and song. It sounded like an old song the nuns had made her learn in the orphanage in New Orleans when she was a child, except that this was more boisterous, perhaps a bit bawdy even. Behind her, she heard Parlen saying to Benton, "There's all kinda businesses and restaurants out on Highway 1 we could check; half a dozen or more use the number one on their logos and in advertising, like the US-1 Grill, Number 1 Golf, Tap One.''

She lifted the phone and just caught Paul Zanek about to hang up at the other end while her recorded voice was asking that he please leave a message. "Don't you people ever answer your damn phones down there anymore, Doctor?'' he said.

"Maybe if you could keep a secretary . . ."

He'd begun calling her "Doctor" again, which meant, for the time being, he was holding her at arm's length, shy of getting burned. "I was in a session with Parlen from Georgia, or don't you recall?"

"Parlen? Georgia?"

"Special Agent Neil Parlen? The Sendak case?"

"Oh, yeah . . . sure . . . how'd it come out? You able to dig anything out of that piece of trash he calls evidence?"

"A little something I think'll be useful for him, yeah, Paul."

He hesitated at the mention of his name. "Get up here to my office pronto, will you? I want to run something by you."

"Sure, what's up?"

"Never mind, just get up here." He hung up.

Left holding the phone and wondering what the call was for, she realized that lately he could speak about anything and everything but what was on both their minds: What was to become of her and her little department now that he'd gone back to his wife?

Paul Zanek had lost all the allure and mystery and luster, all the romantic overtones she'd once ascribed to him. Every woman had a right to be wrong about a man, even a psychic detective on the U.S. payroll. Still, she wondered how she could've been so entirely wrong about Paul. She'd been blind, foolish, childish even. Maybe it had all been because of the death of her Aunt Aileen, the last vestige of her immediate family. Her aunt, only a few years older than she, had grown up in the care of the nuns too, and had taken punishments for Kim. Aileen had always faithfully held to the belief that one day her little niece would become an important person, and she'd encouraged Kim to strike out for her goals. She'd died of a rare, debilitating disease, and she'd died bravely, proud to the end that Kim had become an "important" person.

Kim's loss had sent her into a tailspin of grief, spiraling regrets, depression and self-pity, and Paul had played skillfully on those unhappy feelings. He'd been an easy man to turn to, to seek comfort from.

He had recently separated from his wife of eleven years,

and Kim had found herself working late over cases with him one night, and in the solitary hours past 2 A.M. everyone needed someone to hold, she told herself now. Their love-making had not been so therapeutic as it had been insanely boundless, reckless beyond anything she might've envisioned. Still, his presence had for a time dissipated the darkness that she'd feared coming in on all sides.

She had a right, she'd told herself, to find some comfort, some security and warmth. And hadn't she taken from him as much as he had taken from her?

But that was then . . . and this is now, she reminded herself. "Now I'm an embarrassment to the bastard." She had expected better from him.

She feared most for the foothold she'd gotten for psi studies and psychic investigation within the Behavioral Sciences Unit of the FBI. Paul was in a position to either rubber-stamp it or deep-six it.

Benton was now showing Parlen the door. Thomas Benton was one of a handful of select young psychics recruited to round out the program. He had hardly begun the usual rigorous duties of a cadet in training when Kim had lifted him for duties in her department. According to his file, he was an unusually gifted sensitive.

Now Benton and the others in her department were all threatened, and all because of her. She'd thought Paul above the usual male traits that so often turned a beautiful affair into an ugly nightmare. But now he was doing that bitter danse macabre over the grave of the affair so typical of the male ego—stomping down the dirt. Lovemaking had ricocheted, taking out the innocent with the guilty. Lovemaking had transformed in reverse from butterfly to worm, changing into a guilt-ridden, twisting thing called remorse, poisoning Paul's memory of the incident into something to be ashamed of or hidden from. It became his fall from grace. It was as if she had had nothing to do with it, and yet, she was to blame. He set out trying to fix blame in that arrogant fashion reserved for top-level executives.

Did he fear for his position here or at home? Was he still twisting on the lance, heartbroken like she was, or was he just trying to cover his ass, wondering how much Kim had done to harm his career and his family?

The questions crested, rose and crested again like an unrelenting ocean inside her brain. What did Paul Zanek want now of her? What had he convinced himself of during his isolation from her? Why wouldn't he talk to her? Had he concluded that she had seduced him? That she had manipulated him? That perhaps she had used some psychic's spell on him for Chrissake? Sure, his attraction for her had somehow been used against him to lure him into bed, and she was some black widow spider capable of tying him in an invisible but powerful cocoon to become her helpless morsel. Yeah, right . . .

Bastard, she now thought. How will he do it? How will he rid himself of me? Is this it, she wondered, will this call on the carpet put an end to all that I've built here?

Her fear drove her to the elevator and his office even as it wanted to find an excuse to dodge the SOB. All this while young Tom Benton looked after her with growing concern, sensing that all was not right in her world.

3

A heart is like a fan, and why?—
'Twill flutter when a beau is nigh;
Oft times with gentle words he'll take it;
Play with it for a while, then break it.

—Anonymous

New Orleans, Louisiana

Some goddamned vacation, Alex Sincebaugh thought as he
finished roll one, exposure eight, calmly noting this in his
notepad alongside the crude but detailed sketch he'd made of
the body, its position both in relation to fixed objects at the
crime scene and anatomically. His partner, Ben, always kidded
him about the amount of detail he put into his thumbnail
crime-scene sketches, saying, ''You don't gotta do Gray's
friggin' Anatomy here, Alex.''

''Hey, a d'tail is a d'tail,'' he'd respond, thinking he ought
to have left town, maybe gone to the Bahamas or the Cayman
Islands, someplace where headquarters couldn't have so easily
located him. What good was he doing anyway? There were
better men in the department who ought to have control of the
case, but in the NOPD things didn't work that way. You take
a call here and you're the detective of record and it stays that
way unless the brass steps in and pulls you off.

Ben continued the good-natured ribbing. ''Only d'tail I'd
like to see is my Fiona's—and mine right beside her . . . in
bed . . . at home!''

Alex held a year-round pass to the University of New Orleans's sporting events, for all the good it would do, trying to
match his schedule with the UNO's. Lately, it had become an
impossibility. He'd also scrounged tickets to the pre-season
Saints game for Saturday night, had managed to find a date,
and had had to back out at the last minute due to the pressing
caseload, thanks to a faceless, conscienceless creature stalking

the New Orleans area like some cave-dwelling cannibal with an appetite for human hearts.

Alex's days in pre-med at Trinity at long last were being put to the test now as a detective with the New Orleans Police Department. What he didn't know about the human heart, he was quickly finding out from the library of medical books he kept in his apartment. And the skill required to sketch human organs and bodies in various stages of death had come in handy as well. All this only dismayed his father, who believed that he'd simply thrown his life down the toilet pipes by going to work for the NOPD. His father seemed incapable of understanding how much being a detective on the force meant to Alex. He knew the terrain in and around New Orleans like the rooms of the house he grew up in; he was equally comfortable on the West Bank with its elevated West Bank Expressway, General de Gaulle Drive, Terry Parkway and the old span of the Crescent City Connection to which all arteries eventually led. He knew the outlying counties like Beau Chene, each called parishes, and he had once maintained an apartment in Kenner in the East Jefferson Parish. He had family in St. Charles Parish, where the school system had been crippled by mismanagement when its surplus of $9.3 million mysteriously dwindled to a mere $150,000 two years before. Thanks to the new "Shareware" policy and computers, Alex was no stranger to St. John the Baptist Parish, where right-to-lifers, wanting someone's head on a plate, picketed daily outside the hospital named for the county and the saint. In St. Bernard Parish there appeared to be an overachieving arsonist on the loose. Closer to home, in St. Tammany Parish the enormous, three-hundred-foot gambling boat, *Jewel of the Ponchartrain,* on beautiful Lake Ponchartrain near Interstate 10, had *suspiciously* slipped its moorings, disturbing all at the gaming tables but the true diehards, who'd played on oblivious of the "titanic" nature of their drift, which had very nearly led them into the bridge pylons before some capable someone fired her engines and moved her back to the safety of the pier.

Not surprisingly, the new approach—spending money—meant for the first time ever, cops could get information before CNN and the *Enquirer.* Thank God for technology, he now thought.

Alex had investigated homicides, suicides, accidental deaths and deaths by natural causes in every part of the city. Precinct lines in the Crescent City were seldom a deterrent for a cop, and frequently, what with the Mardi Gras mentality of the population—a parade at the drop of a hat and some sixteen officially slated affairs for the spring and summer months alone—one precinct helped out another when there was a need, and no one was complaining.

Alex knew that in such cities as Chicago, L.A. and New York precinct lines were never crossed. To Alex's way of thinking, the laid-back manner in which the NOPD encouraged precincts to support one another foretold a day when more would be accomplished all across the country with such artificial barriers erased.

Here in the Big Easy, the homicide detective who arrived on scene first, no matter what the precinct, was immediately in charge of the body and the case. It was a system that had its good points and its bad, but cooperation among precincts was never a problem, despite the petty squabbles and bets placed on who was going to catch this Queen of Hearts "asshole" first. A little friendly competitiveness was the lifeblood of the NOPD, but cooperation and collaboration kept that lifeblood primed and pumped.

Alex was forty-seven years old and had made lieutenant sergeant in Vice, doing gainful decoy and undercover work, before transferring to Homicide the year before. Vice operatives got around to all parts of the city, and so he had gotten to know men in the other precincts quite well. Now he was up for a clean lieutenant's rank, and his rise through the departmental hoops and ladders had been steady and appreciated by everyone but his father, the career beat cop.

It was the last thing in the world his father had wanted for him. The disappointment was like a huge bell that tolled in their ears and hearts, standing between them, ringing out its dull anthem each time they shared space. The ringing of the bell had just increased in density as Alex moved up in rank, and it became solid granite after his mother's death two years before.

Sincebaugh now labeled the exposed film, put it away and began another roll. While he photographed the corpse from every conceivable angle and then some, and while he dusted for prints, his partner, Ben deYampert, with the help of a uniformed officer, was pacing off the tape measure to triangulate the exact position of the body, so that Alex could insert more numbers onto his sketch the moment this was determined.

Ben had already measured from the edge of a shoal marker on huge Lake Ponchartrain to the big toe pointing due south, and was now pacing off the distance from the left foot to a nearby road sign that warned of a $500 fine for littering. Triangulation in the woods was a difficult proposition: You couldn't use a tree or a boulder or a road sign; you'd be nailed in a court of law. Even the damned lake might be called into question by a legal-beagle who wanted to talk tides just to play havoc with the prosecution.

"Got to get a more fixed point of reference, Ben!" he yelled out.

"Like what? The fuckin' ruts in the mud?"

"Do the best you can, but vandals or a roadwork crew comes along and we got no sign, and you know what that means."

DeYampert muttered something unintelligible behind his massive form. "You got a rule book up your ass, Alex. Don't that ever pain you, son?"

"Everything strictly by the book, Big."

"Yeah, sure . . . follow rule number one: don't touch a goddamned thing, and then proceed to rule number two—"

"Don't touch a goddamned thing," Alex said, finishing the old cop wisdom for him, quietly laughing at the line, realizing just how unworkable it was.

Alex knew it was impossible to follow the rules here, especially since it was his job to search for any conceivable sign of evidence as well as identification of the victim. They'd found signs of someone's having dragged the body to this isolated, dark and remote location. Someone had less than tenderly covered the body with shrubbery cut from nearby, possibly using the same blade that had felled the victim, since bloodstains had been found on the palmetto stems.

The victim was yet another young, well-tanned, soft-featured male, hardly more than a boy in age, nineteen at the most, more likely seventeen.

They'd found scattered bits of clothing and footprints belonging to a heavyset killer who wore flat, wide sneakers that had made an interesting pattern in the mud, something for the forensics guys to make a cast of along with some fresh tire marks. But neither Alex nor Ben held out much hope of either cast ever being of any particular use.

They'd found signs of animal leavings about the body, defecation to mark the kill in the wild. There was some evidence the corpse had been ripped apart a bit further by animals, but since the insect activity was not too terribly far along yet, the corpse was marked as having come to rest here some twelve to twenty-four hours before a group of blue-haired, retired ladies and gents on a bird watchers' safari had ingloriously discovered the body, reporting it to the local precinct Crimes Against Persons office. The precinct police had put it on the wire, and since it smelled like another Queen of Hearts murder, Sincebaugh had been given a wake-up call and pulled from his vacation.

When Alex responded to the call, he drove a few miles north of downtown New Orleans and just north of Lakefront Airport, along an unnamed artery off Hayne Boulevard, almost at its terminus, where Hayne became Paris Road. It had already been decided for him that he would take charge of the body and the subsequent investigation and paperwork. It certainly looked related to Sincebaugh's ongoing investigation.

Everything at the scene had been happily turned over to him by a detective out of the local precinct, a guy Sincebaugh knew and disliked named Lyle Kellerman. Kellerman's parting shot was: "You can have all my fag meat cases, Sincebaugh. It ain't my kinda case. Don't even wanna be in the morgue with it."

"This meat, as you call the kid, had a name, a history, a past, emotions, a family, Kellerman," Alex had replied as the other man backed off with a pugnacious grin marring his otherwise handsome features.

"Some things you never had or ever will have, Kellerman," Ben had added for good measure.

The discovery was sometime after twilight, the bird watchers, having done their damnedest to log the large-necked, white-ribboned loon here, getting ready to bag all expectations and return home empty-handed. Now it was day watch, definitely the wrong time for Alex and Ben. Alex would have to break Ben's heart; he'd have to put them in for the night shift if they were ever to learn more about this plague of dead boys. Four now that they knew of for certain, and a fifth that Alex clung to as a possible which had occurred over a year before.

They'd been told by Captain Landry that it had been an otherwise dull rotation, only eleven deaths had come on the evening watch, and only a handful were violent deaths, the bulk of them alcohol-related motor-vehicle accidents.

"You'd think Kellerman would've been pleased to get a murder investigation after a night like the one he just had," said Ben, returning to the body now. "What's he afraid of, AIDS?"

"Kellerman's afraid of gays."

"Maybe he's got some latent tendencies toward that direction?" Ben laughed to hear himself say it aloud. "Or maybe he's just got good reason, Alex. Maybe he picked one of those Bourbon Street cross-dressers up once, and he didn't find it too amusing when he got her—him—into bed." Ben chuckled even louder, pleased with himself.

"Maybe. Then again, maybe he's just ignorant."

They worked by the book, the tight-fitting surgical gloves masking their palms. Ben watched his partner's painstaking, careful work. Sincebaugh was officer in charge of the investigation the press had dubbed variously as the "Have-a-Heart," the "Heartthrob" and the "Queen of Hearts" murders. The first two victims had lived in the French Quarter, in the heart of New Orleans, just around the corner from Bourbon Street. An earlier homicide, nearly a year old now, might possibly be linked with the same killer, since the victim too had been a male with a decidedly homosexual lifestyle. No heart had been found in the boy's chest there either, but as the decomposition of the body had progressed and maggots had gotten into the open chest cavity, the illustrious Dr. Frank Wardlaw had proclaimed that the heart had been devoured by maggots. Alex no longer thought so.

The first two acknowledged Hearts victims had actually known one another, and this newest soft-skinned youth looked like the others in all salient features: long, unkempt,

blond to sandy hair, big eyes, powdery flecks of freckles about
the cheeks, small-boned, perhaps five-nine or ten, weighing in
at a mere 130 or 135 pounds. Not much of a match for the
assailant, Alex was sure.

Bruises about the face and forearms and lacerations to the
same areas spoke of a beating and a knifing, defensive wounds
everywhere. The awful carnage had come clear when they'd
rolled the body onto its back. The private parts had been
butchered. The chest was splayed open, carved up surgically,
and missing from the cavity was the boy's heart, replaced by
an unusual diamond-shaped playing card made of a lacy material. Even blood-soaked, the card looked like something
found only in a world long gone, at a time when people made
lace doilies and lace trinkets, very Old World, European-
looking workmanship in the weaving of it. The queen's ornate
costume and lurid features would be found stitched in a rainbow of colorful twine after the thing was soaked and cleaned
of impurities, marking it as the same as those before it. Nowhere, not even in New Orleans, had either detective seen
anything like it. The killer's "calling card," had been wedged
below the ribs. As before, the bold single eye of the queen of
hearts stared back at them.

Was the card a message or a plea? If the bastard wanted to
send a message, why didn't he use Western Union? If a message, what message was the sonofabitch sending? That hearts
were meant to be broken? That gay men had no right to life,
no right to their own heartbeats? That their being gay gave the
killer a genuine rationale, that he was somehow warranted in
stealing the warm hearts from other human beings? That he
had a justifiable right to be heartless? And why the queen of
hearts? Queen suggested that the killer himself might well be
gay—a drag queen—and that he hated himself for the hand
fate had dealt him, and so he was striking out at other gay
men in rage and uncontrolled fury. Certainly, enough rage was
played out on the bodies to warrant this theory, as well as half
a dozen other "hate crime" scenarios, such as perhaps that
the killer was a neo-Nazi who hated gay men so much that he
had to vent his anger.

Then again, if leaving the playing card was some sort of
plea and not a message, what was the killer pleading for? What

did he want Alex—or the NOPD in general—to know? What significance did the queen of hearts hold for the bastard?

And just how damned arcane could he remain and for how goddamned long?

After photoing closeups on the grisly wounds—bodily sites of destruction—and the blood-spattered playing card, both familiar and unusual at once, Sincebaugh carefully lifted the killer's notice—or was it a receipt?—with tweezers. He held the drooping card up to his perplexed eyes for a silent moment, Ben looking on, frowning, no doubt wondering what was going on behind Alex's eyes.

Alex studied the curled and soiled card front and back without touching it or wiping any of the blood away. "It's the same as the others, unique, as if tailor-made for the victim, like the others before."

"Embroidered playing cards. Thought I'd seen it all till now," Ben replied.

"Nothing like you're going to find at the corner dime store or cigar stand."

It was the fourth queen of hearts found in the open chest of victims in as many months. It clinched the fact that this boy was done by the same sadistic killer.

"Damned spooky, Alex . . . damned spooky."

"Sonofabitch's got it bad for young gay men, that's for sure."

"He's also got four spoilt decks of cards by my calculation," Ben dryly pointed out. "And hey, what the hell's he doing with the other fifty-one, or the *hearts* for that matter? That's what I'd like to know, Alex. No evidence the guy hung around long after, so he must be taking the hearts off with him. Why's he taking the hearts, Alex? And why's he cutting out their hearts to begin with? And why's he chopping off their balls and dongs and leaving these damned beer coasters behind? You think he's eatin' the hearts, Alex? You think he's some kinda fuckin' cannibal or something? You think we're going to find a Frigidaire somewhere that's been stocked with human hearts or what, Sincy?"

"Don't go squirrelly on me, Ben. I think this guy just does queens. He's not buying the cards in decks or in coaster sets. I think he makes 'em."

Ben considered this for a moment, each detective aware of what the suggestion meant. *The guy selects someone to kill, creates the lacy card and stalks his prey.* Ben cleared his throat and said, "Squirrelly, me? What's that s'pose to mean?"

"Means we don't sweat the whys and wherefores, remember? We go after how. How does he choose his victim? How does the victim fall into his trap? How'd they come together? How'd this kid get here? What was he doing during the last hours of his life to lead him to this dump site? Who was he with and what'd they talk about? Where'd he have his last meal and with whom? And what'd he eat and where'd he eat it?"

"Sure, sure, I know the routine, Alex, but this . . . this isn't in any way your routine homicide. These mutilations . . . they're . . . they're . . ."

"Hate killings? Lust murders? You going to tell me why before you tell me how, Ben? You're already off track."

"But Alex, if we understood why, then maybe it'd be easier to investigate—"

"And sleep at night?"

"—and we could come up with a faster solution in these particular cases."

"You want to go after it that way? All right, then take a good look at the boy's crotch, Ben. Go ahead, take a closer look."

Ben shuddered even as his eyes went a second time to the area where the boy's sexual organs had been cleaved off, the discarded items lying bloody between his legs like the remains of a gutted chicken. Sincebaugh snapped another picture, this time with Ben in the foreground.

"Something you can show your grandkids, Ben."

"You sick sonofabitch, Sincy. You got a real mean streak in you too."

"Comes of serving with you."

"Let's get outta here."

"Can't, not till Wardlaw or one of his stooges arrive."

"Where in hell're those guys? We called 'em an hour ago."

An ambulance from the NOPD morgue had arrived, but Dr. Franklin T. Wardlaw, M.E. for New Orleans, was nowhere to be seen.

"Call the bastard again. He probably fell asleep somewhere."

Journalists were arriving on the scene now and were being held at bay by the uniformed officers. They wanted all the dirt, and they wanted to know what the NOPD was going to do about the Queen of Hearts killer, and they wanted to know— as always—now. Sincebaugh squarely reckoned that if the killings were ordinary slayings of gay men—without the extraordinary high profile due to the missing hearts—the press would be asleep on the case.

For now, however, the Fourth Estate had cornered Sincebaugh's captain, Carl Landry, along with Lew Meade, the local FBI chief, who'd been dragged from their beds to come down to have a look. All for the sake of the press. What they could accomplish here was zip, save for public relations, but even saving face and saving grace were unlikely at this point with nothing whatever to go on.

"Here comes the circus," said Ben.

"Where the fuck's that drunken coroner?" asked Sincebaugh.

4

A flinty heart within a snowy breast
Is like base mold lock'd in a golden chest.

—Francis Beaumont

Quantico, Virginia

Dr. Jessica Coran, Medical Examiner for the tactical field unit of the Psychological & Pathological Profiling sector of the Behavioral Sciences Division of the FBI, was on twenty-four-hour call to drop everything and go anywhere Chief Paul Zanek sent her at a moment's notice. For this reason, she had a ready bag packed and waiting in her closet at all times. But for the past six months, she hadn't gone anywhere, and obviously she wasn't going anywhere so long as Paul Zanek was the one making the decision.

She had awakened after fitful sleep to her own decision, and first thing after showering and dressing in her most business-like manner, her lab glasses on the end of her nose, she had sought out Eriq Santiva, Zanek's boss.

She found Santiva surprisingly clear on her point of view, understanding her position, nodding throughout and finally agreeing with her. He still wanted special agents with her—to watch her back, as he said—but she argued passionately that this would only harm any chance at luring Matisak back out into the open.

Santiva wanted Matisak badly. He'd just come on as new head of the division when Matisak had escaped.

"Will you clear New Orleans for me?" she asked. "Will you make the whole idea palatable to Paul Zanek? If not, I'm walking out of here, resigning and going back into private practice."

Her threat was taken seriously along with her concerns. She liked, admired and trusted Santiva, who had a sparkling record

31

in the Bureau. He was a lean, tall man with striking dark features.

Santiva shook on it with her. "You'll have New Orleans. Zanek has kept me informed about their wishes, and I think they'll be happy to have you, but you're one hundred percent right about Paul. He'll need to think it's his idea. Keep leaning on him, pressuring him from where you're at, and I'll put it to him from where I sit. Between us, I think we can win Paul over."

She thanked Santiva and left with a sense of accomplishment, a sense that she was finally taking a step in the right direction. She followed this up with a visit to Paul Zanek's office, but there she learned that Paul was as adamant as ever about her staying close to home plate, Quantico.

Zanek, and the others in a position to make choices for her, had stonewalled her since Oklahoma, where the trail for Mad Matthew Matisak had gone cold. Since then, she had been in a kind of "protective custody," bodyguards surrounding her and friends like Zanek shielding her by keeping her cloaked at Quantico. Meanwhile, her life was no longer her own.

Not a single word on Matisak since Oklahoma, no leads, not a clue. The few possibilities had turned out to be false. It was as if the lunatic had disappeared off the face of the earth, and thank God if he had gone down in the light plane he had commandeered at a small Oklahoma airport. Neither plane nor pilot had ever been found again, no wreckage reported, nothing. If they'd run out of fuel somewhere in the southwestern desert, it was possible the monster had died a slow and torturous death, the sort he was famous for inflicting on his own victims. Revenge is mine, sayeth the Lord, and more power to You, she thought now.

She had more than once reveled in the idea of Matisak's dying of slow dehydration, so fitting for a killer that craved the liquid of life, blood. If it had happened, it had not likely occurred before the fiend had fed on the blood of the unfortunate pilot.

She now sat in the darkened projection room, thanks to a busy Paul, who'd come and gone and come back in again. She sat watching the frame-by-frame images of the so-called psychic detective, Dr. "Faith" or Desinor, as she was alternately called by Paul Zanek, whose interest in the woman seemed a bit more than professional. Jessica had pretended she knew nothing of Police Commissioner Stephens of New Orleans, or that he was at Quantico, personally requesting help with the Queen of Hearts killings. She knew now that P.C. Stephens had personally requested her, but that Zanek was doing his level best to sell the man on the psychic detective instead. It was as if Paul had a personal motive in it all, and one that went beyond protecting Jessica from herself.

Paul stopped the camera and in the darkened room, Jessica realized that he'd brought someone else in to view the tape, a tall, older man with piercing green eyes and dyed red hair that she guessed to be Stephens.

Stephens who'd been guided to them by the FBI in Louisiana, was thick-chested, trim at the waist, a man with thinning red hair and a superior attitude that Jessica didn't like in the least on meeting him.

Zanek, a big man, filled the little screening room with his personality and baritone voice. He now said, "We have film on every psychic hit that Dr. Desinor has made since becoming an FBI agent. The woman is nothing short of miraculous. Isn't that right, Dr. Coran?" Paul leaned over and whispered in Jessica's ear, "Back me up on all I say."

He then turned to Stephens while the still shot of Dr. Desinor, larger than life, stared down on them. "I'm sending Dr. Desinor on an experimental basis, rather than Agent Coran here, Mr. Stephens, for reasons already explained to you. Nothing's changed."

"Dr. Desinor," Jessica said, instantly rebelling, "the psychic we're supposed not to have on our payroll? How're you going to get around that? Come on, Paul. It looks to me like they need scientific help down there in Cajun country, not more voodoo." Even as she said it, she was sorry. She knew that the psychic arm of the Behavioral Science Unit was from its inception Paul Zanek's innovation, and besides, she had heard only positive, glowing reports on Dr. Desinor.

"Come off it, Jess," Paul said. "You'd be waving a bloody flag at yourself down there. The press'd be all over the story when they got wind you were pulling into town. Matisak would be at you like a tiger on a kill."

"The last time you used his name, you assured me he was most likely dead! Which is it, Paul?"

"Damnit, Jess, until we find a body . . ."

"And when will that be, Paul? A year, two, three, five? I'm done living this way. I'm through hiding. Do you understand that?"

"I've got a meeting with Santiva I have to get to. We'll discuss this later today. Say about three?"

"All right, all right," she seethed.

Before Zanek retreated, he said, "There's more tapes of Dr. Desinor in action. One in particular you must see, so please, continue without me. Leonard, resume the screening," he told an assistant, and the film began anew.

Jessica wasn't having any of it.

She caught Paul just outside the door. "So, what do you need me here for?"

"To help me convince the man. Jess, we've got a chance to show the combined division chiefs, and the head of the FBI, that psychic detection makes sense here, especially on this one."

"On psycho weird-out cases, you mean?"

"It's just bizarre enough, and I don't know, I just feel it. Will it hurt you to watch the film I've pulled for Stephens on Dr. Desinor?"

Jessica had trouble focusing in on the film now, willing to take Paul Zanek's word for Desinor's feats of acumen and talent in the field of psychometric readings of objects found at the scene of a crime.

On screen, Dr. Desinor, a handsome woman with full features, tall with a proud bearing, now held a ransom note in one hand, lightly moving her fingertips over the surface and going into a trance state. A skeptical agent from Georgia named Parlen had his back to the camera now; he'd come seeking her help in a months-old case involving a kidnapped financier. Dr. Desinor's suggestions came as a surprise, even a shock to Agent Parlen, who doubted her credibility. Jessica could read his doubt in his voice. Nonetheless, Parlen promised to look into the possibility of involvement by an illegitimate daughter and perhaps her husband or live-in boyfriend.

Jessica's mind was filled with its own ongoing film, memories of a soul-warming Hawaii, and gentle James Parry and his touch, flooding in, only to be swamped by the ever-present fear she now lived with: that at any moment, any day now, an escaped maniac whom she had once put away would turn up at her doorstep to seek his long-awaited, carefully planned revenge.

"It's no easy matter living with the knowledge that someone is stalking you." Dr. Donna Lemonte, her psychiatrist, had tried to be reassuring the last time they'd spoken. "Someone who wants more than just your life. Your life's just a symbol to this guy."

"Don't you think I know that? This sonofabitch wants to drain me of my goddamned blood, and drink it before my dangling corpse."

Mad Matthew Matisak, imprisoned for life for the blood-drinking, torture deaths of countless young women and men, had made a daring and intelligent escape from the maximum security asylum that had only held him for a goddamned total of two and a half years. His escape had left a trail of dead and discarded people, like so many empty containers. And that was exactly how he thought of people—containers, buckets of blood, to leave drained in his gruesome wake. The dead included the head of security and psychiatric treatment at the federal facility in Philadelphia, Dr. Gabriel Arnold, who had never understood Matisak.

Jessica had done countless interviews with Matisak, gaining information about where all the bodies were buried. For the past year, Dr. Arnold, head of forensic psychiatry at the facility, had worked with Matisak, and recently he'd begun to make outlandish and foolish claims about small victories scored against his number-one patient: the zookeeper pleased with his most prized possession. Arnold had claimed that the mass murderer had actually become cooperative during sessions with him, that Matisak had become talkative with him, that he had put away all demands and had finished with his "head games" and was a willing subject of study for the FBI.

She might have guessed on hearing such reports that Matisak was playing yet another game out to its conclusion, but she'd had no idea that this time it would end in death.

Jessica recalled now having warned Arnold of her suspicions, that Matisak was not to be trusted, ever, that the fiend cared not a whit for the suffering of the families of his victims. Arnold had only become defensive and angry, sure that she wanted to "keep Matisak breakthroughs" all to herself. Since Paul Zanek had taken over the FBI Behavioral Science Unit, Dr. Arnold had been feeling more and more put upon and isolated at the facility, which, Jessica had no doubt, had further contributed to his death.

Now her predictions had come true tenfold, with the madman's having so completely checkmated Dr. Arnold, making mincemeat of his remains after divesting him of every ounce of blood via a dialysis machine. The madman had made a fool of Arnold, whose so-called "cumulative progress" had amounted to psycho-nonsense.

Cunning and satanically wise, Matisak had not tried to fake an illness, but rather had induced an attack from one or several of the afflictions which wracked his body. He'd done so by not taking his medications, which he'd undoubtably been hiding either in his laundry or on his food tray, if not feeding the stuff to the occasional mouse visiting him in the night. These were medications Matisak had been on for the past two and a half years, medications—supplied via federal funds—which not only controlled his mood swings but his physical abnormalities as well. He had a potpourri of illnesses to choose from. Faking any one of them would have ended in disaster from the start, and knowing this, he'd instead invited a true attack. A calculated risk of his own life.

It had all been carefully planned and thought out. Matisak had lingered in the sick ward for almost a week, biding his time, regaining strength as his weakened condition faded. Security there was tight, but he was out of his cage, and only a short walk down the corridor freedom stood waiting. At precisely the right time of day, using an orderly's robe and badge, the so-called madman—incapable of knowing right from wrong according to some human rights activists who'd fought to keep him from the death penalty—would make the easy walk to deliverance, unafraid of his captors.

So he had waited, and each day had brought a visit from the now-trusting Dr. Arnold, and after the physical therapy sessions, Dr. Arnold would try his uniquely asinine brand of psychotherapy on the killer.

Matisak had cunningly chosen the precise moment of opportunity, when Arnold had filled a syringe and pumped the serum that Matisak needed into his arm. Matisak had grabbed the empty syringe and plunged it deep into Arnold's throat. This had sent the doctor staggering back as Matisak grabbed a scalpel from Arnold's lapel pocket. After a moment's macabre dance with Whalen, the security guard, Matisak had turned the scalpel on Whalen, sluicing through his thick neck in one instantaneous movement.

After wrestling the dying security guard to the floor, Mad Matthew Matisak had easily overpowered an orderly who was new to asylum work and who, frozen in place, had waited for death to easily come.

But the cunning, cool fiend had first ordered the new man to disrobe and toss his orderly whites aside before Matisak took his pleasure with the orderly, slicing through the jugular and carotid arteries. The infirmary had been instantly steeped in blood, which Matisak, at some point, had gone on all fours to lap up in dog fashion. He'd left hand and knee and even tongue prints on the floor in crimson detail, and he'd also left behind the disgusting poem meant for Jessica and written in Arnold's blood across the wall.

Before Matisak was finished with Dr. Arnold, there remained not a drop of blood in his cadaver. The monster had made fiendishly wicked use of a nearby dialysis machine. He'd no doubt planned its use on Arnold all along, and enjoyed watching the blood empty from his body through the transparent polyethylene tube and into the beaker from which Matisak drank his fill, leaving only what he could not consume or take with him. An autopsy had clearly shown that Matisak had used the IV tube and the dialysis machine to pump the blood from Arnold's throat after laying the bound and gagged man across a stretcher. What troubled Jessica most was the thought that Arnold was conscious long enough to watch his own blood streak through the tube, into the machine and out into the waiting beakers.

She held at bay a mental image of the monster hoisting a beaker of blood to his lips before Arnold's crazed eyes.

A reckless trail of victims left in Matisak's wake had led FBI authorities to Oklahoma, and by the time Jessica got there from Hawaii, the manhunt had concentrated on the Tulsa area. It was one of the largest manhunts in recent history. But Matisak had remained elusive, and once the trail had gone cold in Oklahoma, Jessica and Paul had gone back to the federal facility in Philadelphia where Arnold had so hideously died. There she had examined the scene of the murders, which by then had been cleaned and tidied up. Still, she had learned what she could from others who'd swept the actual scene, piecing together the probable string of events that had led to Arnold's death and Matisak's escape.

Once sated, the monster had next assumed the identity of the orderly, named Kenneth Bowden, wearing the young man's lab coat and ID tag. He'd taken the man's car keys, casually strolled out to the car, pulled up to the gate, where he'd blithely signed himself out as Bowden, and proceeded through the gate with a wave of his hand.

Lights came up now in the small screening room behind Zanek's office, and the final film, dated only the day before, ended with Dr. Desinor rushing from the room as if her life depended upon getting off camera. She was neither shaken nor upset by her reading of a ransom note brought her by authorities in Decatur, Georgia.

"She's everything I told you, isn't she? What about it, Stephens?" asked Zanek, who'd returned through his office door at the rear, surprising both Stephens and Jessica. "Tell 'im, Jess."

P.C. Richard Stephens ran thick, freckled fingers through his thinning mop of red hair and allowed it to settle on the bald pate at the back. "She is remarkable, but I had already come to that conclusion just reading of her work from the material you forwarded."

"I think she's exactly what you need in New Orleans," Zanek told him. "Jessica here, well . . . she's got so many duties here at Quantico, it just wouldn't do for us to lose her right now. You understand?"

Stephens, who'd originally requested help in the forensics arena from the FBI, and from Jessica Coran in particular, had heard a great deal about Dr. Coran and how she got results, and all of it had proven to be true. But Zanek had had him waffling between the pathologist and the psychic for a week now, wondering if he should get help in the form of science or seance. All he knew for sure was that his NOPD had its collective hands full with a bizarre string of murders that no one seemed capable of getting a handle on.

"Jessica, you haven't said anything," Zanek pressed, placing a friendly hand on her shoulder. "What do you think of Dr. Desinor? Doesn't she make David Copperfield look pitiful by comparison?"

"I'll admit she's very good."

"Dr. Desinor gets results. She was dead-on in Georgia."

"You know that for sure?"

"Got word just this morning: a major development in the Sendak case. Mr. Stephens here asked specifically for your assistance, Jess, but I've explained to him that you're needed here for the time being. Hell, we've got requests for Jess's help from a dozen different police agencies across the continent at the moment, and I've had to turn them all down, Stephens. Nothing personal. It's just important right now for Jess, for Dr. Coran, to remain close at hand. Now, our Dr. Desinor'll be a fine stand-in, I can assure you, especially on this sort of case, a case involving few clues. Dr. Desinor's your man, if you'll pardon the expression, on a case that requires an instinctive ability to get at the truth."

"She puts on a damned good show," Stephens admitted, "if they have indeed come up with a solution in Georgia based on her reading of that note."

"They have Sendak's daughter in custody, the daughter he never had, and she's told authorities where the body is," replied Paul, obviously impressed not only by what he'd witnessed on the screen but also by the subsequent developments in the Sendak case.

"I'm most impressed," Stephens said. "Dr. Desinor puts on quite a show, but then so do you, Dr. Coran. I read about how—with no more than an arm coughed up from the sea in Hawaii—you were able to reconstruct the awful string of murders there which had gone undetected for years."

"I had a great deal of help there, a support team of the first caliber, and as for detecting the undetected . . . well, James Parry was really the one who broke the case wide open.''

"Modesty becomes you, Jess," said Zanek.

"Parry and his team were superb," she insisted, her stare hard.

"Yes, well, in any event, I wanted to show Stephens here what I've seen in Desinor, and I wanted to show you, since you'll be stepping aside this go-round so as to catch up on your duties here, and since I've long wanted you to evaluate Dr. Desinor's whole operation to see if the Profiling sector might not wish to avail themselves of her services in the future—possibly even think of her department as a new arm, so to speak.''

An interesting idea, Jessica thought. She'd heard of Dr. Desinor's intriguing work. Not many in the upper echelon of the FBI network hadn't. However, Desinor's work was classified top secret, not for public consumption; consequently, Kim Desinor and her small team had kept a low profile themselves. Their budget, it was rumored, was pretty shabby as well.

"Paul, I'd like to talk to you alone for a moment, if you don't mind," Jessica requested.

Stephens flashed a perfunctory frown, his bulbous nose and red cheeks flaring—both frown and drinker's rouge part of his office, she decided—but he quickly recovered, nodded and left the screening room.

Her heart is like an outbound ship
That at its anchor swings.

—Whittier

Paul Zanek fished into his private stock and came up with a bottle of Jim Beam and some water and ice. He made himself a drink and offered it to Jessica.

"You know I've sworn off booze, Paul. If I start drinking now, I might not stop."

"Sorry, no, I didn't know."

"There's a hell of a lot you don't know, Paul, and maybe that's the problem."

"Come on . . . what is this, Jess? I've got eyes. I know what's driving you, but what's all this hostility? I thought we were on the same side of the fence here." His voice changed dramatically as he added, "You look like . . . well, you look like you haven't slept in days."

"You really know how to flatter a girl, Paul."

"I'm sorry, Jess. You know me . . . shoot from the lip."

She waved it off. "No apology necessary."

"No letup to the nightmares?"

She shrugged in answer and plopped into a chair before him.

He gritted his teeth as if afraid to ask, but forged ahead anyway. "Dr. Lemonte's prescriptions of no use?"

All of the above, she silently replied. "No, no . . . nothing like that. I've just been maybe working too long in the lab since getting back."

"I'm sorry about Oklahoma, that his trail went cold and that there's been no change, but the bastard's leery now. We came real close to plugging him up, and he knows it."

"He's had a lot of time to think about when and where he'll next strike, Paul. He went to Oklahoma for a reason, probably to throw us off, but there was someone or something he wanted there. One of the many background files on him said he had been born in Oklahoma in 1948, his family moving to the Chicago area when he was three or four years old. His father became a baker, his mother a factory laborer. The place where they lived in Oklahoma was gone, but he went back there. Why? He has a reason for every step he takes.''

''Maybe it wasn't a conscious decision, Jess. Maybe he just took off running and, coincidentally, wound up in Oklahoma.''

''Where he killed three people in two days.'' The trail from Philadelphia to Oklahoma was littered with Matisak's leavings. They'd gotten a make and model on the car he was using, a white four-door Mercury sedan stolen from his last Oklahoma victims just outside of Tulsa. They'd run the car down with a chopper and squad cars, hauled the driver out at gunpoint and pushed his face into the dirt, but it wasn't Matisak.

Matisak had sold the car to the fool for a hundred dollars. They'd traced back to where the transaction had occurred: at Mohawk Boulevard where it became Young Street, within walking distance of the North Tulsa Regional Airport—where, it was surmised, Matisak forced a pilot into the air at gunpoint to make his escape. Flight controllers had seen the plane take off without clearance and without logging a flight plan with the tower. It was a friendly little airport where people parked their toys and came out on weekends for recreation, and it was not unusual for a man to take his Cessna up, circle the area and return within an hour or two, without having logged any flight plans. The place was small enough that the good old boys in the tower didn't think anything of it until they were alerted by the FBI, too late, about the fugitive in the area.

Actually, the tower had been alerted long before, but a shift change hadn't gotten the message. By now Matisak had vanished without a trace. Still, an army of agents had gone to work in the area. Planes, trains, buses and terminals had been searched, but the monster had simply disappeared. Still, Jessica, on hand in Tulsa, had had the undeniable feeling even then that Matisak had had a specific reason for coming to the area. Something quite specific, she'd surmised, and the taking of an airplane was no spur-of-the-moment decision. She'd reasoned that Matisak had planned his every step, including the theft of the plane, his getaway. But why? Did he have family there that no one knew about? Did someone harbor him during the brief stay in the area? Did he know the guy with the plane? A background check on the pilot, a man named Norman Easthan, revealed nothing unsavory. He seemed just another innocent who'd gotten in the way. Still, she remembered how many people Matisak had used for cover in Chicago, dupes and losers and desperates who'd clung to Matisak for some sense of identity, only to be set up by him.

Was it possible that the madman was still in Oklahoma somewhere? Was it possible that someone was harboring him? Who would harbor such a fiend? It was not entirely impossible, even though every newspaper had carried his photo and every TV set had flashed his face before millions. He'd been highlighted on *America's Most Wanted,* his story retold anew along with his desperate escape. The famous TV program had never featured such a bloody episode in its history. If he was being harbored by someone, that someone must know about it.

She couldn't imagine anyone in the country who could not know what Mad Matt Matisak looked like. But now, for some unaccountable reason, a notion lodged in her brain, and Paul Zanek stared at her, knowing something was running frantically through her mind and looking for an escape route.

"What're you hatching, Jess?" he suspiciously asked.

She was wondering why she hadn't considered the possibility when they were in Oklahoma. "The Indian reservations," she said aloud.

"What?" he asked. "What Indian reservations?"

"Oklahoma is full of Indian reserves. Tribes of half the Indian nations live in the state, are you kidding? What if Matisak knew someone who lived on an Indian reservation down there in Oklahoma, someone who read no papers, saw no TVs, had no idea who or what he was?"

Zanek looked across at her. It made sense. "I'll check with law-enforcement agencies in Tulsa, see if there's been any trouble on any of the reserves. It's a long shot, though, Jess. Don't hold your breath."

"Whataya think I've been doing since leaving Hawaii,

knowing the bastard's stalking me?''

"That's why I've got agents watching you around the clock, kid. I'm not going to let anything happen to my best forensics expert, you got that?''

"I got it, all right, and having men following me everywhere I go isn't my idea of freedom. Ticks me off. He's free to victimize me while I'm . . . well, I'm living in a goddamned box.''

"Look, so long as he's out there and—"

"No, Paul, so long as I'm in here, remember? Hiding behind Quantico's walls? I'm trapped in a goddamned rat's maze that he's knowingly created for me; I know he's thought this through chapter and verse, and he knows me better than you do, better than perhaps I do, damnit. I'm no bloody good to anybody this way, including myself.''

"You're safe, aren't you?''

"Safe's highly overrated.''

"What about life? Is that overrated, Jess?''

They stood now, each having risen along with their voices, and now, staring across at one another, each felt as stubborn as the other. Finally, he broke the stalemate, saying, "You've got everything you need here. We've got enough lab work to keep you occupied for as long as—"

"As long as I like? Well, I *don't like*, Paul.''

"And what do you mean," he countered, "no good to anybody! Why hell, Jess, you're our number-one top field agent. That's the silliest thing I think I've heard outta you yet.''

"Matisak's put me behind bars, don't you see that? I go between this compound and my apartment, from work to bed. I can't even go shopping without the Hardy-fucking-Boys looking on. Ever try on a dress with Bob Waite and Greg Thatcher looking on, Paul? And Sims! What a dull ass. Can't even play gin rummy because it runs counter to his notion of what's in the line of duty.''

He laughed at this. "No, can't say as I blame you for being frustrated, Jess.'' He got a mental picture of Thatcher and Waite in a lady's dressing room, and this led to a grin.

"Nothing funny about those yo-yos you've plastered to me, Paul, and I tell you, I'm through with this warped lifestyle—through. Hell, on weekends, I used to go into D.C., visit the

Smithsonian or just walk the parks and smell the lilacs in bloom, but Waite and Thatcher've made it clear that there'll be no unnecessary risks. I feel like I'm living in a bottle, a goddamned prisoner of some kind of absurd war, and Quantico's become my cell and this . . . this . . . compound is getting the hell on my nerves. It's got to end.''

She tossed back her auburn hair, the long strands curling about her neck, and she went to the window to stare out at the same grounds and the same buildings she had been staring at for six months without letup.

''We're doing everything we can, Jess.'' Paul's response to her outburst came off sounding as lame to him as it did to her, making him frown.

''I know that, Paul, and I appreciate it, but it appears that everything just isn't enough, doesn't it?''

''I can . . . I can send you back to Hawaii to continue field work there, if you like. The hearings being held by the State Department to investigate our part in bringing Lopaka Kowona to justice are coming up soon.''

''No, no . . . not Hawaii,'' she said instantly. ''When I go back to Hawaii, it won't be for any damned State Department hearings, you can believe that.'' Jim Parry was there, and the idea of Matisak in her paradise—and he would stalk her there, as he would to the ends of the earth—made her almost physically ill. She had lost Otto Boutine to this maniac. The fiend would not get near Jim, ever. If the demon learned of their romantic involvement, he might easily target Jim just to hurt her. He was that sadistic.

''New Orleans,'' she firmly barked as she turned to face Zanek. She was as tall as he, her creamy skin taut and strained with her decision. ''I want the New Orleans case.''

''Come on, Jess, we've talked already about this. You can't seriously want to risk your—''

''It's my goddamned life, Paul.''

''You're in the Bureau, and that means it's also our goddamned life you're proposing to waste out there. This organization has invested a fortune in you, you realize, and—''

''Oh, damnit, Paul, don't feed me that crap now. We've been through too damned much together for you to suddenly become J. Edgar on me.''

"Hey, nobody does J. Edgar better'n me," he joked.

"I need a field assignment. I'm no good to anyone the way I am. I want the New Orleans case, this Queen of Hearts thing, okay? I can be effective there. I need to get back to work; I need to know I'm still effective, and I need to know I'm in charge of my life; that I run me, not Matisak."

"But that'd be suicidal."

"Do you understand me? You do, don't you? You'd hate being run around by a creep like this. Confess it. Say it. You wouldn't stand for it if it were you, would you?"

"But Jess, New Orleans would mean opening yourself up to attack. He'll know you're there the moment tomorrow's papers hit the street."

"I'm willing to risk it; I'm willing to bait the bastard at this point, and if that doesn't make you salivate for his head on a platter, Paul, then maybe you'd best get out of this business." She stomped about the room now like a caged animal, her pacing finally making his eyes follow her about. "Besides, you need Waite and Thatcher and Sims and all the others on more important duties. You can't continue to justify the outlay in man-hours to your superiors anymore. We both know that. All those taxpayer dollars so Thatch can stare through binoculars at my bedroom window? Come on, Paul, be reasonable. Come on, whataya say? Let's give Stephens his first choice."

Zanek ran both hands through his thick mat of dark hair and shook his head. It was his turn to pace the room. "It's too damned risky, Jess. I care too much for you to knowingly put your life in danger."

"That's not what I want to hear from you, Paul!"

He drummed his fingers on his desk and finally bellowed, "Damnit, Jess, I don't know. I've been promising Kim . . . Dr. Desinor a shot, you know, to put her theories into practice."

"If that's all you're worried about, don't be. Just send us both—as a team. How better to determine if science and psi can work together?"

"You're so damned competitive, Jess."

"You wouldn't have it any other way. So, what do you say?"

"I can't make this decision without input from above. You know that, Jess."

"But they'll go along with your recommendation. I also know that."

"Do you also know you've talked me into a goddamned corner? I guess you do."

She beamed, her eyes going wide. "Then you'll go to bat for me?"

He gave her a pretended angry glare. "No guarantees but one, Jess."

"What's that?"

"You travel down there with a guard. At least two specially trained agents."

"No, not Thatch and Waite; please, no one, Paul. It'd only defeat us. Matisak won't tip his hand if he smells a trap, and no way can those bozos avoid being spotted."

"You either go with a guard, or you don't go."

She breathed deeply, thinking that she could convince Santiva of the foolishness of this step later on. For now, she must allow Paul to play Marshal to her Saloon Girl.

"Whatever," she muttered. "But I want you to keep me posted on anything happening in Oklahoma," she quickly added. "I can easily get there from New Orleans, if there's reason to."

"All right, then we're agreed. Now we just have to sell Santiva on the idea, and there's the little matter of selling the notion to Dr. Desinor as well."

"I thought you said she wanted to field-test her work? What's to sell?"

"Let's just say she's not anxious to be proven wrong out of the gate, and now with you on board, she might be frightened off; besides, she's very selective about what cases she'll take on. Some, she says, leave her cold."

"I can imagine."

"You think what she does is a hoax?"

"No, I didn't say that."

"What do you think of her work, honestly?"

"The older I get, the longer I live, the more I see in this world . . . the more superstitious I get, I'm afraid to admit."

"But what Dr. Desinor does has nothing to do with super-stition."

"I'm just speaking of my prejudices," she continued, pacing the room again now. "And the older I get, the more sense I make of the old line that states there's more between heaven and earth than dreamt of in your little philosophy, or science, Jessica Coran. And"—she stopped short, seeing that he was concerned, that a crease had formed along his forehead—"and the older I get, Paul, the more limbs I crawl out on, saying things like, I think Paul Zanek's a man of vision for backing psychic detection in the agency, and—"

"You've said that? To whom?"

"And I also think you could take a great fall, Humpty-Dumpty, if she should fail, so I have to believe you're a courageous-type guy to back Desinor."

He smiled at this. "I didn't know you'd formed an opinion. But as I said, Dr. Desinor could be uncomfortable with the idea of working in tandem with you at this stage. We'll have to break it to her gently, in the best possible manner."

"Well, if she's unwilling, then she's unwilling. But I'm going to New Orleans with or without her, you got that?"

"I used to think I made the decisions around here. Celebrity does not become you, Dr. Coran."

Jessica caught a look of deep concentration behind his otherwise smiling eyes. "Tell, me, Paul, is there something going on between you and Dr. Desinor I should know about?"

"No, no . . . nothing between us but a professional relation-ship. How can you ask such a question? You know I'm a happily married man."

Rumor has it your marriage has been on the skids, she thought, and it was easy to believe that rumor. "Hasn't stopped you from hitting on me," she said.

"Well, Jess, that was at a low ebb in my life, and I've apologized how many times now?"

"Sorry . . . shouldn't have brought it up."

"Don't mention it . . . ever again," he joked, and led her from his office and back into the screening room. "Guess we'd better break the latest news to Stephens. I'm quite sure he'll be overjoyed you're going back with him."

"You're kinda taken now with the idea of our baiting Matisak, aren't you, Paul?"

"Hey, what kind of thing is that to say to your boss and your friend, Jess?"

"Come on, admit it."

"Admit it, hell. I'll admit to only one thing, Jess."

"What's zat?"

"After the way you took out Archer from the top of this building two years ago, let's just say that I wouldn't want to be Matisak when you draw a bead on the bastard."

"Well, maybe it's time we turned the tables on him, the way that creep keeps baiting us, leaving those sick, blood-penned notes for us to find. . . . "

"I know it's got to be difficult for you," he said, his mind racing on, "with a maniac like him pining for you like a love-sick calf, only this animal's bleeding others in some unholy exhibition of perverted love . . . delivering his prizes for your approval . . . giving you his twisted valentines."

She thought of the despicable notes, usually in verse, left at the scene of each killing now, written across a mirror, a tile floor or some other surface. All of them were different, but all were the same: Matisak wanted to again taste her blood, to drink her blood. No surrogate would do. *It was an acquired taste*—she'd heard the joke that was going around about her relationship to the convicted vampire killer.

She momentarily thought of his victims, all butchered like swine only after he'd drained off their blood in a controlled fashion from the throat. The precious liquid of life was put up in mason jars like tomatoes, placed in a cooler brought for the task and carried off by the sadistic monster to feed on at his convenience. Jessica had lost self-esteem, confidence and the one man whom she'd loved without reservation up to that point, Otto Boutine, to this madman. Futilely, she had then fought from a wheelchair to see him placed on death row; she had even contemplated avenues of murdering the soulless son-ofabitch herself, but now all that was yesterday's remorse.

While Matisak was incarcerated along with other criminally insane monsters, she had managed to regain not only her physical well-being, the scars from his attack on her healing, but also her mental stamina, and had since proven herself in New

York on the Claw case with Alan Rychman, and in Hawaii on the Trade Winds killings with Jim Parry. But since Matisak's escape, her life had taken a different and ugly turn. The invisible scars had come back like stigmata. And no matter where she was, who she was with or what she was engaged in doing, the signs of those ugly stigmata were always present, just below the surface, always pressing to get out again and overwhelm her again. Even now, standing in the corridor outside the screening room, shaking hands with Stephens from New Orleans again, she was uncomfortably aware of the scars others could not see. She wondered if Dr. Desinor, the psychic, would be able to see Jessica Coran's psychic scars, the thought frightening in itself, for she'd worked so long to keep them invisible to all but the man she loved, James Parry. And even he did not know what awful depths those scars had reached. . . .

New Orleans Police Commissioner Richard Stephens stood dumbfounded just outside the screening room door when he learned from Jessica of his good fortune, that not one FBI operative, but two, would be returning with him to his Crescent City. Both the famous Jessica Coran and Dr. Kim Desinor would each, from her own unique perspective, be looking squarely at the most challenging case in the history of the city.

"Splendid, splendid," he repeatedly said, shaking Zanek's hand after releasing hers.

Zanek glared at Jessica for her having released such information so soon. He still had as yet to speak to Santiva and the upper echelon of the Bureau. Zanek was trying to tell Stephens this now, but Jessica pretended it was merely a matter of protocol at this point, and after saying so to Stephens and catching Paul's unhidden fury, she asked Stephens, "How is New Orleans this time of year? Less crowded, now that Mardi Gras is over?"

"Hot, just like the food, and plenty crowded. There're always parades, no matter what time of year. We celebrate life year-round in New Orleans," he continued.

"Celebrate life, huh." *I'm sure it's well-staged for the tourism industry*, she thought.

Stephens didn't miss a beat. "That's why this monster and

these horrendous deaths must end and quickly.''

Uh-huh, agreed, Jessica thought, her mind wandering back
to Dr. Faith while Zanek escorted Stephens away from her,
talking buddy-buddy to the other man, leaving her standing
alone, the way Paul wanted it. He must be in control, even if
it meant leaving Jessica Coran standing alone in a hallway.

She only hoped that Santiva would have half the luck she'd
had with him.

Now Jessica made for her lab, having neglected work waiting for her there. As she went, she curiously wondered how
the two of them, Desinor and she, would get on. She'd never
worked with a psychic before, and at one time she would have
thought Zanek a madman for starting such a program within
the confines of the FBI. Otto Boutine certainly would not have
allowed it in his division. Still, this woman Desinor seemed
gifted, touched by some power both invisible and divine,
something that Jessica would not mind exploiting, or at least
understanding better and employing. Science had always been
her strength, and yet there was a limit to what science could
do, and there was always that line beyond which you needed
a leap of faith, intuition, instinct. Maybe Dr. Desinor simply
had more instinct and intuition than others. Either way, Jessica
wondered if she could not learn from the other woman some
vital information.

No, Otto Boutine would not have championed a seer, an
Edgar Cayce–type in his unit. Still, Otto wasn't here and the
world was spinning as madly, or more so, than ever on its
axis, and the number of brutal killings, serial murders, spree
murders, rapes and other brands of evil in this world had hardly diminished; in fact, violent crime was up as never before,
even among children. Maybe law-enforcement agencies
needed the assistance of the supernatural and the supernormal
if they were ever to stem the growing tide of murderous rage
in America.

Jessica had never been overly superstitious or concerned
with matters of superstition, at least not until recently, but
events and coincidence had played heavily in her life, and now
with Matisak a werewolf on the prowl, capable of seducing
people at his will, a Jeykll and Hyde of the first order, the
more store she placed in fatalism and common-sense values

born of experience, and the more she'd become interested in what she used to dismiss as superstition.

Perhaps she'd just become more superstitious herself since Hawaii. The beautiful island world had had its effect on her; there she'd discovered a world founded on a faith most took for fairy-tale absurdity about the gods of the sea, the imps of the coral reefs, deities of the volcano and forests and mango trees. Yet as superstitious as that quaint faith was, it had become the real dragon-slayer when it came to ending the career of Hawaii's most notorious serial killer, Lopaka Kowona.

Jessica had once believed that she had seen the future of police detection in DNA fingerprinting, serum and tissue matching. Maybe the real future lay instead in Dr. Desinor's psychic detection. Perhaps police agencies in the twenty-first century, on remote outposts in the galaxy, would be manned by psychics and empaths. Maybe the world would be a better place for it.

Maybe . . . a big maybe, but no one was making any guarantees, and *certainty* was an illusion no one believed in any longer, not the holy men, not the community leaders, not the politicians, not the government and certainly not the criminologists or those who projected into the future of law enforcement.

Arriving at her lab, she gave J.T. a big hug and a thank-you for putting Stephens and her together.

His heart is like a mountain of iron.

—Pentaur

New Orleans

A few days' decay, the elements and the animals had conspired to create a grotesque tapestry over the corpse. Two, possibly three days in the Louisiana heat was enough to turn even the freshest meat into a wormy muck. Internal gases had been baked inside the decomposing corpse, had bloated the body, finally exploding through the skin at unaccountable locations: the cheek turned to the earth, the leg with the most lividity, the forearm where the boy-man had been gnawed at by raccoons or wild dogs.

Degeneration to the once-fine features had created a hideous, repulsive mask which no Hollywood makeup artist could hope to capture. What lay here before Lieutenant Detective Alex Sincebaugh didn't seem human, or rather was a horrid mockery of a once-sentient, lively, active young person. What remained seemed more akin to soiled rags, discarded cardboard, leftovers—''toast,'' as the MTV generation might more aptly put it.

''You think it's Surette?'' Ben asked.

''Can't tell for sure, can you?'' Alex replied to the hulking figure standing over him and the body. Sincebaugh hadn't remembered going to his knees over the victim, but now he found himself staring up at his partner. DeYampert's large eyes looked on the verge of tears, but that expression was one Big Ben carried with him everywhere: the sad, doughy eyes of a basset hound. And like the irises of a calf or a St. Bernard, the glistening, moist eyes meant to reveal no more than a resigned acceptance. Ben, like most cops, kept his feelings tightly balled up. Alex knew that his partner of so many years now had gone to the edge on this one, a missing persons case

53

that had looked to be solved, only to become a murder case.

Sincebaugh too had allowed himself a brief moment of hope that they would locate twenty-one-year-old Victor "Vicki" Surette—but not like this. They'd had every reason to believe they'd find the cross-dresser quite well, alive and unharmed, panhandling or doing johns along the dingy periphery of Bourbon Street. After all, they'd gotten a lead about "Vicki" from Gilreath, a transvestite and a snitch they often pulled over for a mock arrest and street news.

"If this here do be Vic Surette," Ben deYampert drawled in his native Louisiana tongue, "he ain't so much a looker no more."

"It's going to take some time to ID him; take prints, maybe get some dental records to match what's in his mouth—if we can get any records out of the family vault. . . ."

Some families of gay men, cross-dressers and transvestites were extremely reluctant to cooperate with police, even when they loved their offspring, despite the circumstances. And Victor Surette was rumored to have no family, or one so steeped in Old New Orleans values and traditions that no relative would come within speaking distance of him. Gilreath had hinted at old money and modern business holdings. Gilreath had also hinted at a deep-seated hatred there, and since most victims of crime were victims of family, friends and acquaintances, this could not be ignored. But a search of the missing man's apartment days before the location of his body had turned up not one scintilla of information about his family. Gilreath had said that Vicki, as he was known to his dearest friends, wanted it that way. Still, Alex could hardly believe how clean the kid's apartment had been of paper, and without paper, there was no trail back to family, unless one of them picked up a newspaper or heard about Surette's fate on the nightly news and then came forward to claim the body.

"You think it's him, don't you, Sincy?" pressed Ben.

"I'd say the clothes appear to match the last known description." Sincebaugh breathed heavily, his stomach churning, his head reeling from the stench of the corpse, which lay sprawled on its stomach, limbs akimbo.

No one had touched the body, knowing it was Alex Sincebaugh's call since he was detective in charge on this rotation.

He had waited long enough for the M.E., he decided. Wanting to know more now, he slipped on a pair of surgical gloves and turned the body over, his hands instinctively repulsed by the Jell-O–like pressure against his touch. Rigor had come and gone, the body now relaxed and rapidly emulsifying thanks to the heat of a record-breaking week in New Orleans.

"Sincy, you sure we shouldn't wait for Wardlaw?"

Sincebaugh slowed a bit at the use of the nickname his partner had saddled him with, but he bawled in response, "For Chrissake, Big . . . waited long enough for that damned souse."

"Miss Old Doc Whitaker, don't you?"

"Sure as hell do."

They were in a wood on a clear, humid New Orleans night. Nearby, egrets silently stalked the shallows even in darkness, until one broke the silence by piercing the water, spiking a fish with its beak. Alex and Ben were working over a body lying beside the indigo waters of huge Lake Ponchartrain; they weren't in New Orleans proper anymore but had come all the way out to Slidell as soon as it was recognized that this was a murder victim. They'd been out of their jurisdiction, doing a routine rundown on a case involving a pair of high rollers who'd been pumping the area with a new, synthetic drug that was leaving users in various stages of paraplegia and vegetative comas, when the call came over, and since they were so close and Slidell was undermanned, they took it, swinging the car around just before entering the bridge traffic which would've taken them back to downtown New Orleans.

Both men were feeling the tension on the streets in Slidell, where race relations hadn't been so grand lately, and where they felt ill at ease anyway because it was so far from their home jurisdiction and base of operations in New Orleans.

There'd been a riot of a different color than race "o'er t' Biloxi, Mississippi," as Ben had put it in his best Cajun tongue. "At one-a-dem grand 'Sippi casinos der on't da river."

It was a floating palace the size of four football fields, called the *Royal Flush*. The ballroom/concert hall had gotten in the Granite Psycho rock band to add a little allure to the gambling tables, as if there were a need, and things had gotten out of control. Since the gambling casino boat was moored between Biloxi and New Orleans, and the Mississippi legislature had allowed a two-day blue-flu walkout when negotiations failed there, New Orleans police were prevailed upon to respond. So while almost every cop within a six-county radius of Biloxi, including two precincts from New Orleans, had turned out in full riot gear there, Alex and Ben had agreeably driven out to Slidell to follow a lead on Kenny Alvarez and Terrell Foreman, the pushers, only to get the coincidence call of the century, should this work out to be Victor Surette's body, since they'd been doing the M.P. work on him up till now. Ben called it "i-ron-knee."

Dispatch had spoken of a badly decomposed body found at a dump site on a lonely stretch of sand disguising itself as a path. The weeds here were as large as cattails. It was a place that even Alex was unfamiliar with. Alex and Ben had immediately decided as they pulled into the thicket that whoever killed the victim knew the region intimately.

The man reporting the carnage had driven in here to dump a mattress, had spotted something odd among the brush and debris and decided to investigate until he realized that his find was human. After getting the man's statement, Ben had threatened to levy a fine on the fool if he didn't take his damned mattress to a dump, threatening to impound his Nissan pickup as further inducement.

Little good Ben's efforts would do here. The clutter of humanity's leavings hereabouts served to remind Sincebaugh of his father's near-constant drone on how things used to be along the backwaters, amid the swamps and lakes of the region. His father said their great loss was due to shoddy city planning, overwhelming urban sprawl, greedy developers and boating communities now hugging the shores, as well as a general lack of concern for wildlife areas. His father constantly harped on the death of the Old Louisiana, an Emerald City he'd returned to in 1945 after a four-year tour of duty in Europe during World War II. The developers had swallowed up everything his father had remembered in a mad effort to satisfy the rising appetite of the ugly creature called New Orleans. His father called it a travesty of justice whenever he'd had a few too many.

Today, the cityscape was an alien world to the old man. But not to Alex. Alex knew the terrain and felt a certain sense of safety even in its worst neighborhoods.

Still, there was common ground here for father and son to agree on, that pollution in all its ugly guises flourished here, that the gulf waters were losing the battle against industrial waste, that the growing scarcity of game animals in the region was alarming.

Now the alarming cavity flapping open when Alex turned the body over startled him. Even with the surgical gloves on, Alex snatched his hands away from the body; repulsed by a spreading, moving, living creature that undulated inside the enormous, gaping chest wound, which showed clearly how the killer had taken great glee in spreading wide the flesh, the knifing giving the appearance of a lust killing, one in which rage had created an uncontrollable urge to mutilate the boy's corpse. The entire episode, from the moment Alex had touched the corpse and turned it, played over and over in his head at a snail's pace, making him physically ill.

He'd slowly turned the corpse, but it had begun to take on its own momentum, its soupy weight and bones like rolling potatoes in a burlap bag, bursting at the seams. A moment of remorse had flashed through Sincebaugh's mind. He knew that something had ruptured. He'd even heard a faint twiglike snap. Most likely the bone at the base of the neck had just popped, causing what the M.E. would term an undertaker's fracture. Careless handling of a corpse caused breaks, rents and tears. He'd forgotten to cushion the head as one might a newborn's.

Not that he wanted forgiveness, but it was his first mutilation-style murder investigation, and his stomach was doing far more thinking at the moment than his head. Yet his concern for the neck fracture was instantly forgotten now that his penetrating, icy green eyes found the victim's chest splayed open by some awful instrument of destruction, a pool of writhing maggots where the guy's heart ought to have been at peaceful rest.

The fist-sized red organ that once pumped the fluid of life through Victor Surette was missing, only a gaping cavity and the maggots left behind.

"*Sonofamotherfuckinbitchinheat*, Sincy!" lamented de-

Yampert in that curiously poetic tempo that swearing in his melodic tongue took on. Ben's olive and bronze complexion blanched by rapid degrees, his natty but thick hair seeming to stand on end. "Christ on a stick! Geezus, turn 'im back over. Leave 'im for Wardlaw."

"Can't . . . can't do that . . ." Alex heard himself saying as if for the hundredth time, as if from far away.

"Hell you can't," cried Big Ben.

"He's my responsibility, Ben. I'm in charge here, not the M.E., not you, nobody but me, you got that?" This meant it was Sincebaugh's call, Slidell or no Slidell. It was his bloody ugly case, because he was first detective on call, and it was his rotation, and he hadn't bargained it away with Ben or anyone, and therefore it was his call all the way. Any glory to be had out of the case was his, and by the same token, any disgrace would stick to him far longer. Ben knew this as well as Alex.

"Be damned if I'm going to turn the body over before I investigate the scene thoroughly," Alex now muttered.

Ben knew that he was still smarting from a previous investigation into the death of a little boy not yet seven years old who'd been abducted, sodomized and strangled and finally dumped at a site not unlike this lonely place. That case had gone unsolved now for eight months, and Sincebaugh still blamed himself, believing that he'd not been thorough enough that first night at the scene, that he had somehow missed some vital clue. He more than made up for it these days, Ben thought, exasperated with his partner at times.

"I'll let you know when," Sincebaugh muttered now, but even as he said it, he involuntarily turned his eyes away from the gruel in which the maggot life swam within the chest cavity. Doing so, he realized for the first time that the genital area was caked in coagulated blood, and that the genitals had been removed via the same butchery carried out over the chest.

"Wardlaw'll be pleased," he heard Ben saying.

Christ, what a thing to say, he thought.

"Wardlaw loves maggots. Says they speak volumes about time of death."

The insects, still in their larval state, would tell Wardlaw the approximate time of death. "Too bad Wardlaw can't be

as timely about getting here as the fucking maggots,'' Sincebaugh said, struggling to keep his composure.

When he turned to look again on the awful hole in the dead
kid, Alex suddenly tumbled into it, somehow losing his footing over Victor Surette's form, and losing his grip on reality.
Sincebaugh's entire body had somehow plunged into the pool
of mindless, writhing insect life, and he found himself
swarmed over by the decay-eaters, found himself being eaten
by them as well. He tried to pull himself back, tried desperately to find Big, to scream and throw his hand back up for
Big to grab onto and haul him from the cesspool into which
he'd descended. It was a cesspool worse than the bamboo cell
in the water in Nam in which he had endured life for two
grueling months, when he had seen the epidermal layer of his
skin begin to slough off in cascading ringlets.

To this day, he couldn't stand water; in fact, he had an
unnatural aversion to it. He got the shakes just being in a boat.
If he went fishing, it was from a bridge or shore. And to this
day, he still had no idea how he had survived the treatment
of his cruel captors in Vietnam, except that he'd held onto a
shred of hope that one day they'd get careless and he'd crawl
up at night and slit their throats while they slept, as he and
several other POWs actually did during one of those nights of
eternity, he alone finally making his escape stick, finding his
way into a neutral country and eventually getting word out of
his whereabouts.

His father and the U.S. Marines had long before given him
up for dead, and in some ways he was.

Now, here in safe New Orleans he was a prisoner again,
having tumbled into the open wound of a murder victim whose
heart was replaced by maggots. He'd fallen so deep that his
horrid screams couldn't even be heard, and there were no
guards to laugh at him and taunt him back to reality. He wasn't
so sure he wouldn't trade today's cage for yesterday's, and his
screams became one, long, unending shriek.

The howl turned into a shrill ringing noise inside his brain.
It would not go away, and he could not climb from out of the
living quicksand of the army of maggots that were devouring
him alive.

Still, the shrill scream raced through his fevered brain.

It would not be silenced so long as he could feel the insect life devouring him along with Surette's corpse.

Then the sound of the telephone beside his bed reached into his vicious nightmare and lifted him from the maggot pool. He found himself shivering in a cold sweat, his hands covering his chest as if to protect his heart, the beads of perspiration running off in snakelike rivulets. Beside his bed was the open copy of *Gray's Anatomy* that he'd been studying for any useful information concerning the human heart.

He pounced on the phone and just held it tightly in its cradle for some time, feeling the vibration and noise run through him, swallowing in its solid surface, holding on to the reality of it. Relieved to be out of his previous misery, he now drank in the piercing, keening machine sound, thankful that it did not writhe at his touch, that it was genuine and corporeal.

Finally, he lifted the receiver, and out of breath, he spoke weakly and haltingly into it. "Who . . . who the hell's calling . . . at this hour?" All the while his mind screamed, *Thank God you called!*

"Sincebaugh?"

"Yeah, this is me!" he barked now, realizing it was Captain Carl Landry on the other end.

Even as he cradled the phone against his ear, leaning back against the headboard, he realized that his nightmare had told him something important about that hot June morning a little over a year before when they'd discovered Victor Surette's body, that his was not only the first of the Hearts murders—despite what Frank Wardlaw and others believed—but that the proof, missing as it was, had been staring them in the face the entire time. Surette's crime scene had been missing a key element: the boy's missing heart had not been replaced by a playing card because the fucking maggots had devoured the lace. And Wardlaw's protocol had proclaimed the heart muscle ripped away by animals.

Landry said, "You and Ben're up to bat."

"Another heartless one?" He tried to sound as casual as he could without being vulgar about it.

Landry ignored the pun. "I'll be there to run interference for you guys with the press. It's across U.S. 10 over Big Muddy this time."

"Gretna? Why not? He's done everywhere else."

"Well, we won't know for sure till you and Ben check it out and Wardlaw agrees, but we got a body washed up near Gretna's Chantilly Pier looks suspiciously like more work by same mother. Leastways, that's the way it came to me."

Landry sounded tired and depressed.

"Got you outta bed too, huh, Captain?" Alex was still try- ing to regain his own composure, and stating the obvious seemed only to help. "God help us, Captain Landry."

"I'll light another candle."

Ever the good and faithful Catholic, Sincebaugh thought, wishing he had half the faith Landry took for granted. "I fig- ured out why Surette didn't get one of those lacy playing cards left inside him, Captain."

"Really? And how's that, Alex?"

"The maggots, sir."

"What about the maggots?"

"Maggots'll feed on just about anything, including cloth. The playing cards're made of flimsy cloth. They ate the queen of hearts before we ever got to the body, so the killer's calling card wasn't present, so we never knew that Surette was victim number one."

"Hnmmm, now why didn't anybody else think of that?" Landry's sarcasm was so thick it hardly made it through the cables. "That bit of Sherlockian wisdom, Alex, doesn't ex- plain why the killer took over a year off and started up again. And besides, Doc Wardlaw indicated the heart was eaten away by animals, not maggots, that the missing heart in that case—"

"That's just it. Wardlaw was too goddamned busy worrying about the missing heart. Remember? Wardlaw had theorized that animals had gotten to the body, rooted around in the open wound, snatched the organ and run. But Wardlaw was going under the assumption the body was found faceup, remember? But Captain, I—"

"Alex, you've got to get control here."

Maggots mucking out the empty shell . . .

"But I turned the body, Captain. It was facedown and I turned it before Wardlaw ever got there, and I don't know of any raccoon capable of turning a body, and Wardlaw would've known that from lividity alone had he not been stoned that night.''

Landry firmly replied, ''Stick to the present, Alex. The past'll take care of itself. Hell, Surette was fifteen months ago, a missing persons call at that.''

''Who turned into a murder, an unsolved murder.''

''And you're still obsessing over it? Nobody holds you responsible on either the Surette or the Tommy Harkness cases, Alex, no one. There was insufficient crime-scene evidence in both cases, and you exhausted every lead. Now, you have to put this in proper perspective or you'll wind up in Jyl Muller's whatever-happened-to-so-and-so column or on Dr. Longette's foam-rubber couch. Nobody wants that.''

''But Captain, if I'm right, then these killings could date back to even before Surette disappeared, and if that's the case—''

''Hell, Alex . . .'' He sighed heavily into the phone. ''There's not one shred of evidence to link Surette's death to the others.''

''Only because I didn't want to see it; I blocked it out, that whole damned night, but it came back to me, Captain. Came back tonight, clear as—''

''All right, all right. If you can find any connection with Surette, move on it, but let me know first. And if not, Sincebaugh, I want you to move on!''

''But it's related. And maybe it wasn't the first, and if Surette was the first, then he should be the one we're concentrating on. I feel it. I know it is.''

''I know you've got good instincts, Alex, that your intuition is above the norm, but I gotta tell you, Lieutenant, without something more solid soon—very soon—we're looking at a call for help.''

''FBI? Fine, I welcome the help. They can take over the whole damned case file for all I care. I'll happily go back to domestic violence cases, drug killings and tavern shoot-'em-ups, if that's what you'd like, Captain.''

''I'd like you to remain on the case, Alex, to show these bastards upstairs what we're made of, but I'm getting more pressure every day on this one from all sides.''

''I understand, Carl.''

"The hell you do. You might think you do, but no way. You just get me some kind of a pattern in this friggin' case that has more weight than . . . than playing cards and hearts. What else is going on here besides fags getting bumped off by some maniac with a hatred for gay guys in a city full of gay guys?"

"I'm trying, Captain. I've checked with departments in California, San Francisco and L.A. in particular, New York, Chicago, Miami and Key West, Flordia, as well as Panama City, Florida. I've wired Interpol and Euronet, as well as the FBI's crime computers. You name it, I've asked for information on high rates and/or unusual murder rates among the homosexual population, anything at all resembling our case here."

"Any luck along those lines?"

A long, exasperated breath of air was his immediate answer. "A few similar cases reported, one very similar one in Brussels, Belgium, of all places, but nothing of a serial nature until now."

"Oh, and what's zat?"

"A report in from New York. An obvious serial killer there doing gay guys, dismembering them."

"Really?"

"Except whoever this guy is, he's not taking their hearts, just slaughtering them and bagging them and scattering their parts all over the damned city."

"How many victims and how recent?"

"So far, six over a period of two years. I'll get a report to you later today."

"Good, meantime, meet with deYampert at the Chantilly Pier."

"I know the place. I'm on my way."

"Sorry you didn't get away before all this shit hit the fan, kid, but nobody knows these cases like you do."

"And I don't know shit."

"You're doing fine. Hang in."

Captain Carl Landry hung up and left Alex alone again with his perspiration, his nerves and his fear. He sensed he had more to fear than his too vivid, too sensual nightmares nowadays. Captain Landry wouldn't have brought up the possibility of FBI involvement unless he knew something, and

Alex's nonchalance toward the subject had hidden an even deeper fear than he held of maggots and memories of holes into which he had fallen, his fear of failure.

He drummed nervous fingers across his copy of *Gray's Anatomy,* forced himself up and rushed to dress, feeling like a reluctant schoolboy, rushing to a destination he loathed. *Gray's* had only been helpful up to a point. It did make clear to him how, with a little study, anyone might learn to remove a human heart.

"Now that narrows the suspect list down considerably," he told the empty room as he hastened into a pullover sweatshirt and jeans. It was no time for formal attire.

— 7 —

The heart of a man has been compared to flowers; but unlike them, it does not wait for the blowing of the wind to be scattered abroad. It is so fleeting and changeful.

—Yohda Kenko

Quantico, Virginia

People watched her as Dr. Kim Desinor rushed along the busy corridor, young Benton pushing a note in her face. Heads turned, tongues clicked, eyes assessed her with some trepidation, as if she were a freak. News had already gotten around.

"There's been a major breakthrough in the Sendak case in Georgia."

"Really?" she asked.

"And it came as a direct result of your intervention, Doctor."

She stopped in her tracks and stared at the note from Parlen. Back in Decatur, Georgia, Parlen had only had to flash his badge at the right door, and Viola, the long-lost daughter, had crumpled before him, confessing on the way down because the entire enterprise was built on a rickety foundation, a house of emotional cards. Sendak's body had been recovered, and the daughter had fingered the live-in boyfriend, who remained at large, somewhere he felt comfortable and safe, she supposed, like his mamma's place. All Parlen and his men needed to do now was to stake out his known haunts. He'd likely be picked up in twenty-four hours, a few days at the outside.

"Parlen also sent a dozen roses for you, Doctor," Tom Benton said with a smile. "I suppose it's his way of apologizing for the doubts."

"At least the man knows how to apologize," she replied, staring up at the elevator lights now. The car was two stories above, someone holding it. "How did Sendak die?"

65

"Heat exhaustion and heart attack, they surmise. He was locked in a goddamned storage facility, inside a wooden box built to secure him. You were right on, Doctor."

She imagined the suffering of both victim and daughter, not to mention the wife. "I'm on my way to Zanek's office again, so we'll have to talk this out later, okay, Tom?"

"Sure, sure . . . what's it now? He doesn't like the brand of tape recorders we're using? The film, the budget overruns?"

"Leave Zanek to me, okay, Tom? You've got enough to worry about with that test you're running. How's it coming? Am I going to see anything on paper soon?"

"Sure made a mess of it the first go-round. I'm determined to get it right this time, Doctor."

"Don't be so hard on yourself. How could you know about the Y-factor variable? I should've been over your shoulder sooner."

"What you did, Doctor, with the Sendak case . . . well, it must give you a great sense of accomplishment."

"Some, yes . . . but it also gives me a great deal of misery. It's not easy looking into the heart of evil, Tom. And not everyone's suited to doing so." She stared for a moment at her gung-ho assistant, knowing that he wanted to be able to pull off that kind of psychic hocus-pocus, that he admired her a great deal for what she'd done and that he was proud to be a part of her team, but had little idea of the emotional costs involved, despite all her warnings.

"Look here, Tom. Someday, you're going to do psychic loops around me. Just give it time and throw in a healthy dose of patience, and don't forget self-protective measures, all right?" She secretly feared that one day he'd scar himself so badly that he'd leave psychic detection completely. It happened to a lot of beginners.

The elevator arrived and she boarded, Tom waving her off like a dutiful son. Upstairs, she found Zanek's familiar office and pushed through the outer door, her steady gaze meeting Betty's, the secretary another familiar here.

"They're waiting for you, Dr. Desinor."

"They?" *Who the hell were they?* she wondered. Yesterday she and Zanek had come to something of a Mexican standoff, a way to sever ties in an amenable fashion. She had proposed that her minor and inconvenient little shop of horrors, as he'd angrily referred to it, could be relocated under the Psychological Profiling Division. She'd be a step removed from him, he'd be on safer ground with the powers that be and they'd both see less and less of one another since she'd be reporting directly to Jack Santiva, the new head of the entire umbrella division. She thought he'd agreed and that all was worked out, and she was happy with the proposed arrangement. So what was up now? Was Santiva in Zanek's office now? Had Zanek arranged things?

"Chief?" she asked, coming through the door. "You want to see me?"

She assumed the tall man in the tailored suit near the window was Santiva, whom she had never met, but Santiva was supposedly of Spanish origin, and this guy looked anything but Spanish. His hair was red, his face sprinkled with crimson flecks, his skin otherwise a pasty white.

In another corner, like a boxer waiting to be announced, stood a strikingly tall, auburn-haired woman in a beautiful blue serge suit, her gleaming tan marking her as either a model or a princess, her eyes filled with both a keen sense of awareness and a sadness that seemed beyond her years. Neither of them looked like Santiva.

"What's going on, Paul?" Kim asked.

Zanek, a tall, well-built man some years her senior, was showing silver streaks through his dark hair. He cleared his throat, pointed toward the pasty-skinned stranger and began introducing everyone.

"Dr. Desinor, this is New Orleans Police Commissioner Richard Stephens, up from Louisiana."

Surprised, she lifted a hand to Stephens and they shook, her eyes never leaving his, her mind still wondering where Santiva was and what this meeting had to do with her. Outside the window behind Stephens, she could hear a man barking orders at recruits who were doing their morning calisthenics on the parade ground.

Zanek continued the introductions. "Mr. Stephens came here specifically to see you, Doctor, and this"—he indicated the tall woman now extending a hand to her—"well, this is our own famous Dr. Jessica Coran, pathologist in the Psycho-

logical Profiling Division, you know, the division you're as-
piring to join.''

"Jessica Coran . . . I mean, Dr. Jessica Coran?" she asked,
astounded, while images of Coran diving in Maui and bringing
an end to a killer in Hawaii swirled amid visions of Richard
Stephens's New Orleans that came racing in at her boulderlike,
knocking her off balance. New Orleans had been home to her
in a childhood she'd tried desperately to put out of her mind,
and what she knew of Dr. Jessica Coran could fill a textbook
on forensic science and investigation.

She felt foolish, and tried to recoup the words even as she
repeated herself. "What's . . . going on here?"

After shaking her hand vigorously, Dr. Coran offered her a
seat, which she accepted. "I read Bulletin 131, FBI Protocol,
your monograph on the use of psychology and psychic tools
in law enforcement, Dr. Desinor, as has Commissioner Stephens here, and I was greatly impressed in how you related
psychic ability to this thing you call the *blue sense*, the talent
most investigators possess. Anyway, it struck me immediately
that we need your help in New Orleans.''

"You no doubt have read about our Queen of Hearts murders," Stephens added.

"Is that what this is about?" She looked across at Zanek
as she asked the question.

"Right . . . yes, it is.''

"I was impressed with your record for psychic hits," Jessica Coran said.

"She made a real believer outta this guy Parlen in Georgia
I told you about," declared Zanek, fingering a photo of his
wife and kids atop the large steel and glass desk. "Converted
him to her religion, you might say. Led him right to the culprits—the ones who killed Sendak.''

Kim Desinor, staring directly at Zanek now, said, "She—
the daughter—Paul, was just a frightened and cornered kid.
She was in a desperate no-win situation that got out of control,
and she didn't know how to fix it.''

Zanek nodded. "You've heard then from Parlen?" Zanek
had had the information the day before, but had chosen to
withhold it at the time.

"He sent flowers. Anyway, Sendak's illegitimate daughter—despite all the evidence—agonized over what she'd gotten her biological father—a stranger to her—into. The boyfriend had a powerful control over her; he was the dominating force in her life. But it was through her overwhelming remorse, guilt and agony that I was able to perceive the events in the manner I had. And if we weren't working with a KGB/CIA mentality, I could give Parlen a deposition to that effect which might help in the daughter's defense.''

Zanek was unable to respond for a moment, trying to understand exactly what Kim was saying to him. ''Parlen shared this information with you?''

''No. It came to me in bits and pieces after the psychometric reading of the other day. It's information I could share with Parlen, if you're willing.''

He considered this a moment. ''Well, we're not in the business of defending the guilty here, but . . . do you hear what she's saying here, Stephens? Isn't she everything I've said, Commissioner, and more?'' He followed this pep rally up by coming from behind his desk and half-leaning, half-sitting against the edge in a show of friendliness, a kind of male peace offering. Once she pretended to accept the peace offering, he continued. ''Kim, Dr. Desinor . . .''

''Yes, Paul?'' she insolently asked, forgoing his title.

''P.C. Stephens and Dr. Coran both want you to accompany them to New Orleans.''

She looked hard across at Zanek, puzzlement and anger fighting for control within. ''You mean to physically go there?''

''That's right.''

''I see.'' She told herself, *I really do see, Paul*. Just farm me out to New Orleans, allow things to cool here while I'm working a field office as far from you as you can arrange. What's the matter, no murder sprees in Alaska this season? The bastard had found his solution. ''But we're going to be too busy here, what with—''

''Your duties in New Orleans will in no way curtail your work here, Dr. Desinor,'' Paul began, ''as it's only a . . . temporary assignment and while you're gone, we'll find a suitable replacement.''

''But what about the move over to Santiva's division?''

"Santiva's just getting accustomed himself. A big shake-up like that . . . well, let's just give it time, okay, Doctor?"

"This has all been set up for some time now, hasn't it, Paul?" she said, challenging him.

Stephens opened his hands and waved, a gesture he felt awkward with, along with having to plead. "Dr. Desinor, please, we desperately need your help on an unusual and most important case."

"It's to be the test case, Dr. Desinor, for the future of psychic detection within this agency," Zanek drove home his point.

Stephens's red hair was so thin it looked blond, but his scarlet eyebrows were thick. He looked of Irish descent. She knew by now that Stephens must surely have had a careful look at her background via Zanek's information on her, so he must know that her own olive skin and dark features were those of a Creole native of Louisiana. Abused and abandoned by a stepfather after the death of her mother, she'd been a product of a strict Catholic upbringing at St. Domitilla's School for Troubled Children. She'd long since renounced all formal religion as a result of her years there, calling herself a reformed and recovering Catholic. Others might call her an Indoctrinated Ingrate. Either way, she'd find her faith in her own way, and coming to this decision had felt right; it had felt as if the shackles of religion had been lifted from her with this decision made the year she graduated high school from St. Domitilla's in New Orleans.

She'd managed a state scholarship, had spent two years at Louisiana State, going on to Trinity College in New Orleans. From there she'd joined the Florida Department of Criminal Investigation as a psychologist. Unable to fit in "properly" there, she'd entered the police academy, and on graduation, she'd bounced around from one Florida police jurisdiction to the next as a working cop, before she'd returned to psychiatry. Her work had been somehow and almost fatefully noticed by Paul Zanek of the FBI, who'd encouraged her to apply for the FBI Academy. Zanek had brought her along ever since. Little wonder that, when he began to pay attention to her as a woman, she'd responded so completely, allowing her heart to be snared and lost and finally broken, all within the span of a few short years.

"I suggested you for the case two weeks ago, Kim," Zanek said, coming off the desk he'd been leaning on. "It's a chance for us . . . for you . . . to test your theories in an ongoing investigation, show everyone what psychic detection is capable of, including Santiva. It'll take it out of the realm of the laboratory. It'll be more than an exercise for a film. You've got to welcome that."

She knew that Paul had been preparing a paper on the effective use of psychic investigation in the right hands, in the hands of the Bureau, and that she was his secret weapon. For his theories to work, he needed to go beyond research grant money and into mainstream budgeting, to put psychic detection on the FBI grid. These were all aims and goals she herself had wanted along with him, goals they had worked for side by side.

Dr. Coran's whiskey voice filled the room. "You'll have a perfect opportunity to help demonstrate in an ongoing investigation how effective collaboration might be between our usual scientific techniques and your own psychic techniques."

Still suspicious of Zanek's motives, Kim wondered just how much of this show was a put-up job; were Dr. Coran and Paul Zanek close enough to have discussed his desire to rid himself of her for a time? Did Dr. Coran know about Paul's ultimate ambition to become head of the FBI someday? What did Jessica Coran think of Paul's dabbling in the "black arts" in order to get ahead? Was she among those who joked that Zanek was actually on the trail of how to turn ordinary tin into gold through the alchemy of Dr. Faith's mysterious laboratory?

When Kim failed to answer, Jessica Coran said, "No better place to prove a theory than in the field, Dr. Desinor."

Or have you forgotten that you're an agent first? Kim flinched, filling in the trailing thought behind Jessica Coran's dare.

"What's in it for me, Paul?" Kim asked. "Do I get that budget adjustment I've been requesting for the past year?"

He ignored this. "What's the alternative scenario, Kim?" Zanek now pressed the issue. "You sit here in Virginia, waiting for the case to go stale and cold like that damned Decatur mess? Then they bring it all to you in a shoe box? Come on, Kim, this is your big chance. Don't let petty concerns stand in your way.''

She took in a deep, long breath of air, still unsure of his motives and feeling slightly off balance with the others in the room. If he had made the suggestion to New Orleans brass two weeks before, then it was before Paul had decided to go back with his wife. Still, Paul could be lying about when he'd first contacted Stephens about her.

"You're probably the best psychic detective working in America today, Dr. Desinor.'' Stephens's attempt at flattery fell flat.

"But nobody else of consequence outside the Bureau knows that, Kim, not yet,'' Zanek continued. ''And while we're determined here at the Bureau to keep our association with psychism a secret for the time being, there will come a day. . . . '' He turned to Stephens and explained. ''The FBI isn't prepared to go on record as proponents of psychic detection just yet, you understand, so, sir, you'll have to honor our agreement on that score. She enters as a private citizen engaged by the NOPD to help shed light on the case.''

"Maybe after the twenty-first century the Bureau will show some balls,'' Jessica Coran snickered.

Zanek gritted his teeth, a glare slicing across at Jessica which he quickly covered. ''Still, we don't deny the needs of law-enforcement agencies today,'' Zanek continued in his most officious voice.

"To help in your decision, Dr. Desinor,'' Stephens countered, ''please have a look at these items I brought for your . . . inspection.'' Richard Stephens's well-manicured hands now reached for three brown metal-clasp envelopes. He laid them out on Zanek's desk. Two of the packs were neatly creased and lay flat, while the third bulged with what appeared to be and sounded like metallic objects—likely a junk collection from a New Orleans police property room, Kim decided.

Stephens then tore open the first envelope and displayed its flat contents: an array of horrid police photos, one after another, of murdered young men, boys really. Two of the photos displayed bodies in remote, heavily wooded areas, their backs to the lens, faces turned away, features lost. The additional two dead teens lay on brightly colored, silken sheets, lying on their backs, their torsos half covered in bloody bedding. The fifth and sixth victims had actually been beheaded.

"Can you, from these photos, tell me anything at all about these cases?" pressed Stephens.

She inched closer, on the edge of her seat, staring down at the photos now, the others watching her intently. She lifted each photo one at a time, her eyes closing now while her fingers wandered lazily across the placid and glossy surfaces. Something about such crime-scene photos touched people in a mysterious, dark corner of the brain, giving the mind over to the same sensation as when viewing a supposed UFO photo or a so-called ghost captured on film, but here, in a real photo shot of a real victim of violent crime, there seemed to be an aura about the corpse.

"They are all victims of the same killer . . . except this one." She discarded one of the two photos of boys found beheaded and lying in a forested area. Stephens's bushy eyebrows danced in response.

Jessica caught the unconscious body language and saw that Kim didn't miss it either. She quickly grabbed the second photo of the other beheaded boy and tossed it aside as well, saying, "This one too."

"Parlor tricks," remarked Zanek. "Now try her on something substantial."

"The others are all related. At least the NOPD believes they are all victims of the same killer," Kim continued, her eyes closing now, her fingers still reading the photos. "There is some awful common denominator which ties these victims and their killer together. He takes their vitality . . . their energy . . . identity . . . eats from their wounds . . . if not literally, figuratively feeds on them. I see strange crosses . . . black, rising birds . . ."

"Then he's cannibalizing them?" asked Stephens.

"Crosses?" asked Jessica.

"I see large crosses, marching crosses . . . living crosses ablaze with fire."

Stephens's eyes lit up. "What're you saying? That the KKK has something to do with the Queen of Hearts slayings?"

"I just know what I see . . . crosses marching."

"Anything else?" asked Jessica.

"These four were brutalized . . . sex organs amputated, and their hearts were cut out. Killer left his calling card, a queen of hearts."

"All information known to the public," Stephens said, a little disappointed.

"It's an unusual playing card, however," she added. "Not plastic or paper product, something . . . softer, even . . . lacy?"

Information on the nature of the killer's calling card was not generally known, and had purposely been kept from the press and public, held back along with a few other particulars in order that a confession might more easily be dismissed or taken seriously.

Kim looked squarely into Stephens's eyes, reaching into his soul, and asked, "Does the killer make the cards? Does he stitch them out of yarn or silken string?"

Stephens was visibly unnerved. Swallowing became his preoccupation now, but to regroup, he quickly busied himself by placing aside the second flat envelope and going directly to the rumpled third, the lumpy one.

"Well, Stephens?" Zanek pressed. "Is she onto something or not?"

Stephens breathed deeply and exhaled his answer. "Yes, remarkably accurate. Investigators have theorized that the uniqueness of the cards left in the cadavers marks them as personally handmade by the killer. They've been unable to locate their like in any novelty shop in the city. But you missed on one of the victims. He wasn't among the victims of the card-carrying killer, since no card was left with his body."

This left Kim Desinor shaking her head, doubtful.

With fingers growing thicker by the moment, Stephens now shakily opened the unkempt brown envelope, spilling out its contents over the photos. A cascade of seemingly unrelated items skittered across Paul Zanek's desk: trinkets, keys and key rings, bracelets and swatches, rosary beads and necklaces, rings and earrings—one pair a set of crosses, another a purposeful mismatch or mishmash of satanic amulets—New Wave trinkets, skulls and crossbones; added to this were vials of makeup and lipstick, compact mirrors, assorted colorful

combs, brushes, cigarette packs, colorful metal cigarette hold-
ers, intricate and delicate lighters, matchboxes, a broken pair
of pumps, eyeglasses, a grip purse and feminine watches.
Rounding out this montage now littering Paul's desktop were
theater stubs, crumpled granola wrappers and several plastic
playing cards, all the queen of hearts, all fakes, which Stephens now quickly scooped up and put away in a show of
good grace under fire. Many of the items looked to belong to
females.

"More parlor games?" an exasperated Paul Zanek asked.

But Kim Desinor put up a hand to Paul's objections, stepping up to the littered desk and lightly sifting through the
debris of wasted human lives. She picked over it, saying, "All
the victims liked dressing up as women, didn't they?" Still,
she browsed the flea-market items on Paul's desk, trying to
find something that might speak to her. She discarded the grip
purse and several of the jewelry items almost immediately,
saying they were "not genuine."

"Did you bring any of the cards? The genuine ones, I
mean?"

"I didn't have time to get the real ones from the M.E. Crime
lab's still running tests on 'em, but that all seems rather hopeless at this point," Stephens explained.

"Wait a minute, back up there," said Jessica. "Do you
mean you couldn't get hold of any of the cards?"

"No, sorry. I couldn't."

"You've got problems in your lab then," she assured him.

"We . . . we are aware of some problems in the M.E.'s office, yes, and we're working to rectify them immediately, I
assure you, Dr. Coran."

"I can understand why it'd be impossible to get one of the
recent cards, but why can't you put your hands on one of the
earlier ones?" Jessica continued.

"Let's just say that the evidence hasn't always been handled
with the care that it deserved . . . at the time."

Jessica blanched and nodded, understanding only too well,
recalling the intricacies of such problems in the New York
crime lab when she was there, as well as the more recent
political roadblocks she'd faced in Honolulu. She shouldn't
expect less from New Orleans, she silently cautioned herself.

Meanwhile, Dr. Desinor had discarded more than half the additional items before she touched a unique handmade rosary. It held a stunning unusual cross with an inlaid crystal, something your usual Catholic wouldn't wear since crystals were normally associated with mysticism, going counter to Catholic teaching, despite the indoctrinated and institutionalized superstitions of the Church itself. At any rate, the crystal made the cross and beads an interesting, eye-catching piece for Kim. It made the rosary something of an oddity, a maverick piece amid the typical clutter of a victim's pockets turned inside out.

Jessica also wondered about its owner.

Kim found the crystal nicely weighted and warm to the touch, either the mineral stone or her own body temperature the source. Either way, it sent out emanations. She held firmly to it and concentrated.

"Only some of this clutter comes from the victims. This rosary came from the very first victim's neck."

Stephens filled his lungs now and puffed up, feeling relieved that the woman was human, that she was capable of a mistake. After all he'd seen and heard so far, he had almost begun to believe in wizards and witchcraft, and now suddenly he was not so uncomfortable as before. He now rocked on the balls of his feet as if winning a point.

Jessica noticed the unconscious clue, and wasn't surprised to hear Dr. Desinor correct herself. "No . . . not his neck. Found near the body, between the legs perhaps."

"That's very good, Dr. Desinor, but sorry, you're wrong this time. Nobody bats a thousand, as they say. This particular piece belongs to the unrelated, unsolved murder case. The case I mentioned before? Wherein there was no playing card left at the scene?"

She continued. "Crosses. It says look for the cross or crosses, flaming crosses."

"More with the crosses," Zanek mentioned. "That could be significant."

"But I told you," Stephens continued, "that this piece is unrelated, that it's a *control* piece."

"Crosses that madly march on," Kim repeated. *Not hearing him?* wondered Jessica. *Or not wanting to hear him?*

"What kind of crosses?" Zanek pressed on as if he expected to solve the baffling case here and now.

"I would assume New Orleans is full of crosses," said Jessica, unsure of Dr. Desinor now. "Church towers, graveyards, any number of windmill-type displays, crossroads even."

"What kind of crosses are you talking about, Doctor?" Zanek pressed now, as if on a scent, acting as a facilitator, leading her on.

"Living crosses, burning crosses, crosses of blood and bile and tissue . . ."

"Jesus, that sounds like KKK from where I come from," repeated Stephens. "And the KKK are known gay-bashers, but as I said . . ."

"Can't be sure . . . don't know for certain . . . unclear . . ." Kim Desinor was now saying. Suddenly she felt a sharp pang of fear and terror that sent her body into a paroxysm of rigidity. "Oh, Christ . . . God . . . help me! I'm cutting . . . he's . . . he's bleeding . . . I'm cutting and he's bleeding everywhere, God! God's blood everywhere!"

Jessica at first thought she saw Kim Desinor acting out the part of a helpless victim, warding off blows and trying desperately to defend herself with her bare hands against her psychic attacker, but on second look, Jessica saw a much different image: Dr. Desinor had become the attacker now, and she was raining blows with two clenched fists over some imagined victim at her feet. She went to her knees to better destroy her enemy, wielding the rosary still entwined in her grasp as if it were an enormous and powerful weapon in her hands.

The psychic's blows against Zanek's carpeting were so filled with rage, enmity and energy that Jessica was mesmerized by the powerful image that Kim Desinor now presented.

The woman's hands repeatedly flew skyward, and with the power of a U.S. Open tennis player, using both hands, she continued to maniacally stab at some unseen object before her. Then she suddenly collapsed and writhed, until a shocked Jessica rushed to her and worked feverishly to pry loose her grasp on the black rosary beads and the crystal cross.

Stephens, while both overawed and afraid, cried out, "What's happening?"

"Who do you see? What does he look like? Can you make

out his features?'' Zanek pleaded, having gone to his knees alongside Kim and Jessica now he'd wrapped his arms about Kim, forcing her to end it as he rocked her there in his arms, telling her she was safe, that he had her, that they were in his office and nothing could harm her here.

Kim went limp in his embrace, and for a moment Jessica thought they looked like lovers.

"God," Zanek said to Jessica, "I've never seen her react like this before. Something evil about that thing." He indicated the black rosary beads attached to the crystal, dangling now from Jessica's hand.

"Is she all right? My God, I had no idea. . . . ''

"She's all right," said Zanek. "She's all right."

Kim was coming back, but her mouth hung open, slack with fear and gasping.

"It . . . it doesn't make sense . . ." Stephens began, wide-eyed, licking his lips. "The damned rosary came from a murder scene over a year old. Belonged to the victim according to the manifest, a separate unrelated case."

"Well, maybe you better look at it again," suggested Zanek, angry with the other man's reaction.

"No . . ." muttered Kim.

"What?" asked Zanek.

"No what?" added Stephens, hovering now.

"No . . . no," she countered. "It . . . the rosary belongs to the killer."

"Christ, are you sure?" Stephens asked.

"Yes, I'm . . . quite sure."

Stephens's skepticism remained intact, as did Jessica's. Even if Kim were right about the rosary, she might simply have gotten vibes about a separate killer on the earlier case. It was highly improbable that such a killer, so filled with hatred for gay men, would go on a one-year hiatus, unless he'd gone to another territory and returned. And suggesting an actual link between cases on the basis of a psychic seizure didn't seem to Jessica what a detective or a court of law might call concrete evidence.

Jessica and Zanek helped Kim to the nearby divan, where she lay quietly for a moment, trying to regain her strength and composure. "The knife . . . the knife, big as a bloody sword," she gasped aloud. "And . . . and what he . . . what he did with it . . . awful."

Jessica saw a deep concern had come over P.C. Stephens, a shadow about the brow that spoke of disbelief. Was he having serious second thoughts about importing Dr. Desinor to his city? Was he wondering about the circuslike atmosphere that bringing in any psychic was apt to create, or this psychic in particular? Jessica watched the thin-lipped man as he spoke. "That's . . . that's about it with regard to the weapon. Our forensics expert had maintained all along that it's near as big as a machete." He seemed to stare down at Kim with a new and burning sense of wonder. "But . . . but how? How could you know that just from . . . from holding a rosary?"

"I held the knife too. Look . . . look at my arms."

Her hands and arms were red with a crimson hue as if bloodstained.

True stigmata, Jessica thought, amazed, never before seeing such a display. Kim Desinor's skin at the forearms and hands had unaccountably taken on the look of unwashed fresh blood. Jessica could even make out the spatter trails. She wanted to get a photo of this bizarre effect, but almost in a blink, the red hues, stains and stringlets of ghostly blood were gone.

Zanek and Jessica looked for cuts, but there were none, not so much as a bruise, just the red hue against the skin that had evaporated in a ghostly fade-out. Staged trick or real? Jessica wondered.

"I had my hands *in* the boy's chest . . . reached in and cut out his heart . . ."

"My God, she was acting out the killer's part," Stephens raggedly whispered.

"Get her some water, Stephens, now!" shouted Paul, sending the other man out.

He then held Kim for a moment, Jessica backing into a corner, silently looking on before asking again, "Is she going to be all right?"

But it was as if Zanek had forgotten Jessica's presence.

Jessica stared at the sight of a softer Paul Zanek, who was allowing his emotions sway as he caressed first Kim's cheek and next her shining, sun-dappled hair. The other woman had either gone unconscious or was simply enjoying the attention Paul was giving her.

A spasm of nostalgia wafted over Jessica's mind as she looked on from her corner, her thoughts drifting back to the man she loved, the man she'd left in Hawaii, James Parry, whom she'd phoned the night before, assuring him that she was safe and that all was right in her world, lying through her teeth to him even as she wanted him to race to her.

From somewhere far away, Kim heard Paul asking after her well-being in a tone he'd not used since their breakup. She imagined a moment when they were first in love, or at least making love, and he'd been so gentle with her. She enjoyed the feel of his touch again, the sheer strength of it. She felt secure, out of harm's way, if only for this brief, single moment. Relaxing now, her skin tone returning to its normal olive, she opened her eyes on his and found their deep, blue pools filled with a rippling concern.

Jessica sensed the measure of her feelings, the depth of emotion in Kim Desinor, just by carefully watching her, the way she clung to Paul. Jessica could easily empathize with her desire to feel that wonderful sense of being protected, something she herself hadn't felt for a very long time, not since she'd left James in Honolulu.

Jessica thought about her last moments in the airport with Jim, how he'd cleared a room of stewardesses and pilots so they might have a moment of privacy and passion. They had parted vowing to remain in touch, and true to his word, he had called almost daily since she'd left. His phone bill must look like the national debt, she imagined.

Jessica saw that poor Kim was still unable to control her shivering. The fear was tenfold whenever a killer managed to touch the investigator in private places she seldom visited herself, and what was more private than one's own psyche? Jessica had no small measure of experience in that department herself, so she easily slid into sync and empathy with her new acquaintance. Something ugly had leapt into Kim Desinor's psyche, something evil and dominating, and the malignancy had bled her soul and body, not unlike the effect Matisak had had all these years on Jessica herself.

Only Dr. Desinor got it all at once, in one fell swoop, like a giant vulture descending over her.

Kim valiantly tried to put into words the images, telling Paul she had to try. "Flashes of metallic light, a long knife dancing over flesh, maniacal thrusts."

It sounded like Lopaka Kowona, the Trade Winds Killer whom Jessica had helped to corner in Hawaii. Jessica wondered if Kim was not somehow picking up subconscious psychic clues flaring off her, such as the burning, human cross. The image certainly brought to mind how Kowona had died, crucified by his own people. Perhaps Jessica's presence in the room had caused Stephens's little test to go woefully awry, the clutched rosary beads notwithstanding.

Jessica glanced over at the now-clear olive skin along each of Kim's arms, amazed still at the psychic discoloration she'd earlier witnessed now washed into oblivion. If it were some sort of disappearing ink, Jessica's laboratory tests could easily detect as much. She had to know that. And if it were honestly some sort of crime-scene negative played out over her tissues, what then? What did that say for scientific detection? And if it were for real, God, the woman must be nearly as fearful of her own psyche as that of the madman she'd briefly encountered, if she had actually done so.

Still, as far as it having all been a staged hoax, in her soul Jessica knew better. She was an expert at detecting lies and the behavior of liars; she could detect fraud in all its various guises, and there was no duplicity in this room save what she sensed in Paul Zanek and P.C. Stephens, the two men both dancing around a bit, for reasons unknown. But in Kim Desinor, Jessica saw no guile, sensed no hidden agenda.

Stephens now rushed back in with a paper cup overflowing with water, quite unaccustomed to the task, slopping it onto Paul's beige carpeting. The spell between Paul and Kim was at once vanquished.

"You got one hell of a jolt from that rosary," Stephens said, handing the water to Paul, who immediately helped Kim to drink. "But it was placed in as a control item, not a . . ."

Zanek, gritting his teeth, waved the other man off.

After drinking her fill, taking in a deep breath of air and allowing Zanek to help her to the couch, Kim said to Stephens,

"The rosary is hot. I'll want to keep it in my custody for . . . future . . . explorations."

"Hot?" he asked.

"Psychic term," said Jessica, giving herself away a bit, coming closer, taking Kim's hand and asking if she were all right.

"What's it mean, hot?" asked Stephens.

"Psychically hot . . . still warm with psychic emanations," Kim explained. "I think I saw someone named Vic or Victor under attack. In fact, *I* was attacking him."

"If what you're saying is true, then Victor Surette, who was killed over a year ago, was the first victim in the Heart-Snatcher's series of killings," replied Stephens, who'd had time to think about it. "Strangely enough, one of our detectives mentioned the same possibility; at least, it was kicked over, according to my people. But Surette never surfaced as a serious contender . . . never seriously, you know, linked with the others . . . before now, that is. This . . . this is . . . could change a lot of minds, the entire direction of the investigation, in fact, if . . ."

"Killer didn't leave the rosary intentionally," Kim said. "Wore it around the neck. Surette, as you call him, snatched it off in a scuffle. The killer didn't know it was lost until it was too late to retrieve it."

"Jesus, you got all that from those beads?" Stephens asked, his eyes popping.

"I used to be Catholic," she joked.

"What about the killer?" Stephens asked. "Anything?"

"Nothing clear . . . disjointed feelings . . . I wasn't actually in a position to see him."

"What do you mean, not in a position? Are there positions in this invisible world you go into?" asked a curious Jessica.

"I was the killer for a moment, and there weren't any mirrors."

"You were seeing things through the killer's eyes?" Jessica pressed, flashing on Matisak, wondering at this moment what his eyes were surveying.

"Precisely." Kim drank deeply of the water now.

"Can you tell us anything—anything at all about being him?" Jessica asked.

"He's embittered, jealous, vengeful and full of rage all the time. Whoever he is, he's self-conscious. . . . "

"About what?" Jessica pressed.

"His looks, his skin . . . some mark on his skin. And so he wears heavy makeup. It's the only time he goes to a mirror. Self-conscious about his weight and height and general appearance, and he's got a mind full of bubbling hatred and emotional turmoil."

"Anything else?" asked Zanek.

"No . . . nothing else, except for one thing."

"Yes?"

"He intends to kill again."

"Why, and for how long?"

"He doesn't know himself."

"Does he have any remorse?"

"None of consequence, no; the pleasure overtakes him."

"The pleasure?" asked Stephens.

"He derives great emotional release in controlling others."

"Controlling others?"

"The ultimate power trip, complete control," said Paul Zanek knowingly.

Jessica added, "This creep's like that bastard Matisak. A freaked-out maniac who gets high on controlling life and death. He gets his rocks off when he gets to play God, when he gets to decide."

"Gets to decide," muttered Stephens, trying to follow Jessica's train of thought.

"On whether or not you get to live or to die, Mr. Stephens."

"And the taking of the heart?" asked Stephens.

"The ultimate warrior's prize, like eating the heart of the buffalo maybe," Jessica suggested.

"Could be any number of whys for the heart thefts," Kim interjected. "Maybe he's a hopeless romantic, and maybe he enshrines the hearts like so many trophies, signs of his conquests."

"Agreed," replied Jessica, "but it's much more likely the bastard's eating his trophies, that he's a cannibal like the Claw in New York a couple of years ago."

"You've dealt with more of these monsters than I have, Dr.

Coran, so I bow to your judgment," Kim said. "But isn't it also true that each one, while similar in many regards and while despicable and capable of inhuman and unholy acts, is uniquely twisted? That is, perverted in a fashion that is almost surely private and born of a unique fantasy world whose rules only the individual knows?"

Jessica bit her lower lip and considered the inherent warning that Kim was passing along: You don't catch one maniac by presupposing him to be the same as the last. She knew that, had always known that and had proven it time and again, both in the lab and in the field. But lately all the monsters roaming the black patches of the planet had converged into a single satanic creature for Jessica, and as with everything else in her life, her professional acumen had fallen serious prey to the Matisak syndrome she was under. And somehow Kim Desinor both knew this and understood, acknowledging Jessica's painful response.

"Well, it appears we have much work to do," Zanek said, having regained his professional distance on matters. "I believe, Commissioner Stephens, that you will be pleased with the team of Coran and Desinor."

The two women exchanged a final look before Stephens and Zanek shook on it.

8

A wise man's heart is like a broad
hearth that keeps the coals (his passions)
from burning the house.

—Sir Thomas Overbury

The New Orleans police commissioner approached Kim Faith
Desinor where she rested now on Paul Zanek's couch. Jessica
and Paul looked on as Stephens said, "I have one last envelope I would like you to take a look at, Dr. Desinor."

Zanek stepped in protectively, a cold glare for Stephens,
and without a word the other man amended himself, saying,
"That is, if you're up to it?"

"I think she's had enough for one day, Stephens."

"No," Kim breathlessly said, "no, let's finish this now,
Paul." She pulled herself up to a sitting position, took a deep
breath, closed her eyes and silently counted to ten as she exhaled.

Jessica had to admire the woman's courage and stamina.
Stephens now brought the second stack of photos to her. This
time the victims were faceup, having been turned to pose for
the camera, their wounds thrown bare for the camera to catch,
each in his deathly state: each young man's chest ripped open,
each heart removed and replaced by the monster's idea of a
receipt for the large muscle, the eye of the queen on a dirty,
stained and frilled playing card staring up from three of the
photos. Bile and blood had discolored most of the "cards,"
but from closely angled shots Kim could see that the cards
were stitched together with meticulous care, the original colors
a rainbow of tints.

Each of these shots also showed the devastation done to the
lower portion of the body about the privates.

"You see why you must help us, Doctor?" Stephens
sounded even more desperate than before.

Kim wiped her brow with a handkerchief offered her earlier by Zanek. "How are the local guys going to handle help from an outsider, a woman and a psychic at that?" she wanted to know.

"You're not entirely an outsider," replied Jessica. "Didn't you grow up in the city?"

Zanek quickly added, "And so far as anyone will know, you're an independent psychic detective called in by the NOPD. And Stephens will run interference for you with the detectives and the press, if it comes to that."

"It's not the press I'm worried about. They'll paint some lurid pictures, but that I'm used to."

"Anyone else gives you a problem, let us know," Stephens assured her.

Kim looked around at the three high-ranking law-enforcement officials who'd cornered her. "It doesn't appear I have much choice...."

"Then you'll do it? You'll come to New Orleans?"

"Just remember this, Stephens," cautioned Zanek. "We're very serious about keeping Dr. Desinor's association with the Bureau in-house. The Bureau is no more in the business of psychic detection than it is into UFO investigation. Are you clear on that?"

"Completely understood . . . no problem, Chief Zanek."

"Dr. Desinor's introduction into the case must be handled with delicacy and tact, and one hell of a good cover. She'll retain her name, but we've arranged a bogus front, a separate identity. She's been working as a psychic detective out of Florida for the past several years, and since this closely shadows her real life there two years ago, she won't have any problem maintaining this cover. Kim," he continued, turning to her, "we've arranged to open a storefront detective agency in the Miami-Dade area. That meet with your approval?"

Just how much attention had Paul given this step both Kim and Jessica now wondered simultaneously, and when their eyes met, it was as if their thoughts were spoken.

"Here's the paperwork," Paul continued. "Dr. Coran'll run you through your paces, and Dr. Desinor, please make sure you learn exactly who you are, what you've been doing for the past several years, understood? Kept it fairly simple, actually, returning you to your old haunts in Florida."

It sounded like "where I discovered you" to Kim. She had stopped listening by now anyway as Paul turned to Stephens, continuing on. "But it's a no-go if you can't insure that Dr. Desinor will remain incognito. And of course, you'll make arrangements for Dr. Coran's introduction into the case as well."

"Consider all arrangements made, and believe me, I've already sounded out the governor, the mayor and my people on the importance of secrecy, and everyone agrees there'll be no problem. Really, a psychic in our city . . . well, it's really no big deal in the Big Easy."

Kim took a deep breath and stood, finding Jessica's arm and the strength she required. The feeling had returned to her body, but a slight dizziness remained. "I'll have to see to sorting out a few things downstairs first, make sure the lab's in good hands, all that before I go jetting off," Kim said.

"Not to worry," countered Paul. "I've talked to Dr. Tokutsu, and he'll give your apologies to your colleagues, your techs and your trainee."

Dr. Haruo "Harry" Tokutsu was senior assistant in the operation of the unit which had been built around Kim. He was an ambitious man even by Japanese-American standards, and he was a gifted psychic in his own right.

"Time I get back, Harry'll be dug in like a badger," she half joked, and watched for Paul's reaction. But the man's granite features gave nothing away this time.

"Your flight to New Orleans with Commissioner Stephens here has been arranged. You just need to be packed and at the airstrip at 1400 hours, Kim."

"Two P.M.? Today?"

"It's all arranged."

"I'll need more time than that."

"Just pack a bag."

"I'll take a flight out tomorrow morning," she declared, holding firmly to her ground against Zanek, which Jessica found herself helplessly smiling at. She could like this woman. Anyone who could hold her own with Paul Nathan Zanek in the man's own office was to be admired.

"All right," Zanek relented. "We'll arrange a flight out for you tomorrow then."

Dr. Desinor said her good-byes, asking that Stephens leave the rosary beads with its crystal cross in her possession for the time being. "You can leave it with Chief Zanek, if you will." It appeared she didn't relish the idea of handling the object again in the immediate future.

She then exited, still a bit shaken from the session. Jessica didn't fail to miss the long, parting look which lingered between Paul Zanek and the psychic before Kim disappeared.

Stephens next picked up his items and envelopes, all save the unusual rosary. Jessica lifted the long black beads and the shimmering, crystal cross, surprised at its weight, and she assured Paul that she'd personally keep it for Dr. Desinor.

"I think she intends to use it again for insights into your case," said Zanek, shaking hands with Stephens before returning to his seat behind the big desk.

Stephens, in no position to argue, nodded and thanked Zanek profusely. Then he warmly shook Jessica's hand, saying he'd see her aboard the waiting Air Force jet which was due for takeoff in a few hours. Stephens then took his leave, a much-pleased man whose confident step had been somewhat eroded by what he'd just witnessed.

After the door closed on Stephens's retreating form and his bundle of envelopes, Jessica asked point-blank, "What's going on between you and Dr. Desinor, Paul?"

"What hellacious garbage is that you're talking, Doctor? I just went to her aid. My God, she was in a fit of fear. I did what anyone might've done, Jess."

"Paul, I'm a detective. I detect things, remember?"

"Not some things you don't. My relationship with Kim is really none of your business. Leave it alone," he suddenly snapped.

"All right, I'll do that."

"You'll take the flight back with P.C. Stephens in her place, reassure him we'll do everything in our power, all that. . . . ."

"I'm not sure I can be packed in an hour either, Paul, but for you I'll try."

"Hey, this entire crazy scheme was your idea in the first

place, remember? All of a sudden you've got a yen to see New Orleans up close. Damnit, I swear, Jess, if you weren't who you are . . . well, just . . . just be at the airstrip.''

''Fine, but I don't want to see Waite and Thatcher there, got it?''

''Don't leave home without 'em, Jess.''

''Like a Mutt-and-Jeff, Abbott-and-Costello pair tripping over one another everywhere I go? No, thanks, Paul, and I mean it.''

He returned a stern look and said, ''Those men have been specially trained for this kind of duty, Jess, and they've been in position for your safety and for good reason, Jess.''

''They're a drain on the national economy and on my well-being, and they're a pain in the ass, Paul. Now, I thought we were clear on this issue. I usually do as I'm told, just what you wish, but I won't budge on this one, Paul.''

''Don't give me that shit. If it were up to me, you wouldn't be going to New Orleans at all, much less without bodyguards! Going over my head to Santiva on this, Jess, that hurt.''

So he had seen Santiva; so everything was in the open after all. ''Come on, Paul. Admit it, you didn't take me seriously. You weren't listening; you were only pretending to listen. One of your less admirable traits, I might add.''

''That's not fair.''

''You left me no other choice, and Santiva's got the chutz-pah to let me see this thing out.''

''Christ, Jess, you think so? Damnit, I still don't feel comfortable with this. I just don't like the idea of your opening yourself up to a possible attack, using—''

''There's no way I'm going on status quo!''

''Using yourself as goddamn bait for a madman? That Santiva guy's as nuts as you are, and as soon as the New Orleans papers get wind—''

''I'll keep a low profile.''

''—that you're on the case, Matisak's going to be on his way. But you know that. . . . ''

I'm counting on it, she thought. ''I'm a big girl, Paul.''

''You don't make protecting your ass an easy chore, Jessica Coran.''

''Maybe that's the way it should be; besides, it's my ass,

Paul, and it's been damn near six months. Could you live this way for two? I can't and I won't, not anymore. I'm sick to death of dancing to his fiddle.''

"Got it all figured out, do you?"

"No, not entirely, but one thing's for sure. It's either him or me now, and if New Orleans is to be the O.K. Corral, then as the song says, 'Let it be.' "

"Bob Waite and Greg Thatcher'll be glad to hear it put so eloquently. Maybe you can sing the tune to them."

"I got Archer on my own. I suppose I can do the same with Matisak, if he gives me the slightest opportunity."

"Christ, you talk about it as if it were a bloody tennis match or a game of chess."

"Maybe it is."

"With your life in the balance? You've got some nerve, Jess, I'll give you that."

"I'm still the best shot in the division."

"When your nerves are steady."

"I'm absolutely in control of my nerves."

He came around to her and put his arm around her shoulder in a fatherly fashion. "Kiddo, this monster is enough to un-nerve anyone, and knowing he's watching your every move, stalking you like a friggin' werewolf . . . don't tell me it doesn't eat away at you. I know you too well for that."

"I'm ready to have an end to it, Paul. One way or another, I'm exhausted and I want my life back!" She pulled away from him, knowing his reputation for pawing the ladies in the department.

"Don't expect me to like it, Jess, or to approve of this foolish behavior. I can't authorize this, and Santiva's crazy if he does. It's against all policy. If you go without an escort, it won't be my ass they fry in the end. It'll be Santiva's, the new director who should've known fucking better."

"True to form, Paul, ever the 'company' man, clawing your way to the top. I think you like the idea Santiva's gone out on a limb for me. I knew I could count on that. Now you listen to me: I'm ready to face the satanic sonofabitch today, tomorrow, when he comes, but I'm not willing to let it drag on another six months, another year and another. I just can't live like this another day."

He swallowed a large dose of resignation while her eyes bored into him. "No matter my aspirations in the company, Jess, you've got to know how much I care about you. I'm only thinking of your safety."

"Give it up, Paul. It's not your concern anymore. And promise, whatever you do, don't let it get around where I am, Paul, okay?"

"Everybody's going to know, Jess. Soon as the New Orleans press gets wind."

"Just keep it as quiet as possible for as long as possible then, okay?"

He wondered at both her reasoning and her madness. "You can't keep information like that quiet for very long."

"I don't want Jim Parry knowing."

"Ahh, now the truth comes out, I see. You know that he'd be just as upset with you as I am if he knew."

"More so."

"Look, I won't spill it to him, but he's going to learn about it and soon."

"I know that."

Again the look of resignation and veiled disgust wafted across Zanek's features. "Santiva had no right stepping into this," he complained, his eyes narrowing as if hatching some way to get back at the senior man.

"It wasn't his fault. I pushed him into the middle. Let it be, Paul."

He dropped his gaze, played a moment with straightening his desk blotter, in disarray since Kim Desinor's psychic ruminations over what Stephens had placed before her. Under his breath, his voice growing in intensity as he spoke, Paul finally said, "Good luck in New Orleans then, and Jess, be careful down there. Watch your back and stay outta the shadows and hang with the crowd, okay?"

"What's that, water buffalo wisdom? Around the pond? Herd mentality and safety in numbers may not apply. They say in New Orleans you're always in a crowd, that your back is always exposed. That's why so many people go there, to become a part of the 'mob' mentality of the parades and the Mardi Gras and to purposely *expose* their breasts, remember?"

"And you?" he challenged. "You going there to expose

yourself to Matisak is just crazy, Jess.''

She smiled across at him and said, ''New Orleans is the crazy capital of the world. Come on, stop worrying about me, Paul, and start watching out for yourself.''

''And what's that supposed to mean?''

''Whatever you want it to mean. But just you be careful too, Paul. Watch the knife to the back yourself. I'd like to know you'll be here when I get back. I'd like to know some things in life are permanent.''

''Hate to burst your bubble, sweetheart, but there just ain't no such animal as permanent, not in this life.''

''Maybe not in the next either,'' she countered, halfway to the door now. ''All the same, be here when I get back, okay? I'd hate to have to break in a new guy, or gal.''

He only chuckled at the suggestion, saying, ''After Theresa O'Rourke sat in this chair? Don't count on another female chief here in your lifetime, dear, unless maybe you're bucking for the job?''

Now she laughed a hearty belly laugh, something she'd not done in a long time. For all his faults, Paul was quite human, and he made her laugh, and that was a good balm. ''I wouldn't touch your job with surgical gloves and forceps, not even if they threw in my own personal yacht and my own island to sail it around, not for all the perks and bucks in the world, Paul, ever.''

''Hey, it isn't that bloody bad. . . . '' He stopped to consider what he was saying. ''As for the perks, hell, I earn every single one of 'em daily.''

She playfully patted his cheek, stepped briskly toward the door and turned for a final wave, saying, ''I'll just bet you do.''

''I do!'' she heard him shouting from behind the closed door as she passed his secretary's desk, anxious to be finally escaping Quantico, wondering if maybe she'd have time to stop at the local bookstore in town for a guidebook on New Orleans. She knew next to nothing about the city. She'd never visited before. It would prove to be quite an adventure, most interesting and pleasant, she desperately tried to convince herself.

Away, and mock the time with fairest show:
False face must hide what the false heart doth know.

—Shakespeare

Tahlequah, Oklahoma

He'd finished with the old woman whose body weight made
the overhead beam in the barn *irrrrk* with a disagreeing give
and sag. Matisak busily put away the last of the blood-filled
canning jars into the ice-laden foam cooler which he'd earlier
prepared. Teach, as he liked to call himself, had found the
canning jars in the old lady's fruit cellar. He'd emptied the
jars of their tomato, blueberry and strawberry contents, throwing the sugary muck to the hogs, and had washed each jar
thoroughly. The jars amounted to a good dozen, more than
enough for his needs.

Earl and Hillary Redbird had been gracious to open their
hearth and hearts to Matisak, kind to allow him to stay with
them for these many weeks now.

He'd returned to Oklahoma after escaping FBI authorities
not far from here by kidnapping a pilot at a regional airport
and forcing him to take him northeast into a storm. Somewhere
over the Boston Mountains in Arkansas, the plane got into
serious trouble. Unable to withstand storm and wind pockets,
they were forced down in a remote meadow, which the pilot
had called a miracle find amid the mountainous terrain below
them. The pilot, a well-groomed, retired auto executive, was
counting his blessings when the plane touched down, but before it even came to a stop at the end of the meadow, Matisak
had slit the man's throat from ear to ear. His look of shock
was pleasing to Matisak.

After feeding as well as he might on the other man's blood,
Matisak slept like an innocent child in the cradle of the cockpit
beside the dead man who'd called himself Norman Easthan.

The following day, Matisak heard the approach of a helicopter, possibly searching for Easthan, or quite possibly FBI searching more for him than for the now-dead pilot.

He tumbled from the cockpit and worked demonically to force the light plane into the trees nearby. He then went about the business of covering the plane and its markings with debris and brush.

He took as much money as Easthan had in his wallet, sixty-four bucks, and struck out on foot. He went in search of telephone poles, wires, homesteads, a road, preferably paved. He had reasoned that the people searching for him would not expect him to return to the Tulsa area, and so this plan pleased him.

He took his time returning, however, with stopovers in one small town after another, pretending to be a drifter and a hobo, doing odd jobs for people—all the inane work they put off forever. He worked for a place to sleep and, for appearances, a bite to eat. Determinedly, for a time he held his urge for human blood in check. He didn't want anyone discovering a corpse, which would point a dead finger in his direction. The FBI net had come too close for such encounters now. For the time being, he wanted Jessica Coran to wonder and wait, without a clue as to when and where he would strike.

His ultimate goal in life was to have her completely and wholly to himself, just long enough to bleed her, not once but many times. He knew just how much he could take from a victim before she lapsed into coma, and if he continued they'd die soon after; however, if he denied himself for that moment, allowing the victim's body to regenerate a fresh, new supply of blood, then he could take this refill as well. With Jessica Coran, he intended to take such good care of her as to have her produce blood for him as often as he liked, to use her like a milk cow, for as long as her body and soul could withstand the shocks he pledged for her. Either that, or he'd put his quest for her blood to the ultimate test, take it to the max—which he himself could no more survive than she. It would be an end which in truth would be a new beginning, one which promised an eternity with her. He hadn't completely decided which direction their fate would go in, not yet anyway.

But whatever his choice, it would take careful preparation, time and money. Still, nothing so petty as currency should stand in the way of a man's ultimate dream, he reminded himself.

So, his quest had brought him here, finally locating Tahlequah, the old capital of the Indian Nation where Cherokee John Ross held court and sway as the president of the Indian Nation for most of his life during the 1800s. Matisak had some Cherokee blood in him, or so his family history went—relatives in the tribe, distant, yes, but what better relatives to have?

The Redbirds weren't exactly blood relatives—until now, he silently jested—but while they were not kith and kin, the old folks were living in the ancient house where Matisak's mother's mother had been born to Janie Elyse Elkheart, a quarter-blood Cherokee who'd married outside the tribe to Karl Matisak, a German immigrant who became a self-taught doctor who worked among the tribe, and learning just how good he was at faking it, set up practice some years later in Chicago for the better part of his life. Matt Matisak's grandfather had told him tales of how he had buried gold coins in gunnysacks under the floor of that old house whenever they returned. He'd hidden over two thirds of his fortune amassed in Chicago somewhere around the old place.

Matisak's grandfather may well have been telling tall tales for a wide-eyed grandson, but he'd left a detailed map of how to find the old house and its treasure for his grandson. The old man had learned to detest his own son, Matisak's father, who was so overwhelmed by Matisak's mother, a big woman of Irish descent who had a way of making her husband and young son grovel for any and all things.

Young Matisak had never taken his grandfather too seriously, but he was in the area now, and he recalled the exact location from years of staring at a crude map the old man had left him, one which Matisak's mother had thrown into the fire. Matisak had come to Oklahoma to seek his fortune, whatever that treasure might be. But the Redbirds posed a minor problem now that Matisak had come for the coins. Even if it were only a handful of gold coins minted in the 1800s, as his grandfather had said, they would be worth a small fortune, certainly enough to help him in his quest for his newfound love, Jessica Coran. It took money to keep up with the lady. She'd just jetted back to the mainland from Hawaii then to Oklahoma some six months before, and she'd been in the area only a short while, along with a hundred other FBI agents, so it had been too dangerous to get near her then.

Next time, he would choose the time and place, and he'd have the necessary provisions. He must reinvent the spigot, his control mechanism, his instrument of choice, the mechanism by which he could carefully drain her of every ounce without spilling so much as a drop, or he must acquire a new, high-tech mechanism which only money could buy. Either way, it would take some doing.

But first he had to look around the old farmhouse where he'd been doing odd jobs for the Redbirds. He'd been fortunate that the fools in law enforcement had been circulating photos of him as he'd looked when he was first taken into custody so many years before in Chicago. He looked quite different now, what with a full beard, glasses, a road map of wrinkles and sunken eyes in deep shadow. He'd put on some weight about his middle, somehow making the hunchback less pronounced nowadays, giving him a harmless Yoda or aging-old-man appearance, his graying hair brittle as fence wire.

The people around the reservation didn't ask questions. The Cherokees here were a displaced race, and miscegenation had done the rest so that there were hardly any full-bloods remaining, and so the small amount of Cherokee blood that flowed through Matthew Matisak's veins had been enough to suffice, getting him past old Mr. Redbird's threshold into one of the oldest standing homes on the reserve.

The old place was mightily run down, chimney heaving to one side, roof faded and worn, shutters half on, half off, and the barn lived up to the old saying that you could throw a cat through any wall, but the Redbirds worked harder than most to keep their yard and front porch free of clutter: no used appliances sitting beside the front door, no rusted-out bikes on the lawn, no cinder-block sculptures or half-built outhouse shells, everything neat but the overgrown weeds, save for the ancient rusted hulk of an old, useless Ford touring car on cinder blocks and below canvas out back.

The house with its small barn needed fresh paint, and he had promised to do the work, if they'd get the materials, which they had been scraping together. In the car port a usable old Chevy rust bucket of a pickup waited now for Matisak, the keys in the ignition.

Old Redbird, in his khaki pants and red plaid shirt, had stepped into the barn that morning, curious, wondering if his visitor had finally chosen to move on. He'd told neighbors that the younger man's father had been his brother-in-law, which wasn't true, but even the People felt foolish nowadays to take in a stranger from the outside world, and the old-timers in particular felt they had to present some excuse for such behavior. If they followed the old custom of never turning away someone on their doorstep—a custom Matisak's grandfather had mentioned a thousand times—nowadays they risked the ridicule of the younger generation, even their own children. But of the Redbirds' three children, two had died young, something to do with booze and a joyride, and a third had somehow gone from the res years before to take up a life elsewhere.

Most of the traditionalists simply accepted the fact that Redbird must house the man who showed up on his doorstep claiming a kinship. It was taboo, long-standing tradition; you never turned away anyone who knocked at your door unless he was a known enemy. It was a custom begun generations before and perfected by the great and famous chiefs who opened their own homes to any and all who traveled great distances to see them.

Such was the case with the last of the great chiefs, Keeowskowee, or John Ross, who prospered well here in what was once Indian Territory as both a businessman and the Principal Chief of the Cherokee Nation. His Light Horse Guard still rode, but nowadays they were on motorcycles and in Toyotas and were known only as Res Police. The Res Police seemed very interested in the stranger at first, and had asked Redbird many questions when he had gone into Tahlequah to the Cherokee Feed & Grain Store. They had told him to expect a squad car out at his place before he went to bed tonight. The old fool had stupidly confided this to Matisak, telling him that if he had anything to fear from police, he'd better "skee-daddle."

Matisak only nodded, went outside without any breakfast and disappeared. He waited in the shadows inside the barn for Redbird to come out to milk his single played-out old cow. Matisak had some milking of a different color in mind.

It was then that the old man felt a slicing, blood-letting blow to his right temple, just barely seeing the business end of the spade before he blacked out. His final thought was a worry, a worry for his bride of forty-seven years—Hillary.

From inside the house where she was preparing a chicken for dinner, Hillary had watched her old man amble bowlegged into the barn, swallowed up by the darkness there. When she'd first married him, he was doing the southwest rodeo circuit. He'd been so handsome and such a fine horseman, and he'd spoken of one day owning a big, fine ranch filled with horses, but he could never get enough money together, and after the trampling he'd received when that bull named Angel's Breath in Ardmore threw him under its pounding weight, well, neither he nor his long-held dream was ever the same again. Still, she'd continued to love Redbird, despite the arguments of her family, and she made a good home for him, and she was the best wife she could be for him, and they had had a good life together, despite the most heartrending moments, as when they'd buried their two sons, who'd run their car into the Ver-digris River and been too drunk to swim out, or when Aaron had left for college and never returned.

She was brought back from her reverie on hearing the an-noyed whine of one of the plow horses and the wail of the milk cow, but nothing else. She, like her husband, was glad to have seen the last of their "nephew" by marriage. Jack Thomas Elkheart Mankiller, he'd pronounced himself that first night, laying out a string of tenuous details connecting the family to him, despite his obvious whiteness, which he claimed was due to some sort of illness similar to what Mi-chael Jackson, the famous singer, had. And there was something around the mean eyes that reminded Hillary Clay Redbird of Big John Mankiller, who'd been married for near thirty-four years to Winnie Elkheart over near the Arkansas line, but both John and Winnie were years in the grave now. John, though, had been a massive fellow, nearly three hundred pounds, when he'd died of a heart attack, while this man was sickly by comparison. Of course, if the man could be believed, he'd been orphaned in Chicago, shunted about from foster home to foster home, as many a poor Indian child had been, hardly able to fend for himself. Little wonder he bore such scars and the crooked back. His face was sallow and etched with pain and menace, however, and Hillary felt too old to become anyone's fool, despite her good Christian upbringing.

Hillary had confided to her husband in their bed the night before that she'd taken to sleeping with her gun below her pillow from the moment the stranger had arrived. This had somewhat shocked Earl, but he'd seemed all of a sudden to understand her need. He'd drawn a hickory ball bat he kept in the closet closer to the bed that night as well. She'd asked him about it, but he'd just grunted something about the Res Police looking in on them and their newfound relative tomorrow.

But now it was morning and the birds were chattering away, chasing one another in the apple orchard, the light dancing along the leaves, a brilliant blue sky made the more blinding by great billowy Oklahoma clouds that hung so low she thought even a little woman like herself might reach up and touch them.

She looked up again from her work, expecting to see Earl come out of the blackness of the barn with the eggs and milk she'd requested. Couldn't make a proper stuffing without either. He'd also said that he had to fetch a hoe and a rake, to do something with the cucumber and squash patch alongside the house. So where in tarnation was he now? Had he forgotten what he was doing again?

She grew impatient, and thought again about Jack Thomas Mankiller. Mankiller was an old, even ancient tribal name, and there were Mankillers up and down the hills here, spread across the state. One of them had been the first Cherokee woman ever to become Principal Chief at the longhouse. So, why didn't this Jack stay with closer relatives who might better know him and who surely had more to give a passing stranger than they? She didn't mind being charitable, but there was a limit, blood or no, custom or no.

Still no sign of Earl.

The damned stuffing wasn't going to make itself. That hoeing wasn't going to take care of itself either. Where the deuce was he?

She placed the cleaned and waiting chicken aside in a large pot of water to allow it to rinse in herbs and salt water, an old recipe handed down by her mother to her. Washing and wiping her hands, she decided it was too lovely a day not to step out into it, at least for a moment. She did so with the ulterior motive of looking in on Earl. He was getting up in years, and there was no such thing as being too careful. Suppose he'd fallen inside the barn there, hurt or cut himself? This might account for the uneasy neighing that old swayback was putting up, and the racket Merleen was still raising with her mooing was going to put the old girl off her milk for a month.

Strange that the dog wasn't right in there with Merleen, making harmony, she thought as she neared the barn aperture, which was bathed in black shadow, a stark contrast to the light of the outside world.

"Earl . . . Earl, honey? Are you aw'right in there?"

She stepped into the shadow and into horror. Earl was hanging by his tied heels from a large tenterhook at the end of a pulley, his throat slashed at the jugular, the blood pumping out in large coughing spurts like a poorly pressurized pump. The blood settled into a pool of red inside a sterling-new bucket Earl had brought back from the feed and grain store just the day before. Earl's dead arms dangled, limp tendrils trying halfheartedly to touch the blood-soaked earth and straw-strewn barn floor. His old dog lay dead half in and half out of Merleen's stall.

The horse was whinnying wildly and kicking at its stall. Merleen continued in distress. Chickens scattered and nervously paced. The only light she saw was that which streamed in through cracks and at the rear of the barn, and she wanted to race for the light, afraid to turn or back out the way she'd come, sensing that Mankiller—living up to his namesake—was in the shadows behind her. At the same time, she was wholly unable to move, frozen in place, her fear and disbelief overwhelming, cutting like a cold blade into her soul, and here she was . . . caught, trapped like this . . . without a weapon or a plan of any sort . . .

Matt Matisak stepped from behind the barn door and easily draped his arm around the old woman in a firm manner, squeezing her shoulder and indicating Earl's corpse as if he'd brought her a gift to show off, pleased and proud of his demonic accomplishment. Hillary's scream was cut short by a swoon, a dark blotch of redness filling her brain at the moment Matisak's bloody hand streaked her forehead.

"War paint," Matisak joked as she fell into a dead faint on the straw. Earl's dead form swayed in response.

Matisak next lowered a second tenterhook. The hooks had held an ancient carriage in the air which he'd earlier lowered and rolled to the rear of the barn. There were four hooks, one for each axle of the carriage, but he had only two bodies to drain.

Maybe he'd wait for those Res cops the old man had warned him about. . . .

While he hadn't quite enough jars to accommodate the two additional blood-givers, he believed leaving four bodies rather than two dangling here would surely make a greater and more lasting impression on Jessica Coran and send her racing back like a yo-yo to the Tulsa, Oklahoma, area in search of him. And as she hunted, so too would he. . . .

He was ready for her to make her appearance this time, for he'd located the coins, a small sack of gold eagles, circa 1879. He'd have enough ready cash to do a complete and thorough job on Jessica. His thoughts continued to race as his hands busily worked to remove the old woman's clothing, revealing her leathery skin.

He now tied a small-link chain around Hillary's ankles as he had with Earl, and then he attached her to the J-hook and hoisted her wizened old body up. She dangled like a slaughter animal, her morning chores and dinner preparations going unattended forever now.

"No more care in the world," he assured her pliant form. But even as he hoisted her up, he realized she'd have to wait a bit, until he finished bleeding old Earl first. There was only one bucket in the place sterile enough for his needs, unless maybe he could find something new in the kitchen to assist in his endeavor here.

Serendipity had played its pixieish part in his vampiric orchestration of events. He'd been wondering and even worrying how he was going to get Jessica to come to him, while doubly worrying about what sort of containers he'd use to bleed his host and hostess. All senseless worries now, he thought. All things to those who wait, he told himself, and then the old man had shown up with his shiny new, silvery bucket, still fresh with the red and blue Chickasaw brand-name label along its front.

With Hillary now secure, the blood rushing to her head, Matt Matisak now began dipping the mason jars he'd confiscated from the old lady's fruit cellar into the bucket. He quickly filled each and screwed on the lids as he went, until Earl had no more to give.

Hillary was coming around.

He emptied the remaining fluid from the bucket and into another jar, using a Rubber Maid ladle he'd stolen from the kitchen earlier, until the bucket was completely drained of Earl Redbird's blood. He then looked into Hillary's upside-down eyes as they blinked open in confusion and terror, which spread through her quivering old frame. He smiled in a kindly manner and said, "I didn't get a chance to thank you and Earl, ma'am, for all your kindness. I'm doing that now."

"You bastard! You godawful son-of-a-creature of Satan, you son-of-a—"

Her words were cut short when he severed the jugular, and the rest of her epithets came out in a spittle of gibberish and gurgling and blood.

Matisak stepped back to watch the action of the blood as it pumped itself snakelike down into the silver bucket. He again calculated he had enough jars.

"It's not the best of blood, but it's carried you two a long way," he said to the now-silent corpses. He marveled a bit at the way Hillary's corpse flinched and jerked toward the end. Earl had gone much more quietly, but then he'd had a rather bad contusion to the head. A lot of the blood was spilt over

the straw and dirt floor, which was a shame, he felt. There
was little to do for it; he hadn't the kinds of controls he would
prefer. Bleeding a person ought to be more an exact science,
as it had been with Dr. Gabriel Arnold back in Philly. Now
that dialysis machine, he thought, that was control. He meant
to purchase or steal a portable one of his own, no matter what.
He meant to be ready for Jessica when she at last came to
him.

But here in the rickety old barn, given the conditions, the
fact he was a fugitive, the primitive tools he had to work with,
he hadn't done so badly. His former care and technique over
his victims would, in time, return to him. "Just give it time,"
he assured himself, patting and jingling the little canvas bag
filled with precious coins, "and I'll be back, stronger than
ever."

He drank down one of the pint jars filled with Earl's blood
now, gulping, feeling sated for the first time since his arrival
in Tahlequah. The blood fix soothed his frayed edges, calmed
his mind, lulled him.

He knew he couldn't stay. The Redbird farm was seen by
people going by every day. They'd look at it and instantly feel
something odd, sense something out of kilter, see the lack of
smoke in Hillary's chimney, smell no baking odors and sense
a hundred other things out of sync here. Pretty soon the flies
would come and the all-too-natural odor of the corpses would
waft out over the little patch of corn that Earl had planted in
the spring.

He'd been with the Redbirds for nearly a month now, and
they'd finally accepted his story that he was indeed related to
them. Some of the neighbors wondered about him, asked nosy
questions, but no one recognized him or seemed to want to
recognize him. He had altered his appearance, growing a full
beard, coloring his hair, sporting glasses, but still he'd imagined that someone might be smart enough to figure him out.
If no one else, then Earl.

He knew the lay of the land and the customs here, but old
Earl was no more related to him than was the President of the
United States. But his grandfather had lived in this old house
built of stone to last the ages, and the Redbirds had bought
the place, Grandfather first deeding it over to Matisak's parents

in the final, feeble moments of his life, as a favor to his son and daughter-in-law, whose idea it was to sell the worthless place. Matisak recalled how his mother, gaining access to the property at last, had talked of better days for them at last. Now, for the Redbirds, their transaction with the Matisak family had come full circle.

Soon he'd come full circle with Jessica Coran too, soon after she received his latest poem to her, after news of how the old Earl and Hillary had ended their days together on this hardscrabble plot of land. She'd come to have a firsthand look at his handiwork; she'd have to. She wouldn't be able to keep away, not even if she wanted to. He was as much in her blood as she was in his, he reasoned.

And when she came . . . he'd be waiting. . . .

He was angry with Jessica for having left Oklahoma in the first place, for having given up hope of their reunion. Where was she now? Why hadn't she stayed in Oklahoma to hunt him down as she'd promised in the press? Where was the bitch whose blood he most savored now? He'd once again been wronged by the one person whose blood he most wished to devour, and she called him evil, her with her torturing innocence. Always filled with that sickening sense of righteous indignation; the self-righteousness of the pampered and pedigreed, as if she were completely innocent, as if she had nothing whatever to do with his obsessions and his blood lust.

Still, he must admit that she didn't know evil quite so intimately as he'd like her to know it.

But by the god of all that was perverse, she had excited and inspired him. She'd been the catalyst to stimulate him to new heights, since his first contact with her, his first all-too-brief taste of her blood, when she'd first hunted him across the Midwest and throughout all of Chicago. She was the reason Dr. Arnold had to die; she was the reason he himself had to escape, so that he might see her again, touch her again, listen to that melodic voice once more, but this time without cameras or recorders or bars or six-inch-thick glass partitions between them.

He now dipped his index finger into the last jar of crimson fluid extracted from Hillary, and in her blood he wrote across a smooth #2 pinewood board he'd nailed to the joists beside Earl and Hillary his latest sentiment toward Dr. Jessica Coran. He started by drawing a scarlet T, the first line reading:

Time to renew, Jess

Soon he was entranced by his own poetic vision, the words and blood flowing in tandem, as if inspired, his finished product reading:

> Time to renew, Jess
> All devotion to you, Jess . . .
> Come to renew
> Our love which grows here
> With each drop that flows here . . .

Then he was sated for the moment, sipping on more of Earl's blood from one of the mason jars, when he heard a dull *rumble-against-stone* noise coming from outside, either a faraway plane or a car coming along the hardscrabble surface of the dirt road. A peek out into the bright day hurt his eyes, but he made out the black and white trappings of the Res Police car fast approaching.

Matisak grinned in the darkness.

He had the res cops in his sights now the entire way. They pulled to within six yards of Hillary's kitchen window, one of them shouting from the car while the other hammered the horn. When they got no response, each man got out, both looking trim and muscular in their green serge uniforms.

One went for the house, the other coming directly toward the barn and other outhouses.

Matisak's grin widened. He felt like the ghoul beneath the bridge, prepared to pounce, his eyes wandering back toward the carnage over his left shoulder where the two remaining tenterhooks and halters begged for weight. He raised the blood-caked spade he'd used on Earl.

His single worry was where to find more mason jars and an additional cooler.

10

Brothers and Sisters, I bid you beware
Of giving your heart to a dog to tear.

—Kipling

Quantico, Virginia

She was damned if she did, damned if she didn't, and she bloody well knew it. Even getting on the Lear jet provided her by Paul Zanek and the Air Force at Quantico, she knew there was no hope for it.

If Kim had said no to Paul and the New Orleans assignment, she would have handed Chief Zanek the first official stake to drive into her heart—or the heart of her fledgling division. Insubordination still weighed heavily at the unofficial "court-martials" carried out all the time at Quantico. It would take more than a disagreement about assignments to do her completely in, but it would be a start, a first blot on the record to inevitably lead to another and another until the "evidence" indicted her.

And if not New Orleans, he'd find another "bazaar" for her to be banished to. Still, in accepting the dual challenge brought her by Commissioner Richard Stephens and the presence of Jessica Coran, Kim knew that she could do far worse damage in the Big Easy than she might have in refusing an assignment offered her by a superior of Zanek's rank.

Suppose the psychic trail was now too cold to follow. Suppose the killer had moved from the area. Had been arrested on other charges and was serving time far from the city sprawled crescentlike along the winding Mississippi. Suppose she could get nowhere on the case. Suppose this hardly heartless monster went into some den to hibernate. Say, an asylum in Louisiana's up-country area. She could come up pitifully wanting, unable to detect useful clues or any information whatsoever, and such a poor showing, leaving everyone dissatisfied, would only bring unwanted attention and notoriety to her department, and from this all would crumble. The FBI funding would dry up and they could all pack their bags; the powers-that-be were already paranoid over knowledge of the FBI's research into the use of psychic detection falling into the wrong hands. Either way, Paul Zanek might actually have manipulated her into a corner that she didn't deserve to be in. God forbid the newshounds got wind of the story; if so, her work and her place within the safe confines of Quantico would be history, especially if she wound up on *20/20, 48 Hours* or, God certainly forbid, *Hard Copy*.

She tried to get comfortable in her seat, the roar of the engine like a banshee wail, a warning, an unclear yet persistent premonition of tumult yet to be sensed, seen, heard, swallowed and felt internally as well as externally—to be fully realized both physically and psychically.

She settled back as the plane began its desperate race to meet the wind; lifting, it took on the weightlessness that always made her a bit disoriented yet exhilarated, not unlike the first pangs of fear on a descending roller coaster. She rested her eyes and felt foolish to be the only passenger aboard the six-seater, momentarily wondering about the cost in jet fuel and manpower to the taxpaying public she secretly served.

Soon cruising at thirty thousand feet toward home, she wondered what she would find in New Orleans. She'd been away from the Mardi Gras capital of the world for almost eight years now, and nothing changed faster during one's absence than a major American city. "You can't go home again" was a very real and poignant experience for most people, but for her it meant little, for going home was the last thing she wanted to do. She'd been remarkably successful at closing out that part of her life, hiding her Cajun blood and even her childhood from herself; you only remember what you want to remember. In fact, her childhood was little more than a big, dark screen with an occasional gray image wafting across from a broken-down projector. She supposed that a shrink—someone other than herself—might help her to deal with that inner wasteland of the soul that she'd battled to ignore her entire adult life, but she really didn't want to go home. Her conscious mind had successfully and thoroughly blocked out her subconscious mind on this score, the two in a quiet, even contest, holding one another at bay, grappling in that inner cosmos, each with a headlock on the other and no way to continue the combat. But going back could change all that, and she had reason to fear the outcome, knowing that some awful creature from the dark past lurked there, waiting for her return.

Not wishing to think of the possible consequences, she opted to dig through the case files left her by Richard Stephens, who'd gone back to Louisiana with Jessica Coran the day before to pave her way by preparing an elaborate hoax to keep her attachment with the FBI concealed. She kept coming back again and again to those minutely detailed and thorough police reports by Lieutenant Alex Sincebaugh. She had searched the stack for a file on the Surette case, but there was none, for as Commissioner Stephens had said, this case was not considered a relative of the others, despite frequent references to it which Sincebaugh had made by way of comparison. He seemed the only one who'd kept an open mind to the possibility of a connection.

As she continued going through the files and photos left her by Stephens, she also thought about how she might be a disruption to Sincebaugh and others working the case. She'd faced resistance to psychic detection before many times when she'd had her own psychic detection agency in Florida. A part of her wanted no role in the absurd concealment of her true identity as a psychologist and paranormal investigator with the FBI, but it was politically incorrect these days to spend the taxpayers' money on frivolity, and unfortunately, too many Americans still believed that anything to do with the psychic world was frivolous.

Psychic detection had a long and lurid history, dating back to the time of Solomon, who, many scholars were now convinced, had a psychic power of his own. Some had gone so far as to suggest that Christ and John the Baptist were both gifted psychics, not to mention other world-renowned religious leaders such as Buddha. Psychic surgeons and fortune-tellers from the famous Edgar Cayce and Nostradamus to the infamous Rasputin, along with an array of charlatans, frauds and freaks, all made for a fantastic and colorful history of psychic phenomena, a history which left many people more comfortable with herpes or hemorrhoids.

She was by no means convinced that all psychics through-out the ages were true blue-sense people, that they actually possessed the gift that had been granted her, but she was certain that psychics came in all shapes and sizes, that many were indeed frauds and charlatans, and that while the history of occult phenomena was also a history of criminal activity, scams and hoaxes, there always emerged that rare psychic or seer who could actually perceive with indelible clarity the details of events yet to come, or reconstruct time and events from some netherworld inside the cranium. It was rare to find the true psychic who could reveal details of a murder which had occurred in the past—*post-cognition*—and rarer still to locate a seer, one who could foretell the future—*precognition*. But it was that singular individual who gave credence to the fact that there existed, somewhere in the vastness of that inner universe of the human mind, the ability to tap into an undeniable sixth sense.

She found some coffee in a pot at the rear of the plane, poured herself a cup and returned to the case files to study, the steady hum of the plane soothing and tranquil. In her lavish seat in a conference area, with a circular table in front of it, she again began to finger through the files. The more she learned now about the crimes, the victims, their family backgrounds, their circumstances, the more convincing she'd be before a room full of cops who would, more than likely, be hostile toward her entering the investigation months after the first body was discovered. Natural resentment was always difficult to overcome.

"What do you prefer?" she asked herself in the empty cabin, feeling terribly alone. "Unnatural resentment?" To a suspiciously regarded psychic there really wasn't any difference.

She tried to concentrate instead on the kind of rage the victims of the Queen of Hearts killer had faced in their last moments on earth. Whoever the killer was, the level of sheer hatred for the victims was shockingly extreme and intense; given the sheer number of stab wounds, the evisceration of the heart muscle and the mutilation of the private parts, it was no great leap of faith to ascertain that the killer was exceedingly and agonizingly enjoying his knife work. An extraordinary, killing energy fueled by dementia had left the bodies hacked apart by an enormous blade.

"Why a blade?"

A large blade; a hefty meat-cutter's blade, something that was made for cutting upward, like a butcher's specially designed, serrated knife for cutting and deboning carcasses. At least that was what the coroner, a man named Wardlaw, was suggesting in his reports. Perhaps more importantly, why was he taking their hearts? She recoiled from the obvious, that he cannibalized the hearts, both because it was repugnant and because it was obvious. Were there secret reasons that only a madman might have to fulfill, a longing no one in his right mind could possibly ever understand, even if the maniac were willing to share such reasons? Furthermore, did it matter what this alien mind did with the hearts, since the end result was always the same, a vicious mutilation murder with lustful, sexual overtones? She thought of a line from a long-forgotten poem which she must look up again, a line that spoke of the heart in relationships between men and women that went something like:

> Often with gentle words he'll take it;
> Play softly with it, then rudely break it.

Did the killer suffer from a broken heart? Was he trying to rebuild or repair his own, using assembled "parts"? "And what is the significance of the playing card?" she asked aloud to the hum of the Lear. "And what the devil kind of card is it that's made of lacy material?"

Every particular, every item, every article of information she might learn now would help her to convince skeptics—whom she was bound to run headlong into later—that she was a genuine psychic, capable of magical feats of mental agility and supernormal abilities. Dazzle them first; get them off your back, and then you can go to work, she reminded herself.

Going to work, however, wasn't so simple, not for her. Going to work, a phrase that meant boredom on the horizon for most people, a phrase that conjured up a nine-to-five nightmare, was just the opposite for her. Going to work for Dr.

Kim Desinor meant both opportunity and anxiety, elation and depression, courage and fear all tenaciously wound together like the strands of a tightly packed baseball below its leather coverlet. It meant she must take that first step beyond, and each time she had to take that step, it was as if it were her first time. She tried to conjure up that first time, but she'd had the sight for so long, since she was so young, that she could not recall ever being without it. Still, she never knew where her second sight might next lead, whether she would find her way or become lost, dead-ended, or if she'd fall over the edge of the labyrinth, or psych herself into a meaningless corner filled with useless images and symbols of no apparent or corporeal value; or if, on the other hand, she might discover revelation. And she never knew going in if she'd return intact and unscathed, for within the netherworld she visited, angry monsters freely roamed, searching for psychic prey of their own. Often psychic scars resulted, invisible to others, but painfully obvious to her, scars which did not heal so easily as fleshly ones. Scars which often must be denied so strongly by the psyche that they were healed over only by forgetfulness, though forgetfulness got in the way during an investigation of this sort. What she'd felt in Paul Zanek's office the previous day, when she had literally become the killer, she wanted more than anything to forget, yet she must court the memory, tease it back, squeeze every detail from it, if she were to crack the case of the Heart-Taker of New Orleans.

Her work often meant facing terrors and unimaginable suffering, yet unlike many a burned-out psychic who'd looked into the mind of a killer or through the eyes of a victim, Kim had always been fortunate to have a strong hold on the here and now, on current time and reality. As a result, she was able to hold at bay the dogs of fear, at least to the degree that, even while in trance, one small part of her mind knew the truth of her situation, that she was in no real or immediate danger, however horrid or graphic her psychic visions might become. She likened it to reading a Geoffrey Caine archaeological horror novel, which was among her favorite pastimes; she could always set the lurid motion picture of the terror tale aside and say to herself that it was foolish to fear the images contained and controlled by a higher force—the author—within the pages of the book; so too with the pages of her mind, where she was author and authority, where she was in control, molding from chaos some semblance of order, however dastardly and grotesque that order might be. Until now, until this time. Holding this killer's rosary beads had shaken her faith in herself to stand on an objective baseline and direct and orchestrate what her trance-self should next do. There was always the chance that she could become lost inside a vision, and in Zanek's office she'd lost all control.

That control had always been the one saving grace that kept her fit for such work as this. Many psychics far more gifted than she were unable to divorce themselves from the physical violence played out on a victim, or to withstand the mental pressure of having to climb around inside the mind of a fiend in order to think like a killer. She could, doing both in her career as first a cop for the Miami-Dade Police Department, when she'd first learned of her special talents, and later as a self-employed psychic and psychoanalyst, and finally now as an agent for the FBI.

Just then Kim's thoughts and her peace were suddenly interrupted when the cockpit door opened outward and Dr. Jessica Coran stood before her in a pleated and pleasant lime-green suit, a pleased half smile on her face as she stared at her surprised colleague.

"What, you didn't sense I was aboard?" Jessica said, attempting a wan joke. Then she pointed at the display of files scattered across the table. "I see you've leapt right into the workload."

Kim Desinor tried to regain her composure first by quickly closing her gaping mouth, a signal to Jessica Coran that she had taken Kim by total surprise, a lesson no psychic wanted pointed out to her. Was Jessica intentionally testing her? Kim wondered. Was she here as Zanek's watchdog? If so, Kim reasoned, she'd have to give the bitch enough leash to hang herself. For now, however, Kim was merely trying to hide her complete bewilderment on learning that she and the pilot were not alone on the plane after all.

"Why, Dr. Coran, I thought you'd already left for New Orleans with Stephens . . . yesterday."

"Learning to pilot one of these things; never know when the skill might be useful, and I've been wondering where to put some of my money. Ed—Lieutenant Sand up front there—let me take a turn at the controls. Sorry if I startled you."

"You mean that takeoff was . . . was your doing?"

"Sorry. I know it was a little rough."

"No, no . . . I hadn't noticed," Kim lied, still angry with herself for being so totally taken in.

"Now you're lying like a rug, Doctor."

"No, really . . ."

Jessica closed the door behind her and said, "Don't tell me you didn't sense me nearby?"

Kim could not tell whether Jessica Coran was being facetious or straightforward with her innocent question. Stalling for an answer, Kim caught her breath and, staring up at Jessica from where she sat, replied, "Actually, you were the furthest thing from my mind."

"Really?"

"Yes, really."

Jessica came closer, seduction oozing from her along with the faint odor of alcohol. That Jessica was consuming a great deal these days took no great psychic knowledge; it was common gossip among the FBI family, along with the feeling "Who can blame her?" Still, if she'd actually been flying the plane while juiced, Kim would make sure to file a complaint with the powers-that-be. She didn't care to have her life placed in danger by Jessica Coran or anyone else whose judgement was impaired by either despair or booze or both.

Kim had done a little digging on Jessica Coran before she left for New Orleans, where they were to ostensibly work in tandem. She wasn't altogether sure she could trust the other woman, at least not in her current state.

Now, rather than entering from the opposite side of the semicircular seat in the alcove here, Jessica nudged Kim to move over, joining her on this side and brushing past the files that Kim had laid there moments before.

"Really," Kim said, echoing her last remark, not knowing what else to say to Dr. Coran.

"Hey, I wanted a chance for us to get to know one another better before we get embroiled in this *brouhaha* down in New

Orleans, you understand? 'Sides, once we're there, we're to look like we aren't on the same team, right? Don't want you getting the idea that I'm some cool, scientific type who has all the answers, but that's the part I'll be playing down there, so . . .''

Her cool tone and the silky voice placed Kim somewhat at ease, but did not completely convince her of Jessica's sincerity. "Yes, it would be nice to get our Indians in a row."

"I see you've been doing just that." Jessica fingered the medical examiner's reports and pawed at some of the photos. She'd already studied the same information in duplicate at her apartment.

"There's another reason you lagged behind to come away from Virginia with me, isn't there?" Kim pointedly said now.

Jessica visibly stiffened, but said nothing.

"You . . . I sense some dread in you," Kim went on. "Nervous energy and a joking demeanor don't always hide the truth, Dr. Coran."

Jessica dropped her eyes, and her head followed easily into her hands. "I must look like shit. I haven't slept in days."

"If you wish to talk about it, please do so."

"It's just that . . . well, you'd think I could get used to it . . . but it's ruining my life. Every waking moment, knowing this madman is stalking me, knowing he will never rest until either I'm dead or he is . . . or both of us . . .''

"Matisak . . . the one who's become obsessive about you. Yes, I've heard the story. Escaped the asylum, killed his doctor there and masqueraded as an orderly to gain his freedom?"

"He's since murdered many more, and from time to time he checks in."

"Checks in?"

"Part of his goddamned sick game of hide-and-seek. It's all a freaking head game to him."

"A head game?"

"With the intent to drive me crazy, I suppose. He's doing a pretty good job of it, wouldn't you say?"

She disagreed instantly. "No, not at all. In fact, when I met you the other day in Paul's office, I thought you quite composed and in charge."

"Ever hear of Prozac?"

"I hope you're not popping them like Excedrin."

Jessica ignored this. "Do you think New Orleans'll be interesting this time of year? Kinda off-season of the Mardi Gras, isn't it?"

"Well, we're not going for fun and frolic, now, are we?" Kim felt the knifelike edge to her voice and knew she was sounding bitchy, but was unable to help herself. *What does she want from me?* she wondered. *I know she wants something, but what?* "Do you think it's really safe for you, going there like this, I mean . . . now? Isn't Paul Zanek worried in the least about your safety there?"

"I've convinced the brass over his head that it's the only logical step at this point; probably the only way to lure Matisak out of hiding. I've been under guard and surveillance since his escape, since I stepped off the plane in Oklahoma from Hawaii. Zanek had an army surround me there at the airport. Now it's been near six months of sheer hell; imagine it, all that time without any semblance of peace or sense of privacy. I told 'em all that their bodyguard duties toward me were over. I'm sick of being watched—even by them. You understand that?"

"Sure, I can understand that, but—"

"I can take care of myself."

"I'm sure you can, Doctor."

"Jessica . . . call me Jessica, or Jess if you like."

"Very well, and I'm Kim."

"As for Matisak . . . he's vanished, just as if he'd fallen off the globe. Not a trace." She breathed deeply, wiping away a tear. "Some tough FBI lady, huh?"

"Hey, I understand completely. God, I can't imagine having someone stalking me, and knowing the man's a blood-drinking sadist, knowing he's after my blood, that no one else's will ever completely satisfy him. God knows, I don't fault you in the least for showing natural emotions, Doc—Jess."

Jessica wiped her face with a tissue and cleared her throat and continued. "There's an ulterior motive for my having talked Zanek into teaming us up, Kim."

Kim thought, *Here it comes,* the truth. "Oh, really. And what ulterior motive is that? Something Paul put you up to?"

"I thought at first I should just keep it to myself, but I was raised to believe that two people going into a venture as important as this must completely trust and understand one another.''

"Here, take some of this coffee," Kim offered.

Jessica sipped from the foam cup, thanking her for the lukewarm offering.

"Now go on. Out with it."

"I had hoped . . . after seeing what you're capable of . . . I'd hoped that perhaps you could . . . I mean. . . . ''

"I know you don't want anyone watching your back or sitting on your shoulder at this point, so what?"

Jessica sniffed back another tear and laughed. "You are intuitive."

"So you traded in your FBI trained bodyguards for me? I suppose I should be flattered. Perhaps it would be flattering, if I gave it much thought."

"Look," Jessica began anew, "yes, I was hoping that with a few private sessions between us, you might help me locate that sonofa-satanic-bitch before he locates me, but if it doesn't sit well with you, then . . . then—"

"You're not even *sure* I can help you locate him before he locates you; Jess, it seems to me that you're clutching at straws here . . . not to mention presumptions not in evidence, and for a woman of science . . . well . . ." Kim paused, saying nothing further, searching the sun-drenched clouds out the porthole to her right. The dense white mountain of cloud which stretched outward forever looked like a pillowy glacier onto which she might escape. However, real glaciers were not storybook-smooth on their surfaces, but rather pitted and treacherous. Between Zanek's sending her back to face her childhood home and Jessica Coran's undeniable need, Kim herself might surely need an escape route, or at least a friend. *Pour it on,* she silently thought.

Still, she managed a pleasant enough smile, turned back to face Jessica, took her hands firmly in her own and said, "I'll do whatever in my power to help keep you safe. I can't actually promise you anything, but if you think a psychometric seance with me will help, I'll certainly arrange one . . . if you're sure."

"A seance . . . really?" Jessica hadn't expected such a commitment so soon. "I'd . . . I'd like that."

"You wouldn't by chance have brought along anything once belonging to Matthew Matisak, would you?"

"I've collected a few items, things left in his cell, some of the evidence used to put him away, that sort of thing, but . . . but . . ."

And you of course carry the scars he inflicted upon you, thought Kim.

"Damnit, all that stuff's packed away and in the cargo hold," Jessica said.

"Well, then, what about your . . . your well-publicized ankles?"

"My ankles?"

"The scars he left on you. Would you trust them to me?"

Jessica kicked one of her heels into the air in response. "Does that answer your question?"

"You must've been impressed by what Paul had to say about my abilities, or you wouldn't so readily place yourself in my hands," Kim replied, a look of surprise fading over her brow.

"I saw some tapes on you. I was impressed."

"Best hurry then and do this, yes? Before you change your mind." Kim's self-deprecating smile was meant to put Jessica at ease, but the FBI's most famous M.E. remained aloof.

"I've tried everything else. I'm desperate."

Everybody's desperate when they come to a supposed miracle worker, Kim thought. "Jessica, you needn't apologize to me. I understand."

"I'm sorry, I didn't mean to sound ungrateful or as if I . . . I . . ."

"Never mind, forget it. I've long ago become accustomed to dealing with people who doubt me but at the same time want to believe I can help them, Jessica."

"I suppose God gets a lot of that too."

It was said with the venom born of frustration and drink, as spiked a phrase as Kim had heard in a long time, but for some reason, it was also funny, so Kim, unable to respond any other way, burst out laughing. Jessica, surprised by the outburst, suddenly joined in, and together—unable to completely stifle the nervous edge to the laughter—they sputtered like old friends reunited.

Jessica's eyes wandered now, and she felt incapable of saying more; she felt vulnerable, as if she had opened up her soul to this near-stranger. She'd worked for years with Dr. Donna Lemonte, who'd suggested that she seek other help since Donna had begun to feel that their therapy together had come to a standstill, that while Jessica teetered at the precipice of complete discovery and peace, she was too afraid to take the leap. Donna Lemonte had cut Jessica loose—telling her it was for her own goddamned good, telling her that she'd taken Jessica as far as she could go in a psychoanalytical sense, telling Jessica that any further sessions would just be highway robbery on her part, saying she was too much Jessica's friend now to lie to her or string her along. *With friends like that, friends who abandoned you,* Jessica thought, *who needs enemies.*

Donna had said that Jessica was as obsessed with Matisak as he was with her, and that until that obsession could be resolved or at least controlled, any further attempts at resolutions and order in her life were futile exercises, draining both patient and therapist of energy in a no-win battle for Jessica's sanity.

Jessica now confided some of this to Kim Desinor. All the ground that she and Donna had fought so painstakingly for, all the strides, all the wins—all effectively demolished by one act on the part of the madman, *his escape.* Matisak's escape and his insidious notes to her, his ugly poetry, had with one fell swoop unleashed all the shadows and horrors that for years now she had fought to control and put away forever.

"In all truth, it was Dr. Donna Lemonte who suggested I get together with you, but I didn't think it right, unless I could do something for you in return," Jessica confessed now, feeling better at having the deception out and in the open.

Doesn't like to feel obligated, Kim thought, to anyone. Is afraid of long-term commitments, and this is killing her, to have to ask for help, so she barters instead.

Jessica continued speaking. "I urged Zanek to give you this chance; it's your chance to come in with us at the profiling team, a chance to take a giant step ahead for psychic profiling and detection at Quantico.''

Kim's smile was an embrace. ''Donna's a great friend and colleague. She mentioned you might be seeking me out professionally someday. I just didn't expect it quite in this . . . fashion. You know, Jessica, you could've just come to me.''

''Call me selfish. I wanted to get back to work too. They've had me caged up at Quantico. The bastard's out there free to kill and kill again, and I'm the prisoner now. Well, to hell with that.''

Kim admired her fire, the spirit that inflamed her soul, so visible in Jessica's vivific aura.

Jessica almost shouted, ''I'm not going to play the part of some rabbit in a warren, waiting for that sonofabitch to snare me. I won't do that; I can't, at least not anymore.''

Kim said nothing, her face stern and emotionless, but her eyes fastened to Jessica's. Jessica feared how much of herself she'd already given away. ''That sounds like a healthy attitude to me,'' Kim finally replied. ''Look, Jess, if you want to start chasing this monster immediately, why wait until we're in New Orleans with all the complications there. Let me have your ankles.''

Jessica breathed in deeply, and she slowly nodded while kicking off her second heel at the same time. ''You really mean it? I mean . . . here, now . . . in the air?''

''I can't think of a more peaceful environment in which a psychic might work, can you? Close as we're likely to come to the stars, the planets, God . . .''

''Well . . . yes . . . I mean, if you're sure it's all right.''

''It's actually very freeing, being among the clouds like this. So then, why not get started?''

''Those scars are pretty well healed,'' Jessica said as she placed her stockinged ankles across Kim's lap.

And what about those of your heart?

''All right . . . whatever you think best . . .'' Jessica kept talking as Kim's eyes closed, her hands going over the nyloned ankles until she abruptly stopped.

11

Now that my ladder's gone,
I must lie down where all the ladders start,
In the foul rag-and-bone shop of the heart.

—Yeats

Kim asked that the cabin lights be shut off and all the window portholes be closed against the sun. She then told Jessica to go to the rear of the plane and remove her panty hose before returning her ankles to Kim's touch.

This done, Jessica returned, her natural skepticism returning too, for now she sat across from Kim and placed her bare legs across the coffee table between them, atop the file folders there. Kim then placed her hands around the old scars inflicted by Matisak some three and a half years before when, after sedating her, he'd cut her Achilles tendons and hung her up like a side of beef to be bled from the throat until dead.

No one before now, not even her lover in Hawaii, James Parry, had ever caressed the scar tissue about her Achilles tendons, not since "Teach" Matisak.

Kim's tender touch alone brought memories welling up inside Jessica, memories of a horrid night in Chicago when she first encountered and was snared by the maniac who signed his notes to her as Teach. He had fixated on her blood that night, and every night since his incarceration. She wished now she had killed him when she'd had the chance.

Kim Desinor got immediate psychic impulses, her jaw tightening and her face contorting with what she saw behind her closed eyelids. After almost five minutes of eerie silence in the plane, Jessica's mind pleaded to know if Kim could help her.

She had tried hypnosis without effect. She had tried medication and shrinks. Nothing. She had tried drink, and that had failed miserably.

"He will come . . . he is driven to come for you. His only comfort now is in you. . . ."

Jessica's mind screamed through her mental hallway, *Tell me something I don't already know!*

"When the sky falls . . . he will come . . . when the sky falls."

"What?" Jessica was confused, wondering if the other woman might possibly be joking. "Isn't that a bit extreme, like Chicken Little?"

"All I see is debris from a falling, black sky. Glass shards, water, lightning, the falling of planets . . ."

"Planets?"

"Stars and moon will fall. . . . When the sky falls, he will attack."

"Beware the falling sky. . . ." Jessica's lingering skepticism got the best of her. "Really?"

"He plans to die with you; a suicide pact. Wants you to want him; wants you to end it with him . . ."

He was saying as much in his fucking blood poetics. "Is there any indication where he is now . . . at this moment?"

"A dark, large area, perhaps a warehouse? Barnlike . . . yes, light unable to penetrate. Others . . . other eyes looking on . . . perhaps animal eyes, lurid eyes all around . . . Large-eyed demons, cat's eyes, blackbirds or crows descending and rising and descending again . . ."

"What, now we're talking about an aviary or a zoo?" Jessica's cynicism broke harshly into Kim's decidedly foggy vision. She'd not gotten much, only bits and pieces sluicing by like krill in the sea of her soul.

"Matisak's a careful SOB; he's not going to try anything in a public place," Jessica stated.

"I'm sorry . . . that's all I'm getting. Perhaps later, I can do a psychometric reading on the items you brought along."

"So watch for falling skies, huh? Cats and crows with big eyes. That kind of thing . . ." Jessica's look was verging on disdain. She'd hoped for and expected far more; she'd offered up her own body as catalyst for the reading, and what she'd gotten was hardly worth it.

Kim cautioned her. "Often what I see, Jess, is merely a symbolic representation. The black crow, for instance, could be in reality an undertaker or a booze label, in which case this information must be taken with *great* care. A cat's eye could be a child's marble, a face mask, a brand of cereal or a logo for a paper mill. On that level, the image, say, of the falling planets, well, it could mean any number of things.''

''Such as the end of the universe? The Big Bang returned?'' Jessica pulled back her legs and located her high heels.

''Anything,'' continued Kim, ''in an allegorical fashion.''

''Oh, then we are talking Chicken Little.''

''No, we're talking about a falling billboard sign with a sky backdrop, say, or a theater backdrop coming down, a ceiling, a roof caving in . . . or—'' She abruptly stopped short of what she'd failed to plan not to say.

''Go on. What?'' Jessica pressed, seeing Kim's fine features ravaged by concern. ''If I see the roof caving in and I'm under it, he's got me?''

''For all I know, you are the roof, Jessica.''

Jessica's face blanched white. The fear of a complete breakdown hadn't been totally ruled out by Dr. Lemonte either. She wondered just how much Lemonte had confided in Kim Desinor, psychic and shrink, just how much doctor-patient privilege meant to her so-called friend when confiding in another doctor about an interesting case involving a homicidal maniac recently escaped and seeking revenge and a release of his perverted lust against the doctor's patient—whose own fixation on and fear of this unholy human had led Jessica to a near-collapse of personality.

She stared at Kim Desinor, her mind turning to granite over the thought, the single question she feared asking the other woman: Am I an interesting guinea pig for you two shrinks to ponder over? Is that what I've become?

Jessica snatched up her panty hose and returned to the cockpit, where Ed Sand, a person she could talk to without any fear of psychoanalysis, might keep her laughing, at least until they landed in New Orleans.

New Orleans

If they were expecting a quiet reception on the ground, Kim knew the instant the plane landed that such an idea was literally gone—out the window, so to speak—when a motorcade of police vehicles careened up to the plane, causing her to wonder and stare.

Once the plane had safely landed and was taxiing for the hangar, Kim tore open the cockpit door to find Jessica and the pilot embracing. Kim had two sweeping sensations at once: a feeling of chagrin and a certainty that Jessica was behaving irrationally and out of character, not simply for Kim's benefit but because she could not help herself. Kim covered by shouting, "What the hell's going on outside the plane, Dr. Coran? I thought we were going to be 'secreted' in, remember?"

"Don't know," replied Jessica, sitting opposite the pilot in the copilot's position, her panty hose draped over the back. "We're trying to get information now." She had raised a hand for Kim to remain silent while Ed Sand, the handsome, uniformed pilot, talked into his microphone, then listened, snatched off his headset and began explaining. "There's been another Hearts killing. They want you, Dr. Coran, to get in the limo provided by the city and go with the motorcade. The two of you will be staying at different locations in the city to keep your cover, Dr. Desinor, so you're to remain on board the plane until all the hubbub dies down."

"Then what?"

Lieutenant Sand looked at her quizzically for a moment as if the question was beyond him, then stated, "I . . . I assume then someone'll be along to pick you up as well, Dr. Desinor."

"You mean I have to sit here and wait?" Kim complained.

"Sorry . . . some welcome to the Big Easy, huh?" The pilot's dark eyes then flashed on Jessica. "Later, Jess, I'd be happy to show you some of the nightlife. Whataya say?"

Jessica looked from Ed Sand and back to Kim Desinor, and with a near-mean grin, she said, "Sure, Ed . . . I'd love it."

Kim, unsure why Jessica's attitude toward her had so quickly and coolly changed, stepped away from the door and allowed Jessica and Ed another private kiss, which Jessica seemed to initiate for Kim's benefit, as if to show Kim that Jessica was far more woman than the psychic who'd frightened off Paul Zanek. Or was it part of the self-destruction which Jessica seemed bent on?

Kim didn't bother closing the cockpit door.

· · ·

On the shimmering cracked concrete surface of the taxiway, P.C. Stephens was standing in a bright wash of light in a beige suit, waving at the plane and signaling Jessica Coran to dash for the limo, where his entourage stood all around him, men in dark suits, all looking quite official and important. Some of the others looked like dignitaries and luminaries of New Orleans, prepared to hand Jessica the keys to the city. "Yeah, that bastard Stephens sure knows how to keep a secret, doesn't he?" Jessica said, snatching down a carry-on from an overhead compartment.

From the carry-on bag, Jessica pulled the strange black rosary beads with the crystal amulet that had so unsettled Kim in Paul Zanek's office. "Thought you'd want to get this back," she explained, handing the rosary to Kim. "Use it carefully and wisely, right?" She sounded kind and gentle when she said it, her mood swings perhaps partially due to medication she was on, Kim silently decided as she took the dubious offering.

"See you in the media," Kim replied. "And so will Matisak, Jess. But I have no doubt your pilot friend will make you feel safer."

"Hey, if I wanted safe, I . . . I'd have stayed in Virginia, surrounded by guys a lot bigger and tougher than Ed in there."

"You see any media out there?" Kim asked.

"Where there's cops, there's media. But by the time Stephens pulls out with me, you'll be in the clear. Ed'll see to it you get to the scene if no one shows, so never fear. Who knows, Ed might even loosen you up a bit, Doctor. And remember, from here on, we don't know each other from Adam, okay?"

Jessica was about to deplane when Kim reached out and held her firmly by the forearm. Their eyes met. "I didn't mean to imply any more than what my signals tell me, Jessica—about the falling sky, I mean. *You* came to *me*, remember?"

"Yeah, I remember, and maybe I'm already regretting it."

"Come on," shouted Ed. "They're getting real antsy at the bottom of the ramp for you, Jess. Got to get you into that limo quick's possible. Soon as the door opens, go, and I'll see your bags make it to the Hilton."

"Later and good luck, Dr. Coran," Kim told her as Jessica dashed from the plane. Kim cautiously peered on from a back window at the scene, feeling an overwhelming sense of detachment from the ballyhoo below, yet also a great, rising concern for Dr. Coran. At the same time, she wondered what the other woman wanted or expected of her.

She watched Jessica Coran now as she raced for the limo, and in a moment she was swallowed up in its plush interior, seated alongside P.C. Stephens and Lew Meade, New Orleans area FBI chief, a bland, squat little man who looked more politician than policeman, making a nice counterweight to Stephens only in build.

Kim wondered just who they'd send for her—and how long she'd have to sit here pretending she didn't exist before someone came for her. She still wondered about the fanfare below, why Stephens had made such a to-do of it all.

"When're they going to send someone for me?" she asked the pilot.

Ed Sand's boyish, even devilish, grin flashed over her. "Not to worry, Dr. Desinor. No one's likely to overlook you, not in the least."

She ignored the innuendo and the glint in his steely eyes, saying, "If the fools wait long enough, the crime scene'll be so cold, I'll make a complete ass of myself."

"Hardly likely from what Dr. Coran tells me about you, Dr. Desinor."

She wondered what Jessica had confided to the pilot and why. "Well, if this is the way they want to play it out, then maybe I'll just be on the next plane for Quantico and be back in my lab before lunch. Whataya say?"

There was a call from the tower and Ed Sand retrieved his headphone set, taking in the message. He finished with a look of ebullient pride showing. "They told me to tell you that your ride's on the way, an unmarked vehicle and no cameras. They'll take you to the crime scene, and like I said to Dr. Coran, I'll see your bags get to the Mississippi Marriott downtown."

"Thanks, Lt. Sand."

"No problem, Doctor."

"Say, Lieutenant, how long has she—Dr. Coran—been flying?"

"Not long. Just took it up, in fact."

"Is she any good at it?"

"Fact is, she's damned good . . . got a natural gift for it, I'd say."

Kim nodded. "I've heard she's very good at whatever she takes up. How long have you known her?"

"Well, not long really . . ."

"Not long?"

"Well, we just sorta met on takeoff."

"Jesus, Lieutenant, and you allowed her to take off? You didn't let her land this thing, did you?" *How damned persuasive the woman is,* she thought.

"Told me she'd flown with other pilots out of Quantico," he replied as if this explained everything. "And the way she handled the controls, and given who she is . . . well, I just didn't see any reason to doubt her."

"Did she? Land the plane, I mean."

He hesitated before lying, worried now about the kind of trouble Kim could get him in.

Letting him off the hook, she said, "Ed, will you do me a favor while you're in New Orleans?"

"Well, if I can, sure."

She picked up a trace of West Virginia in his drawl. "Watch her while she's here in New Orleans, will you?" she told him.

"Sure . . . I intend to . . . intended just that." He smiled widely now at the task Kim had given him.

"How long can you stay in the city, Lieutenant?"

He cleared his throat as if he had to think about this. "I got some leave coming. Thought I'd requisition it by fax this afternoon. Maybe a week . . . maybe more. Depends what's cooking . . . at the base, I mean."

Kim breathed heavily, the motorcade a dim sight, the sirens now a whisper in the distance. "Where the hell's my ride!" she moaned. Then down below, an unmarked car pulled into the gates facing south and skirted amid the shadows of a series of nearby hangars until it came to rest below the Lear jet. Ed was careful to keep himself and his uniform from sight, and there were no markings on the jet to indicate to the casual observer that it was in any way connected to the U.S. government.

Kim grabbed her own carry-on, and from atop the ladder she tried to make out the occupants of the car, but the front windshield was masked in a stark, tropical glare until Kim put on her Coasta Del Mar sunglasses. As she made her way down the Lear's carpeted steps, her Polaroid lenses cut cleanly through the daunting glare sprawled across the windshield. Her glasses, the same as those used by Virginia State Troopers, allowed her to see the Hoss Cartwright lookalike in the passenger seat and the handsome features of Alex Sincebaugh behind the wheel.

Somehow she knew they'd send Sincebaugh for her.

"Alex Sincebaugh?" she called out, extending her one free hand through his window.

"Yeah." He held onto her hand for a moment. "But how'd you know?"

"Been reading your reports on the Queen of Hearts killer."

"There's nothing in those reports to tell you a thing about me."

"Oh, but that's not true. They told me a lot about you."

Ben deYampert had leapt from his side of the car, and was now opening the back door of the sedan to her and taking her handbag, a leather Gucci satchel, which he placed on her lap after she climbed in. With a smile, he said, "Welcome to New Orleans, ma'am."

"And you must be Sergeant Detective Ben deYampert?"

"That'd be me, yes, Miss . . . ahhh, Dr. Desinor."

"What're you, the welcome wagon, Ben?" Sincebaugh snapped. "Time's wasting, Big, so let's have at it. Climb in. We got police business to attend to." Sincebaugh sounded as annoyed as a delivery man whose time schedule had been thrown off, and the officious use of the phrase "police business" was a sure sign of his ire. It was highly unlikely that he'd wanted to make the detour to pick her up.

"What can you tell me about the latest death?" she asked from the rear.

"Today's?" asked Sincebaugh with a rough laugh. "Nothing yet. Yesterday's? You can read the report. Bastard's escalating's all I know."

Ben, half turning to look into the rear and meet her eyes now, cleared his throat and added, "Escalating his mutilation technique too."

"Meaning?" she asked.

"Severed yesterday's guy's head near clean off 'long with his . . . everything else, ma'am."

"And today's discovery, also headless?"

"No, don't reckon this one's missing his head," said Ben. "If that were the case, it'd be all over the police band by now."

"On top of all the other atrocities," she mused aloud, "he's now added to his repertoire of mutilation?"

"Is that supposed to be a joke?" Alex muttered. "On top?"

She didn't think Sincebaugh's remark was funny, and Ben seemed not to get it, and now Ben had become strangely reserved as though Sincebaugh had jabbed him in the ribs and into silence.

"We've got another body . . . washed up out of Big Muddy this morning . . . looks like the work of the Hearts guy," said Stephens to Jessica Coran as the motorcade moved over an enormous bridge spanning the Mississippi, the dappled light and shadow of the bridge cables creating a mosaic of fleeting images through the tinted glass windows. "Thought you may's well set right to work, Dr. Coran. You should've come ahead with me yesterday," he finished, chastising like the polite headmaster of a boarding school.

"We heard you had another yesterday as well. Kinda getting crowded in the morgue, no doubt. Déjà vu for Dr. Wardlaw, I'm sure."

Stephens was silent for a moment. "Wardlaw'll be around for a week or so, hand over the baton, all that, but he's officially off the case."

"Off the case?"

"We felt it best that you take complete control at this point, Doctor . . . for the time being at least, and he . . . well, he didn't like the arrangement, so we severed ties with the man."

"Whew . . . what happened, Stephens? What really happened? Out with it. You don't fire an M.E. for no cause."

Stephens ran a hand through his thinning red hair and

sighed in exasperation, echoing her words. "What happened . . . quite . . ."

"I'm a big girl, Commissioner. Tell me straight out."

"Look, suffice it to say that the man's become unglued, and it's spilled over into his work and, well . . . having the eyes of the nation bearing down on us, thanks to this case, we just can't have any slipups at this point."

"Unglued? As in a nervous breakdown?"

"Not precisely. Perhaps you might call it a drug dependency."

"Alcohol?"

"You are perceptive, Doctor."

"It comes with the territory, sometimes. The drug dependency, I mean . . ." She felt for this faceless, unknown Dr. Wardlaw. Many good M.E.s, and doctors in general, had faced the same problem he faced now, she included—although hers was of a short duration, exacerbated by two men in her life, Matisak and Jim Parry, the one she feared and hated, the other she feared and loved.

What difference would it have made had she stayed in Hawaii, she told herself. If she'd remained, she would have found a way to destroy what she and Jim had anyway. Dr. Lemonte had told her as much. Not until she could rid herself of the damage caused by Matisak could she be fully free of her crippling fears, which included a fear of commitment and a fear of happiness.

"We're here to assist in any way we can, Dr. Coran," said Lew Meade, introducing himself and shaking hands with Jessica. "Frankly, I long before lost all faith in Frank Wardlaw, and I also place little store in psychics, even if they do work for us, so I was more than pleased when I learned of your coming."

Stephens quickly countered with: "But we are at our wit's end here, and the local police have exhausted their leads, so . . ."

The limo ride was like glass over a silken pond.

"So, why not give hocus-pocus a chance?" Jessica asked.

"Thought you'd appreciate my candor, Dr. Coran," said Meade, a thick man whose girth spread across the limo. "Sorry, I don't mean to offend in any way."

Jessica wondered why she'd felt compelled to defend Dr. Desinor in her absence. "No offense taken," she lied, taking an instant and irrational dislike to the man, feeling uncomfortable with the way in which he and Stephens had chosen to handle matters, waving a red flag at the press. And yet isn't that what she'd wanted, to signal to Matisak her whereabouts, to lure him out?

"Tell me more about the specific reasons for taking Wardlaw off the case," she said.

Stephens ran down the particulars, citing numerous lab errors which Wardlaw had made, finishing with: "Really not much more to tell. The man simply couldn't cope with it any longer—emotionally, I mean. In any case," he continued, "you're pretty much in charge at the NOPD crime lab for the moment, Dr. Coran."

It was a thought that made her happy to some degree, to be in charge, not to have to tiptoe around the local chieftain at the crime lab, to be able to simply plunge in without the usual bowing, scraping and posturing, to just have everyone in the place following her orders. The idea held out great charm and possibilities to her. Maybe Wardlaw's loss was her gain; maybe Wardlaw's alcoholism was her redemption . . . maybe now that she had a handle, she believed, on her own problems . . .

The motorcade had drawn onlookers and a crowd of reporters, just as it was intended to do. Some had snapped off shots at the airport, but this wasn't enough for many who'd followed on their heels, and now as they pulled in under the enormous, rusting metal bridge spanning the Mississippi, reporters were not only taking snapshots of Dr. Jessica Coran but of the crime scene itself.

Stephens and Meade had, for their own reasons, staged a media circus, and Jessica found herself in the center ring.

"You got public-relations problems with this case big time, don't you, Commissioner?" she asked as she climbed from the limo, dragging her hefty black valise with her. The two men in the limo admired her legs before following her out.

A suspendered politician with a young and hungry look rushed to them and took her hand, shaking it like a pump, saying, "I'm second deputy mayor of the city, Leroy David

Fouintenac, Dr. Coran, and anything—I mean anything the
city can do to make your stay more comfortable—please,
please don't hesitate to contact me. Call me at this number,
day or night, you got the least problem, understood?" He
slipped her his card, which she took with a heavy dose of salt.

"I'd like to get to work over here," she told the men, stepping away from them, allowing them to roost here at a safe
distance where they might posture for the public all they
wished. She went straight for the body. It felt good to be
back. . . .

She was soon over the corpse, standing, sizing up things
from afar. The body, which had already been disturbed by
others, was now draped with a policeman's sheet, one that
could've been cleaner—old blood smears from previous cases
staining it. The coverlet was meant to protect the deceased's
integrity, but it did very little to protect the integrity of the
crime scene, most likely having come from somewhere in the
back of a squad car.

From her black valise, Jessica pulled forth a full-length
white lab coat and placed it over her shoulders to protect her
lime-green pants suit. It was extremely humid already though
it was still early morning, the day promising a record-breaking
heat. She saw an unmarked police car coming off the bridge
now, and in the rear seat she could dimly make out Dr. Kim
Desinor's pretty profile.

"Good," she muttered to herself, "give the men something
else to stare at for a while."

Overhead, Jessica saw a sign for the Jax Brewery, and beside this an even larger billboard advertising live bait, beer
and snacks in that order, along with excursion boats and fishing charters, all below bold letters that read: "TOULOUSE
STREET WHARF."

12

One by one, and two by two,
He tossed them human hearts to chew.

—Shelley

Alex Sincebaugh felt the wave of burdensome humidity leisurely insinuate itself into his pores as it wafted across the pier
where the body, pulled from the water by men and machines
moments before, was still dripping and not likely to dry out
anytime soon. As early as it was, the heat had settled in like
God's angry breath on their faces, necks and any exposed skin,
sending a perspiring reminder to one and all that mortality was
ever present, while promising up a scorching day for the radio
announcers to bitch about, a day of blown-out tires and blis-
tering metal fatigue for automobiles, all in the wake of a
record-breaking Louisiana heat wave; in other words, misery
and a wall of super-heated air to exist in and to move through.

Louisiana's summer heat killed things: potted plants on win-
dowsills—all but St. Augustine grass—and the small hearts of
rabbits, raccoons, and overwrought birds that didn't stand a
chance, couldn't cope. Dead opossums floated downriver in
the Big Muddy, their teeth, gums and bone exposed, water
turning their hardened, furry forms into tarlike slicks. Only
time and the water might clean up such debris; the fish didn't
seem to want it.

It was nearing mid-morning at the Toulouse Street Wharf,
where the first rays of the sun glinted and winked between the
paddle wheels of the steamboat *Natchez*. From where Alex
stood, the angle of the paddle wheel lifted over the bridge,
making passing cars disappear on the Jefferson Highway on
the east side of the river and U.S. 18 on the west. Here was
a Mississippi River stopover with restaurants, a Texaco station
for boat traffic and another excursion cruise ship called the

Bayou Jean Lafitte, which departed every two hours for the Bayou Barataria, once home to the famous pirate.

Across the river from where she stood, Kim Desinor, her sun-drenched hair glistening in the New Orleans morning, could see a levee and a canal, which in the old days might well have connected up to others and, if followed carefully, might take one to Lake Ponchartrain—but that was before economic progress had covered over many of the canals.

Still, there remained literally hundreds of canals that criss-crossed the city, meeting the perpetual downriver flow of the Mississippi at the city's northernmost tier. New Orleans was a city of canals and intermittent pumping stations. Below sea level, half the city's land mass was perpetually under siege by water, and when it rained hard, as it often did, water had to be pumped from canals which fed into Lake Ponchartrain, else the entire city would flood.

Sincebaugh and Ben deYampert, along with Kim—who was feeling like the psychic interloper or psychic saint, however the myriad perceptions might mold her—now joined the crowd of authorities on the wharf where Jessica Coran had already started to work. It appeared the aftermath of yet another seemingly mindless, unreasonable and bestial desecration of a person, the body belonging to a young man, his exact age and identity yet to be determined.

All too obviously to Kim, as it must be to Jessica's FBI-trained eye, the brutalization of the body had filled a raging need in the monster who'd inflicted such wounds in his attempt to get at the heart, ripping wide the chest and viscera from the hapless victim. Kim, also trained to some degree in criminal-profile procedures, could read all that in the stark evidence on the wharf. No great or mysterious or powerful trick in that observation, she told herself now; certainly no sixth sense required, she continued to mentally remind herself, wondering again why Jessica Coran should be acting so bitchy toward her. Perhaps it had all to do with the fact that Jessica's mind, as well as her entire life, had always been predicated on the search for scientifically proven fact, indisputable, hard, tangible evidence. It was what a medical examiner staked her life on; it was her worldview. Yet here Jessica was on bended knee, and not bending too gracefully at that, groveling in her mind's eye, no doubt, to a woman whose worldview was in direct contradiction to her own, having to ask Kim Desinor for help. She had been so far reduced by her continuing fear of the phantom stalking her that she'd arranged a secret moment alone with a psychic for answers, and then what did she get? The sky is falling . . . shit . . .

Kim was angry with herself that her reading had gone so badly. It might color their relationship from here on out, should Dr. Coran make assumptions based on what had occurred in that Lear jet.

Kim watched the other woman now in the shadow of the big riverboat *Natchez*; Jessica's sable-like, auburn hair and alluring features were startlingly set off by the white lab coat she now wore, a pair of silver-rimmed magnifying glasses framing her enchanting hazel eyes. Besides appearing lovely, Jessica looked adept, competent, knowledgeable, experienced and in charge all at once—all those good things which Kim at the moment was wishing she felt. Jessica and the NOPD principals on the case, Sincebaugh and deYampert, did their work while tourists looked on from the deck, preparing for an excursion upriver and down.

A light fog veiled the scene, but not enough to offer cover from prying eyes and the high-tech photo lenses of curious journalists and people with home cameras. Officials were rightly concerned that they might wind up on *I-Witness Video* in coming weeks, and from Stephens's behavior, he'd welcome it. Word had already gone out about the heinous nature of the crimes to both the locals and nationwide. Facts in evidence: There'd been a string of male prostitute deaths in the French Quarter; these deaths were caused by massive lacerations to the upper body; each victim had later had his genitals excised; each victim had had his heart removed, some people speculating that it had happened before death set in; the killer had struck five, possibly six times and had escalated his attacks; the killer had attacked both indoors and out. And now he was escalating the frequency of his attacks, according to police; only the day before there'd been another discovery of a body floating in a Mississippi backwash, the headless cadaver that Sincebaugh had only hinted at. Everything known about the killer culminated in one frightening truth—the phantom remained unapprehended and he would kill again and again until he was stopped.

Sergeant Detective Ben deYampert ambled over to where Jessica worked, almost stepping on her black valise, he was that clumsy. He started talking as if they'd known each other since childhood.

"You know, I've lived all my life in New Orleans, and I've spent the last six years on the NOPD, working my way up to sergeant detective, Homicide Squad. Guess it takes a case like this to make you wonder why a man'd subject himself to this line of work, huh?"

When he got no answer from Jessica, whose attention now was riveted on the body, deYampert merely continued on. "I got a wife and kids at home; they don't hardly know me anymore. I'm telling you, if something doesn't bust loose soon, well . . . I ain't so sure I want to keep on as a detective."

She finally looked up at the doughy-eyed, large man and offered a half smile of reassurance. "Hang in there, Sergeant. We're going to get this bastard and soon." Even as she spoke the words, she realized how cold and routine they must sound, but she only made things worse when she went on. "But if you're looking for psychoanalysis, see Kim Desinor over there. I understand she's a shrink as well as a psychic."

"Is that your idea of a consoling word, or do you have something concrete or useful to share with us?" asked an acerbic man now beside deYampert who quickly introduced himself as the principle detective on the case, Alex Sincebaugh.

She looked over her shoulder from the kneeling position she'd taken alongside the horrid corpse. The fire in Alex Sincebaugh's eyes was a sharp contrast to the cold, watery yet barren gaze of the corpse.

"Why'd he leave this one's head intact?" asked deYampert of her, as if she had some magical dust to spread which would reveal the answers to all his questions.

"I don't think he's really interested in heads as trophies," she coolly replied.

"We figured with yesterday's vic," deYampert continued,

as if still hoping for the pixie dust, "that he was increasing his attacks, but we never figured on finding another body within twenty-four hours."

Jessica had no reply for such a statement, certainly not here and now. She'd need considerable time in the lab to look over the evidence of both recent kills. Out of the corner of her eye, she saw that Dr. Kim Desinor was pacing the wharf, seeking out an area where she might receive some psychic emanations, Jessica supposed, but the doctor of head and haunt seemed at the moment only to be frustrated. Continuing to gather what trace elements she could from the waterlogged victim, scraping out the nails, knowing that the water had likely already gotten her real trace evidence, Jessica made short work of the preliminaries. At the same time, she kept an eye on Kim, who had now reached into her purse and pulled forth the rosary beads but seemed hesitant to clutch them, dropping them back into her purse instead.

"So, do you have anything of substance for us? Dr. Coran?" Sincebaugh pressed.

"Wardlaw, your M.E.," she began to Sincebaugh's audible groan, having to forge ahead over the man's pained expression. "Anyway, he tells me yesterday long-distance that he was able to get some semen from the previous victim's mouth which he's running DNA scans on now. He theorizes that it could be from the killer, and if so . . . who knows, maybe we can learn something about this guy's physical makeup—racial identity, probable height, weight, color of hair, eyes. . . ."

"Wardlaw's just as likely to botch a DNA test as any other test he runs."

She looked up again at the rankled cop. "Well, I see there's no love lost between you, but amazingly enough, there were some hairs and fibers found *inside* the corpse which didn't belong to the victim."

"Semen? None of the others had any semen in their mouths." DeYampert was working on this puzzle.

"Exactly . . . and none of them had had their heads severed either, and nor does this morning's package. Everything intact except the missing heart and genitals."

Sincebaugh was nodding appreciatively. "I'd had similar unanswered questions about yesterday's 'package' as you call it, Doctor. So, Frank's on top of that one, huh? Going at it through DNA testing. Just where is ol' Frank Wardlaw this morning, Dr. Coran?'' Sincebaugh asked while struggling with some inner turmoil that Jessica couldn't quite put her finger on.

''I assume he's at his crime lab. I really couldn't say.''

''I would've assumed he'd be *here*. How're you two getting on, then?''

''We actually haven't as yet met—face-to-face, that is, Lieutenant.''

Damn thorough of Frank to catch the semen, thought Sincebaugh. *Wonder what's up. Now that the famous Jessica Coran had hit town, was Frank going to finally do his job?* ''Just the same, Frank ought to be out here, don't you agree?''

''He . . . he wasn't called out, so I'm told.'' She blinked in the morning glare in P.C. Stephens's direction, her long lashes like butterfly wings.

''Wasn't called? Really?''

''Yes, really. He's . . . well, guess you'll hear soon enough, but it's not my place to tell you.''

''Tell me what?''

''He's currently under some, I don't know, attack. . . . ''

''What the hell's that? FBI euphemism for investigation of misconduct and impropriety?''

''Both in and out of the lab, I'm afraid.''

''Damn, so you're taking charge altogether on the forensics end? So we trade off Frank's alcoholic problems for your . . . press-magnetism?'' He pointed to the array of cameras on the bridge, the reporters held back by uniformed cops.

''I didn't invite the press, but for the time being, yes to your question, and in particular on this case. Wardlaw's staff will see to the routine calls.''

Ben and Alex exchanged a glance. Things were happening fast.

''So Frank let the Hearts case blow him out of the water,'' Alex mumbled to deYampert.

''Maybe his bleeding heart did him in,'' said Ben, and both men laughed at the inside joke.

She knew how callous and jaded cops were, that it came

with the territory, but she empathized strongly with the unknown Dr. Wardlaw, who'd fallen prey to the case he was working. She imagined it could happen to any M.E. or pathologist who got too emotionally involved in a case, and without thinking, she blurted out, "The man's hurting badly both emotionally and professionally, gentlemen. I don't suppose you two have ever been there?"

"It's hard to muster any sympathy for Frank, Doctor, so don't even try," replied Alex curtly.

"Is he, you know, psychologically impaired over the case, or did the booze do him in?" asked Ben.

"That's the common belief, yes," she replied, leaving her response purposefully vague because she didn't herself know all the particulars. The M.E.'s predicament made her wonder if someone would one day be speaking the same epitaph over her when she finally flipped out over a case.

Sincebaugh was now also thinking about Wardlaw's emotional response to the Hearts case, the ramifications of it all. Not only had the case had a powerful emotional effect on Alex, but on others as well. He had given little consideration to its impact on Wardlaw or Landry or even Benjamin deYampert, who'd been beside him the whole time, so wrapped up was he in his own reproach and turmoil and the damnable nightmares plaguing him thanks to the most bizarre case of his tenure as detective in the NOPD.

Something in Jessica's steely, glinting eye made Alex now look over his shoulder at the psychic, Kim Desinor, whom he'd been ordered to fetch and bring here before he and deYampert had even had a chance to view the body. It stuck in his craw that he and Ben were sent like a couple of welcome-wagon ladies to greet the psychic whom Landry had notified them about.

Landry had said that it was out of his hands, that the Department's top people had requested it of the mayor, for Christ's sake, and that the mayor, a superstitious SOB, had readily gone along with the idea of hiring the psychic to come in to do her touchy-feely thing over the case evidence. But nobody had warned him that the psychic would be allowed here at the crime scene, to rummage about as she liked. What the fuck had happened to proper protocol? And what was the famous FBI forensics guru, Jessica Coran, going to think of the Department, or how a backward police precinct in New Orleans conducted a murder investigation? He momentarily thought of all the evidence-gathering he and Ben had done, his thick notebook filled with detailed drawings of the crime scenes, notes and sketches which he'd pored over and stared at at all hours of the night, none of it giving up anything remotely helpful to determining the killer's identity.

Alex was involved in the same process now, drawing a thumbnail sketch of the body where it lay on the pier, noting its condition down to the smallest detail. But as he worked, he continued to think about Kim Desinor and the psychic connection the city had made with her. Word was that Kim Desinor was a doctor, a psychologist, as well as a psychic, which for some made her legitimate, but proved not a thing with Alex. Word also had it that she hailed from the Miami-Dade area, where she'd done some "incredible" work with police agencies. Word had it that she was a psychometrist, that she took readings from the evidence in a case and imaged out possibilities and scenarios, which ordinary cops like Ben and Alex couldn't possibly be expected to do. Word had it that the woman was strikingly good-looking as well as "gifted" with a "sight and vision" beyond normal. Part of the word according to the cop-vine was certainly true: She was a strikingly beautiful woman with an olive tinge to her skin, full red lips and penetrating eyes, her smooth complexion and shoulder-length hair enticing.

Yes, the word was right about her features; she was a good-looking woman, as was Dr. Coran, who continued to kneel over the body, her gloved hands busily working, her black case beside her. Coran certainly looked to be a lot more in control than Wardlaw had ever been on any of the Hearts cases. Coran was taking little pieces of the victim and putting them in tubes and vials and below glass on slides; she was cutting nails and hair samples, taking scraps of flesh from here and there.

Alex watched her work over the corpse. The pier had long since come to life. Fishing boats went by in convoys, the deck-hands curiously staring as each boat headed for open sea. In the distance, birds sent up a screeching racket as they followed

the shrimpers. All around the death scene were signs of humming, buzzing life as cars sped across the big bridge overhead,
and squealing children—like birds at play—scrambled after
one another between their parents' legs amid an anxious, restless crowd waiting to board the ferryboats, some of the families now leaving for a less dubious adventure, thus causing
consternation among the boat personnel, who'd pleaded with
officials earlier to hasten their cleanup before the crowds arrived. But all had remained intact for Jessica Coran and for
Kim Desinor's plane to touch down clear across the city.

But there was also around the crime scene an aura of ancient
bloodletting, the people on the bridge and at the yellow tape
line ever the Roman spectators, crying for more intensity and
shock and gut-wrenching horror so they could investigate
death in all its guises from the safe distance of the armchair
enthusiast. Add to this the sickening sight of the mutilated
corpse and the pungent aroma of the wharf itself, a place
which saw the slaughter of fish and blood with every incoming
fishing vessel—a demonstration which the crowd also appreciated on a daily basis here—and what did Alex expect. An
aroma of decay and death forever sniffed at by people and
roaming cats, like the one now representing its wild brethren
as it slinked silently and unseen to the body for a curious sniff
and inhale, making Jessica Coran shout, "Will somebody get
this freakin' contaminating cat out of the crime scene area?"

Ben deYampert reacted immediately, chasing the cat off
with a kick, which gained a wave of sympathy from the onlookers, a few elderly women hissing at Ben something about
cruelty.

~ 13 ~

Fiend behind the fiend behind the fiend . . .
Mastodon with mastery, monster with an ache At the
tooth of the ego, the dead drunk judge: Wheresoever
Thou art our agony shall find Thee Enthroned on the
darkest altar of our heartbreak Perfect, Beast, brute,
bastard. O dog my God!

—George Barker

Dr. Kim Desinor recalled the last time she'd come down to
the Toulouse Street Wharf area, barely thirteen years old. She
was in the company of a busload of others from the two
schools at St. Domitilla's, the boys' and the girls' reformatories. It was a rare occasion, an event, a field trip. They had
been given an opportunity to go aboard and take an excursion
on a paddle wheeler like the one now over her shoulder, only
hers was called the *Creole River Princess* and was far less
elegant, and along with her was a young man whose features
and sexual proclivities were not completely unlike those of the
victim over which Jessica Coran was now working. The young
man's name was Edward Mantleboro, and he had his sister in
tow, a strange and silent girl who stared not at you but through
you. Edward had introduced her as Edwina, a twin sister, although they didn't look very much alike. Edwina was unpleas-
antly swollen, her skin wrinkled badly for one so young, her
eyes puffy, as if some fluid were below the surface, but it was
her distant irises which seemed lacking soul that had most
disturbed and intrigued the young Kim. She'd forgotten about
the queer girl, along with so much else in this city, until now,
and she wondered, why now? What brought such fragments
of memory to the surface? Was it her surroundings, New Orleans, the wharf, the steamboat or the vacancy in the dead
man's eyes? Perhaps it was a combination of them all.

Edward, the young boy, by contrast to his odd sister, seemed to possess all that his sister lacked: health, vitality, soul, charm, wit, sensitivity, and he liked and flirted with young Kim, in fact spending most of the trip hanging and hovering about her, often apologizing for having been saddled with his sister, while Edwina spent most of the trip either staring out at the river or at Kim, as if she'd like to set fire to her. Kim found it both disturbing and interesting that the other girl, without really knowing her, harbored such an unreason-able hatred for her. It had been a memory that Kim had suc-cessfully put away until now, but here it came galloping back at her like an angry Headless Horseman, like an indelible mark that had never gone from her memory at all.

She wondered what had ever become of Edward and the girl, who had both also attended St. Domitilla's, he in the boys' school, she in the girls' school. Kim had thought them both odd when Edward, perhaps fifteen at the time, had con-fided that they weren't parentless or abandoned, but that their parents had placed them into the orphanage to be "straight-ened out." He'd muttered something about it all having been "bought and paid for."

The memories were vague and confusing now, but the Tou-louse Street Wharf brought back vivid images. She hadn't ex-actly been on a date with Edward Mantleboro. It had been more like two desperate young people looking for someone to be with and cling to. That was how their friendship had begun, before it turned into something bigger and more confusing, and before Edwina had attacked Kim with a broken bottle in the shower.

Kim still had the scar from the deepest wound to her upper back, which had required eight stitches. Edwina had later dis-appeared, no explanation given, and life at St. Domitilla's had gone grinding along without her, much to Kim's relief.

As for Edward, one day after her fourteenth birthday, she'd agreed to secretly meet him in the anteroom off the cafeteria located between the two buildings. Far into the night, refugees from a painful world, they'd lain in one another's arms, obliv-ious to the hardwood floor, and Edward had made love to her. But soon after, he too had vanished from the school, never to be seen or heard from again. She'd never told anyone about the incident except for her aunt, the only friend she could trust.

She had since had relationships with men, but most were frightened off by her powers of "darkness." Men, for the most part, didn't want a complicated woman, and being gifted or cursed with psi energies was one hell of a complication in a relationship. Looking around the pier now, she recalled a similar romance and an excursion boat in Florida when she lived in the Miami-Dade area. John Keys was his name, and he was her watch commander when she was a police detective there, when she'd been fairly successful at masking her potent ESP. At first John was delightful, a real prince whose acerbic wit never failed to make her laugh, and he was so good to her and so very shy about asking her out that first time. Once they had arranged their schedules and gone out, it was necessarily a daylight cruise out and back in the cerulean waters leading toward the placid Caribbean, because neither of them could get an evening free. It had been one of those blindingly bright, brilliant days only found off the waters of Florida, a lingering ocean breeze sweeping over the blue calm, the only clouds far off to the east, menacingly aligned against the crystal clarity of blue on blue sky all around them, the huge army of clouds awaiting the call to battle, yet strangely holding back for them and them alone. The battle came later that night when a terrible tropical depression brought on a downpour the likes of which the city hadn't seen since Hurricane Andrew in '92. But that day, as they'd disappeared like a pair of Huckleberry Finns aboard the cruise ship *SunGod's Dream*, floating slowly beyond sight of Miami's crime-ridden streets and its golden skyline, she had felt closer to John Keys than anyone she had ever known, and his embrace had been so very warm and comforting. She had fallen deeply in love with Jack, as she'd come to call him, but rumors had started circulating about the Department after an unusual bust and collar—not rumors about them, but rumors about her; rumors about how she'd conducted herself, how she'd second-guessed her partner and how bloody accurate she'd been, and how she could read minds.

Jack began to wonder at first, and soon after he confronted her, and when she confided in him her strange, unexplainable power, he soon began a somber campaign to distance himself from her. It started slowly at first, like a rape victim's partner who was unable to cope with the situation, but step by pains-taking step, he surefootedly waltzed away and into the background of her life without giving her the courtesy of an honest explanation. When she confronted him, it became achingly clear that he was unable to deal with the new reality that lay before them like a granite stone in a Dali desert vision. There was no reviving the lost life of their relationship. Put simply, he was frightened off.

It wasn't long after that she was unofficially drummed out of the Department and off the force, and this compelled her to go into private practice as a psychic while she finished up her doctorate in psychology. She'd gone from a member of the force, where she'd been accepted, to a lone wolf, called in on cases all over the country, but seldom if ever in Florida, and never in the Miami vicinity.

That was why Paul Zanek was so damned attractive to her when he'd first proposed that she go through FBI training and become an agent. He'd been in Miami on a case in which FBI assistance was needed, and somehow he'd gotten wind of the woman who, in cop circles, had come to be known variously as a Psi-co cop, a Private Psi, 3rd Eye Psi, Cop Hazel, Spooky K.D., Taro-Cop, Ol' Faithful or the Psi-clops cop.

Given the circumstances and the time element, Paul Zanek dared not speak of a psychic division being contemplated by the FBI, but it was obvious he both knew of her reputation and was not put off by it. Little wonder, a year later, she was in his arms.

Now this, she thought: New Orleans and a bloodthirsty killer feeding on hearts, and Paul thousands of miles away, getting his staid life back in order while her own was once again a shambles. Even before the plane had landed and the limousine filled with dignitaries sent for Jessica Coran, with Sincebaugh sent to bring her along as an afterthought, she'd sensed trouble in the air over New Orleans, that this bright morning would find a large and ugly stain upon the sun-drenched mecca for party-goers.

"Bastard seems insatiable and the guys at headquarters have placed odds on what the creep's doing with the hearts," said Alex Sincebaugh, who'd drifted from Dr. Coran to her now.

"Ten to one down at the precinct says he's doing a Jeffrey Dahmer thing with them, 'fry pan and biscuit gravy,' you know."

"I'm not so sure," Kim managed, her mind elsewhere. She now forced herself to think about her first impression of the body. She'd had to lean far out over the dock to stare down at the cold spot in the water where—she'd been informed—the body had bobbed like a bloated cork for an hour before they could get a diving team prepped and in the water to place the halter over and around it. He was nude from the waist up, his chest cavity picked clean by feeding fish, the heart long since gone. The pasty, white skin had sloughed away, leaving only the dermis layer, which would make fingerprinting more difficult for Jessica, but thanks to new technology, not impossible. The body was in one piece, and the teeth also might help in identifying the victim.

No mean trick for the divers earlier in the water to handle the body with any gentility, even here in the Old South, Kim thought now, wondering how many of the psychic emanations had been bled off by both the watery environ and the earlier handling of the body. At the same time, she was wondering just how difficult it was going to be working with Jessica Coran, wondering what kind of miraculous expectations the woman anticipated from Kim, and if Kim's calls should fall short of Jessica's expectations what the other woman's reaction might be. And again Kim helplessly wondered if Jess'd be reporting daily back to Chief Paul Zanek.

Agent Coran had already said she'd become desperate, that Kim was something of a last resort. But Kim knew she had to shake loose from these constricting, petty concerns if she was to be of any use whatsoever here this morning. She worked hard now to mentally compose herself, to locate the necessary serenity required within herself to receive whatever slight message or messages she might from the corpse. Now that Jessica and the evidence-gatherers were out of her way, she came closer to the body.

The victim's features were larger than in life, as the facial skin had bloated to blowfish size, along with the fattened limbs. The torso was flat, not at all swollen, more in the manner of a deflated balloon, what with the huge gash there.

While Kim hadn't been present at the time, she was receiving playback images of the body as it was removed from the river: The total effect when the body was raised on the crane's cables was that of a hideous, grotesque crab, a lifeless marionette.

The body was judged to be tall, rangy in life, and like the previous victims, he'd been young, early twenties, late teens maybe. He'd likely prove—once they learned who he'd been—a lively, vivacious and good-natured young man, liked by all who knew him, with family of one kind or another who loved him, either despite or because of his lifestyle. All previous victims, save yesterday's, had been identified as known gays living in and around the city.

It all reminded Kim of a case she'd worked some years before in Florida, where a madman had decided that seven women had to die to pay the price of his having been born a seventh son. In each case the heart had been removed, but jammed into the victim's mouth in a sinister twist on an old cliche about one's heart rising to one's throat.

Another psychic photo from the more recent past now rushed in at her: Envisioning the crane lowering the body too quickly onto the wharf, Kim felt a sudden wave of revulsion on a primal level sweep over her as the body slipped and came to rest with a *splat,* like a tarpon hauled off a boat and onto the dock.

"Get some more photos, Lieutenant! Then I guess we can wrap him; call in the attendants when Dr. Desinor here's finished, okay?" Jessica Coran's resonant voice and the ever-present hum and throb of the awakening city, its heart at a full beat, no longer disturbed Kim. She'd reached that level of being in which she might hear or see only on a psychic level, in a realm closed off to most humans. Her every conscious, outward sense was turned down, the world around her tuned out, while simultaneously her subconscious or inner senses—which ancients called the third eye—were turned up and tuned in. Fortunately, Jessica and the others had moved off and had not called in the ambulance attendants just yet.

Kim, now in a trancelike state over the body, kneeled, her pose strikingly similar to Jessica's before her; her eyelids half closed, eyes rolling back, hands closing over the rosary beads, she silently chanted a mantra to herself. She'd learned to do so silently so as to not put off those around her, or to give the appearance that she was some ordinary fortune-teller with a deck of tarot cards and a Ouija board. She looked to the outside world and to that part of her which hovered over the scene and her own body like a woman in supplication over the deceased. Her third eye and her second self also saw a wondering, curious crowd of onlookers, none more intent than Jessica Coran herself, staring on. Only Alex Sincebaugh seemed distressed and unforgivingly skeptical, pacing now like a cornered panther, occasionally glaring at the body and the soothsayer and back again at photographers on the bridge, who'd begun a new wave of snapshots at the strange behavior exhibited by the psychic. Kim easily sensed Alex's distress over what he felt to be a Barnum and Bailey atmosphere orchestrated by Stephens, Meade and other brass.

All around her, Kim had to fend off the remarks and taunts, both spoken and projected via thought, like piercing arrows directed at her but interfering with her procedure. There were no doors to close here, no shades to draw, no cushion between her and the public, no barriers to ward off the skeptical or the mental flares fired at her. The psychometric reading suffered in turn. She had come to find comfort in her props and in controlling the environment in which she worked. Maybe the lab had softened her.

She cursed herself deep within her soul to find a solution. But the seance was awash in a sea of disbelief and twisted emotional cinders coming in at her from various sources, including Jessica Coran and P.C. Stephens as well as Alex Sincebaugh. Stephens had never actually wanted her here; she'd been pushed on the bastard by Paul Zanek. Stephens's secret desire was simply to have Jessica Coran follow him back to New Orleans. He had no real desire to have Kim. At least that was the garbled message she now received over several others entwining themselves snakelike about one another.

Too damned many people here at odds with the situation, she told herself. She couldn't possibly focus, not here, not like this, and so she removed herself from trance, opened her eyes and stared down at a new horror awaiting her. *Something's alive inside the corpse,* her mind shouted.

She saw the odd, slick, reflecting ripple of movement first, like an unseen shadow out the side of the eye, odd but definitely there. It was a little glimmer of movement in the intestines deep within the body cavity. Maggots? Yes, a nest of them, swirling about now, covering the entire abyss before her. But these were psychic maggots, not real, nothing to be alarmed about. She didn't know what the image meant or why it had come to her, but she held firm to the real world, breathed a sigh of relief and saw that the maggots were indeed gone. There was no way maggots could've gotten at the body anyway, given that it was in the water all this time. So, just an illusion, part of her vision trying to take form? A symbolic representation, lingering on after her trance? But again she saw movement inside the corpse, making her start. Was this some easily explainable muscle spasm that would garner laughs all around from Dr. Coran and Sincebaugh and the others should Kim so much as twitch again in response? She maintained her stoic posture, but suddenly this snakelike movement shot to life, leaping from the body toward her. She started and fell back, tripping on the wet planks.

"Jesus!" she shouted. "What is it?"

Everyone was instantly staring at her where she lay, the oozing, slick eel slithering over her legs, leaving a trail of gruel on her pants leg. The six-inch eel, a baby by Louisiana standards, which had embedded itself inside the body, now slapped furiously about the wharf until it found an escape, flailing itself back into the Mississippi and sinking quickly into the depths from which it had come.

Still startled and shivering, shaken to her core, Kim was suddenly grateful to feel someone's strong arms go round her; the sensation of warmth and caring that careened through her entire being from the man's helpful hands served to help her regain her composure along with her feet. With the forgotten rosary beads, cross and crystal amulet dangling loosely in her hand, she felt herself being turned like a toy top in the large, caring grip, fully expecting to meet Ben deYampert's brown eyes.

"Are you all right, Dr. Desinor? Are you all right?"

It was Alex Sincebaugh's eyes she gazed into, and when her eyes found his, she realized how completely sincere and concerned Lt. Alex Sincebaugh was, although she was unsure just why.

She also realized how many eyes were on them, and so she quickly pulled away, saying, "Yes, yes . . . fine. I'm okay; rascal just caught me off guard's all."

"You shouldn't've let yourself get talked into this case, Dr. Desinor." His protest was almost a whisper, a confidence between them.

Alex, for his part, continued to stare deeply into her mysterious eyes, thinking how like his nightmares this scenario with the eel had been, except here it was one large, giant worm instead of thousands of small ones.

"Oh?" she finally replied, breaking the bond created between their eyes. "I suppose I should check with you each time I decide to take on a case? Is that right?"

"Someone like you . . . it's just—"

"Best I stick to missing-persons cases? Dogs and cats up trees? People wishing to be reunited with their dear and dead departed? What?"

"I'd think you'd want to spare yourself the . . . the discomfort of . . . of such a . . ."

"Heart-wrenching case?" she quickly filled in for him, imagining he'd like the macabre humor as much as any cop might. "Don't worry yourself, Lieutenant. I can pluck at the old heartstrings with the best of 'em. Might even teach you a tune or two." She worked up a smile for Sincebaugh.

He didn't return the smile, and he didn't care for the brand of humor she was doling out. "Yeah, something like that," he sullenly replied.

"Sorry if I don't live up to your image of the damsel in distress, Lieutenant, but there you have it. Thanks for the helping hand, but don't try to tell me how to run my business, okay?"

"All right, if you're sure you're not hurt. Guess I was wrong to put myself out on your behalf, Doctor."

"As I said, I appreciated the hand up. . . . "

"Sure . . . whatever you say, Doctor."

She felt his ire and frustration, and turning away from him, she also felt him leave. Her oval eyes now returned to the victim. Her hands clutching the rosary, she felt little or no psychical movement about the body, merely a handful of shrouded, dark flashes of energy, smoky images of the knife-wielding murderer, the monster's rage so strong and overpowering that all else was blotted out. The killer was striking out again and again at the victim, and she felt his presence. The monster was close, somewhere nearby, very much within the confines of the city. But the image was as momentary and as fleeting as Sincebaugh's moment of concern and compassion had been.

Nothing was forthcoming, and she knew that pressing it here and now would prove futile. The eel and Sincebaugh had taken the day. Unfortunately, she'd gleaned nothing of great import for P.C. Stephens and the others, and if things went as they appeared, Jessica Coran and scientific observation had won the first match.

Jessica came over to her now, not to gloat but simply to ask if she were finished, telling her that the morgue attendants were waiting and that the body would be at her disposal at the morgue later, should she wish to continue there. She even offered a consoling word, saying, "Perhaps in the solitude of the morgue, you know . . . without so much to distract or disturb you . . ."

Taking a deep breath, the sun glinting stonily in her eyes, Kim Desinor replaced her dark glasses on her face and backed away from Jessica with a swift nod, returning to the sanctuary of her escort's car, where Ben deYampert told her he'd be happy to see her to her hotel.

Sincebaugh had disappeared in the crowd, tugging someone away from Commissioner Stephens. Kim's eyes followed Sincebaugh out of curiosity, and now she realized that Alex was suddenly ensnared in what was a quiet but bitter discussion with an unknown man.

"Sure, yes, Detective," she replied to deYampert. "Say, who's that with your partner over there?"

"Oh, that'd be Captain Landry, ma'am."

"I see. Maybe on the way to the hotel, you can tell me what you know about the previous victim found—where?"

"At the Chantilly Pier in Gretna," he replied. "Tell you all about it."

"How's your partner going to get back?"

"Don't worry about Alex. Landry and him have some differences to iron out."

"Me, you mean?"

"Hey, it's nothing personal with Sincy . . . Alex, ma'am. Just that he doesn't believe in changing horses midstream, if you get my drift."

"And what about you, Ben? You consider me a risk?"

"Me? Well, ma'am, I told Alex that seems to me that we're not riding a horse but a two-humped camel at the moment, and if switching from a camel to a horse midstream has any merit, then by God . . . well, I'm willing to give it a try."

She laughed lightly at this. Ben she liked instantly. "Tell me about Gretna, and after that tell me about Victor Surette."

"Surette? You know about Surette?" Ben's voice rose audibly, displaying his amazement on his sleeve.

"I know a little about him, yes."

"Really? You thinking like Alex?"

"I don't know. What's Alex thinking like?"

He hesitated, holding the door for her. "Ahh, maybe best not to discuss it just now with you; it's kinda between partners, you know."

"Sure . . . sure, I can respect that."

"Good . . . good . . ."

He marched around the car, grimacing at himself as he went, and in a moment they were pulling away from the wharf and all its excitement, heading for the bridge that would return them lakeside. To the locals, to simplify life, there were four directions in New Orleans: lakeside, riverside, uptown and downtown.

Once over the Mississippi again, a few blocks into the bustle of the city, she said to Ben deYampert, "Alex thinks that Surette was the first, doesn't he."

"What, huh?"

"Alex believes that Surette was the first Queen of Hearts victim, doesn't he, Ben?"

"Christ, Dr. Desinor, you're good. Got to hand you that. How'd you come to that reckoning when you've been in the city for what, less than two hours?"

— 14 —

And I find more bitter than death the woman,
whose heart is snares and nets, and her hands as bands.

—Ecclesiastes

Jessica Coran marched up to Stephens and said, "I want to see yesterday's victim immediately."

Stephens turned from the reporters who were pushing forward, attempting to get a word from the woman they only knew as Special Agent Jessica Coran of the FBI. He took her aside while his aides dealt with the press. "Wouldn't you care for a break, something to eat maybe, a chance to unpack?"

"Right now, no, just yesterday's body. Can you get me to the morgue without a lot of hubbub and press on my heels, Commissioner?"

"Sure, sure . . . we can arrange that easily enough. You've got to transport the evidence of this crime scene anyway, right?"

She nodded, agreeing to the protocol that said she must at all times be under guard so long as she was transporting medico-legal evidence.

"I must say I was a bit disappointed in our psychic friend this morning," he confided in what seemed an unnecessarily conspiratorial tone.

"Yes, well . . . no one bats a thousand, as they say, and being upstaged by the eel . . . well, it effectively shut down the show, didn't it? What is it actors say about working with animals?" Jessica immediately regretted the theatrical comparisons, knowing that Kim didn't deserve this and wondering why she felt so compelled to view the psychic detective as her competition.

Stephens now led her to a police car, ordering the uniformed officers there to see that she and her evidence arrived safely and efficiently at the precinct, where every item would become part of a manifest of murder. The integrity of the evidence depended upon a scrupulous cataloging of each article and substance she'd collected at the scene, all of it then placed under lock and key to maintain the integrity of the data.

This was quickly done after a ride across the city, and from the evidence room, it was a short walk to the morgue via a tunnel that ended at the lower depths of the Tulane University Hospital extension, a highly regarded state-of-the-art teaching facility.

Inside an hour and a half, she was standing over a stainless-steel, revolving slab on which yesterday's nameless victim lay cold and earthen to the touch, the flesh and features turned to a claylike caricature of what they had once been. Into the room stepped Dr. Franklin Wardlaw, and for a moment the large man with his piercing, steel-gray eyes simply stared over his mask at Jessica as if she were lost.

"The autopsy was only begun yesterday when I was interrupted by your superior Meade, P.C. Stephens and a political hack by the name of Fouintenac," Dr. Wardlaw began, his voice like a biting metal file in her ear. She'd ostensibly replaced the man in his own hospital.

She didn't know quite what to say, but she could empathize with the scene he described. "Removed while in the middle of an autopsy? That's unconscionable, really."

"Fouintenac—whom I've never seen before—did as nice a job on me as this poor slob got." He indicated the decapitated body lying before them. "I was curious about the decapitation, you know, since it was such a departure from the other victims and—"

She agreed instantly. "My thought too, absolutely."

"So here I was, staring down at the wounds, when P.C. Stephens had me bodily removed. My lawyers are fighting that action now, and have gotten a cease-and-desist order against the city and Commissioner Stephens until we go to court. The injunction holds for the time being, Dr. Coran, and so we are stuck with one another, I'm afraid . . . at least for now."

She didn't miss a beat, replying, "In the meantime, then, I will assist you as best I can, Dr. Wardlaw."

This only made him stare even harder at her, as if he suspected her of some false pretense—and to a degree, he was correct. It was a standard line meant to place the local M.E., pathologist or crime lab technician at ease. Still, she felt some compassion for the older medical professional who had slipped from grace. So she continued, saying, "And I can only hope you will accept my presence here in the spirit in which I've traveled here, to offer my full cooperation and that of the FBI."

"You have no idea the embarrassment, the shame they've caused me. Well, I'm not taking it lying down, and Stephens will be sorry for the day he sided against me."

"I was M.E. in Washington, D.C., some years before I became an agent, Dr. Wardlaw. I know about the ugly political aspects of the M.E.'s office."

"You were on staff at what hospital?"

"Washington Memorial."

"As a junior pathologist?"

"No, no . . . I was their M.E., the designated city coroner for D.C."

"Really? I must say that's impressive for one who looks so young."

"I started young, and believe me, all my life I've witnessed how narrow and stupid the bureaucrats can be." She quickly recalled for Wardlaw's benefit a time when even her father was "let go" by a city as its M.E. In this respect, New Orleans was far behind the times; no municipal employee, including the mayor of the city, ought to have the right to summarily fire the city medical examiner. It smacked crisply of conflict of interest. An M.E. should answer to only one god—scientific truth. Knowing little of Wardlaw other than what she'd read in his reports, Jessica withheld any personal judgments about the doctor. However, it was true that his paperwork, at least on the Hearts case involving Victor Surette, was lacking.

Her attitude seemed to have surprised Wardlaw, who was prepared with an angry, hell-raising speech but had not prepared a conciliatory word. He hemmed and hawed a moment before Jessica added, "Dr. Wardlaw, I'm glad to see that you've chosen to fight. There're too few of us M.E.'s in the country willing to fight for our basic rights as is."

"Your concern, Doctor, is deeply touching." His bitterness had dissolved, any earlier sarcasm now dispelled by her charms. Now only his annoying smoker's cough and drinker's breath filled the room.

"It was never my intent to have you removed, sir, I promise you that."

"Very well, then. Shall we go to work before that snake doctor they hired comes poking around?"

She smiled behind her own mask at his theatrical allusion to Kim Desinor. "My sentiments exactly." In fact, she'd rushed here to get to the body before Kim had a chance to do her psychometric reading.

"Science can't possibly outmaneuver the ramblings of a psychic, and certainly we can't hope to outpace the witch," continued an irate Wardlaw. "Science and truth take too much time for the press, the public and the powerful concerned with holding office."

"I don't know her well enough to call her a witch, Dr. Wardlaw," replied Jessica. "However, it was my intention to get as far and as fast as possible here before she arrived, yes."

"Then we agree on something."

"I hope that we can agree on many somethings here today."

"Hmmmm . . ." He contemplated this, then reached out and snatched the dull white sheet from the cadaver with one even thrust, the sheet spiraling up and away like a ghost. "Then examine the neck wounds and tell me precisely how this fellow lost his head."

She smiled at the challenge. Wardlaw was tall with hard-edged lines, an Abe Lincoln cast in granite, sorrow molded to him like some stone shroud. He was weary of seeing the kinds of atrocities that big city crime had routinely to show him, and she could well believe that the recent flurry of unholy terror which came to him in the form of cut-up young men whose hearts had been removed for God knows what unnatural cause or ritual might easily have thrown the man into a tailspin of self-destruction.

His surgeon's hands were as large as a pair of cast-iron skillets, thick blunted fingers, dark, gray, sensitive and cold as the casket itself, she thought. She guessed from his features, particularly the flat, flaring nose and natty hair, that he was certainly as much African-American as he was white, perhaps some Creole or Cajun blood there.

He pointed with his scalpel to a camera on the ceiling which had been activated with the push of a button. "We're on, Dr. Coran. Want to smile for Big Brother?"

She wondered if one of Stephens's lackeys was watching at the other end of the TV monitor somewhere; wondered if the commissioner had Dr. Wardlaw on video film in an inebriated state here in his own operating room—not that he could do much harm to the ''patient patient,'' though he could easily harm the evidentiary proceedings. If so, Wardlaw might well save his lawyers' fees.

Jessica rattled off the requisite information for the camera: time of day, cadaver tag, age, height, weight and sex of the victim, finishing with the victim's name, John Doe for the moment. After only a few minutes of close scrutiny over the neck wounds, she saw that the greatest gash was to the rear of the neck at the base of the skull rather than below the chin, so that if the killer had used a meat cleaver, he'd chopped at the head in execution style, from the rear. But it was by no means a clean cut; in fact it was a ghastly tear that'd made several strange rents, none of them looking like clean incisions. Either the killer had used a very dull blade and had had to repeatedly hack at the victim's neck, or something entirely different had occurred to John Doe.

''This looks like the work of a . . . a machine of some sort,'' she said.

''Go on, Doctor,'' he urged her.

''A . . . like a propeller . . . a small but powerful, three-bladed propeller.''

''And you may recall that the body was found by a group of fishermen, and fishermen do as much drinking as fishing, and they're not always careful about watching where they're headed, and none of them follow the speed rules, striking floating manatees and gators all the time.''

''A boat propeller . . . the propeller severed the head,'' she decided.

''Not completely, but damned near, and the poor handling of the body from water to shore did the rest, but like the fishermen who left out the fact they'd hit the body where it bobbed in the water, no one wanted to own up to the fact that the head later tore loose. Honesty's hard to come by.''

''Well, they might've saved your office a lot of time and effort, and nobody wanted that.'' Her sarcasm, which he seemed very much to appreciate, was met with a hearty laugh on his part. Not likely that he'd had much to laugh about lately.

''Nobody much thinks about the demands of my office,

Doctor. You don't actually know anyone who really, truly gives a damn out there, do you, Dr. Coran?''

"No, I'm no longer gullible about people, not any more than you are, Doctor.'' She breathed in deeply the pungent odors of the room. "No . . . leastways, I shouldn't be.''

"Still, truth dies hard . . .''

"Okay, so the victim wasn't beheaded by the killer.'' Score one up for science over seance, she thought. Although Dr. Desinor hadn't been up to bat on this one yet, both M.E.s were confident that the psychic couldn't possibly know how the head was severed from the body. Jessica silently and secretly felt good about this, that only science could clearly show the way to truth. She recalled an old and wise saying that went: In art, truth is a means to an end; in science, it is the only end.

"Would you care to wager that this fellow is not one of the Queen of Hearts victims?'' asked the grinning, eccentric Wardlaw, whose single gold tooth shone brightly beneath the tensor lamp where they worked.

"That's quite a leap.''

"Don't tell me you didn't have instant doubts yourself when you heard about the head being severed.''

"Yes, but now we know the killer didn't sever the head, had nothing to do with the decapitation, so . . . so why're you still contending that this one died differently than the others? The heart was taken, after all.''

He only grinned at her like a nebbish.

"What else do you have?''

"I wouldn't want to prejudice you, Doctor, but give some consideration for this man's age and the semen found adhering in the throat. Just minute traces, but rather interesting since none of the other transvestite and gay victims were sexually molested.''

"He's older, maybe early to mid-thirties?''

"Precisely.''

"Someone killed him and tried very hard to cover the murder by using the Queen of Hearts cases as a model? A copycat killing? But this killer didn't count on the beheading, and only guessed at the semen since he knew all the victims were gay.''

"In my estimation, all true, yes.''

"Interesting premise.''

"More than a premise.''

"Really?"

"The seminal fluid found in the mouth has been matched."

"Matched? Matched to whom?"

"To the John Doe here."

"You're telling me that the semen in his mouth was his own?"

"That's right. Now you must ask yourself who was close enough to this poor SOB to have that kind of access and control of the man's own semen?"

"Someone damned close to him, I'd imagine."

"You play this game well, Doctor."

"Now if we only knew who he was. Fingerprints turn up anything?"

"Not so far, but I think they will."

"Really, how can you be so sure?"

Wardlaw pointed out a cheap, half-botched tattoo on the man's right biceps with the word "Beau" spelled out across a heart. "A prison tattoo perhaps?" she asked.

"Almost appropriate, heh?" asked Wardlaw.

"Just be careful, Dr. Wardlaw. If they're out to get you, just remember that an error is more dangerous the more truth it contains."

"An ancient proverb?"

"Call it the M.E.'s creed nowadays."

Settled into the bustling downtown hotel room with its balustrade balcony overlooking beautiful Lake Ponchartrain, where a late afternoon sun painted broad-stroked shadows over the water, Kim Desinor had managed to shake the jet lag and the unsettled stomach which the eel had left her with. A pleasant shower and a leisurely nap had helped restore her scattered energies, and thankfully yet strangely, no one had interrupted her here with a phone call.

The very authorities who'd gotten her here weren't particularly anxious to spend time with her; at first she'd thought perhaps she was being overly sensitive, paranoid, but now she knew better. Stephens and Meade had purposely avoided her, casting their lot with the known commodity, Dr. Jessica Coran. Whether they wished to be or not, apparently she and Jessica were in some sort of competition here.

She changed and called for an escort to the morgue. She

wanted more time and privacy with the murdered man she had seen at the wharf.

When the unmarked police car carrying her across town arrived at the morgue, she learned that Dr. Coran and Dr. Wardlaw were just finishing up an autopsy on the victim of the day before. She heard scuttlebutt that this particular victim of the Queen of Hearts killer might not be another Hearts case at all, but rather a coverup, what they called a copycat killing, in which the murderer masked his moves by duplicating those of a previous murderer.

She asked around and located the autopsy room where the two doctors were just emerging. Not wishing to see or confront anyone at the moment, wishing to remain in a calm and undisturbed state, Kim ducked into an adjacent, empty room where cold-storage freezers lined the wall. Hearing the doctors pass by, she bided her time, and then surreptitiously entered the autopsy room from which they'd emerged.

A tag hung limp from the dead man's toe, the only visible portion of the body below the Dacron-sheet shroud. She moved closer, knowing that at any moment a lab assistant might walk in to claim the body for one of the freezers in the next room.

It was cold in here, a constant seventy-two, the hum of the A.C. and the outtake fans, which kept a steady, healthy flow of air uniformly and continually moving through, doing nothing to dispel the odors of death which permeated the walls. She lifted out the curling, black rosary beads which seemed to have a life of their own, wishing to slither from her grasp, the shining crystal cross blinking at her. She clutched the beads tightly to her chest in a firm ball made of her fist. With her other hand, she reached out and lightly placed her fingertips atop the dead man's chest, feeling the prickly sutures beneath the sheet, placed there by Jessica Coran. Even the light force she next placed against the chest caused it to sag a little. The touch was like that of a worn beanbag.

Wait a moment, she silently told herself, an ugly image of a headless man flashing before her mental eyes. "This isn't today's victim, but yesterday's."

She pulled back the sheet far enough to reveal the truth of her belief. She had gotten the distinct impression from all she'd read and heard about yesterday's beheaded victim that he was somehow different, but aside from the severed head, she didn't know what about him was so unusual until now.

Sincebaugh and Coran had both discovered differences, following along varied paths. She sensed the truth of this. She concentrated, moving toward trance state, asking the dead man to reveal to her these differences.

It became a mantra in her mind: What's different . . . what's different . . . what's different . . .

She knew that Alex and perhaps deYampert had seen that this one was dissimilar to the others, especially since the victim's head had been severed, but there were other peculiarities as well. Her brief and curtailed reading over the other dead man on the wharf had conjured up images of furious rage and sexual repression, lust killing and mutilation, but here with her hands firmly against this John Doe, she was getting a quiet despondency, a despair and a disbelief that rose off the corpse like the saddest of whale songs.

Despite the obvious similarities, this man's means of death was not at all the same as the death faced by the victims of the Hearts killer. This fellow had died peacefully, calmly, not knowing his fate, his wounds and mutilations coming long after death had set in, no doubt as the pathologists' combined reports would be reflecting. This man had not seen the eyes of his killer or the knife as it was wielded. He'd been astonished at his killer, amazed, overwhelmed in a deep, psychic sense, completely awed far more than he was frightened, and he'd died in disbelief at the actions of his killer. While there'd been no suffering like the brutalization played out over the other victims, his death being a relatively easy one for he'd been poisoned by an overdose of barbituates, the victim remained confused and painfully inconsolable at what she had done to him. His killer was a woman, a woman he'd loved. Something Coran's thorough autopsy could hardly show. Kim wondered who here would believe her.

She peeled the sheet back further, indulging her eyes at the line of neat sutures that had put head and torso back together again, the stitches creating a patchwork mosaic against the alabaster skin. *All the king's horses and all the king's men,* she thought, *couldn't put Humpty-Dumpty back together again.* She didn't know why, but she had the sensation that he was kiddingly referred to by his friends as an egghead or thin-shelled.

She studied the body further, examining it with eyes and fingers until she was stopped by the tattoo on the biceps.

She only felt a cold, hard-eyed creature staring back from afar, and beyond these ice green eyes indistinct and distant images of a rough-hewn log cabin and a woman who was several hundred miles away. Who was the woman, where was the cabin? It wasn't in or around New Orleans, possibly not even in the state. She was sure of only one thing, and to set Alex Sincebaugh on his ass, maybe she ought to confide it to him now.

She heard someone behind her start and gasp, taken by surprise at her being in the room. The young assistant looked too frail and juvenile—her hair done up in a ponytail—to be here doing this kind of work. But the young woman found her nerve and demanded, "Just whoooo are you? No one's 'sposed to be in here without proper authorization." She came directly into the room now and thrust the sheet back over the cadaver, asking again, "Who are you?"

The spell was broken but not before Kim knew who the killer was and what her relationship to the dead man had been. She wondered if sharing her newfound knowledge with Alex Sincebaugh might not help their already teetering relationship. Listen here, Lieutenant, she wanted to shout, yesterday's victim, the headless one . . . "Yeah, what about it?" he'd gruffly reply.

"You can't be here!" The M.E.'s technician was pulling her away from the body now. "Do you know the deceased?" she asked. "We've been unable to identify him. You'd better talk with Dr. Wardlaw."

"I am Dr. Kim Desinor. I was told that I could do a psychometric reading over the body of the Hearts victim. I was given clearance to do so."

"Nobody told us down here a thing about it, Dr. . . . ahhh—"

"Desinor, Dr. Kim Desinor. I'm going to be on the case for a while, and I'd like your—and everyone's—help and cooperation, Miss . . . ahhh—"

"Penwarren, ma'am, Amy. Still, I think you should come away with me to Dr. Wardlaw's office."

"That'll be just fine, Amy. I think I've got what I've come for."

•   •   •

She found Jessica Coran in Wardlaw's labyrinthian laboratory located just off his office, the two of them finishing up reports, prepping tissue and blood samples, discussing the case like old friends, obviously having formed some common bond, M.E. to M.E. she gathered.

"The Hearts killer didn't do yesterday's victim," she announced to them. "Someone answering to the name of Beau, a woman, killed him, very likely someone who placed a missing person's report on him. I'm calling Sincebaugh to ask him to follow that lead."

The two medical doctors stared at her, wondering. The technician spoke behind Kim, saying, "I found Dr. Desinor in with yesterday's John Doe when I went in for the body. She was . . . examining it."

Jessica's look of astonishment dimmed quickly. "Ahhh, you saw the tattoo, then." Jessica paused long enough to introduce Wardlaw and Kim to one another.

"I did more than read the man's tattoos, believe me," Kim said now. "You'll find that he was poisoned by his live-in lover or wife. She did the rest of the damage after death, all meant to cover her tracks."

Wardlaw's jaw went slack and Jessica's awe crept back across her face. Wardlaw said, "There's no way you can know either fact."

"There is one way. The dead man told me so. Can I use your phone, Dr. Wardlaw?"

It was late afternoon now, and Kim was told that Alex Sincebaugh had gone off duty and wasn't likely to return. So she asked for his captain.

Later, in his office, Landry was polite, listening to what she had to say, and he promised to follow up on her information, saying that he'd get Missing Persons on it immediately.

"I think you'll find some surprising results," she promised.

"You're convinced then that the man pulled from the river at Gretna yesterday has no bearing on the Hearts case other than in gross and superficial similarities?"

"Absolutely and well put, Captain."

"Interesting . . ."

She heard more in this single word than he'd wished to convey, she was sure. "You've theorized as much already?" she asked now.

"Not me . . . Alex Sincebaugh."

"Really? He does sound like a remarkably intuitive detective, Captain."

"That he is . . . that he is . . ."

"I'm sure the age difference and the decapitation must have instantly alerted him."

"Yes, but what alerted you, Doctor?"

"Of course, I saw the same when I looked in on the body this afternoon."

"We'd already put out a call to Missing Persons, knowing of the tattoo and other distinguishing marks," he told her, which explained why he'd been so calm about her revelations.

"Yes, understandable," she replied, "but did you also know that the man was poisoned?"

"Poisoned?"

"And that the mutilation occurred after death?"

Landry asked, "Does Coran have any scientific proof to back you on this call?"

"She will, in time."

"She'd told me that it was highly unlikely that the Queen of Hearts killer would suddenly escalate to beheadings and then not repeat the performance on his next victim. Said the usual escalation signs would be repeated, and then when we got this morning's cadaver, well, neither she nor anyone else could tell me which man was killed first, the Gretna body or the Toulouse Wharf body."

Kim stood up and paced Landry's office, a place filled with bric-a-brac—supplied almost entirely by his wife, he'd said. She took in a deep breath before plunging ahead. "In time, Dr. Coran and Dr. Wardlaw will discover that yesterday's victim was killed by some poison, most likely downers, barbituates ingested with a meal."

Landry could only scratch the back of his head and wonder at the chutzpah shown by this handsome woman before him. She had just climbed out on one hell of a shaky limb, unless she had somehow gotten information out of Wardlaw or one of his assistants as to how they were leaning in the lab. He made a mental note to check with Coran and Wardlaw the moment he was finished with Dr. Desinor. Most likely the so-called psychic had simply picked up some clues from Jessica Coran and had merely extrapolated from something she might have been guessing at or mulling over.

"We've been running this through our Missing Persons Department since discovery yesterday, but nothing's come of it. As I said, I'll give it a push."

"Widen your sweep. Include surrounding states—say, Texas. Something about Texas clicked in earlier, something about a lone star . . . steers . . . a Texas penal colony . . ."

"All right, will do, Dr. Desinor. Anything else you think I should know about?"

She could hear the skepticism in his voice even as he choked it back.

"Obviously, you weren't instrumental in getting me on board here, Captain," she said.

He waved that off, saying, "Now hold on. I've extended you every courtesy."

"Crazily enough, you've extended me far more courtesy than those who are paying my fee."

He raised an eyebrow at this, but only repeated himself, asking, "Is there anything else you'd like to add to your . . . ahhhh . . . report, Doctor?"

"No, that's it, except when your men check, have them look for a Beau, someone answering to that name."

"Gotcha, Doctor."

"Could be a nickname, and as I said, I believe he was poisoned by a wife or live-in lover. Could be her nickname."

He waved her out the door, nodding in an officious manner. She stepped out into the squad room, and instantly knew which vacant desk belonged to Alex Sincebaugh. It was far neater than any other in the room. When she raised her eyes, she found herself staring up at Jessica Coran, who was leaning against an entryway doorjamb, looking exhausted but pleasantly pleased with herself. She must enjoy her work thoroughly, Kim thought.

"So, do you think we're all on the same wavelength, Dr. Faith?" asked Jessica.

"Yes, matter of fact we all are, including our reluctant Lieutenant Sincebaugh."

"Really?"

"Want to get dinner and talk about it?" Kim offered. "I'm buying."

"Frankly, I need to get away from it . . . altogether for a while. Besides, I have a date."

"The pilot?"

"Yeah . . . so, maybe a rain check?"

"Jessica." Kim stopped her colleague as she was about to go.

Jessica turned and looked demurely back at her. "Yes?"

"We're not in any sort of . . . competition here, are we?"

"Why, no, of course not. We're on the same side, right?"

"I had hoped so, but I haven't felt so."

"If I've seemed . . . distant . . . well, it's for the benefit of the charade actually, to keep your association with the Bureau our little secret, remember."

She's lying . . . covering up her true feelings, Kim instantly realized.

Jessica continued, running a nervous hand through her hair. "What would it look like to the others if you and I were . . . chummy? Well, I've still got to freshen up, meet Ed by eight."

Kim nodded and breathed deeply. "Yes, you're right, of course. But listen, any time you want, I'd be happy to handle those items you took from Matisak's cell, as a favor to you, Jess."

"Maybe tomorrow. Good night, Kim."

"Night, Jess." Now she's so reluctant, Kim thought, when before, on the plane, she was so anxious.

It appeared that Wardlaw had beaten them both out the door, for he was nowhere to be found either, and Kim felt terribly hollow and unconditionally alone.

15

Egyptian Proverb:
The worst things:
To be in bed and sleep not,
To want for one who comes not,
To try to please and please not.

—From F. Scott Fitzgerald's Notebooks

Alex Sincebaugh felt the summer breeze cascading through his hair as his car sailed over great Lake Ponchartrain's shallow, brackish basin, the hum of the car in sync with Hank Williams's most melodic ballad, "I'm So Lonesome, I Could Cry," the D.J. asking for callers to ring him up with the bluest blues they'd ever felt, something to top the line about the whippoorwill that "sounds too blue to fly." Alex switched off the radio for the golden silence of the waters here, waters which served the city in countless ways. In winter, they warmed the frigid air coming in from the north before it chanced to the city's perimeter; in summer, the lake served as an ideal playground for boaters, fishermen and picnickers, although most of her waters were now too polluted to allow swimming, particularly along the southern rim by New Orleans. The northern area, however, remained a prime source for hefty trout, crab and shrimp any time of year. Named for Louis XIV's naval minister, the huge lake connected via narrow straits to the Gulf of Mexico, and little wonder it was a favorite dumping ground for mafia hits.

To clear his mind, Alex liked to drive, so he'd taken off early from his apartment and meandered about the city streets, gathering his thoughts, honest to himself about not wishing to be alone in his place. He'd become fearful of sleep, and to banish it and the creeping boredom, he'd even driven the twenty-four miles from the Jefferson Parish shoreline to Mandeville. The roadbed, perched just a few yards above the waters of Lake Ponchartrain, was blatantly advertised as the

166

world's longest bridge, and at midpoint Sincebaugh could see neither shore from the famous causeway. However, the near-blinding, brilliant sunset was plain Southern beauty, like a fire in the sky, the light dancing arcade-fashion along the giant catfish scales created by low-lying, slow-moving vapor clouds which mirrored the bay waters. It was nearing eight P.M., and he was too exhausted and frustrated to sit around at his place.

Lake Ponchartrain, forming New Orleans's northern boundary, was in fact more of a bay than a lake; still, nobody—especially the tourists—had to know that, he told himself as he fished out his two dollars for the toll, reentering the city at the now-famous Lakefront-Bayou St. John district and City Park, where jazz and food spiced up life.

From there, Alex drove to a nearby coffee shop where he'd found the lights dim enough to go easy on his eyes but bright enough to read the *Evening Star Gazette* and the *Times-Picayune*. He didn't feel like going back to his place, at least not directly, and he knew that sleep would evade him, and he feared the recurrent dream he had been having since the death of the first Hearts victim, young Victor Surette. He also knew that he looked like hell, that he was not working on all four burners, and that soon his C.O. would call him in for a complete dressing down, now more than ever since he'd made a public spectacle of himself, infuriating Landry in the process at the Toulouse Street Wharf before the press moments after Dr. Desinor had left the scene.

They'd argued openly and loudly about the psychic, and Lew Meade's high-handed FBI forensics guru, Coran, as well.

Alex felt alone and confused and at odds with everyone. At the same time that he was glad to learn of Frank Wardlaw's dismissal, he found something about the self-assured Coran which equally rubbed him the wrong way. It wasn't anything he could put his finger on, just her officious manner, the way she conducted herself, maybe the way she took control and that emotionless exterior. Where had she put her feelings? Were they something she took out from that black bag of hers only when the occasion called for it?

Maybe he was just being foolish, childish and petty even; maybe none of it mattered; maybe Coran and maybe even the psychic detective could do a better job than he and deYampert. Fuck it all.

It wasn't that he hated women by any means, but maybe he did harbor a little fear of women who came on so bloody strong as Coran—and perhaps Kim Desinor as well. The two women had much in common, he surmised, and each was as talented or as crafty as the other—cunning folk, they'd have been called in the days of the witch trials. And each was al-luringly attractive, each as beautiful in her way as the other.

Damn. He cursed the thought of feeling in the slightest at-tracted to Kim Desinor, though he knew he was. He'd felt something between them, some intangible and fairylike spark of intense desire that rose so quickly it was extinguished in its own rush to escape the moment he'd taken her in his arms there on the wharf. She too had to have felt it, despite her words and her coolness.

Yes, he was physically drawn to her, but at the same time, for some goddamned unaccountable, unexplainable reason, this Dr. Desinor's very presence on the case had him recalling in glaring and vivid detail the Vietcong doctors in that hell-hole of a concentration camp where torture and human exper-imentation were routine, daily occurrences. Why such horrors should return now so vividly, he did not know, but he felt that she was the catalyst, the one who let loose the horrors. He didn't know why she had this effect on him, and no doubt it was totally unintentional on her part, but she did, and it was unpleasant, and yet there was something so erotically appeal-ing, seductive and charming about her that he wanted to pursue her, no matter the consequences. He wanted to learn more about her, and this strange paradox of feelings had had hold of him from the moment he saw her step off that Lear jet today.

Alex had managed to endure the gross indignities and suf-fering placed on him in Vietnam largely through the process of mind over matter. After a while, he was no longer present, freed from the pain and humiliation by mere will and a kind of mind control his captors had no notion of or cure for. It infuriated them, challenged them, took them to new heights of cruelty, but he was no fun for them any longer since he felt not a thing.

He looked down at his scarred hands where the nails had grown back, covering the now-tough tissue beneath. He seldom thought of those times nowadays, because the moment one such image came even remotely close to his consciousness, it was extinguished by a fail-safe mechanism which he didn't fully understand but did truly bless.

The tortures were beyond cruel and sadistic; his scars attested to that. His ex-girlfriend, Allie, was one of the few women he'd allowed close since Vietnam, and even then she'd only seen him in the dark. He was careful to be up and dressed before dawn whenever she stayed over, except for that last time when she'd gotten him drunk and talking and sleeping in the next day. She must have seen the scars, understanding for the first time his total sensitivity to her touch, for while she hadn't said a word about the ugly tattooed back, they'd never again slept together. And soon she'd disappeared altogether. Since then, he'd been unable to feel comfortable around any woman, until that moment when the eel had so frightened Kim Desinor and he'd instinctively taken her into his arms to comfort her.

He'd pulled over to the coffee shop, gathered his newspapers up, and stepped inside. The old friend behind the counter had his usual coffee waiting as he liked it the moment he walked through the bell-clanging door, having seen him park on the street out front. As Alex now read his newspaper and sipped the rich Peruvian black coffee, he grew increasingly depressed over the stories now beginning to appear in the press with lurid headlines about the "Thief of Hearts Circus" being conducted by the city, and the cops were the clowns. Speculation, theory and conjecture of every stripe filled the pages of the *Times-Picayune* alongside shots of Dr. Jessica Coran, whose purpose on the case was fully outlined. In a sidebar piece, there was a smaller photo of Kim Desinor and a story on the psychic "connection" citing the *fact* she was called in to help the bungling cops.

Sincebaugh scanned what he could stomach of the stories, gathering in what little information was released to the press about Desinor, his curiosity aroused. He went on to read the press versions of the killer's supposed motive and modus operandi, and most of what the press carried was nonsense verg-

ing on supposition about the heart-pounding case, little of it
founded in fact. Still, Sincebaugh detected one truth: There
were enough half-truths and twisted logic among the stories
to know that the rumor mill was operating at peak efficiency,
despite a gag order in the Department. Leaks were being fed
to the press, and he placed blame for the unplugged hole at
Frank Wardlaw's doorstep, for the few details that were true
were all technical in nature, items that could only be gotten
from the coroner's reports, items only he and deYampert and
a handful of other cops working these cases knew about, all
of whom were sworn to secrecy.

His blood boiled when he found details about the type of
weapon used in the murders embedded in one story, details
that were accurate: a cleaver-styled cutter in one murder, a
specialized butcher's knife in another, a possible rib-cutter?

Such information was crucial to the case and should remain
confidential; now that it was public knowledge, every butcher
in the city was a target for his neighbor's fears, suppositions
and allegations, and every nut case with a Swiss Army knife
would want now to confess. They'd be showing up in droves
tonight and tomorrow at every precinct sergeant's desk with
cleavers in hand, stories well rehearsed about precisely how
they did it, all chewing up valuable investigative hours.

True, every precinct in the city had at least two men working the case, separately and without task-force unity, and any
one of these men might have spilled information to a shrewd
reporter, but Sincebaugh wondered about Dr. Frank Wardlaw
in this respect since he'd been under such fire from both above
and below, and especially since the most vital information
leaks had coincided with Wardlaw's being dismissed. The man
certainly had more friends in the Fourth Estate than in the
NOPD.

Sincebaugh felt like putting his hand through a window, felt
like hitting or arresting someone, but he instead sat granitelike
and lowered the headlines just as the shop bell rang and two
young punks dressed in natty, moth-eaten army fatigues
stepped in. The fatigues were army-surplus issue.

Sincebaugh had never liked the wholesale wear of army
fatigues, not since it had become the in thing; he believed a
man should earn the right to wear them. Aside from this dis-

gruntlement, he sensed trouble welling up from within the two
punks the moment he saw their eyes.

One's eyes roamed about the place while the other's eyes
fixed on Tully, the old man behind the counter, who'd started
his shop here in 1962 after moving from New Jersey. He often
told Alex he missed his family "but not a damn thing else
there."

Sincebaugh knew he'd have to time everything to the second to take out the two punks without anyone being hurt. He
pretended to laugh at one of the comics and carried the paper
over to Tully, saying, "Here, old man, you gotta read this.
This Calvin and Hobbes kills me. Read this."

"No time for papers," Tully dourly replied. "I got customers, Alex."

"Take a look. Will it kill you to take a fuckin' look?"

"Hey, Alex, easy, friend . . ." Tully eyed him suspiciously
and ambled over. The old man had started to grab the paper
when Sincebaugh brought it crosswise into the eyes of the
closest kid. The other one, closer to the door, turned and ran
without hesitation. Alex decked the first punk, still fighting
with the newspaper, before he could bring his gun to bear.

"Call a cop, Tully!" Alex shouted over his shoulder,
snatching free the punk's concealed weapon.

"What? What for? You *are* a cop! 'Sides, what'd they do,
Alex?"

Alex pushed the kid's weapon into Tully's hand. "They
tried to knock over your place! I'm going after the other one!"

Sincebaugh had seen the direction the second young fool
had taken, and he was now in his car, in pursuit, calling it in.
His adrenaline rush was exactly the fix he'd needed. A good
collar might do wonders for his sagging spirits, he thought
now, his eyes scanning the urban jungle for his prey. He saw
an army-green and brown blur dart down an alleyway just as
his car passed. The kid's camouflaging fatigues blended into
the cityscape. But Alex's twenty-twenty vision fixed on him.
It was him. He just knew it.

He called in his location and the fact he was leaving his
vehicle in pursuit of the kid felon. Behind him he heard sirens,
other cops rushing to the scene, but he wanted this one all to

himself. He wanted to bust somebody, anybody, maybe belt the creep around a little while he was at it.

He found himself rushing too fast through the alleyway and out the other side where he could have easily met with an ambush. Instead there was silence all around. He saw nothing, no one, only a deserted courtyard, a high, wooden fence badly in need of repair, still swaying from someone's having recently vaulted over it. There was a padlock on the gate.

He inched forward and pulled himself to the top of the fence, eyes in windows following him now, a light Louisiana downpour, silver and fresh, cascading from nowhere and everywhere at once, drenching him in its warmth and calm, making him feel alive.

He now leapt over and onto the other side of the fence and into the alley. A cat scurried from behind some rubbish and pails.

"Toss the goddamn gun away, kid, and come outta there with your hands showing high! Now, goddamn you!"

No response.

"Do it, damnit, or I'll fire through the cans! So help me, punk!"

No response.

"Does this sonafa-lowlifin'-bitch think I'm playing games with him?" Alex shouted to the sky, his months of frustration bubbling dangerously to the surface. All his training as a police officer told him no, but his finger on the trigger said yes. He aimed at a can, pulled his aim to the bottom, fired and sent up a powerful thunder from his .38 which rocked the trash can, the bullet going harmlessly through the lowest point of the metal trash bin and into the earth below it, no doubt leaving a gaping hole through the bottom. Instantly, in response, a gun came flying out over the trash heap, landing at Alex's feet.

"That better be all you're packing, kid."

He saw the boy's hands, white and pale, come trembling up over the top of the trash. Shaking, the kid stepped out into the open, pleading for mercy.

"What kind of mercy did you two have in mind for Old Tully back there, kid?"

"We . . . we needed the money."

"Shut up and turn around and spread your legs." He hand-cuffed the kid, who looked to be perhaps eighteen or nineteen, younger than the other kid. Then he Mirandized the boy, his anger subsiding.

The boy kept talking the entire time. "I didn't want to do it. It was Will's idea, all his. He's done time."

The familiar phrase was like a red badge of courage to the young street punks of New Orleans. "Sounds like *you're* going to do some time now, kid. Hanging out with the wrong crowd, son." God, he hated sounding like his father. "Come on. You can tell it to the judge."

Only now, coming out of the alley and handing the kid over to a uniformed officer, did Sincebaugh realize that he'd actually not seen either boy's weapon at the time he had struck out with the newspaper, and that neither of them had actually made a truly threatening gesture before he himself had acted on instinct. Alex knew that a smart lawyer could get either or both off, especially since there were no witnesses to the so-called "crime." In point of fact, there had been no crime. Still, Sincebaugh knew that he was the only one who knew this, and that all he needed to do was call it a crime in progress.

Yet there was one witness, Tully. He'd seen the whole thing, and by now the old man had pieced it together clearly enough in his mind that he'd provide the necessary details. And with the younger kid squealing so loudly, no one would be any the wiser. Still, Sincebaugh wondered: How did I know? Was it their movements? Their clothes? Their eyes? A combination of all of it? Or did it just come with years of experience on the force, a second sight or blue sense as some called it? Was it any different from the second sight which Dr. Kim Desinor purported to both have and control, or was there an intrinsic difference?

Again he was reminded of Vietnam and how he had survived capture while better men had succumbed to an eternity there.

Ben deYampert was almost home from Little League practice with his kids when he heard the radio call come over, instantly alert, recognizing his partner's involvement. It was as though Alex had gone out looking for trouble and found it, like he was playing James Arness in *Gunsmoke* or something. Sonof-abitch is just spoiling for trouble with Landry and the brass. It figured with all the anger he'd been bottling up inside and no place to loosen the cork. Something had to give.

Ben rushed his kids home and didn't stop for so much as a biscuit or a kiss from Fiona, shouting that he had to take an emergency call. He heard one of his kids telling his wife it had something to do with Uncle Alex.

Ben hadn't taken time to change out of his sweat-soaked coach's uniform. He worried the entire nine and a half miles through traffic to the scene, his siren blaring atop the family van.

Was Alex flat on his back, a bullet hole in him? Would he be hauled off in an ambulance before Ben could get there? Was he critical? What was going on? Nobody seemed to know.

Alex was a good partner and a fine man, someone Ben had confided in over the years, a man whose opinion he'd sought in all things, from purchasing his first home, to speaking to a divorce lawyer, to his daughter's taste in guys. They'd part-nered together for so long, they'd become what cops called an old married couple. Ben had picked Alex as his partner after Alex's last partner, Keith Tyler, had been killed in a running gun battle, the wound opening up a grapefruit-sized hole in Tyler's head thanks to a single cop-killer bullet used by the backwater creeps that Alex and Tyler had gone after.

Some said that Alex, in those days, had a death wish, and that Tyler's death was the result, that it was somehow on Alex's head, due to his irresponsibility, but Ben didn't believe it, and when he visited Alex in the hospital, he was doubly sure. Alex had taken two hits behind a Kevlar vest, but Alex had also taken out the men who had killed his partner, a pair of wild-eyed drug dealers. Ben greatly admired his partner and while Alex confided very little, Ben often found himself con-fiding a great deal, about his kids, his wife, problems at home, money woes, almost everything.

Now he greatly feared for Sincy. No news was coming over the radio. No one could tell him what was going down, what had happened, nothing.

He raced demonlike to the scene.

"You sonofabitch, Alex! You'd better be okay!"

When his van couldn't get past the congested street filled with police cars, their strobes menacing the night, Ben leapt from the passenger seat and raced the half block remaining, huffing and out of breath before stopping just outside the big plate-glass window of the coffee shop and staring in, seeing that Alex was alive and well and calmly going over the shooting with Internal Affairs detectives inside. Ben took a deep breath and pushed through the door.

"What the hell happened, Alex?"

"Little simple armed robbery attempt's all."

"This camera operating?" asked one of the IAD officers.

"Sure . . . sure," said the old man, Tully. "We got the whole thing on video! I shoulda thunk of it myself. Now youse guys'll hafta see we're tellin' it just the way it happened. Right, Alex? Wonder if that *I-Witness Video* or maybe *The Crusaders* program would be interested in this?"

Alex realized only too late that he'd painted himself into a corner.

"Who knows, Tully." Alex's reply came out flat and heartless, his fear of the tape rising in his constricted throat. He could only hope that the angle was with him, shielding his and the kid's hands.

The IAD cop, a thin and sallow man with no upper lip named Hanson, asked Tully for a ladder. Ben sensed the sudden uneasiness in his partner.

"You guys got what you want?" Ben barked at the IAD men.

The other IAD man grumbled that they did, for now.

"Then I'm going to buy the lieutenant here a drink. So, if you don't mind?"

The IAD guy on the ladder fumbled about with the camera's mechanism near the ceiling. Finally, the machine released the tape, freeing the two IAD cops to leave. Hanson rushed out ahead of his partner, an even younger guy who gave Alex and Ben a sophomoric grin and a big thumbs-up sign, saying, "Looks like a good collar, Detective; fairly simple, cut and dried. We'll just file our reports. Say, aren't you the two guys who're on the trail of the Heart-Taker? Some disgusting creep, huh? Boy, what I'd pay to be in your shoes; real police work.

This crap with IAD is driving my balls numb.''

Alex and Ben exchanged a knowing look. Most IAD guys were so young and inexperienced because no cop wanted such duty, and so the NOPD had taken to putting its best and brightest and most recently finished Academy types directly into Internal Affairs. That way no one knew them and they had no conflicts of interest, or so the thinking went. Of course, the Department was losing in the long run.

Big Ben nodded, smiled at the clean-shaven kid and said, ''Maybe some day, kid. What's your name?''

''Hirschenfeldt, sir.''

''We'll keep you in mind when something comes open, Hirsch-felt, how's that?''

Alex turned into the booth where most of his newspapers still lay, trying to hide the uncontrollable laughter erupting volcanolike at Ben's nasty little tease.

The IAD guy was all wide-eyed and smiling now, stumbling for the door like a lovesick suitor who'd just asked his secret love to go to the dance with him and been surprised with an acceptance.

''Terrific . . . wow,'' he sputtered, ''great . . . really . . .'' He backed from the coffee shop, the bell announcing his departure.

Ben immediately turned to Alex. ''Now, you want to tell your fat, old wife what the fuck happened here, Sincy?''

⟞ 16 ⟝

> . . . after they have . . . lost all this fear, they are
> so artless and so free with all they possess. . . .
> Of anything they have, if you ask them for it,
> they never say no; rather they invite the person
> to share it, and show as much love as if they were
> giving their hearts.
>
> —Columbus

Ben deYampert telephoned his wife Fiona, letting her know that all was well and that he and Alex were going to have a few beers and he'd be straight home from there. Ben insisted on taking Alex to a nearby tavern, a place called Maxine's, where the music was country and western, the clientele generally down on their luck and toasting to better days. Alex recognized the neighborhood—fairly seedy, the streets lined with shops of every size and stripe, signs littering the doorways and windows as far as the eye could see, all vying for attention and gaining none, save maybe the Root Mon's store, Root Heaven. Alex pointed it out to Ben as they were entering Maxine's, and together they laughed at the memory associated with Root Heaven.

Once inside and sipping dark Guinness beer, Alex asked Big, "You remember the call we got on that place?"

Ben laughed heartily. " 'I know where the hearts are bein' kept. And I know what they're doin' with 'em!' Slow down, lady, I told her. She almost busted a gut having to give me her name. Never did get an honest answer to that one."

" 'Too 'fraid of the whoo-doo mon. Him make yo' life hell or him make yo' life heaven.' "

"Took those damned shriveled, dried-up old hearts all the way downtown for Frank Wardlaw's inspection."

"Frank'll never let us forget that."

Ben, eyes watering with laugh tears, gulped his beer.

"Turned out to be goddamned big buffalo hearts! Where you reckon the Root Mon got buffalo hearts, Alex?"

"Don't ask me."

"Oughta be a law . . ."

"Probably is . . . somewhere . . ."

Alex thought back to the day they'd stepped into the Root Mon's world, to confront a lanky, huge-handed black man with a Jamaican accent and polished white teeth, two of them gold, each with an initial on it: R and M for Root Mon. Inside his shop hung every imaginable item from pegs and ceiling, half on and off shelves filled with vials, boxes, jars and baskets.

"What yooooou gentlemens need for? Whatever it is, you come to de right mon."

"Hearts," Alex had said.

"I got plenty of dem, mon, but what kind you need?"

"What kind you got?"

"Come on back to de back, Officers, and we see what we can find, mon." He looked nervously around as if expecting someone to come rushing in. At that moment, someone did. It was a well-dressed TV newscaster whom Alex had seen many times before both on the tube and at crime scenes. She was generally a pain in the ass.

"How the hell did you people find out about this call?" asked Ben, glaring at Edna Lowery of *It Takes 2 News*.

"It's our business to find out," she curtly replied as her camera team began to set up in the shop, one with a large but portable camcorder panning the amazing array of items found in the collection of herbs, spices, cures, medicinal potions and magic lotions.

Alex knew at once that the entire call was a publicity ploy for the Root Mon's store. "You better have some recently hocked, hot hearts," he warned the tall, smiling proprietor of the shop, who flicked on his CD player, rushed the camera and began a spiel like nothing Alex had ever heard before. He broke into a reggae singsong of poetry and commerce, further underscoring the bogus nature of the complaint that the store dealt in human hearts. The owner's "rap" went on and on, and he did a little dance for the cameras as he spoke of his Root Heaven, saying:

''You carryin' a curse? Got urgent pain? / Can't make de water? / Jus' you come down to Root Heaven, / the famous Root Mon's store!''

''That's enough of that,'' Alex began in his most serious detective's tone.

But Big put up a hand and said, ''No, Alex, I want to hear this.''

The Root Mon smiled wide and continued, playing to the cameras. ''Here's a broth, / here's a stew. / You want both, mon, / for what you gotta do. / You got needs? / Plannin' big sac-ro-fice? / We got seeds / and chickens on ice. / We got bugs, scrubs, herbs, / all kinna spice. / Need dem magic words? / Hav' a dose-a-crawlin' lice. / Eat a canna magic rice, / a pinch of snuff for dat ol' wart, / jus' 'nough for de heart.''

He was on a roll now, unstoppable.

''Toad sweat'll get you up'n fit / with no shivers, shingles or sneeze. / Get whatever you please / wid *heavenly* ease.''

As he droned on, Alex stepped through the curtained rear and began digging amid an amazing assortment of ancient and filthy artifacts stacked on shelves and boxes here too. From the other side of the curtain he could hear deYampert's amused laughter. Meanwhile, the camera panned from the proprietor to a huge wall sign which was a poetic listing of all the services and items provided his customers. Later that night, when Alex would see himself on the late newscast, they also flashed the big sign, which read:

ROOT HEAVEN CREDO

We got fat slugs
and tobacco plugs.
Got fuzzy cut worms
for cuts, scrapes 'n burns.
For fever it's de poltice
and de crucifix Christ.
Got many things for stings:
herbs, toots, roots 'n strings.

Go-head, make your day

wid dat fat bottle
of turtle-nip spray.
Toss the snake rattle
over your left shoulder
onto a big boulder
beside a flowing river
at the midnight hour.

Get whatever you need.
No talk, guilt or greed.
Join de Root Club!
Special on de belly rub,
Special on de herb'n'potion.
Jus' whisper who gets
dis notion, dat lotion,
hex on/off jus's you wish.

Got stalks and stones
minerals and bones,
cat tails in pails
wid good'n'plenty snails.
Got a clip of royal bangs,
eyelashes from Queens,
nose hair from de King,
Bob Marley's gol' ring . . .

Take dat magic tobacco,
wrap it in fine calico,
tie it wid de cat gut.
Finna fine ol' cemetery,
dig dare a big rut,
an' quick bury it up.
Wid dat per-scription filled,
you got your enemy
killed . . .

Fix you up wid a hex sign!
Tack to the nearest pine.
Throw a magic lotion
into the closest ocean.
Come back for more

when you're cravin'
de additional cure
from your Root Heaven . . .

COME TO ROOT
HEAVEN

"Guard your fleas. Curses comes in threes, / missy! Get even how eva you can, / and Glory be, see me, mon. / So, if'n you wants / to regain de health, life an' prosperity, / den listens to me! / forget dat 7-Eleven, mon, / get yow-self to my Root Heaven!''

He finished with a flurry and a full, rich laugh. Ben de-Yampert and the camera crew joined in the laughter, several of them poking about the curious shop as Alex announced, "Are these the hearts you got us down here for? You got anything fresher?"

This only cracked everyone in the place up. After the laughter, the Root Mon, Anton Eugene "Mystick Ruler" Dupree, said, "You want fresh, you got to go to de butcher, mon."

Everyone laughed heartily again.

Anton Eugene approached Alex, grabbed up two of the larger hearts and said, "Mostly dese are use for grinding into powder."

"Powder?"

"Big hearts like dese help the fine ol' wife dat's gone slack wid the rheumatoy back. Also for ill odors and to end de ol' man's snores.''

Ben, tonight on his bar stool, remembered every line and every laugh from the time in Root Heaven as it all came back to him now. Alex had to catch him when he fell off the bar stool while they both helplessly laughed together.

"Newspapers and TV guys had a lot of fun with that one too," Alex added. "Come on. Take yourself home. I've got to get some sleep myself."

"You're okay then, Alex?"

"What's not to be okay about, Ben?"

"Nothing . . . everything . . . hell, life."

"Life's a bitch."

"Got that right."

They said their good nights back at Tully's place, which by now was dark and empty, closed at past midnight. Alex located his car and drove home, the voice of the Root Mon playing in his head. They'd played out the voodoo angle on the Hearts case, and if anyone had his ear to the voodoo grapevine, it was Anton Eugene.

"Try de KKK, maybe," was Anton Eugene's last suggestion on the day they'd returned his buffalo hearts to him.

The music at the Blue Heron was ear-wrenchingly loud, wonderful for private conversation. It was also a terrific place to meet old friends and make new friends in more ways than one. It wasn't unusual for Thommie Whiley, a.k.a. Mademoiselle Marie Dumond, to be approached by a stranger, but seldom one as good-looking as the one across the table from him now. He thought it a little quirky, the way their conversation had gone from the drinks the guy had bought him and the band to a dead guy he'd known only briefly a year ago, a guy named Victor Surette. He wondered if the pickup was a ruse, if this guy was an undercover cop or something, looking for dirt among the gay and transvestite world of the French Quarter; the guy knew immediately, even though Thommie was in full regalia as Marie, that he was hitting on a cross-dresser, as if he had some sixth sense about such matters.

But suddenly all such suspicion was put at bay when the guy said, "I'm Vicki Surette's brother, Emanuel."

"His what?"

"You didn't know he had a brother?"

"No, I swear, I had no idea. . . . "

"I'm surprised; you might've guessed. Look closely, the high cheekbones."

Their conversation was funneled through the cacophony of noise coming from the band, the wailing sounds of Janis Joplin and Judy Garland wannabes and female impersonators, live on stage, the house packed so full that to communicate you had to shout, yet no one could possibly overhear any single conversation, unless the table were perhaps bugged—and even then it would take a sound expert to clarify the words from the cascade of gibberish all around them. But somehow Thommie Whiley could hear every word spoken by the guy who'd asked to buy him a drink, the guy now claiming to be Victor Surette's brother, Emanuel.

"Well, I heard a guy took his apartment soon after his death," Thommie said, "but no . . . I never knew you were his brother, no . . . and nobody around here seems to know anything about you either."

Thommie glanced about the room, his fake eyelashes catching everyone's attention. "Vic . . . he never spoke about you either, man. Said his family pretty much disowned him. Did say they had money, but that was all."

The other man giggled lightly. "He wasn't always proud of me or the rest of the family. Look . . . look closely, around my eyes, the cheekbones, the way my lips are always pouting." He posed for Thommie. "Now you see the resemblance, don't you? Don't you see it?"

The noise of band and screaming performers filtered in one ear. "Yeah, now you mention it . . . yeah, you do look a little like Vic."

"He never liked being called that, Vic, you know. Never really liked Victor either. He preferred Vicki or Victoria, but never Vic . . . never."

"Yeah, you're right about dat; he surely didn't like being called Vic, no. He sorta put up with me calling him Vic, though."

"He was tolerant of others."

"Yeah, he was . . . and he was really a sweet guy, really. I loved him for that."

"You loved him?"

"Yeah, anybody would," Thommie said.

"You took a piece of his heart, didn't you?"

"Yeah, you could say that, but he took a piece of mine too. It works both ways, but you probably know that, right?"

"Took his sweet heart and you broke it, I'll just bet." He puckered and feigned a kiss at the air, and this excited Thommie.

"Well, it was an amicable split, actually. You see, we both wanted out of the relationship. You know how it gets a little too heavy at times, so you back off's all."

"Broke his heart according to his diary."

"He say that in his diary?"

"That and more, yes."

"I'm not so sure I want you or anyone else reading about me in Vic's—Vicki's diary. Cops couldn't find it. How'd you get it? Fact of the matter is, the cops didn't ever say a word about you either." Thommie's natural suspicions reignited.

"They didn't know about me." Emanuel drank from his pink drink, shrugging at the same time. Even his shrug was alluring, coquettish, Thommie thought. "And as for the diary, well, Vicki sent it to me a few days before his horrible death, almost as if . . . as if he knew, as if he'd had some sort of strange premonition, you know?"

"Did he say anything about a premonition?"

"No, never."

"Not even in the diary?" Thommie was curious. He thought hard on Vicki Surette's face and recalled it with great fondness. He was so gentle, meek even in bed. The meek shall inherit the earth, he silently chanted. "So, you didn't at first know—that is, hear about his death?"

"Not until I came to visit, no."

"God, that must've been tough. Getting it in the face like that, I mean."

"Learned it from the landlord of his building," Emanuel almost sniffled.

"So what're you doing now? Staying on in the Big Easy? Sorta doing your own thing?"

"Sorta conducting my own, you know, unofficial investigation, if you want to know the whole story?" Emanuel's lips were large and full and sensuous, Thommie thought, the more so when he spoke.

"Gee, that's kinda neat, like in the movies or something, kinda romantic in a way. But don't the cops notify next of kin?"

"How could they? He was living under an assumed identity. His family would have nothing to do with him. He was completely cut off, alone, except for his lovers . . . except for you and the others."

. Thomas Whiley dropped his gaze. There was so much fire in this guy's eyes, so much pent-up energy. He did remind Thommie of Victor Surette; he brought back old memories which had haunted Thommie on and off since Victor was found mutilated a year ago.

"Well I guess you read the papers," Thommie said. "You know about the others since your brother, don't you . . . others like us found murdered?"

"Their hearts dug out of them with some kind of nasty carving knife, yeah . . . I know all about it now. I've been interviewed by the cops, a million questions about Victor's friends, acquaintances."

"Did you give 'em the diary?"

"Yeah, sure . . . soon as they asked for it. But I kept some of the information, like about where you live and where you hang."

"Jesus, you don't think I had anything to do with Vic's getting killed, do you? The cops talked to me; they must've told you I'm in the clear."

"They're actually worried about you, Thommie."

"Worried? Whataya mean?"

"They think whoever's doing this Jack-the-Ripper number could come after you too."

Thommie shook his head slowly from side to side, his mouth for the moment not working. Finally, he squeezed out his thoughts. "I . . . me, no . . . nobody's getting me like that, no way."

"Whoever this maniac is, Thommie, he likes sweethearts like you. Frankly, I can see why."

"Whataya mean by that?"

Thommie felt Emanuel's hand rising to his groin below the table. After a brief massage, Emanuel said in a heaving voice, "I wouldn't mind digging around a little for your tender heart myself, Mademoiselle Dumond."

Thommie smiled coyly and leaned in over the table, asking, "Why, sir, what are your intentions?"

"Strictly dishonorable, madame, I can assure you."

"Then maybe I'll take a piece of your heart too."

"Hey, you've got some line, Marie."

"So do you, Emanuel. Pretty name, Emanuel . . ."

"So's Marie . . . I much prefer Marie to Thommie."

"Really? Good ol' sweet-tassled Vic . . . Vicki, in a way it's like he's working from the grave, you know?"

Emanuel looked strangely at him, eyes questioning.

"You know, the way he's led you to me?"

Emanuel smiled, eyes alight with fire now.

"Come on," said Thommie, finishing his White Grenache. "I know somewhere where we can be alone."

Emanuel countered. "I know a make-out spot where we won't be disturbed."

"Why not my place?"

"Is it nearby, because I'm extremely horny."

"Getting very hot in here myself, hon. It's just around the corner."

"First, I need to use the little boy's room."

"C'mon, you can take a leak at my place."

"All right, if you insist."

"I insist . . . and if things work out, I may insist again."

The stranger laughed sweetly at this, and Thommie Whiley laughed with him. Others seeing the pair took them for lovers having a good time in one of New Orleans' oldest gay night-clubs, but no one paid very much attention when they got up and left together, as everyone was after his own conquest to-night.

They couldn't wait for the privacy of Thommie's bedroom, or at least Thommie couldn't, and in the elevator he tore at Emanuel's clothing with his hand, and then his mouth with his own, but E, as Thommie had teasingly begun to call the other man, kept him at arm's length, saying, "Calm down, baby . . . whoa . . . you want to have the neighbors complaining? Take it easy . . . we've got all night. Besides, like I said, I need to drop a loaf. But I did bring something to wear."

Emanuel snatched a red teddy from the brown leather bag he carried slung over one shoulder resting on the opposite hip. "How'd you like for me to wear this?"

"Jesus, I like . . . I like . . . think you can fit into it?" Thommie half joked.

"Don't worry, I'm slim at the hips and I brought falsies."

"Good . . . good and plenty and sweet . . ." Thommie's mouth was watering now. "Maybe later, I can try it on?"

"Sure . . . sure, sweet thing. Whatever turns your crank."

The elevator deposited the would-be lovers at the top floor

and Thommie worked the lock open with nervous fingers. He kept talking nonstop. "Vic ... Vicki was a tender guy and a great, great lay, and we respected each other tremendously, like I told the cops, but like I said, we just grew a little apart ... you know ... shit happens ..."

"Grew a little apart," Emanuel repeated, nodding. "Sure, I understand. Don't worry about it, Thommie Marie."

As soon as the door closed behind them, Thommie Whiley, a.k.a. Marie Dumond, was at him again, forcing him against the door, kissing and caressing, his tongue finding Emanuel's deep throat, jabbing in and out, enjoying E's intoxicating, provocative perfume. E knew how to give what he got, and he smelled so damned good.

"Wait ... easy ... back off and let me get situated and dressed for you, Marie ... and Marie, get out of that dress ..." He spoke through gasps and kisses.

"Sorry ... just so ... I don't know ... turned on by you. What's that perfume you're wearing? God, you're good-looking, you know that?"

"Thank you; now, I'll see you in a moment. Why don't you get undressed and pull the covers down, huh? Got anything to drink? Why don't you pour us something to drink?"

"Coming right up. Bathroom's that-a-way."

Thommie Whiley impatiently and breathlessly waited, going naked about the room, pacing and moving several times from the bed to the bathroom door, almost knocking, speaking through the door, asking if everything was all right inside, wondering how long E was going to take and just what he had to do to freshen up. He'd never known a guy with so much cool and restraint before.

"Everything all right in there, Ms. E? Am I going to have to come in after you? Spank your behind? Can I call you EZ?"

"Just a minute," Emanuel repeated in his most feminine voice for an insufferable third time.

When he finally came out, E was stunning with long, smooth legs and an incredible shape, dark, alluring eyes and sensuous mouth, filling out the little teddy like a pro on the runway at the Blue Heron, Thommie thought as he went for him, or rather her, Thommie's hands outstretched, the drinks he'd poured earlier forgotten, the ice in them melted.

"Wait," she said, "my bag . . . bring me my bag."

Goddamnit, he silently cursed, but with a little frown of impatience, he glanced around and then retrieved her bag, a large, leather Gucci. "Jeeze, whataya got in this thing? It must weigh a ton."

"The icing on the cake," Emanuel replied in a soft, purring whisper as *she* now pulled forth first a vibrator to his delight, allowing him to take charge of this, and then she pulled forth an enormous carving knife with serrated edges, the blade glinting in the half light of the room.

"What the hell's that for?"

"Like I said, hon, I'm after your heart."

"What the fuck's that supposed to—"

"*Ayyyyyyyyyyy!*" Emanuel screamed and lunged at him with the blade, but Thommie dodged the blow, lunging for the floor beside the bed where he tore from below the bed a baseball bat which he'd kept there forever for protection.

He brought the bat to bear, but he was twisted round in such an awkward position that he couldn't negotiate it properly, unable to get his weight behind it. With the swing, however, he lost his footing, and E was rushing at him a second time with that damnably huge knife, trying to find his chest and his heart, and all in that one instant, Thommie realized that Surette had been butchered by this motherfucking fiend who claimed to be Victor's brother, and that this monster had also killed and mutilated all the other Queen of Hearts victims, so Thommie put what force he could into a backswing blow from a kneeling position, lashed out at the raging madman's hairless legs, but E just kept coming, and suddenly Thommie felt a sharp pain to his temple, the bone crack sound reverberating in his brain, and next Thommie felt something sharp penetrate the skin beside his ear and sink almost to his left eyeball before he passed out.

When Thommie came to, he was lying on his back in bed, where E had placed him, blood caked at his temple; he was disoriented and seeing through a thick blur, the sound of his own blood and pounding heart in his ears, threatening to send him into deafness so loud was the sound of it along with a sentient ringing noise, as if his own internal alarm clocks were all going off at once. When his eyes fully opened and focused, he realized that Emanuel's red teddy and enormous, blood-smeared breasts were dangling pendulum fashion over him, and E's curly head worked back and forth, *her* hands doing something up and down along a slippery path.

Christ, atop every other indignity, he really is a she!

Thommie's eyes coming clearer now, he saw E reach into an enormous cavern that'd opened up in Thommie's chest, and he felt the other's hands tugging at his beating heart when Thommie suddenly saw only a blinding white light which he allowed himself to fall into; it was not a natural light but a light that blinded both his vision and his feelings, like a shower of mercy and Thommie gratefully retreated into it. All life was severed with the connections between his heart and body and Thommie stepped into a never-ending sleep.

The world stands out on either side
No wider than the heart is wide;
Above the world is stretched the sky—
No higher than the soul is high.
The heart can push the sea and land
Farther away on either hand;
The soul can split the sky in two,
And let the face of God shine through.
But East and West will pinch the heart
That cannot keep them pushed apart;
And he whose soul is flat—the sky
Will cave in on him by and by.

—Edna St. Vincent Millay

IAD had advised Alex to remain home until the incident at
Tully's was officially declared a righteous bust, and that he
was cleared of any wrongdoing in the discharge of his weapon.
Still, he reasoned that since no one was so much as grazed by
a bullet, and since he'd wounded only a trash can on firing in
the line of duty, Sincebaugh took them at their word: Advised
meant advised.

He had too damned much to do at headquarters to slack off
now, and so at precisely three P.M. the next day, the beginning
of his new rotation, he was standing in the middle of the squad
room with all eyes upon him. From the cold stares, he knew
something was up.

Dr. Jessica Coran had no doubt filled the captain's ear with
a lot of technical forensics jargon that he'd need to catch up
on, to see what he could learn from her about yesterday's vic.
He was anxious to look at Coran's reports on the latest heartless corpse, believed to be the latest victim of the maniac he'd
been pursuing since June, hoping she could provide more than
Wardlaw had in the past.

He immediately sought out Ben and found him at the coffee machine, where he was on his second caffeine hit and finishing up a Snickers bar.

"Hey, Alex, how's it hanging? You all right after last night?"

"Couldn't be better; actually slept. Now where's the goddamned coroner's report on the body fished out at the Toulouse Wharf, which was going to be on my desk when I got in this morning—and I quote?"

"Complications at the coroner's is all. Slow up, pal, will you?" Ben was sleepy, unaccustomed as he was to the new rotation.

"What's that supposed to mean?"

"You ain't heard yet?"

"Goddamn it, Big, heard what?"

"They're not so sure anymore that the Gretna vic is one of the Queen of Hearts killings. I thought you were told by now, that Landry would've informed you."

Sincebaugh recalled the victim. "So what're you saying, Ben? That yesterday's victim wasn't number five?"

"Not if they're right. If they're right, the Toulouse body's really number five since Gretna was a copycat job."

"What're they going on, Ben?"

"A little of everything, I think. Either way, should make you happy. This means they're going over everything with a fine-tooth comb, going over every word you and me put to paper, and—"

"You don't write more than a thimbleful, Big."

DeYampert pretended not to hear. "Every lab report Wardlaw's done on the case. Hell, I'd have thought you'd be pleased."

"Maybe I am."

"Got a queer way of showing it."

"So, they're finally thinking the Gretna body's a copycat killing now, huh?"

"You called it first, Alex. Landry knows that you beat out Wardlaw, the FBI M.E., and the psychic on this."

"Sure he does."

Alex stood there seething, wondering, trying to guess the

enemy's next move. Ben tried to make light of it.

"It's no biggy, Alex, really."

"Christ, Ben, are you out to lunch on this? It's time you woke up, partner. They're replacing us on the case and you're doing a tap-dance routine."

"Landry wants us to stay on the case. He told me so. Besides, would it be so bad if we were reassigned, Sincy? Hell, we'd both sleep better."

"Landry . . . how long do you think Landry's going to remain in charge of the investigation now that the FBI's involved, Ben? What planet are you living on?"

"Well, goddamnit, Alex . . ." Ben's voice was an angry whisper. "If they want the case, I say· give it to 'em lock, stock and barrel. Would it be so freakin' bad? Hell, you know how it's been like with Fiona, the kids? And what about you and your damnable inability to sleep, pal?"

Sincebaugh stared across at his partner, saying nothing.

"We're burned out on this one, Alex. We both know it."

Sincebaugh gave his partner a glare, wondering what was on his mind and with whom he'd been talking. "So, that's the latest opinion poll?"

"Maybe you'd better just talk to Landry or . . . or go see this Dr. Coran for yourself." A strange look flitted birdlike across Ben's eyes.

"Something's up. What is it? I felt it the minute I walked in."

Ben frowned, looking as if he'd been caught in a lie. "Seems the captain's called in our medium to lay hands on the body, and yesterday Alex, she told 'em all that the Gretna guy was poisoned by someone close to him and hacked up later. Said his head was cut off after death too."

"She put it on record, just like that? When?"

"Late yesterday."

Alex looked away, shaking his head in disbelief.

"At least you two agree . . . seem to be on the same, you know, wavelength. Coran's report's going to back her contention too. Least that's what Carl Landry told me."

"What the hell do we know about this Dr. Desinor, Ben?"

"What, you want a full background check? She's a psychic . . . a trance medium . . . a psychic detective out of Florida . . . Miami area . . .'' Ben watched him closely as he continued to speak, waiting for any sign of an explosion.

''What else?''

''Has her own detective agency it seems . . . an independent, freelances, you know. Did you really get any sleep last night, Sincy?''

''Will you quit staring at me, for Christ's sake, Ben?'' Alex moaned the words. ''I don't need your mothering or your psychobabbling to add to this goddamn three-ring circus we already have here, okay?''

He rushed off for the nearby hospital police morgue in the basement at Tulane where Dr. Coran must have done her work beneath blinding fluorescent tubes in rooms without windows. Alex went for the stairs that would take him down and through the lonely tunnel, too impatient and upset to take the elevator. When he got there, the dingy old facility, normally empty and silent save for a wandering technician or two, was packed full with people, Captain Landry at the center along with the police commissioner, someone from the mayor's office—that deputy mayor by the name of Fouintenac—and the New Orleans FBI Bureau Chief, Lew Meade, a man who'd hounded Sincebaugh for months now on details about the Hearts case but would give nothing back, preferring to deal at a higher administrative level that kept him from getting his hands the least dirty.

Dr. Coran stood in the rear beside Dr. Wardlaw, the medical examiners both obviously distraught and displaced by the psychic, Dr. Desinor, who was center stage amid the dignitaries, all hovering over the latest corpse, the one snatched from the Toulouse Wharf section of the Mississippi. It took Alex a moment to realize that Dr. Kim Desinor's hands were actually inside the open chest wound of the latest victim. Obviously, she'd gotten over her fear of eels, the slimy intestines causing her no compunction. She looked in a state of raw ecstasy.

''Captain Landry,'' Alex began. ''What the hell's going on here, Captain?'' He heard the others shushing him, and he now saw the strangest light dancing deep within Kim Desinor's luminous eyes. She didn't look like the same woman.

Her eyes—which were not hers at the moment—rose from the corpse to him with shimmering intensity, a magnetic surge going between the psychic and the cop, a vivific fire which he could not fully comprehend, and yet he felt that she'd taken something from him.

"Shhhhh!" Landry placed both hands on Alex's chest and hustled him back through the double doors of the autopsy room. "I thought you were advised by IAD to stay out for a while."

"You know damned well I've got too much invested on this case to slack off now or to—"

"That's enough, Alex. You don't own this case anymore. It's gotten too big!"

"—or see it turned over to Stephens"—he didn't slow down or hear his captain—"and . . . and some psychic clown he's brought with him."

"Lower your voice or shut up, Alex, now!"

"To hell with it, Captain! What's going on and why wasn't I advised about your bringing in a damned psychic in the first place, and by God, if you're going to hold a frigging seance in the morgue—"

"You were advised!"

"Bullshit."

"When's the last time you took a reality check, Alex? What the hell'd you think I was talking about to you in my office the other day or when I sent you out to the airport to pick her up? This isn't a game of backgammon, and it goes without saying that we don't work in a goddamned vacuum either. We've got the eyes of the nation on us now."

"So Stephens calls in a psychic and the press? Then he holds a . . . a bloody seance over a dead guy in the morgue with Wardlaw and Coran displaced and looking on?"

"She's made significant hits, Alex. She's extremely good!"

"You know how this already looks to the press, Captain? How's it going to look when word leaks out about her doing a reading of the corpse down here, huh? Answer that one, Carl. You, me, all of us are going to look like we're freaking out, that we're so fucking desperate that—"

"We are desperate, Alex . . . we are!" Landry, a stocky man with a large neck and broad shoulders and smoldering, yet sad gray eyes, gritted his teeth and said, "You don't get it, do you, Lieutenant. This case is going into a new phase. Now you can either be a part of that new phase, or you can be phased out, all right?''

"No way you're taking me off the case, Captain."

"Well, that's a relief! What a change of heart, Lieutenant. Believe me, at this stage, that decision is not entirely up to you anymore, Alex."

There was a long moment of silence between them. Alex held his jaw firmly set.

Captain Landry continued hollowly. "IAD brought me some interesting footage today in which you play a major role."

"It was a simple bust, Captain."

"Simple? You read those guys like a book, presupposed their actions and stopped them cold before they committed an unlawful act, Alex. Now call that what you want, IAD could make trouble for you. Hanson and Hirschenfeldt wanted to bust your ass the moment you walked through the door today, believe me."

"Those clowns? That's bull and you—"

"They think they've got the crime of the century in their possession, Alex, and you are the star. I convinced them to let it be for now; I convinced them good."

Alex calmed a bit. "I suppose this is where I say thanks?"

"And I showed the tape to Dr. Desinor in there."

"What? You had no right to—"

"And she was as impressed as I was with your . . . your foresight about those punks. She wants very much to work with you, Alex, and I think you ought to graciously accept her invitation to do so."

"Or else?"

"Or else, damnit, that's right."

"You'd sic those snot-nosed IAD punks on my ass? You'd see to it I was forcibly yanked from this case, and maybe from the Department?"

Landry's fists were balled up now, and he breathed heavily through dragonlike nostrils. "I hope it won't come to that, but yes . . . if I have to . . . yes."

"This case has blown a lot of relationships to hell, Landry. I guess one more is just one more."

"Hold on, Alex. Just think about it, damnit. And give Dr.

Desinor a chance. She's good . . . she's damned good," Landry self-consciously admitted.

"Real good, huh? Is she really telling you any more than what Wardlaw has already leaked to the press?"

"Considerably more."

"Is that right?" Alex countered.

"That's right."

"She's just snowing you, the commissioner, Meade, all of you."

"She's revealed to us that the Gretna victim was, like you said, a copycat killing."

"Information circulating about since I suggested it, yes."

"That the heart was taken only after the man was poisoned, which has now been confirmed by Dr. Coran's preliminary tissue and blood tests."

"A wild guess, maybe."

"She even gave us a name this morning, said it came to her in her sleep afterward."

"A name . . . came to her in her sleep . . ."

"Lennox, she said, and it checks out with Missing Persons in Texas where a Marie B. Lennox reported her husband as missing six weeks ago. According to Dr. Coran, the body was between six and eight weeks dead, kept in a frozen state for some time and only recently dumped in our territory in an attempt to make it look like one of the Hearts killings. The killer, Dr. Desinor says, knew the victim well. The victim knew his killer as either Billy or Beau. The wife's middle name is Bolinda with two nicknames, Beau or Billie. Kansas police this morning confronted her with the fact a psychic identified her as her husband's killer, and guess what?"

"She crumpled, no doubt."

"She was told his body had been fished from the Mississippi in New Orleans."

"And I suppose she confessed on the spot?"

"She did, and interviews subsequently place her in our area, driving a van, about the time the body would have been disposed of here. Hell, she sent postcards to the folks back home, the cards dating her trip, placing her extremely close to the Toulouse Wharf area. Photos have given us a definite I.D. on the victim as one Samuel Wayne Lennox, who had some heavy-duty insurance policies taken out on him in the past year. Asked about the beheading, she told authorities in Kansas that she hadn't cut off her husband's head, only his penis, in keeping with what she knew of the ruthless Heart-Taker in New Orleans; she claimed not to know how his head was severed from the body.''

"Then how the hell did his head get separated from his body?" Alex had listened intently, unsure where to attack next.

Captain Landry informed him of how Wardlaw and Jessica Coran had put that piece of information to bed.

"Sounds like the interlocking pieces of the puzzle fell very neatly into place then."

"Yes, yes, they did."

"And you're satisfied with this Lennox woman's confession?"

"Completely, and it all tied in with your theory, Alex, that the Gretna victim didn't fit. I tell you, it gave me the shivers. Desinor's . . . well . . . uncanny."

"So was my prediction, based on what my eyes and my gut told me, only I couldn't prove it."

"Maybe your reading up on those Headless Horseman murders in New York last year had your nose twitching."

"So Mrs. Lennox took the heart and the private parts to simulate the Queen of Hearts killings, not knowing that some drunken fishermen would hit the corpse with their propeller. She poisoned and butchered her husband for the insurance bucks."

"And because she could no longer stand the wimp, or so she says," Landry added.

"Impressive of Desinor and Coran to put this all together," Alex admitted with a heavy release of air.

"Frank played a large hand in it too. He figured out how the head was severed."

"I thought Frank was out of the picture, Captain."

"Ever hear of an injunction? He won't go quietly." Landry walked Alex a little way down the institutional-green cinderblock hallway. "But you're still skeptical, aren't you, Alex?"

"Nature of the beast, I guess . . ."

"Seems Mr. and Mrs. Lennox had vacationed here when she first read of the Queen of Hearts cases, and later when she

saw the latest Hearts case break into print back in Texas, she
began to concoct a copycat killing. She'd read Canon's piece,
the one that speculated there would be more killings, remember?''

"Who could forget that piece of journalistic masturbation."

"Anyway, this tough old Texas babe gets it into her head
that she could kill hubby, remove the heart and privates with
no flinching, and when the serial killer was caught, she'd be
home free with a hell of an inheritance in insurance bucks.''

"If it was so well planned, why'd she fold so quickly when
confronted with the information?"

"Who knows . . . crime makes you stupid. The word psychic to some people is instant truth and enlightenment . . . who
knows?"

"So, you're impressed by Desinor."

"I damned sure am, and Coran for that matter."

Alex wanted to argue, to tell his captain that there was more
to it than met the eye, that perhaps Jessica Coran and Wardlaw
and Desinor were cohorts, in some magic show together now.
Maybe Coran had studied Wardlaw's files on each case from
top to bottom, seen the oversights and the sloppy work, talked
with Desinor, and the two of them had cut Wardlaw in. Then
they had all conjured up Samuel Wayne Lennox, whose name
had most likely surfaced some time before, since the killer
herself had put out a missing-persons report on the man she
had killed. Somehow Alex had to put a rational spin on the
scenario, as he had with the incident at Tully's.

"What's so hard for you to accept, Alex?" Landry finally
said.

"Look, the business of the body's not having been destroyed in quite the fashion of the other victims . . . the rib
cage intact, the fact it was a different sort of weapon used to
open Lennox's chest, all pointed to another perp. Hell, even I
knew that. As to the Beau Lennox story, Kim Desinor could
easily have read about the disappearance of the Texas man, in
a state right next door, and from the general description put
two and two together. As any good detective might, she
bluffed and won."

"She's on the case, Alex. Get used to it."

"I'm out of here for now. Maybe I'll just take that time off that IAD suggested. I'm beginning to feel unnecessary. Besides, all this has got me feeling like I need to find the closest bar.''

''I'm conducting a meeting this evening, my office. Be there at six.''

Alex didn't reply, and Landry's leathery face creased into a look of concern and worry, the wrinkles dancing across his forehead. He wondered if Alex, whose instincts were better than excellent, could be right about Dr. Desinor after all. He'd never believed in psychic hocus-pocus himself before Desinor's recent revelations, which Alex had somewhat effectively fired silver bullets through.

Still, Bolinda Lennox was behind bars in Kansas thanks to Kim Desinor, and so far, in New Orleans, Alex had made no score with respect to the Heart-Taker. Results were what City Hall and P.C. Stephens were now after, results before the next Mardi Gras season, results that would reassure a nation of potential tourists that New Orleans was a safe fantasy land into which they might securely snuggle for a while, long enough to unload their ready cash; that it was a wondrous place to spend their money and enjoy the local pleasures with complete peace of mind, a commodity that seemed all too rare in the city these days.

Landry couldn't blame Stephens and Meade and Leroy David Fouintenac and all the other politicians, not really. All they wanted was for New Orleans to return to the days of Huey Long, to be left unmarred by the terror of a sadistic lunatic roaming the same streets where lovers strolled arm-in-arm to the strains of Louis Armstrong's jazz legacy, which poured out into the street from the numerous bars. They wanted New Orleans to be free again, free from the barbarism of an illness that was supposed only to grip bigger cities such as L.A., Chicago, Miami or New York. They wanted their gleaming cash-cow touristy world back the way it had always been before—before some maniacal butcher with an enormous appetite and an even larger blade had begun to stalk his unique prey for the pleasure of taking human hearts from their cradling homes.

All the brass wanted was a return to normalcy, a return to sanity—so far as sanity could be mustered—in the Big Easy.

While lunacy of the Mardi Gras sort was tolerated, while excessive drinking and nudity were played out on the streets of the French Quarter nightly, this other sort of lunacy simply had to end. A return to normalcy in a place where there was no norm seemed a contradiction in terms, and Landry wondered if such a day would ever come again in this town.

Kim Desinor had seen something frightening in Alex Sincebaugh, something that had brought her from her trance state, something that had also taken her breath away, all in that instant when he'd entered the autopsy room. A fire went around the man, a fire of energy and life naked to most people's perceptions but blinding to her own.

It was more than the noisy interruption, more than the anger and frustration enveloping him and dispelling the trance state she was in, sending her hurtling back to real time and place. She had sensed his presence before she had seen him; in a room full of men, she had felt him.

She now recalled where she was, finding herself surrounded by the men who had brought her here, men who'd been frightened and awed by her recent revelations. Even Jessica Coran, the other single woman in the room, the one to whom she'd hoped to become allied, perhaps even find a binding friendship with, was now hesitant with her, uncertain and distrustful of her.

Even when they believe in you, they don't accept you. She heard an inner voice giving her familiar notice, to take heed. No one here any longer saw her as one of them. And maybe that was why she liked Alex Sincebaugh, despite his obvious disdain for her in particular and for psychic investigation in general; because he wasn't about to treat her as special or unusual or as some sort of freak, she admired his genuineness.

She had previously I.D.'d the victim and given authorities a pair of names to search for, an unusual "gift" to receive from a corpse murdered so long before, but Lennox had a strong will that his killer be known and somehow that information was implanted in his every cell, the tissues crying out with their own decaying march toward oblivion, his permeating plea rising from every pore. Lennox was unusual, or at least his corpse was; the man's cadaver was a fluke, a fount of information, giving up information in such a cascading tide that she could not take it all in at once, as it was offered, as if there were a time limit involved.

Kim had suspected the single name she kept getting from Lennox was the endearment used for a girlfriend or possibly a wife . . . and she had told Landry to follow up, and later that night she'd telephoned Captain Landry again with the name Lennox, which came to her in a dream sequence, a kind of "aftershock" to the initial reading. But no one, Landry included, had as yet today confided anything to her about what had been done with the information.

A second "reading" of Lennox's body might reveal more evidence, or so P.C. Stephens had hoped, aside from wishing to be on hand when such revelations occurred, perhaps to show her off to the mayor's man, who'd come expressly to see the reading of the body. However, with the flood of information released initially to her, the corpse had turned stony and remained now stubbornly silent, like a granite mass, still and cold and suddenly lacking all the psi energies so powerful just the day before.

Still, with the P.C. on hand, alongside the mayor's stooge, the "show" had to go on in order to clearly determine if there was any connection to the other deaths.

At one point she was asked directly, "So, what do you think, Dr. Desinor?" It was the balding, broad-shouldered Lew Meade, New Orleans FBI Bureau Chief and one of the few men in the city who knew that she too worked for the FBI.

"Nothing . . . coldness . . . emptiness . . . loneliness and isolation. This man has no connection to the other victims," she said before Sincebaugh had burst into the room, "and my feeling is that neither did his killer, as I've earlier informed Captain Landry."

"So you continue to maintain that this man was killed by his wife, and that his death has no link to the Queen of Hearts killings?" asked the mayor's man, Leroy David Fouintenac, a regal and robust man who appeared to enjoy Bourbon Street's finest restaurants. He'd obviously been coached long before on what she'd imparted to Captain Carl Landry.

"Wife, girlfriend, live-in lover," she muttered absentmindedly as her hands searched for any hot spot on the body. Finding none, she faked it, her hands shaking like a pair of dowsing rods.

"What is it?" asked Stephens while the others stared on.

"All the earlier information, all corroborated . . . nothing new, however . . ."

"With such remarkable results," began the mayor's man, a tall healthy-looking, rugged John Carradine lookalike, "perhaps the good doctor can—"

"What remarkable results?" Kim asked, staring now through Carl Landry. "I've heard about nothing that has come of my report."

"You made a number of major hits on the Lennox body, Doctor," replied Landry. "I wanted to tell you earlier, but . . . well, let's just say that we wanted to be sure and these things do take time. We have a woman named Beau Lennox in custody, and she has confessed to her husband's murder. She's being extradited from Texas as we speak."

Kim turned to stare at Jessica, silently asking, "Did you know about this?"

"At any rate," said Leroy David, as Meade called his political friend, as if nothing of consequence had happened, "might you now be persuaded to do a reading on one of the certain victims of the Heart-Taker? After all, that is the case you are being paid to . . . to help solve."

The comment made her wonder if the mayor's people were out of the true loop here. Perhaps they weren't informed about her actually working for the FBI.

Dr. Coran came forward from the corner where she'd been standing in shadow. "Well . . . why not? It's not as if we have to exhume a body for the purpose; we had a victim wash up just yesterday."

All the men looked from one to another. "It could look awkward in the press," suggested Captain Landry. "So, unless we can keep it to this room . . ."

"What the hell," said the P.C. "This is New Orleans. Anything goes, right?"

"Anything within reason, but this . . ." Landry began to counter, a certain feeling of unsureness creeping over him.

Fouintenac stopped Landry cold, staring across at him, sternly saying, "There's no reason the bloody press need get hold of any of this, is there, Carl? I say, give it a try with the last victim, but we do it in complete secrecy.''

''What about it, Dr. Desinor?'' asked the P.C.

Kim looked about the room at the faces all pinned on her reaction, expectant and hopeful. They all wanted a miracle and she was supposed to supply it. ''I'll be happy to . . . to do my best, but I can't possibly guarantee or promise any startling revelations, as you know. Still, I will go along with whatever you gentlemen and Dr. Coran and Dr. Wardlaw decide.''

That was how it had ended before Sincebaugh's arrival, the body of the Toulouse Street Wharf victim wheeled in only moments before Alex Sincebaugh had come crashing through the door as if to save her from both herself and the company she found herself in.

She now found herself thinking only of Alex Sincebaugh, half wishing he'd stayed, glad he'd gone all at once. She wondered what it was about him that so attracted her, despite everything.

◄18►

Heartily know,
When half-gods go,
The gods arrive.

—Emerson

Kim Desinor looked from one to the other of the men before
her. Landry and Stephens were dissimilarly built, Landry being a short, stocky squared-off cop who hadn't lost the rough
edges of his profession. With too much around the middle, his
brown hair graying before Kim's eyes, she guessed him to be
in his mid-fifties, and from the gnarled little hands to the way
he walked, she surmised that his body was riddled with ar-
thritic pains from fingertips to back and leg muscles, all of
which he denied, even to himself. He had suffered some injury
as a youth, something to do with being in a place he shouldn't
have been, and he'd also suffered a knee injury in college,
where he played a defensive linesman, no doubt, given his
heft and size. She recalled some chance remark he had made
with regard to Richard Stephens's ambitions and he'd served
up a football metaphor, something to do with an end run that
fooled no one.

As for Police Commissioner Stephens, while not so tall as
Alex Sincebaugh, he stood extremely tall beside Landry, and
while he was not a slim man by any stretch, against Landry's
bulk he appeared so. Still, Stephens's single most distinguishing characteristic remained his obviously dyed full head of
flaming red strands which entwined one another in a series of
wild dance moves. Where Landry's jaw was set in what
seemed a perpetual, teeth-gnashing, concrete half snarl, PC
Stephens sported a painted grin, born of campaigning. Stephens's henna-colored temples and fine features marked him
as the best choice for higher office—more politician than cop
and obviously made for the office. It seemed he'd go to any

length to protect his personal citadel. Maybe he'd long since made up his mind that he would sit out his last years in office, content yet ever watchful, ever fearful of events that might topple him, such as this case.

Stephens's tailored beige suit gave him the image of a modern-day Huey Long, replete with suspenders beneath the stylishly rumpled suit, in a breezy New Orleans way an expensive item in anyone's estimation, yet relaxed and loose-fitting. Stephens's nails were professionally done. But then, so were those of the guy from the mayor's office, who actually wore red suspenders and a checked tie with an angora-sweater poofiness to it which marked him as not only politically correct, but far more up on fashions, even down to the ridiculous sideburns. There was little else to distinguish the thin man named Leroy Fouintcnac who'd been throwing his title—deputy mayor—around the room along with the hungry, darting eyes and the beaked and sniffing nose which led Kim to the image of a kind of malnourished buzzard, a sickly scavenger bird, as opposed to one who successfully hunted. He was thin and priggish, in imitation of a David Niven character she'd once seen in an old black-and-white movie.

Rounding out the foursome was the staid FBI bureau chief, Lew Meade, a stony observer who seemed detached from everything but the arrangements and connections, always at the ready with the introductions, however, and always anxious to know the latest. He'd obviously called in the mayor's man, since they shared many more whispers than P.C. Stephens enjoyed with Fouintenac. Meade had an army of agents to see that Dr. Coran was made comfortable for her stay, while he'd totally ignored Kim, in keeping with the incognito approach she was to take here, her detachment from the FBI seemingly complete.

She suspected that it had been Meade's idea to have Alex Sincebaugh pick her up at the airport, obviously to rub salt into Sincebaugh's wounded ego. She'd sensed the animosity Meade held for the lieutenant even at the crime scene the day before, but even more so here when Alex had entered the room.

Meade was an observer, a watchful man who kept his cards extremely close to his chest. And Kim had no notion of what

Meade meant to accomplish with his presence here. But Lew Meade's closemouthed approach had already alienated Kim and only made his blandness of character the more bland.

Dr. Jessica Coran, by comparison, was a woman of color in every sense of the word, but her mysterious eyes held no warmth or clue at the moment as to what lay behind them. What did she think of all this talk of doing a psychometric reading of the last victim's body? It had been taken now from its refrigerated tomb by Wardlaw's young, female assistant, who'd wheeled the cadaver into the autopsy room and efficiently replaced the Lennox body with the nameless, hapless true victim of the New Orleans Mardi Gras Hearts Thief—as one newscaster that morning had called the killer.

Kim herself was immediately worried by the idea put forth by Fouintenac and heralded now by Stephens. In fact, she hadn't particularly cared for the idea of doing a hands-on reading of the other so-called latest victim of the Heartthrob Killer—as others in the press had dubbed the phantom monster.

She had to go along with it, she knew. Hell, Stephens and the others had taken a giant step forward with regard to her work. They accepted her ''gift'' unreservedly now, accepted the fact that extraordinary, extrasensory perceptions and detection were possible. Perhaps even Wardlaw and Coran had grudgingly accepted to some degree that some things which science had no answer for must be taken on faith alone, by sheer instinct alone. Kim was a purely instinctive individual, working out on a frontier which science might never fully comprehend or explore, a frontier of emotion and mind over matter which galled most scientists and pragmatists. Given their imperatives and natural liking only for that which proved empirical, she well understood why both the doctors in the room were far from convinced of her often startling and uncanny abilities.

She unnerved people, she knew. People in general feared her, which was a far cry from admiration or awe. She sensed fear in Wardlaw and something akin to fear in Jessica.

''Perhaps we should allow Dr. Coran and Dr. Wardlaw time to prepare their findings on the victim before I—''

She was instantly cut off by Fouintenac. ''If we wait for

laboratory reports and findings, it could be weeks. Please, Dr. Desinor, do what it is you do.''

''The deputy mayor came here to see you work, Doctor,'' added Stephens. She read into his remark that he'd confided in Fouintenac exactly who she was and how he himself had witnessed firsthand what she was capable of.

Obviously, due to her psychic hits on the Lennox body, she'd made believers out of some in the room. Still, Kim felt the air in the morgue close in on her; there was a stifling anger welling up from Wardlaw which Jessica perhaps contributed to.

But Fouintenac and the others waited with eager eyes and ears, with obvious disregard for the delicate nature of such an undertaking, without regard to the two M.E.s in the room, without concern for protocol, without fear of the concerns of family, friends of the deceased, without much thought given to possible negative outcomes—so dazzled had they become with her gifts, little suspecting that half or more of her insight came through normal means: intuition born of education.

She'd had ready access to knowledge of the previous victims— enough to fake what she must—thanks in large measure to Alex Sincebaugh's absolutely thorough and meticulous examinations of the crime scenes and Wardlaw's forensic examination records and subsequent discussions she'd had with Jessica, Stephens and Landry. Jessica's detailed report on this victim in particular, and those earlier reports made by Detective Sincebaugh, had been invaluable, so much so that it was obvious to her, as it must be to coroner and cop, that the supposed victim with the severed head was out of the ordinary for the killer, possibly a setup of some sort.

As to the flashes of psychic insight, she didn't entirely know where they had come from. She sensed and heard and saw images which sometimes were letters, road signs, maps leading her from one sensory input to the next, from one intuitive leap to another, and sometimes each led her along a direct line and sometimes quite the opposite. In Lennox's case, it had been a straight arrow shot. She'd heard the mewing, clicking, humming sounds of a barnyard, the distinct noises of a chicken ranch coming out of the muffled, mysterious soundings given off by Lennox's body, that meaningless, whale singsong; then images had grown from the more distinct sounds. She'd seen a child everyone called Billy or Beau chasing terrified chickens, grabbing one and wringing its neck until it was dead. This had led to ugly little scenes, the same faceless girl in a frayed frock playing cruel games with some of the animals, both carnal and unnatural. She'd next seen Billy as a large, awkward girl, and then as a gargantuan woman in her mid-twenties, hard-bitten and tough. As Kim's hands had moved over the dead man—in one time and place—her mind had moved across another time and place, to a wedding, to a fight in a bedroom, to a dark closet and a pair of scissors she'd failed to use on him, to a new honeymoon during which all seemed peaceful and harmonious.

Jessica and Wardlaw had proven that all the wounds were superfluous, even cosmetic, to ape the Hearts Killer, all fabricated to mask the barbital poisoning which might well have been overlooked had not Jessica Coran been asked in on the case. Even the severing of the head had come long after death, Kim had rightly guessed, as Jessica had confirmed.

Still, Sincebaugh and Jessica, even Frank Wardlaw, had gathered as much from a quick perusal of the body and the wounds. So Kim was not surprised that Jessica, like Alex Sincebaugh and most assuredly Frank Wardlaw, knew that she had simply picked up on the same immediate clues as they had when they'd first viewed the body. Just because she possessed psychic power, this was no reason to discard common sense as a tool either.

Still, she desperately wanted Jessica to remain on her side. As for the severing of the head, it'd been the result of a motor blade on a boat, the boat filled with drunken fishermen who'd found the body.

As for Mrs. Lennox in small-town Texas near Austin, and as to her husband's mysterious disappearance, reported weeks before, Kim knew that she might well have recalled some particulars of the case from the hundreds of such cases that crossed her path in the line of duty every working day, but how she knew this was Lennox, and that he had died in the fashion he had, she could only attribute to a power she herself had no control over, nor anywhere near a complete understanding of.

She had learned to live with the power, a power without definition, without boundaries, without reason, or rather outside of the realm of the normal meaning of such words as reason, rationality, sanity, normality. What was normal about speaking to the dead and having them speak back? Yet in a very real sense, it was precisely what Dr. Jessica Coran did with her probes, DNA tests and electron microscopes.

"Will you do it, Doctor?" asked Stephens again.

"I would like to see an exhibition of your . . . your laying on of hands," added Fouintenac, curious, pressing.

"I will do what I can," she began. "I will do my best but can promise nothing, gentlemen. . . ."

The laying on of hands over the last of the Heartthrob victims yielded very little that Kim Desinor didn't already know. Even clutching the killer's strange rosary beads brought little or no new information, although the attempt exhausted her, for in the vision she once again became the killer wielding the knife. She had to be pulled from the cadaver, and so savage did her attack on the corpse become that she broke several ribs that had managed to remain intact until now.

Still, the yield was slim. She tried to explain that while she was the killer, a part of her was not given over to the monster, and did not wish to be. Still, there was so much that remained blocked; so much was shut out.

None of the principals in the room wanted to hear this, however. She finally said in a moment of desperation, "The killer uses a disguise of some sort. It's one of the reasons I can't quite get a fix on what he looks like."

"What kind of disguise?"

"I don't know . . . something frilly and elaborate, like a stage costume."

"Clown costume?"

"Some sort of Mardi Gras outfit perhaps?" pressed Stephens.

"That's enough!" Jessica boldly stopped their questions. She had been the one to move in and grab hold of Kim and soothingly talk her down from her vision. She now wrapped her arms around Kim again. "You've already pushed Dr. Desinor to limits no one should have to endure. Allow her time to recover, please.''

''This just isn't enough,'' said Meade, disappointed along with the others.

''We need more specific details,'' added Stephens.

''There might be another way,'' suggested Landry with a pained expression, but then he quickly corrected himself, adding, ''No . . . forget it . . . too much of the taxpayers' money involved, not to mention the emotional costs.''

''What?'' asked Fouintenac.

''Go on, Carl,'' said Stephens. ''Spit it out.''

Jessica knew what Landry was driving at, knew it from her readings of the files, from Alex Sincebaugh's earlier requests, and yet when she spoke Carl Landry's thoughts, no one thought she had mind-reading abilities as they might have if Dr. Desinor had spoken the same words. ''Exhume the first body, the first victim.''

''Oh, I don't know . . . no, I think exhumation's out of the question,'' replied Stephens, suddenly animated. ''Papers get hold of that one, the family learns of it . . . we're talking major lawsuits and legal crap up to our hips.''

''We can get the family to agree,'' countered Jessica, who knew the difficulties inherent in what she said. ''And if they refuse, we go ahead anyway. This is a murder investigation. They can't interfere. Nor do they have grounds for legal action. Besides, from what I read, the first victim's body was never claimed.''

''It just leaves a bad taste in my mouth,'' replied the deputy mayor, halfheartedly agreeing with Stephens.

''Then we'll leave you out of it, sir,'' countered Landry, who now seemed hot on the idea he'd first posited before them.

Jessica took up the slack. ''If the killer knew any of his victims, if he's closely connected to any of his victims, it'd most likely be his first victim. A likely hypothesis and one worth checking into.''

''Then we do the first. What was his name?'' asked Meade. ''Stimpson . . . Kenny Stimpson, wasn't it?''

''Some of us think Stimpson was the second,'' countered Landry.

"You're not seriously thinking of exhuming the Surette corpse," replied Meade, his eyes going wide while Fouintenac chewed on his lower lip and Stephens's slack-jawed expression displayed his own surprise.

"And why not?" Jessica said. "We have good reason to believe that there was missed evidence in the case which would have pointed to its being the first Queen of Hearts killing, and that was over a year ago." Jessica pushed the point. "What is it you're afraid of? That you might've saved some lives if you'd taken this step sooner?"

Kim was slowly coming around to the meaning of the words being bandied about the room. All but Wardlaw, who stood stonily against one wall, were heatedly debating whom to exhume for her to psychometrically read, but Jessica wanted her shot at the Surette body also, while Wardlaw likely wanted his mistakes to remain buried.

"Somebody want to ask me if I want to do this?" Kim finally asked.

"You are getting paid well for your services," said Landry with a grim poker face.

"There would be very little disturbance to the grave or the coffin," countered Jessica, "since we're talking New Orleans, where everyone's buried aboveground; we merely have to unseal the crypt, and I don't truly see that family would be involved since he was buried in a paupers' yard, right? Why would there be objection now, a year later?"

"Dr. Coran is right," added Landry, defending the move now with surprising enthusiasm, though Kim quickly realized he was happy with the consternation he was getting out of the other solid citizens in the room, including a nervous Dr. Wardlaw.

Wardlaw cleared his throat and jumped into the fray, saying, "But also in New Orleans, Doctor Coran, death—the grave, rather—is viewed as final and sacred. You will find opposition, family or no."

"Either way, there's no guarantee," said Kim.

"I say we give it our best try, Dr. Desinor," countered Landry, seemingly anxious for the event. Or was he simply enjoying himself now at the expense of Stephens and Meade before the mayor's man?

God, Kim thought, now they're calling for an exhumation of an earlier victim, long since deceased and decayed, and Jessica, along with a supporting cast of Stephens and Landry, was suggesting that Kim could perform her "magic" over the exhumed corpse. Was Jessica Coran being catty? Was she trying her best to undermine Kim, believing that a poor result in such an endeavor was virtually assured? Should Dr. Coran get her way, Kim might easily be sent packing, and Jessica could take over full rein on the case. Was that what she wanted? From what little Kim knew of Jessica Coran, she assumed that getting her own way was what had made her so invaluable to the FBI.

Kim tried to imagine the unimaginable, no doubt a first for psychic investigation: a psychometric reading over a body long since gone cold in every sense of the word. Could anything come of it? It was one hell of a lot of trouble and turmoil to go to for what might well be *nada*; it was also one hell of a challenge engineered by Jessica, who obviously had thrown down the gauntlet.

Kim felt certain that such a "show" would result in nothing save a handful of theatrics she could call on. The results would be pitiful at best. Psychic impressions left in the wood of old haunted houses was one thing; psychic energy might linger for years where spirits roamed, but what sort of ghostly impressions might remain in a decayed and entombed body or the porous concrete of an aboveground tomb? It was the ultimate challenge, as when the famous Pierce Reeves had psychically "attacked" the mummified remains of Tutankhamen, the boy king of Egypt, never recovering from his encounter and dying a disheartened and shriveled man in his late thirties. That event, which had fueled the fire of the infamous curse of King Tut for yet another generation, was still fresh in Kim's mind as she considered the ultimate disturbance of a body in its grave.

She was hardly certain that she was up to such a task, nor had she had any idea that she'd be boxed into such a position.

It was one thing to read the body of the recently deceased, but to snatch a corpse from its long slumber . . . The very idea repulsed and unnerved her, and to some degree—old habits dying hard—went against the few teachings of the Church she yet believed in, about the sanctity and piety of the grave.

Jessica Coran, by comparison, was eager to go ahead with an exhumation. It was scientifically a logical step, to ensure that what the NOPD had perceived as indeed a series of killings by the same man was in fact correctly dated to its inception.

According to an inner logic which Jessica herself followed instinctively, seldom were things as they seemed on first glance. But for the moment, Kim almost believed that Jessica was delighting in the psychic's discomfort.

She hadn't had time to fully assess Dr. Coran, or why her own presence here in the coroner's domain should make her antsy and uncomfortable, but uncomfortable was precisely the word for Jessica now. She could see that Jessica's usual sea-blue aura—the fiery glow that encircled the cranium to flutter about all living forms—usually a serene moon-glow aqua-marine around her, was now shooting off orange sparks of blood red, a sure sign Jessica was upset.

Still, Kim realized that her form of magic made a lot of people—most people, in fact—uncomfortable. In almost every case, she made men and women, and people with iron wills and concrete world views in particular, unsettled in their beliefs and generally unhappy as a result. It was the nature of the beast, as Detective Alex Sincebaugh so exemplified.

Sincebaugh was obviously threatened by her, and so too was Jessica, perhaps to a lesser degree. Paul Zanek, for a number of reasons, had been terrified of her, not that he would ever have admitted it, not even to himself. The other men in this room, while not particularly believers, were desperate, all save Landry, and they had already made up their minds that they would go to any lengths for a breakthrough in the Hearts case, so why not a seance over a corpse?

Apparently, she had stepped into a hotbed of political intrigue that P.C. Stephens and Lew Meade had conveniently not explained to either her or Jessica. Either man had had plenty of opportunity to catch them up on Wardlaw's flaws, for instance, and on Sincebaugh's reticence and reluctance, on the politically charged environment—the shaky situation with respect to the detectives working the case who were ready to explode. Even Meade, who was supposedly on their side—

their FBI man in New Orleans—had failed to inform either of them, but why had he failed to do so?

Was it because Meade and Stephens didn't want her to know what kind of shit she was about to step into? Was Stephens or Meade fearful that she would pull out at the mention of any trouble? Or was it more basic than that? No doubt the duo of Stephens and Meade wanted her to stay focused on the case, and not the peripheral nonsense surrounding the case.

"Will you do it, Dr. Desinor?" pressed Landry. "If we get the order to exhume? Will you do a . . . a reading?"

"We'll be happy to meet your price," added Jessica, like some cheerleader with ulterior motives now. "Whataya say?"

At that moment Wardlaw chose to leave the operating room, calling out that he wasn't feeling too well. The other men exchanged knowing looks, aware that Wardlaw was fighting off the d.t.s, doing all in his power to keep off the booze, and now was further upset by talk of an autopsy of the Surette body. No M.E. wanted to admit to a single oversight, much less the possibility of a series of errors.

No one stopped Wardlaw's retreat, which was followed by an assistant coming into the room to wheel the body of the latest victim away once more. Meanwhile, Captain Landry, who'd so recently become awed by Kim's insights over the Lennox affair, only stared across at her.

She swallowed hard, wondering how much she might trust Landry, remaining upset at his having earlier withheld the Lennox information from her. She realized now why the Lennox corpse on second reading had so abruptly ended communication with her. Its need to communicate had been ended long before, and they had all known this in advance of coming into the morgue today—Jessica included.

"You've done very well here, so far, Dr. Desinor," said Fouintenac. "What an enormous gift you have to offer law enforcement. Now you must do whatever's necessary"—he meant the exhumation, which he no doubt would skip—"to help us locate this maniac who's feeding on our city."

"All right," she abruptly agreed. "If it can be done in a sterile, well-lit environment, okay?"

"That's the only way to go with an exhumation," Jessica commented.

"We'll arrange everything," assured Landry, who seemed suddenly to be in control, running the show.

Stephens quickly put in, "All you need do is be here." It was, after all, Stephens's show.

"Good . . . good," agreed Landry, who seemed to have boxed Stephens into a corner. "Then I'll begin the paperwork for Victor Surette's exhumation."

"Surette?" countered Meade. "I still think we should do the Stimpson body or the Lawton body, at very least the Trent Fischer body, since . . ."

Stephens waved Meade down, took him aside and explained things to him in a whisper the others could not hear. Meade erupted once with: "Who the hell is Surette? We're not even sure his death is related to the case."

"Surette is very possibly the first victim, Chief," Landry explained again.

"First victim, says who? Alex Sincebaugh? I still say Kenny Stimpson was the first."

"New evidence on the Surette homicide has recently surfaced," began Landry. "We have reason to believe that the killings date back at least as far as Surette."

"New evidence has surfaced regarding the Surette death?" asked a surprised Stephens.

"What kind of new evidence?" Meade pressed.

"We'll know more after the exhumation," Landry assured the other two men. "Suffice to say that Surette was known by the other victims."

Stephens and Meade exchanged a look of surprise before Stephens replied, "You'd better have something a hell of a lot more compelling than the fact these fags knew one another, Carl."

Captain Landry nodded, his large jaw firmly set, allowing his cocksure expression to do the talking for him.

"I know what's going on here," Meade said. "Landry here seems to think that his Detective Sincebaugh has some sixth sense about this case, don't you, Carl?"

"I'll take Alex Sincebaugh's instincts and stack them against anyone you've got in your whole damned agency, Lew."

"It's on then. Let us know when and where, Carl," Stephens declared with little enthusiasm for the idea.

Meade gave Stephens a menacing look, and Stephens fired back a volley of words in reply. "I have other reasons to see this through, at least to determine if there ever was a . . . connection, Lew."

Kim knew that Stephens had been made curious over the Surette case due to what he'd seen her do in Virginia when he'd placed the Surette case in as a decoy, only to learn it was, in her professional opinion, related. She wondered why he had chosen the Surette case to use as a decoy when he'd visited Zanek's office in Quantico; had it been merely coincidental, or had there been motivating circumstances that she was unaware of?

Jessica Coran stepped between the men and said, "From what I've examined of the Surette case file, one which Dr. Wardlaw only reluctantly revealed to me, I had the immediate impression that there was a connection which Dr. Wardlaw at the time, for whatever reasons, chose to overlook."

"Overlook?" Stephens was incredulous.

"The report claimed that the heart had been dug out by animals and taken off, that the body had been in the woods for weeks and was maggot-infested, but other, more easily accessible organs and parts of the body showed little to no sign of animal contact, only the extremities where rats, field mice and perhaps raccoons had got at the decaying fingers, hands and toes. It seemed odd to me that only the heart was removed from the viscera. That runs counter to logic."

"Since when are animals logical?" asked Meade. "But even if you're right, why? Why would a respected M.E. of Wardlaw's obvious, ahhh, caliber . . ." Meade was cut short by Stephens, who jokingly told him that his final argument would lose his case.

"Perhaps the idea that someone cannibalized the heart, or took it off for some other perverted pleasure, simply got the best of Dr. Wardlaw," Jessica replied. "Or Wardlaw had other reasons not yet before us."

Kim quickly added, "There's no accounting for what turns a normally functioning adult human being into a child filled with fright—psychologically speaking, that is. For some of us it's the touch of a spider's leg along the ankle, the sight of a snake, a maggot pool. For others it can be an odor associated with some long-ago hurt. Or a few words which conjure up a reproaching parental voice threatening us with God's divine punishment.''

"What're you saying, that Frank Wardlaw's ready for the funny farm?'' asked Meade.

"No, no . . . not at all,'' Kim replied. "I'm telling you that for some people . . . well, the very idea of . . . of, say for instance, a murder victim's hands being severed at the wrists becomes a torture to contemplate, much less work over, examine and touch. Such a terrible trauma came for a colleague of mine in Chicago once, and perhaps . . . just perhaps the idea of a man's heart being ripped from his chest might not put you into an emotional tug-of-war, Chief Meade, but it may've found some long-protected chinks in Dr. Wardlaw's armor, possibly placing him in an emotional upheaval which you and I only can guess at by comparison.''

"Well,'' began Jessica, "suffice it to say that Dr. Wardlaw obviously was in no state of mind to want to deal with what his eyes were telling him at the autopsy. Call it human error, frailty, emotional turmoil, oversight if you like.''

"Bullshit. The man's a cutter himself,'' said Meade, obviously impatient with the psychoanalysis of a friend.

Stephens stepped in. "Just do whatever's necessary, Dr. Coran, to get that exhumation order on this . . . what's his name . . .''

"Surette,'' added Landry a bit impatiently, knowing full well that Stephens knew of the suspicions that had cropped up around the Surette case.

"You run into any goddamned problems or red tape, Doctor,'' Fouintenac said directly to Jessica, his eyes blazing now, "and you just have the asshole who gets in your way give me a call, or you may call me yourself at this number.'' He extended another expensive-looking embossed card.

"Carte blanche? I like doing business with you, Mr. Deputy Mayor, Commissioner Stephens, Chief Meade.''

The mayor's man made a feeble attempt to impress Jessica further, looking as if he were on the verge of asking her to dinner when he instead said, "You'll find us all here in New Orleans most cooperative, Dr. Coran . . . Dr. Desinor. If the

FBI's best can't he'p us, then God he'p us all.''

"Just keep those good wishes flowing our way, Mr. Fouin-tenac," Jessica said for both Kim and herself.

"Will do . . . will do, ladies . . .''

Kim saw that Jessica's tone was mild but that her aura was a pulsating flare and her eyes, boring into Kim now, were driving home spiked shards, projectiles of uncertainty. Something was nagging at the other woman, something like a shadow that crawled up from inside Jess and took up a position along the wall, camouflaging itself there, waiting with infinite patience to snatch her whenever she might be alone.

And she was clumsily, awkwardly seeking help from Kim, yet unable to negotiate the uncharted waters, having no prac-tice at asking for help from anyone, especially from a psychic, thanks most likely to her upbringing. Jess worked heroically, tirelessly at being the professional that she was, but she was also working overtime at keeping the shadow at bay, but it climbed up out of her at times—even here—casting a pall over her eyes, and deep within those shadow-cast eyes lay the most fathomless and nameless emotions Kim had ever seen.

Kim suddenly grabbed Meade by the arm, saying, "Let's have a private word, Chief Meade, now!''

19

I hear it in the deep heart's core.

—Yeats

Meade followed Dr. Desinor's march through the heavy double doors and out into the two-tone yellow tunnel—a perverse twist on the road to Oz, leading as it did to the autopsy room. "I want to know just what the hell is going on, Lew."

"What're you talking about, Doctor?"

"Hey, the mayor's guy, the P.C., you, a captain . . . who's next to take an active role in the case? The goddamn governor?"

"As it happens, the governor has taken an interest in the case, as have two senators."

"Why? Is this going to be an election issue?"

"I believe the governor's genuinely interested. I think it's the heart thing . . . just like what you said with Wardlaw before . . . simply got to him. I don't know. Maybe a lot of us are squeamish about the heart. All I know for sure is that he wants to see a quick, speedy resolution to the problem."

"So does the Chamber of Commerce, I'm sure."

"Well, hell, yes! Tourism's the biggest industry in the city, and this kinda thing's no good for tourism. Not to mention a pending government contract that'll bring in jobs if—"

"And that's what propelled Stephens to come see us in Virginia in the first place, isn't it?"

"Don't trivialize our concerns here, Doctor. We all want to see an end to this before it gets any worse. Nobody in that room"—he pointed a chunky finger—"nobody wants to see another murder. It's as simple as that."

"I see. Then it is electioneering. Can't start too soon, right?"

"It's not about politics, Doctor."

"Could've fooled me. Besides, everything's about politics in our business, isn't it, Lew?"

"In a manner a speaking, I 'magine, yes, but—"

"The tension in Wardlaw's lab, the fact Frank Wardlaw's

out before we're in . . . just doesn't sit well. We . . . Jessica and I didn't come here to take a scalpel to people's lives.''

''Wardlaw's been on the bottle; he dug his own hole long before you arrived here. Let it go at that.''

She gnashed her teeth together, sighed and leaned heavily against the wall.

''We all have our reasons for wanting a speedy resolution to this madness in our city, but that doesn't lesson our concern for the victims, their families or future victims, Dr. Desinor. And I can tell you this Surette nonsense is just going to waste everyone's time. It's a Landry-Sincebaugh ploy to throw us all off, to give Alex and Landry more time.''

More time to do their jobs? she almost shouted. ''What's so damnably wrong with this Lieutenant Sincebaugh being allowed to pursue leads, Lew? Are we all at odds here, Lew? I want to know the truth.''

''Sincebaugh's a rebel and a bastard. And he doesn't play well with our office, never has. He gummed up a case for us a year ago that we're still trying to untangle. Hadn't been for him, we could've screwed over this drug czar working out of the Quarter a long time ago, but Sincebaugh likes to play cowboy, so he ran his own scam and it blew up in *our* faces; some innocent people got hurt. I didn't want you running the same risks.''

I'm touched, she thought sardonically. ''And so everyone's on Wardlaw like he's been the problem all along, and now that he's out of the picture, we cut Alex Sincebaugh off at the knees, show good faith with the press that a shake-up has been ordered, that every little thing's going to be hunky-dory? And Captain Landry? Is he next? Stephens and you intend to throw him to the wolves too? Then who's left, Chief? Who's the mayor and the governor and the FBI and the P.C.'s office going to point a finger at next? Who'll be your final scapegoat? Dr. Coran, me?''

Meade clenched his teeth and stammered.

She realized now why the air in that autopsy room was so thick with the smell of tension; no wonder Alex Sincebaugh and Captain Landry were both so on edge.

She stared hard into Meade's beady eyes and firmly said, ''Now that we've blown it with Landry and Sincebaugh, the two principal cops on the case, I don't think we've got a chance in hell of working together.''

"Just as well. Sincebaugh's not gotten anywhere, I tell you, and going back to the Surette thing . . . "

"But Landry has a lot of respect for him, and just because the guy seems to think differently . . . well, Sincebaugh does have reasons to believe as he does, I'm sure. The snitch trail I've only heard snippets about, for instance."

"It's a dead end."

"What's a dead end? Fill me in, Lew. Keep me informed. I want to know everything—everything."

"Something about the killer's having known all his victims, about his gaining their trust before dispatching each, a cold-blooded, deliberate bastard who takes his time getting to know each of the men first."

"I got just the opposite feeling, that the killer didn't know his victims at all."

"As I said, you'd just be at odds."

She shook this off. "At odds doesn't frighten me, but I'd be hard-pressed to do my best with that man around."

"Good, then it's settled. I'll see to it that Stephens yanks Landry's chain and we snatch Alex Sincebaugh off the case; replace him with someone suitable to you."

"No, no! That'd be the worst thing we could do right now. The chief medical examiner for the city's already been cut out from the herd for slaughter." She breathed a deep sigh of resignation. "There's enough right there to fuel problems between us and whoever's left. I don't want everyone in the NOPD thinking that I'm any more knowledgeable about this case than anyone else; hell, leave that act to Dr. Coran, who I suspect wants the privilege." She was instantly sorry she'd made the remark, wishing she might take it back.

"But Dr. Desinor—"

"Believe me, nothing can be gained if the detectives working the case are given the impression that the investigation has been turned over solely to a psychic detective, Lew. I know this from experience. This case is going to take time, Lew, time and teamwork."

"You'll be reporting to Stephens and me directly, in any case."

"You know how the locals feel when a normal FBI operation takes over in a case. We've got to remain light of foot here."

''I've requested D.C. allow us to fully take charge of this investigation.''

She raised up off the wall, let out an exasperated breath and waved her arms, saying, ''That's no good unless the FBI's been invited in to take charge, Lew. Don't you see?''

''The request is in and under advisement,'' he replied patly. ''While it's being reviewed, we've opted for the forensics help which Jessica Coran will provide, but officially, so far, the case is still in the hands of the NOPD. And officially, you don't exist as an arm of the Bureau, so you're ostensibly working for the NOPD, and our conversing here like this only jeopardizes your cover.''

''So if there's a screwup, the FBI comes out smelling rosewater-fresh either way. I get the picture, Chief.'' She saw it all completely, that top officials in New Orleans and in the state were scrambling to control that which was uncontrollable, not unlike the desire to preserve in coffins that which was impossible to preserve. Meanwhile, none but perhaps Sincebaugh understood the whole and soul of the case.

Jessica Coran had stepped through the doors, and she'd heard the tail end of the discussion, so she quickly jumped in, saying to Meade, ''Lew, we don't want to rock the boat any more than we already have, do you understand me? We don't need or want any macho-shithead FBI gonzo tactics, Lew. By replacing the chief investigating officer, we'd only be building more walls of resistance against Kim, not to mention me, understood?''

Kim felt instantly better, having Jessica aligned with her so perfectly.

Meade now took a long, deep breath. ''Yeah, okay . . . guess you're right, if you two want it that way.''

Anal-retentive, Kim thought, picturing a baby Lew Meade in a sandbox, fighting. ''You sure you're objective where Sincebaugh is concerned, Lew?'' she asked.

''Oh, good Christ, now you're questioning my sense of duty? Listen, Doctor, no one with the rank of lieutenant in a frigging city police force has the right to keep files on a case all to himself, which is what Sincebaugh has been doing.''

''Come on, Lew,'' Jessica said with a frown, ''that's how all cops operate; we all know that.''

Kim fired her heaviest guns. ''The press leaks have saturated the public mind on this case, and you're concerned about a lock on Sincebaugh's files? Maybe if more cops were like Sincebaugh, your governor wouldn't be feeling so much heat over the case.''

''That's all well and good, but we at the FBI have a legitimate interest,'' Meade countered.

Inside the autopsy room behind the double doors, the P.C. was badly dressing someone down. Landry, she imagined.

''You hear that?'' Kim asked. ''My fears are already coming true.'' She returned to her frontal attack on Lew Meade. ''What gives with this character Stephens, Lew? It's a murder investigation. It belongs to Sincebaugh, but Stephens wants maybe to grandstand, to use it as a means to gain attention for himself? To razzle-dazzle the press and the public with his intelligent, up-close and personal, hands-on handling of the crime? Or what? Why's the P.C. so bloody upset with Landry's handling of the case?''

''Stephens believes the press leak is coming from somewhere inside Landry's precinct.''

She nodded, frowned and knowingly breathed this information in. ''I see. And is it?''

''It appears so, yes.''

''You don't think it's a disgruntled Wardlaw, then?''

''Wardlaw has cooperated with us. It's only through him and Stephens and the damned press that I've learned as much about the case as I know,'' Meade replied. ''Stephens provided me with a set of the same files you got. Sincebaugh stonewalled doing so, put it off again and again.''

Jessica Coran stared back at the autopsy room, the shouting inside having risen to a crescendo, Landry getting his licks in now. Jessica then turned to Meade and asked, ''Who officially called us—the FBI—in on the case originally? Stephens?''

As a federal agency, they had no jurisdiction over murder cases without having been called in by the local authorities. Kidnapping was a federal offense, but murder was a local affair.

''Yeah, yeah . . . Stephens first contacted us. I encouraged him to request you, Dr. Coran.''

''You're not being honest with us, Lew,'' Kim countered. ''You want to start over?''

He was unnerved, not by what she said, but by the truth. ''I . . . I'm not completely at liberty to—''

''You saying the governor called us in?'' Kim blurted out, already having guessed the truth and now sharing it with Jessica.

"Let us just say, ladies, that the highest officials in the state are extremely and compassionately concerned."

Lew's usual tight-lipped style had burst with the words. Still, Kim and Jess knew there was more going on behind the story than Lew wished to discuss, but for now, the women chose to say no more. Suddenly Carl Landry stormed from the autopsy room, not bothering to say anything to anyone, disappearing down the yellow tunnel. He was followed by the commissioner and Fouintenac, who each in turn thanked Kim and Jessica for their combined efforts on the case. Fouintenac's handshake was limp as lettuce, while the P.C.'s was sweaty.

Meade raced to catch up with the two high-ranking officials.

"For obvious reasons," Jessica told Kim, "I'd take Sincebaugh for the lot of them."

Kim watched the officials disappear ahead of them. "Now you're reading my mind?"

Together, they walked down the long, silent corridor, going for the elevator.

"So, how is Dr. Wardlaw holding up?" Kim asked Jessica.

"Oh, as well's might be expected under the circumstances."

"They had to throw somebody to the wolves."

"Yeah, you got that right."

"And it looks like they're lining this Detective Sincebaugh up for the next fall."

"Maybe . . ."

"You have anything on your mind, Jessica? I mean about me, about us working together? You having any second thoughts about this whole operation?"

"No, none at all. If I seem a little distracted it's . . . well, it's about something that happened last night."

"Oh, your date with Wing Commander Sand didn't exactly sing?"

This made Jessica laugh, a sound which Kim had not heard very often.

"Ed Sand turned out to be a handful—and I do mean a handful—of trouble. What is it in a man that makes him think your one function on this planet is to be a receptacle for his bodily fluids and parts? Yeah, Ed Sand's allure tarnished rapidly after the flight, trust me."

They now boarded the elevator, the small cubicle barely able to contain the emotions running back and forth between them. Kim felt it as kinetic energy, and saw sparks in the other woman's aura and eyes. Jessica was vibrant, strong-willed, disciplined, but circumstances were chipping away at her.

"Then after I got rid of Ed, an old friend called from Quantico with some disturbing news."

Someone named J.T., Kim thought, reading a flashing thought which belonged to Jessica. "Oh, I'm sorry to hear it."

"Quite disturbing."

"Well, if there's anything I can do, Jess. You know, I'd like to be your friend. I'd like for us to get on . . . if that's possible, of course."

"What do you mean, if it's possible. Sure, it's possible. It's just that . . . we . . . well, I wouldn't know where to begin on this particular bit of news."

"Why don't you start at the beginning. Go ahead, unload."

The elevator opened on the main floor, where a corridor led back to the precinct building and the parking garage where they might find transportation back to their respective hotels. Jessica started ahead of her, as if to walk away, but she stopped, turned and stared for a long moment into Kim's questioning eyes.

"Just how close are you and Paul Zanek?" Jessica's question came like a body blow.

"Close . . . well, we're . . . we've been friends right along. He fairly well ushered me into the Bureau, ushered in psychic investigation with me, you know."

"There just seemed to me to be a lot of . . . tension between you. Look, all I want to know is . . . is he capable of lying to us . . . to me, I mean? Do you think he's capable of lying to me?"

Kim started walking again, now with Jessica keeping up. They passed along the gray and unfinished walls of the concrete tunnel which connected precinct to hospital and morgue. Finally, Kim answered. "I'm not sure what you're driving at, but in answer to your question . . . yes. Yes, he knows how to lie if it serves his purposes, yes."

"Yeah, I might've guessed as much."

"Have you ever been romantically involved with Paul?" asked Kim now, her question taking Jessica by surprise.

"No, not ever, although it wasn't for lack of trying on his part."

"I see. Then this lie he's told you is not of a personal nature?"

"No, it isn't . . . well, yes, it is quite personal to me. . . . "

"Then it has to do with a professional situation?" Kim asked. "The case we're currently on?"

"No . . . I mean, yes . . . I mean, yes, it is about a case, just not this case."

"Matisak?"

"Yes."

"He lied to you about some aspect of the Matisak case?"

"I'm sure he'd call it something other than a lie, but yes, it's what you might call a lie of omission."

"Something's come up and he's failed to alert you; meanwhile, this friend does so?"

"This friend assumed I knew. Four bodies found on an Indian reservation in Oklahoma, hushed up by the local authorities, FBI called in . . ."

"Four bodies?"

"All drained of their blood, a poem written in blood, a poem penned for me, found at the scene."

"Oh, dear God, Jess. I'm sorry. I know how you must feel."

"No, you couldn't know. No one can know this feeling. No one's ever had this kind of a brutal monster stalking her, no one."

"We've got to continue that reading for you, and soon."

"Do you really believe it'd do any good?" The resignation in her voice was a clear bell. She'd not believed any of the images which Kim had related to her during the psychometric reading on the plane coming down; Jess hadn't suspended her disbelief of Kim's powers long enough to consider the symbolic or literal meanings she might ascribe to the reading.

"I've decided to play out Zanek's little game," Jessica said. "He's managed to black out any news coming out of Oklahoma on the killings; he thinks I don't know. If I fly up there to have a look, I tip my hand and maybe he pulls the plug on what we're doing here. Leastways, he pulls the plug on my participation. At any rate, I've sent my own message to Matisak."

"That sounds very dangerous and maybe a little foolish, Jess. What have you done?"

Another look of doubt flitted across Jess's brow before she

carefully chose her words, making Kim wonder if Jess thought her some sort of stoolie or spy for Paul Zanek, sent here to inform on Jess's behavior.

"Tomorrow's headlines," she began. "I gave an exclusive to the *Times-Picayune* about the headway we're making on the Queen of Hearts killings. There's likely to be another photo on page one, and it'll hit the wire services tonight."

"Is playing to the press going to help our case here?"

"I believe so. The Hearts killer, in my estimation, is as anxious to read about himself as everyone else in the city. If we can alert people to the type of killings, down to the victim profile, then maybe we can save a life in the bargain, and maybe . . . just maybe someone out there's run into the Queen of Hearts killer but doesn't know it. I gave them enough to know one way or the other."

"You did this without Meade's approval, didn't you?"

"Wardlaw's given the press very little. All anyone knows is that the gay community is being stalked by a crazed individual who has some sort of vendetta against gays and cross-dressers in particular. That he's blond-haired, possibly balding, or that he wears a human-hair wig, and that on occasions he wears a dark animal-hair wig is all new; he's also right-handed, of medium height but possessing a lot of brute strength."

"Information gleaned from the crime-scene evidence, I gather?"

"Hairs, fibers left at the scene tell us one thing, the angle and depth of the original penetration wounds during initial attack, another."

"Then we know more about this degenerate than I thought." Kim took in a deep breath of air, clearing her head.

"Precisely, down to the kind of carving knife he uses, and the unique playing cards he alone seems to possess, perhaps because he knits them himself."

"I see. A kind of retaliation to Zanek. And in this way you virtually insure that Matisak will come to New Orleans in pursuit of you."

"Not very clever or subtle, but it should get results."

"A little clever and a little crazy, yes."

"What alternative do I have?"

"I see." Kim's tone had become matriarchal. "So, you've exhausted all avenues, have you?"

"Yes, damnit, I have."

"No, Jess, you haven't at all. Let me help you."

Jessica shook her head, replying, "Don't you get it? I'm a scientist, Kim, pure and simple. I thought for a time I could believe in you and your . . . power. Like everyone, I strive to find someone or some thing to worship, but for me it always comes back to science. You've got to understand me to understand that I mean no disrespect, but when I lifted my ankles to you, I was high on medication and not thinking clearly."

Kim half smiled at this and simply said, "I think it was John Tyndale who said that religious feeling was as much a part of the human consciousness as any other feeling; and against it, the waves of science beat in vain."

"Very clever, Doctor, but nonetheless—"

"And Jesus of Nazareth was a scientist."

"Really? I would've guessed you'd have called him a psychic, Doctor."

"Actually, he was the most scientific man who ever walked the earth."

Jessica frowned. "Give it a break, Kim."

"Because he did what you do, Jess. He plunged beneath the material surface of things and found the spiritual cause."

"Spiritual cause, huh? I haven't seen or understood any spiritual cause for some time, Kim. I . . . I . . ."

"I know how lost you feel at times, Jess. How out of touch you become at times with your feelings, your own best impulses. But there is a spirit within you and there is a spiritual cause underlying both the Matisak case and the Hearts case, twisted though it all seems. And God is here with us, on our side, I promise you."

Jessica only stared back at her, biting her lip, on the verge of venting a tear. Instead, she reached out a hand to Kim and firmly gripped her by the forearm: a silent thanks. "I've got to get out of here, get some air. Want to join me?"

"Fact is, I really need to see Alex Sincebaugh," Kim replied.

Jessica nodded, saying, "Keep me apprised," and left.

Kim stared down corridors within corridors, wondering where she might find the tall, striking lieutenant detective. She went in search of the detectives' squad room.

— 20 —

I am content to live
Divided, with but half a heart.

—Henry King

The Old Remorse Bar & Grill was alive with off-duty cops as early as three P.M. when the rotation between day and night duty was made. It was here that war stories were told and old wounds were, if not healed, layered with an alcoholic balm or two, or three. Cops coming on often stopped in before their watch to catch a glimpse of old partners and friends from the day watch and grab a Coke, a burger and cheese fries along with the latest dirt bubbling from the precinct, while guys going off duty loaded up on gin, whiskey and rye.

The precinct today was abuzz with the news of the quite feminine super-sleuth psychic detective who was going to do Alex Sincebaugh's job for him, put a burr under Big Ben deYampert's butt, get the old "Heart File" up and "pumping" like never before (some of the clowns now humming the musical theme of *Entertainment Tonight*).

"Maybe do a triple byyyy-pass!"

"Tug at the ol' heartstrings."

"Ba-dum, ba-dum, ba-dum."

"Get the ticker tickin'!" someone openly shouted, bringing a round of laughs to a table.

The debate was raging when Sincebaugh entered. He'd long since become sick of guys in the department slipping little heart-shaped candies into his drinks, on the seat of his car and elsewhere; he'd grown accustomed to the childish pranks, from crude drawings of hearts with arrows through them to some yokel's idea of heartfelt poeticisms written on the bathroom walls both here and at the precinct. He'd become almost desensitized to the callous and hard-hearted black humor revolving around the Hearts case like onerous flies about raw meat left on a backyard barbecue.

He'd heard the joke making the rounds, all about the Achy-Breaky Heart NOPD-fashion, and now he caught the drift of the conversation long before everyone was silenced by the whisper-wave that had begun to spread through the semi-darkened room, news that Sincebaugh had entered.

"It'll take some kind of voodoo witch to locate a devil like that bloody heart-eatin' bastard. . . ."

"She's a voodoo princess, all right . . . some looker."

"Sincebaugh's a fool. Wouldn't mind if she did a little psychic readin' on me."

"Aren't you worried, Malloy, that she'll find out you can't get it up?"

"Fuck you, Bennett."

"Been a real kick in the nuts for Alex, though."

"Newsies are havin' a field day with this."

"Psychics—*woooooooo*—here in New Orleans—*woooooooo*—so, what else is new?"

"This one's no ten-buck swami with a crystal ball. She's damned good."

"She's no back-alley palm reader's what I hear."

Then total silence as everybody realized that the lieutenant had entered and stepped to the bar. "Give me a beer and make me a ham on rye, will you, Stubby?" Alex ordered more than asked. "I'll be at my desk." He indicated his usual back booth, but before he left the bar, he turned and said to the assembled cops, "You people have any idea what the fuck you're talking about? Do you?"

A guy named Bennett, who'd gotten smashed here the night before and had been talked into singing "I left my heart in the Mississippi," stuttered and replied, "Hey, Alex . . . it's only talk, man. Guys blowin' off steam."

Alex targeted Bennett, locking him into place with a cold stare as he said, "Psychics may be of use when somebody's pet Persian cat is missing or when a dog is the only eyewitness, so you need someone to communicate with the dog. It's fine if a jewelry store wants to hire a psychic and post a sign saying this store is under psychic surveillance. I got no problem with that. But read your goddamned criminal investigation and interrogation manual, Bennett. It's a popular fallacy to think that a clairvoyant can give valuable information with respect to a homicide investigation. They've got no damned business in a homicide investigation.''

No one disputed the lieutenant. He stood there, wanting someone to dare disagree. Bennett just went back to his drink.

This only made Alex more determined and angry. He began to pace about the bar in nervous-tiger fashion, the others watching out of the sides of their eyes for him to make the next move.

He settled himself against the bar and said, "Fact is, these so-called psychic people just arouse the hopes of the family members, and to justify the dollar/man-hours to follow up on a bunch of empty leads . . . well, enough said.''

"Well, Lieutenant,'' said one young officer, "seems to me, you're telling it to the wrong crowd.''

"Yeah,'' agreed a second, taking some courage.

"Why don't you tell it to the captain?'' suggested Bennett.

"Carl Landry knows how I fuckin' feel. No matter how sincere a so-called psychic may be, the actual hits she makes are usually due to some bit of information she was previously exposed to.''

Still no one disputed him. *God,* he thought, *I'd really like to throw a punch at Bennett. That'd feel great.* Instead, he continued to shout his opinion. "These psychic detectives are con men, or con women, even if sometimes they don't recognize their own con. They're cunning people with photogenic memories and steel-trap minds, no doubt. Their lucky guesses are far from lucky guesses. They use open-ended thinking, seeing multiple end points to a case, just like any good detective, but the bozos who're taken in by them confer on them this incredibly wide margin for error that no cop is afforded ever.''

"You ever work with psychics before, Lieutenant?'' asked Stubby from behind the bar, listening intently, curious.

"Where's that ham sandwich?'' Alex sharply countered.

"Gettin' it . . .''

"Whataya mean, wide margin?'' Bennett asked of him.

"Psychic says!'' Alex mimicked the famous host of *Family Feud.* " 'I seeeeee a bodyyyyy . . . a bodyyyyy of water . . . yes, water . . . near the body.' So figure it out.''

"You mean like a lake?"

"A lake, the Atlantic fucking Ocean, a roadside puddle, a doggie dish with mosquito eggs germinating in it, or maybe a mailbox with the name Walters, Waters or Pond on it, or maybe a goddamned billboard with the words Aqua Velva printed across it, and since aqua is Latin for water and the sign just happens to be fifty feet from the body, or a hundred, or five hundred, the psychic is *right on.* What the hell does 'near the body' mean in exact feet, Bennett? You got any idea?"

There was some laughter at this.

Alex kept on talking. "It's anybody guess, but you can bet that somewhere in the vicinity of a body you'll find some water somewhere, somehow, and 'cause the psychic says it's so, it's called a psychic hit! Same goes for when the con man calls for a large tree near the body or a whole damned forest. How large is large, and maybe a billboard has a plantation oak pictured across it, so that'll do just as well as a large tree, or the subdivision being advertised is Oak Lawn Lake, so you get two hits with one psychic stone—an oak tree and a goddamned lake!"

More laughter filled the bar, and a few cops hoisted their glasses in a toast of agreement and cheer.

"It's not mystical so much as it is the law of truly large numbers. So every goddamn year there are thousands of cops nationwide hunting down missing persons who can be found near water and a large tree. No big surprise when some place a psychic actually locates a dead or alive, every year or so."

"What about the ones who're really good, Lieutenant? You know, the psychics who've repeatedly been right over and over?" asked one female cop from a booth across the room.

"They're better at it, smarter, more cunning. 'I see a body, near an old church . . . a windmill . . . a road sign.' You know how many damned old churches and waterwheels are out there? These guys, they shotgun information, scatter it about rapid-fire, all generalized until they see some naive cop like you, Bennett, raise an eyebrow, and then they lock on, knowing what you know. They play twenty questions with you and they win every time."

"You've worked with 'em before, haven't you, Lieutenant?'' asked Kellerman, who was way off his turf for some reason.

"I have, and without useful results. Bastard says to us, 'You'll find the boy in a shallow grave.' Christ, stands to reason! I mean, if you murder some little kid, you don't go out and buy a coffin and dig a six-foot grave, now do you? Besides, how many murderers you know carry a shovel around with them. Ever try to dig a grave with your bare hands?''

This brought on another bout of laughter while some people were leaving and others entered. Sincebaugh, allowing all his pent-up frustration over the case to bubble over, kept on talking. "Meanwhile, a lot of wasted time, wrong leads, raised hopes, all for nothing except the almighty dollar, the taxpayers' money, which goes direct to the psychic.''

"No wonder you're not too happy with this.'' It was one of the Internal Affairs guys he'd met at the diner where he'd jumped the gun on the two would-be robbers. He hadn't seen him where he'd been sitting in a booth with a couple of other cops, one being the other IAD officer. "You're talking about the Tommy Harkness case a couple years ago?''

Jesus, these assholes've been climbing around in my file for days, Alex thought "Sleight-of-mouth, that's all this voodoo crap's about, trust me,'' he said aloud.

"Clever, cunning, able to outwit men and leap tall buildings at a single bound; sounds like maybe you're a little afraid of her, Alex,'' quipped Kellerman, a man Alex's size and build.

"Sandwich is up,'' shouted the man behind the counter.

Sincebaugh, frowning at Kellerman, now with exactly the right face to punch standing before him, knew he could do nothing, not with IAD men in a nearby booth just waiting for him to do something stupid.

It was all so much like a setup, he began to feel a creeping paranoia come over him. He turned to Stubby, paid for his drink and sandwich and took in a deep breath of air. He was trying desperately to peel back the layers; not only did the onion here stink, but layers of it had to be carefully stripped and pared away to find all the underlying meaning.

When he turned, he had control of himself. He'd once been told by Big Ben that if you felt paranoia down to your bones in a given situation, you probably had good reason to be paranoid, that sometimes paranoia was the healthiest response, the first warning bell on the bullshit detector.

"I'm not afraid of any goddamned spoon-bender, and maybe now I've said enough on the subject." He stepped away from the bar, went to his booth and began to slowly consume his meal. Others in the bar sensed his need not only to be alone, but to be left alone over the matter of both the Heart case and the new guns in town, particularly the psychic gun.

Still, he wondered who'd sicced IAD on him, and what connection the young vultures had with Kellerman. Did they have something on Kellerman to force him all the way over here from his precinct to get into a confrontation with Alex, provoke a fight and ultimately send Alex on an undeniably long vacation, maybe land him on the police shrink's list of incorrigibles? If so, Kellerman wasn't trying very hard. At least, not yet anyway.

Through the door bounded Ben deYampert, his hands filled with the files they'd talked about going over. Both men knew they could get next to nothing done at the desk with the phone ringing constantly, so they'd agreed to meet here for something to eat and to glance over some of the documentation on the Hearts crimes. He waved Ben over, and Ben almost made it before Kellerman got in his face with a crude joke he'd heard about the Hearts cases, something to do with the missing organs having been crammed up the anal canals of each of the gay victims and Frank Wardlaw not wanting to get his hands dirty searching there. Ben shoved past Kellerman, ignoring him, but Alex could see the purple anger in his partner's eyes.

Stubby called out for Ben's lunch order.

"Send those guys over some artichoke hearts on me, Stubby," shouted Kellerman, drawing a little nervous laughter around the darkened bar and grill.

"Lame-o, real lame-o, Kellerman. Set me up with one of your famous pig barbecues, Stubby," Ben replied before squeezing into the booth opposite Alex.

"This place is crawling with paranoia, pal," Alex warned him.

"Is-zat right?" Ben gave an appreciative smile and a wink. "What'd I miss?"

"You missed the IAD guys at the other booth."

"Didn't see 'em, no . . . but I wondered what Kellerman was doing so far off his stomping grounds this time a day."

"He and his squeaky partner Bennett've been doing their level best to pick a fight. I think they're hoping I'll throw the first punch."

"Setup?"

"Yeah, and it almost worked."

"Restraint, Alex . . . restraint in the Old Remorse," replied Ben in a balladeer's voice, finishing in his best imitation of Andy Rooney with, "I . . . like . . . that . . . So, how'd it go in the morgue?"

"I was thrown out."

"Thrown out of the morgue?"

"Carl got pissed." Alex looked across at his friend and partner, a growing smile coming over him until both men laughed heartily, causing others in the bar to wonder what was being said between them.

After a few minutes, the IAD boys left. Not long after Kellerman motioned Bennett to the door and they too disappeared, leaving the place in a pleasant stillness, people at the various tables talking animatedly now among themselves. No one was disappointed that IAD had vacated their watering hole, leaving it the sacrosanct place that it was.

"You think they bugged the booth?" asked Ben.

"No, I don't think so."

"But they were here before you arrived?"

"Yeah, they were."

Ben was equal in his suspicions. He called Stubby over to their booth with a conspiratorial grunt and a large, curling finger. "Anybody use this booth today before us?"

"Nobody."

"You lie to me, Stubby, and I swear you'll be too damned short to be called Stubby ever again, understood?"

"I'm telling you, nobody was in here before you guys, not today, not in this booth, no."

"Whataya mean, not today?"

"I don't know . . . couple of guys were in here last night

asking questions, or so Wanda told me. Wanda said they asked when you guys come in here and where you usually sat.''

"Christ, they did bug the damned booth.''

"Find it.''

Stubby had come over with a bowl of soup which neither of them had ordered. He now placed it on the table, and he dropped a small metal device into the soup, the device sinking like a lead weight. "Not to worry, gentlemen, not in my place. Enjoy the soup, Ben. It's on the house. And as for you, Lieutenant Sincebaugh, you haven't been in touch with your old man for weeks. He's worried about you.''

"How the hell would you know, Stubby?''

"He's on the phone over here.'' Stubby indicated with a curt motion of his head. "We had a nice, long chat. Great guy, from what I could gather. Got some idea you're in over your head with this Hearts case thing.''

"Oh, please . . .''

"He's like any father . . . just worried about your health. Go on, talk to 'im.''

"Whataya saying, Stubby? He's still on the line, holding for me?''

"Yeah, now go talk to the man.''

Frowning, Alex slid from the booth and located the phone behind the bar. He talked amiably with his father for a long time, the old man allowing him the freedom to get a few things off his chest, and Alex felt good at having had his father to use as a sounding board. Before hanging up, he promised to come by and see his dad at the first available opportunity. His father agreed with everything he said about the Department's putting a psychic on the case.

"You take some time off and we'll go fishing, like the old days, son. Don't let the bastards wear you down, Alex'' were his father's last, reassuring words.

Alex almost allowed his paranoia to kick in again when he cradled the phone back into place. If that asshole Meade could touch IAD and guys like Kellerman and Bennett, then why not put Alex's father on his case? When was the last time his father had asked him to go fishing?

— 21 —

O heart! O heart, if she'd but turn her head,
You'd know the folly of being comforted.

—Yeats

Sincebaugh looked up from his unofficial desk—the end corner booth at the Old Remorse—to see that it was Dr. Kim Desinor casting an intrusive shadow over the dossier he was reading, information on a drug case he had been working off and on now for the past several weeks in addition to the Hearts case.

"Well . . ." he began, sizing her up. "So, Doctor, is it? Whatever you were peddling back at the morgue to the yo-yos won't wash here, so don't waste your time or mine."

The place was fairly well filled with cops, both uniformed and plainclothes—obviously a favored watering hole of the NOPD, she'd surmised the moment she had entered.

"Joseph Wambaugh could do a story about this place, no doubt. Call it the Onion Room, maybe."

"It doesn't smell that bad." Alex momentarily reflected on how he had himself said to Ben before Ben had left to return to the precinct that there was so much deceit and mendacity in the air that it had to be peeled away like an onion. But he didn't dwell on the coincidence. "Like I said, what're you selling here, Doctor?"

He made his final word sound like a racial slur. She asked if she could take a seat across from him.

"Yeah, sure . . . sit down."

"Look," she began as she slid into the booth, "I can understand your reluctance to accept me—or any psychic—here on your case, but why not at least give it a try? What can it hurt?"

"Nothing ventured, nothing gained, you mean? Isn't that

what you so-called psychic detectives count on? So long's you get paid?''

''You know, Detective, I see no reason for your hostility or your judgmental—''

''I've been a cop for over twelve years, Doctor, and I've worked some pretty bizarre shit that would curl your pretty hair.''

''Is that right?''

''And I've worked with your kind before, and you're all alike.''

''Is that right?''

They were becoming loud; others around the room were staring.

''You throw up a smoke screen of predictions and clairvoyant visions, virtually all vague and self-fulfilling prophecies any high-IQ Mensa type might count on to come true, and you squeeze all you can from these so-called pre—''

''You mean like when I named Lennox and his killer?''

''Give me a break, lady. Odds-on guesswork, the significance of which is only colored in later by gullible cops, ESP advocates and a public only too willing to believe. In this case Stephens and Meade and that clown from the mayor's office.''

''Funny you don't include your captain in that group.''

He sat in stony silence.

''Naturally,'' she continued, ''we all have a built-in wish to believe, fed by the media, which has a tendency to exaggerate psychic claims.'' She sounded as if she agreed with him and this threw his timing off.

''Yeah, right, the press so sensationalizes you people that you're made saints, heroes, because sensational sells. You think the NOPD hasn't used psychics in the past? In every department in the country there's at least one cop wasting his time and the taxpayers' money by remaining in touch with a psychic . . . ahhh . . .'' He hesitated.

''Go on!''

''A psychic dick.''

''Maybe I need you to talk to my . . .'' She stopped herself from saying boss, angry she'd almost revealed the fact she was working for Paul Zanek. ''My shrink.''

''That's a good one, a psychic who goes to a shrink.''

"Just like cops," she said coyly. "Psychics have problems in their relationships too." Her eyes were beautiful, lustrous, and they glistened even as they bore into him like two small harpoons. "I know how important this case is to you, that it's consumed your life, your every waking moment, not to mention your subconscious."

She saw him tense before she felt the rising wall around him come back up like an ascending shield or cloaking device. She'd come a little too close in her assessment of Alex Sincebaugh, and this understandably made him uneasy. Any normal person would be a bit paranoid as a result, but a cop was doubly so. A cop was trained to reveal deceit, and who could blame him. She tried to counter what she'd said by adding, "All cops can be obsessive; it's the nature of the beast, isn't it?"

"You're smooth; I'll give you that much, Dr. Desinor."

"Check with Miami-Dade. I was once a cop myself before I became a professional psychic. Check my record. Ask about the Hughes case. I knew the killer—a failed medical student— had cut off the little boy's ears after the boy was dead and that his kidnap ransom request would only yield a corpse. Ask about how I pinpointed the identity of the mad doctor who kidnapped the kid, not for ransom but for vengeance against his father, who'd been chiefly responsible for keeping the killer out of medical practice."

"All hits an ordinary cop like myself could have made, no doubt."

"No doubt . . ." She took in a deep breath of air. "All right, okay . . . agreed, but none of the other cops made the connections."

"So, now you take yourself seriously, and you figure there's more money in being a psychic consultant than in being a cop. I get it. Now, if you don't mind—"

"Do you have some hang-up against making money?"

"Only when it corrupts."

"Cops . . . you're all alike."

"What's that supposed to mean?"

Stubby came to the table and asked, "Alex, you going to buy somethin' for the lady or what?"

Sincebaugh asked her what she'd like.

"Tea, if you have any."

"Tea . . . lady, this is a bar."

"Glass of chablis, then."

Stubby nodded, jotted down the item on a notepad as if it were the U.S. Constitution he was putting down and finally stepped away.

As soon as he left, she leaned in over the table and said to Alex, "When a psychic succeeds, you guys are unwilling to admit that any psychic guidance is responsible, but the moment a psychic fails, you abuse her with ridicule and blame."

"Oh, I'm sorry if I've offended your delicate sensibilities, Doctor." He laughed a bit mirthlessly at his own response.

She bit back her anger and let his sarcasm pass. "As for quitting Miami-Dade, well, that's a long story."

"I've got time and Stubby's going to take all day with that wine you ordered."

"All right. My leaving had to do with Florida's gung-ho, fundamentalist-Christian, hell-and-brimstone state's attorney, Don Q. Weaver—Weavil, we called him. Guy announced his own personal belief regarding psychic powers and denounced them as coming from the Evil One."

"Satan?"

"Weaver almost single-handedly pushed through an order to prohibit all law enforcement in the state to refrain from doing the Devil's work, forbidding any future consultation with psychic detectives."

He'd been trying not to laugh, holding it back as Stubby arrived with the wine. "Anything on the menu you'd like, miss?" Stubby asked.

"No, nothing for now . . . thank you."

The greasy little man ambled away with a pronounced limp, and she continued. "Anyway, Weaver started to invoke scripture, since he was a part-time Baptist minister."

"You're kidding. The state's attorney was a part-time minister?"

"Baptist. And in his faxes to the department, he began quoting from Deuteronomy eighteen, verses ten and eleven. To paraphrase: God's followers are forbidden from using divination, or an observer of times—that's me—or an enchanter, or a witch, a charmer, a consulter with familiar spirits or a wizard or necromancer.''

"Maybe the Reverend Weaver was right. You do have an enchanting way about you, Doctor.''

"Are you kidding? He went on to tell us we shouldn't be dabblin' or experimentin' or doin' nothin' on the fringe of occult powers. 'Ultimately nothin' good ever came of it,' he said."

Alex laughed, and his smile was infectious.

She smiled in return, sipping at her wine. "Weaver finished his fax with, 'I feel the success of my office in the courtrooms across this fair state of ours is the direct result of the Holy Spirit working His word through me, and I don't want any other spirits to undo that good work.' ''

"You quit being a cop on account of that double-talking bozo?''

"Not exactly, and I'm glad you don't object to me on religious or moral grounds. You see, Weaver had heard about me. Some of the other cops called me the psychic cop; you know, good record, strangely successful, all that, not unlike you, Alex. Anyway, Weaver made it a vendetta to get rid of me.''

"Jesus, sounds like a hard-ass.''

"More to the point, he was a real prick," she corrected him. "Anyway, he went so far as to contact the Committee for Scientific Investigation of Claims of the Paranormal.''

"Yeah, I've heard of them. Somewhere in Ohio?''

She hesitated. It wasn't everyone who knew of the infamous committee. "Buffalo, New York, but they have centers all over, and they don't take any claims of the paranormal lightly. They're a dogmatic Scientism group that some call the New Inquisition. They made life hell for me. Still do from time to time. Imagine, a fundamentalist in the Bible Belt calls on a Yankee science group to sic them on a lone psychic—me.''

"I guess it comes with the territory if you're going to make supernatural gestures like hanging out a shingle that tells people you can speak to the dead, Doctor.''

"Supernatural is a theological term; refers to all those miraculous intrusions into the material world: deities, spirits, all that. Paranormal is processes and laws observable in nature, but which have not yet been scientifically explained.''

"There's a significant difference?'' He did find her fascinating and beautiful to look at.

"Damn straight there's a difference. The paranormal is no more scientifically unexplainable than a certain disease or area of the brain we lack knowledge of. The fact we can't explain something doesn't mean that it's invalid.''

"So far I'm with you, Doctor, but remember you are dealing with a cop, so let's take it slow.''

"Psychic functioning is merely an unexplained biological sense, rather than necessarily a communication with a spirit world, you see.''

"Aha, I think. Does it go something like this? A psychic doesn't perform miracles, she just does the miraculous?''

She frowned but went on. "Critics and people like Weaver, and perhaps you, have intentionally blurred the distinction between what is truly supernatural and what is purely paranormal.''

"I see,'' he said without conviction, sipping at a light beer.

"Anyway, I returned to school, got my degree in psychology, parapsychology, and psychic research—some call it *psi.*'' She pronounced the word like *sigh,* and his thoughts lingered over her lovely intonations.

"And I'm presently a member of the Parapsychological Association of Amer—''

"So you've since legitimized your telepathy, your clairvoyance and your precognition through the accumulation of doctorates . . . I see.''

She let the remark go by, sipping again at her wine while he finished his beer.

"Actually, I'm primarily into *retro-cognition,* dredging up images out of the past, although I get flashes of the future, and PK and psychometric observa—''

"*Peee Kayyy,*'' he said, repeating the letters. "Don't tell me. Psychokinesis.''

"That's right.''

"What State's Attorney Weaver would call laying on of hands?''

She laughed now, and he enjoyed her smile, allowing his eyes to linger.

She felt a definite attraction for him, and what now seemed a permanent half-smile or cocky snicker on the parted lips seemed both natural and boyish. She sensed his interest in her was growing.

"Tell me this," he said. "How do you know when you're actually seeing some so-called truth come out of this fifth dimension you people speak of, and when you're just maybe reading the mind of the cop or the M.E. who's standing alongside you? You know that Wardlaw and Jessica Coran were already thinking the Lennox man was no victim of the Bleeding Heart killer, same as me, and it may well be that Frank or Dr. Coran knew of the disappearance of a man named Lennox long before you arrived here. Maybe, Doctor, you'd better leave for home while the gettin' is good. We po' boys in the NOPD may not be's dumb as them what's in Dade County, Miami."

"Either way, whether I read the M.E.'s thoughts or was truly clairvoyant in that room, Lieutenant, I got it right, and that's what's bothering you, isn't it?"

"I know it's got to bother Frank, and for that I'd pay your fee out of pocket, but going for the real killer isn't going to be fun and parlor games, Doctor. I know New Orleans, and when the collective *they* find out what you really are, you'll be looking at an old-fashioned witch hunt. Superstitions die hard here."

"I know all about New Orleans, and as for going home, Lieutenant . . . well, I am home. I grew up not far from here."

He was momentarily taken aback by this. "Really?"

"That's right."

Now he saw the Cajun blood clearly, and he wondered why he'd missed it before. She'd done a great deal to conceal it, he now realized. Maybe there was more to her than he'd previously thought.

"Where'd you attend school?"

She recognized it as the prying cop question it was. "None of your damned business."

"Okay." He guessed it to be St. Luke's or Mark's, where the parish was made up of the poor. She didn't want to be reminded of it, he mentally noted. That was *her* business, as she said, but if it had a bearing on her being here with her nose in his case, it was his business as well, and maybe he'd look into it on his own time.

She seemed to be reading his thoughts, so he superstitiously cut them off, asking if she'd like another glass of wine.

"Oh, no, no, thank you. One's sufficient for this time of day, and having had no lunch, well . . ."

"No lunch? We'll have to remedy that. Stubby!" he called. "A menu, please."

"No, please, it's a bit late to eat anyway, and I really have to be going."

She got up, preparing to leave, and he politely stood across from her now. "I'm sorry if I come on strong, Dr. Desinor, but that's the only way I know how. Landry's going to regret ever calling your hotline. They're already calling him Captain of the Kook Squad, and you're already front-page news, and by tomorrow who knows what the press'll be saying about you, me, the Department. Either way, when the circus comes to town, the media is first at the center ring."

"I didn't expect to remain hidden here."

"Well, no, I should expect you'd want all the publicity you could get, right alongside Dr. Coran. I heard about her press conference through the grapevine. Another reason I was against you and her . . . your coming in on the case, rather. More publicity is one thing this case doesn't need, despite the arguments you no doubt have heard on the other side, that the public should be warned. Hell, the public has been warned!"

"I think you should know we're conducting an exhumation of the Surette body at dawn."

"What? Whose idea was this?"

She bit her lip. "I'm not a hundred percent on who first suggested it, but I'd hazard a guess it was your Captain Landry. The P.C., Meade and Fouintenac were reluctant, but Jessica and Landry pushed hard for it and got their way."

"And what about Frank?"

"Dr. Wardlaw left somewhat abruptly when the discussion turned to exhuming Surette. As I said, Chief Meade wasn't too keen on the idea either, but your Captain Landry fought for it. Said your investigation keeps leading back to Surette, that is. He gave you due credit."

"So what will Dr. Coran be looking for on exhumation?"

"Not her . . . well, not her alone anyway . . ."

"Wardlaw?"

"No . . . me."

"You?" He stared so hard she felt it like a blow. "You're telling me you've talked those idiots into an exhumation for the purpose of a fuc—a blasted seance?"

"Well, honestly . . . it really wasn't my idea, and neither is it technically a seance, but rather a psi reading. In a seance—"

"Wasn't your idea? And I suppose it wasn't your idea to psycho-feel and psychobabble your way across Lennox's body either? That you were just an innocent bystander who happened to be drafted by Stephens, Lew Meade and the others to perform?"

"Wait just a minute, Lieutenant! I'm doing my job. And the reason I came looking for you was so that—"

"Yeah, I'm not so clear on that. Why did you come looking for me, and wait just a minute, lady! You're not doing *your* job. You're trying to do *my* job."

"That's nonsense. I wouldn't have your job for the world."

"Oh, really?"

"Really! Now, if you've got a legitimate complaint or a problem with this exhumation tomorrow morning, take it up with your captain, Lieutenant!"

"Damn straight I will."

She gracefully turned on her heels and exited, momentarily bathing the place in light as she pushed angrily through the door, muttering a curse under her breath.

Alex started for the door, stopping halfway, and from the corner of his eye he saw Dr. Jessica Coran staring fixedly at him, something smoldering within her which he could not here and now fathom. He realized only now that he'd rushed toward the retreating Dr. Desinor like a schoolboy in pursuit and was left standing in the middle of the room and rooted there for the moment, with everyone's eyes on him, but none so piercing as Dr. Coran's.

"Just who in hell does that woman think she is?" Alex asked Jessica Coran as he approached her darkened booth.

"She's quite amazing, really," replied Jessica in a calm

born of a double whiskey sour. "If you'd stop fighting her long enough to look clearly through to what's right for your— this case, Lieutenant, you'd see that she's far more an asset than a liability. She was right on with the Lennox case, and I've seen amazing footage on her back at Quantico. You hear about the kidnapping and murder of that banker in Decatur, Georgia, name of Sendak?"

"You telling me that Kim Desinor was instrumental in solving the case?"

"And she did it long-distance. Never left her lab . . ." Jessica hesitated, realizing what she was saying. "In Florida . . . where she works out of an old, remolded lab . . ." *God, that sounded lame,* she thought.

He considered this in silence, sliding into the seat opposite Jessica. "You're a scientist, a reasonable person, Dr. Coran."

"I like to think so."

"God. I mean, an exhumation of the Surette corpse, followed by a seance. What the hell's next, Doctor?"

"I don't see that it'd be much different than what went on today."

"But how can you, a person of science, possibly go for this kind of theatrical display?"

He'd noticed Jessica's ongoing interest in Dr. Desinor, and he wondered if they'd arrived at the bar together, and if so, why Coran hadn't joined them from the outset. Had she been watching their conversation from here, how much Kim Desinor and he had had to drink together, the length of the other woman's stay? Obviously, she'd witnessed the blowup.

Jessica's eyes were sending pinched little darts in his direction, but now her head dropped, and she pretended to have seen and heard nothing. Just like a woman, he thought, wondering if he should not make a hasty retreat back to the false security of his booth.

"Well, are you going to answer me?" he said. "How can you stand aside and allow a body to be exhumed for such purposes?"

"My reasoning's simple enough, Lieutenant. If the body is exhumed, I'll have an opportunity at it as well, and we'll know for certain if this Surette character was in fact our killer's first victim or not. That's where my interest lies, and if getting it done via Kim Desinor works, then so be it.''

"You're smarter than I thought."

"So's your captain."

"Landry's running with the foxes at the moment."

This instantly angered her. "Is it me, Sincebaugh, or does everybody rub you the wrong way lately?"

"You got no idea what you're talking about, Dr. Coran, so don't start on me, okay?"

"We've got a lot in common, you and me."

"Jesus God," he moaned.

She downed what remained of her double and stared hard across at him. "You're a walking raw nerve, Alex, but you can't treat everyone like . . . like . . ."

"Look, if I want a dressing-down, I'll call Ben back in here." Ben had put it to him much in the same way as she was doing now. "What I don't need at this point is another *wife*." His icy glare was unmistakable. He wanted to be left alone. When she held her ground, he got up, returned to his own booth and snatched open one of the files he'd been looking through earlier, tilting it toward what little light he could find and leaning back in pretended peace.

But something told him that Coran wasn't going to go away, and in fact he felt the dagger of her stare penetrating deeper and deeper into him, twisting just enough to make him squirm. He looked up to find her standing over him.

"What?" he asked.

"I saw the way you two were looking at one another. You could work well together, if you gave her a chance."

"Are you kidding? She knows I have no regard for the black arts and no respect for the way she earns a living."

Jessica tensed visibly, the veins in her neck throbbing. She wanted to set him straight about Kim; she wanted to tell Sincebaugh the truth about their relationship. Perhaps it would bring him around if he knew that they both worked out of Quantico. And since Paul Zanek had lied to her, she wanted to hurt the bastard too, and this might be a way, but it could also backfire and hurt Kim as well.

"That's bullshit, Alex. She does the same kind of work as you. I know about that tape of you in the diner and frankly—"

"Damn that Landry. What's he doing, holding a daily screening for everybody at the precinct?"

"He had Kim look it over. She was impressed by your psychic guesswork prior to the robbery attempt. She wants to work with you, not against you . . . and she's . . ."

"She's what?"

"Sincere."

"Sincere . . . sincere? What're we playing at here, Dr. Coran? Is sincerity supposed to make everything in New Orleans all right tonight?"

"You are insufferable, aren't you? Meade tried to warn me."

He tossed aside the file and raised his hands as if shot through the heart, apologizing all at once. "It's me, I guess. It's my life right now . . . it's an unholy mess and . . ."

"You're maybe letting this case overtake your life?"

He declined to answer, granting her a brooding stare instead.

"Listen," she said, "I happen to know how that goes, and trust me. Somewhere, somehow, you've got to hold onto some corner where you can get away from it."

"So, you ever take your own advice, Dr. Coran?"

"Sometimes . . . not often enough, but sometimes."

"As with this Matisak thing? That's what the press conference was all about, wasn't it?"

"The press conference was on the Hearts Killer, and I'd like you to be present at my next conference for questions."

"Everybody wants me around and for what? Window dressing?"

"No one knows this case like you do. We both . . . we all know that from just looking over your meticulous case file notes."

"Look, Dr. Coran, you know the score; you've been to hell and back; you know what it's like to be given a case, to get involved in it heavily only to see it snatched away. It's my case, they tell me, my responsibility from the outset, right? But every time I turn around someone else's nose is in it and her nose . . . this ridiculous miracle approach . . . well . . ."

"I pushed for the Surrette exhumation, and so did Landry. Kim was against it." She slipped into the dark booth.

"Yeah, Carl's a great one for going along with whichever

way the wind blows these days.''

"Look, if nothing else, it'll give me an opportunity to compare the scars on the Surette corpse with the more recent ones. You may well be vindicated in your own hunch that Surette was the first victim.''

He nodded, conceding the point. "Maybe something good could come of it. I just hope the press doesn't get wind of it.''

"They will. But there's no foundation to your belief that Kim Desinor is a charlatan, now is there? What're you basing your opinion on? Past experience? Kim's not like anyone I've ever known or met.''

"What, you think because someone puts the word psychic after her name that she's automatically directed by some divine light?''

"No, I'm thinking you've got a hell of a lot to learn about women, and one woman in particular.''

"Ask Ben, my partner.''

"Ask him what?''

"He'll tell you straight. I haven't been fit company for anyone since . . . since . . .''

"Since the first Hearts victim, I know. But together we can help you get through this, Alex, if you'll let us.''

"You've been talking to that damned deYampert, haven't you?''

"Yes, about you,'' she confessed. "He's very—''

"Nosy, an old washerwoman, I know.''

"Concerned is what he is.''

"I know. The big bastard.''

"Ben's your friend and so am I. What's so wrong about accepting help where it's offered, Alex? No one . . . no one should be in this . . . alone.''

"Is that how it is with you, Dr. Coran? You feel out there . . . alone?''

She forced a phony smile and lied. "No, not really. I have the backing of the entire FBI, remember?''

"Yeah, right . . . the entire FBI.''

"Thanks Alex,'' she said, getting up. "I'm glad we had this little talk. Thanks for listening.''

He thought he saw a tear drop, but she turned her head away

as she made for the door. He started to call her back, but she was bent on racing out.

Stubby frowned from behind the bar and shook his head in wonderment. "No luck with the ladies today, huh, Lieutenant?" he called out. This made others in the room laugh. "What gives?"

"None of your goddamned business, Stubby."

"Sure, sure . . . Lieutenant."

"Thanks for understanding, Stubby."

"Hey, Alex, *no problemo,* sure . . ." Stubby went back to wiping glasses and picking up loose change and refilling the pretzel dishes while humming "Achy-Breaky Heart."

Alex thought about how he'd alienated Dr. Desinor; he thought about how he'd alienated others recently, including, to some degree, his partner, Ben, whom he hadn't wanted to trust with the truth about his nightmares—and now he knew why he'd waited so long to even mention them.

"See the Department shrink," Ben had advised.

He had told Ben to go to hell, so Ben, being the wise guy that he was, took his partner's problems to Jessica Coran!

Christ, everything was screwed around. He thought about pulling himself off the Hearts case, putting in for some time off, getting the hell out of New Orleans altogether, taking his father up on the offer of a fishing expedition, renting a house boat maybe, lying in the sun for days on end.

"Where would you go if you did?" Ben had earlier asked.

"Don't know . . . maybe the peninsula. Anyplace with lots of water, sand, sun, someplace where they've got only one cop, and he rides a bicycle."

"No cops, huh?"

"No cops."

"You trying to tell me something, pard?"

"No cops."

Maybe the notion wasn't so wild after all, he now thought.

Just then Big Ben rushed into the bar, his eyes darting in every direction until he nailed his partner at the phone, where he was about to dial his father, make plans. "We got a call, Alex. Could be another vic."

"Oh, Christ . . . where?"

"East Canal Street apartment, just above Robert E. Lee Boulevard."

"Indoors, you mean?"

"Indoors."

"Thank God for small favors. The usual M.O.?"

"That's the message received, yeah."

"Better get the hell over there."

"I brought the squad around."

Stubby, watching and listening from behind the bar, shouted to the retreating figures as they barged out, "See ya later, fellas. Don't go wearin' your hearts on your sleeves."

22

Man with the head, and woman with the heart.

—Tennyson

Sincebaugh and deYampert uneasily stepped into a completely new yet familiar, expected nightmare at 34 East Canal Street, which was in an older section of the city where unkempt, weedy courtyards dominated along with boarded-up windows and going-out-of-business signs. The streets here were dirty and narrow, but quaint with cobblestone pathways. Here the old stone buildings had French windows that cranked by hand and hung out over the street, black wrought-iron gates in sad need of repair about each front and rusted-out terraces leaning out overhead. Sincebaugh thought that while it was not the loveliest area in the city, neither was it the most squalid. The racial mix here was predominantly black, Cajun and Spanish, and if you blinked you might see the ghost of a Conquistador standing in one of the dark courtyards.

Neighbors had heard nothing, seen nothing. The entire scene reminded Sincebaugh of the *Murders in the Rue Morgue,* down to the dapper little man with mustache and suspenders who called himself the superintendent and who had discovered the body when, after two days, he had not seen Miss Marie Dumond, a light-skinned mulatto/Cajun, in or out of the building. When he'd begun to notice a foul odor coming from within, he'd used his pass key and found the blood-spattered scene. Even then, perhaps due to the hysteria that overtook him, he still had no clue as to the true nature of his tenant.

Lying half on, half off the bed was a young man. Mademoiselle Dumond was no more a woman than deYampert, although he was far prettier and frailer. The corpse was a man whose fine features and torn underclothes marked him as extremely interested in his own feminine side: He was a cross-dresser.

Eyes closed in what seemed a peaceful sleep were at horrid odds with the mutilation played out over his body. The chest was splayed open as if some enormous bird of prey had settled atop him and begun ripping with talons, painting the bedclothes and walls with his blood. In fact, there was a message scrawled across one wall in blood, presumably in the victim's blood, presumably penned by the killer—a sure departure from the monster's earlier M.O. as he'd not left anything of himself behind before, save the now-familiar calling card.

The two cops stared at the blood message for some time before turning away, each recalling how the beheaded victim of two days before had turned out to be a copycat killing. Over the bedposts the letters, snaking trails of dripping blood, formed three words:

Queer of Heart

This was an absolute departure for the usually reserved, cautious killer, sending a warning signal that this again could be the work of a fiendish copycat killer, another mooncalf altogether. But peeking out from the victim's rib cage, deep in the heart cavity where the large red organ was missing, was the familiar doily card displaying a bloodied, fouled queen of hearts. It seemed to leer up at them in a mocking fashion as if miming a single word: *Gotcha.*

"I thought you said she . . . he . . . was a woman?" Ben teasingly asked the superintendent, desperately seeking a way to lighten the moment when the super had crept in behind them, curious as a muskrat and about to lose his lunch.

The man was dumbfounded. "But she . . . she *was* a woman."

"Not anymore," Ben said in his driest tone as he removed the bloodied sheet farther down the torso to reveal the young man's severed private parts.

"*Oh . . . mydearLordyGod'nHeaven'boveJesus,*" moaned the super.

"Don't need to ask if the husband did it, do we?" Sincebaugh said to Ben, eliciting a belly laugh from his partner, further disturbing the superintendent. Others from the building had begun to jam the doorway, so Alex shouted for the uniformed officer there to keep everyone out.

"Let's start the routine, Ben," Alex said.

Both men knew the importance of the appearance of dedicated police work, even if they also knew that usually nothing came of the measures they took at the scene. Ben dispatched two uniformed officers to do a neighborhood search for any discarded knife or hatchet that might have been carelessly tossed away by the killer—doubtful since this had not occurred in any of the previous Queen of Hearts killings. This in essence meant the uniformed cops had to sift through trash cans and in sewer grates, a task few but rookies threw themselves into.

A second pair of uniforms were sent out to canvass the building, asking questions about the deceased and his relationships to others. Since he was a transvestite, Alex held out little hope that others in the building had much to do with him or that he actually had a family that kept in touch. Later, after all the canvassing, Ben and Alex would ask the officers who did the initial legwork if they had spoken to anyone who had seemed unusually rattled or nervous, or seemed to have known more about the victim's personal habits than the super obviously did. Such steps would build public confidence in the Department, if nothing else, to show that they were moving on the case.

Interviewing witnesses was a contradiction in terms on such a closed-door homicide as this, an oxymoron. If you interviewed a witness in a case of out-and-out brutal murder carried out in such a cold-blooded, calculated fashion behind closed doors or in a dark place, you were in effect interviewing the killer or killers, the only witness being the killer. Still, someone might have heard something, might have seen a stranger in the hallway, on the front doorstep.

Dusting for prints would likely reveal nothing useful; even if a usable print were found, if it didn't match one on file with the Department or the FBI, it remained useless until an arrest match was made. Still, if a print were found to match one identified at an earlier scene, then it did tell them that they were dealing with the same beast. All such attempts and effort had to be made, so Detectives Sincebaugh and deYampert went about the business of evidence-gathering and note-taking and measuring.

At the door the police photographer waved his way in, a good man whom Alex and Ben had worked with on countless other cases. Yancy Rosswell was his name, and he'd photographed most of the handiwork of the Queen of Hearts killer. Whenever he was unavailable, Alex had done his own photos, which Rosswell had once called functionally okay but lacking in artistic merit. Rosswell's walls at home were hung with crime-scene photos dating back as early as the 1890s.

He was long and lean and his every bone was just below the surface, prepared to create an angle on his body somewhere. He had a Clint Eastwood edge to him and a Jack Palance profile. He was as tall as the two actors as well.

"Damn . . . damn . . . damn." He punctuated every shot with the expletive.

"Get plenty of shots," Alex instructed, unnecessarily, just wanting to hear himself, to see if his vocal cords were still operational after looking at the sight before him. "We make it the same bastard, Rosswell. Whataya think? From a cameraman's point of view, that is."

"The camera don't lie unless you lie to yourself," he said with a philosophical wheeze.

As had been the case with all the Hearts victims found indoors, and those caught up in the confluence of river or lake, the body had been left in a "posed" position by the killer. All of his outdoor victims had been placed facedown, requiring police to turn the body to discover the hole cut into the chest, while those killed indoors were always laid unceremoniously and indignantly across their beds, no matter what room they were killed in, with their faces and chests facing straight up, with a sheet or a blanket gently pulled up over the hideous wounds, hardly hiding them since blood matted the sheet to the wounds in an indigo pool. It was as if the killer held some sort of odd fetish about tucking them into their beddy-bys when he killed them indoors.

These were the few strands or patterns the killer had left them until now, with the blood message on the wall. It was indeed a departure from the killer's usual reserve and caution.

"Queer of heart." Alex curiously read the words aloud as

if aloud would make more sense of them.

"Bastard has a sense of play, doesn't he," said Ben.

"Yeah, maybe, but we've never seen this before."

"Must've really been pissed off by the copycat killing maybe, wouldn't you say?"

"Maybe . . . yeah . . ." Alex considered this thoughtfully. "So perhaps, after all he's done, he wants us to know that he can laugh at himself? Or he just wants recognition for his handiwork? I don't know, partner."

"Whataya saying, that it is another copycat? But there's the card. If it is another copy, Alex, it's far better than the Lennox Xerox. Nobody but us knows about the cards."

"Yeah, you're right . . . has to be the same freak. We've searched all over New Orleans for those kinda cards in every novelty shop. Has to be him."

"So, it just doesn't set well, the whole message-on-the-wall thing, huh?"

"No, it doesn't. And if it is him, he's . . . evolving."

"Evolving?"

"I read in the police bulletin once about how some killers' M.O.s evolve, change with the evolution of the fantasy that the guy's working out, you know. This could be something like that, Big."

"You think so, Sincy?"

Alex nodded. "Yeah, maybe, Ben." Alex turned to the photographer and called for him to get the wall shot. "Can you get the whole thing in a wide lens?"

"Sure, no problem, Lieutenant." He coughed into a handkerchief he'd been holding against his nose. He was also wiping sweat from his brow. It was an ugly kill and he'd had to do his artistic best with it.

He worked like a pro, however, and soon had shot after shot of the message on the wall, from every angle.

"How you doing, Rosswell?" asked a second cameraman who'd suddenly gotten past the police barricade at the door.

"Who the hell're you?" Sincebaugh blocked the man's path, taking him for a reporter.

"I'm with the FBI—Dr. Coran. She's right behind me, coming up the stairs."

"Really. What, she doesn't trust us to do the fuckin' job?" Sincebaugh shouted.

"I got the call, was told to be here, guys. What can I say?"

"One way or another, looks like Lew Meade's going to wrench this case loose," said Ben. "Just waiting for us to fumble, Alex."

The FBI photographer shrugged. "I only take orders, gentlemen." He then went straightaway to work. He talked as he fired away over both the body and the wall, commenting on the grotesque nature of the crime, saying he'd thought that he'd seen everything until now. He seemed to need to talk in order to work; it seemed to be a way of calming his nerves.

The FBI fingerprint guy and Dr. Coran followed, and she went straight to the detectives, saying, "You were wearing gloves the whole time, I hope, so we don't pick up any unnecessary prints, gentlemen?" Satisfied, she went to work without looking at the body because she was stopped stone cold by the bloody writing on the wall. Alex watched her for a moment before he and Ben moved off, deciding to comb the little two-room apartment in the meantime, checking into cupboards, drawers, the refrigerator, staring at photos of friends, family, anything they could find.

Finding little of use, Sincebaugh returned to the bedroom to find a jittery Dr. Coran seemingly unable to concentrate on her work. She dropped a vial, swore and began a procedure over. From time to time, she stared up at the message on the wall. This seemed only to further upset her. Meanwhile, the fingerprint man said he'd done all he could, and so he began huddling with the two photographers, who knew one another from previous engagements. Each man promised to have prints of one sort or another to Sincebaugh before his shift was over tomorrow. The two photographers and the dust man left together, speaking of locating a watering hole after each dumped his evidence at lockup.

Alex went to Jessica Coran and asked if she were okay. She looked up into his eyes and said, "Nobody said anything about the writing on the wall. It took me by surprise."

"Yeah, us too."

"It's him, Alex . . . Matisak."

"What? Whataya mean?"

"It's his new thing. He writes poetry in blood on walls after each of his kills."

"But his M.O. is completely different from this. He wasn't here, Jessica." He tried his most reassuring tone.

"You don't put anything past Matisak. He may've killed this boy just to get me here to see this!" She pointed to the blood message on the wall. "That's his doing, his handwriting."

"You can't know that."

"It's his way of telling me that he's here, close by, watching me."

"You're jumping to conclusions not in evidence, Jessica."

"Get hold of myself, right?" She glared up at him. "He shadowed my every move on the Claw case in New York from his jail cell. This . . . this would be a cakewalk for him. I'm telling you he's been here, in this room. I can sense him. Hell, I can smell him."

It was then Sincebaugh heard a clamor from outside in the hallway and going toward the noise, he saw Dr. Kim Desinor pushing forward through the crowded hallway, followed by Lew Meade and Captain Landry. Alex could only drop his gaze and shake his head in a gesture of defeat. He had one badly shaken M.E. working the scene, and now he'd be forced to deal with a psychic on the premises.

"Stand aside, Alex," ordered Carl Landry at the doorway, and Alex dutifully did so, casting a worried glance in Ben's direction. Kim Desinor followed his eyes for a moment before going toward the bed and body, noticing immediately the blood communique over the bed. When the psychic stepped away from the horrid scene at the bed, she went toward the kitchen, trying to come up for air. She came face-to-face with Alex instead. He hoarsely whispered into her ear, "Doesn't look like we'll need an exhumation now, Dr. Desinor. We got a body right here for you to psi over."

She captured his gaze and drew it into her own for a millisecond, finding a firm strength in this man, some anchor for her reeling senses. This death scene wasn't like anything she'd ever faced before. It was so bloody, not at all like the body fished from the river the other day with its hideous wounds bathed and washed clean. Here the full horror of what the

Queen of Hearts killer did was full in your face.

Captain Landry pushed into the small kitchen, wondering what was going on. "Let Dr. Desinor do her job, Alex, without interference, please."

Alex watched in dismay as Landry and Meade guided the psychic to the corpse for a second time like a couple of vultures to pick over found prey. Meade ushered the shaken Jessica Coran aside while Landry whispered some encouragement in Dr. Desinor's ear. Kim looked faint, forehead sweating, hands trembling and nose twitching with the stench of the two-day-old corpse. Even the seasoned, hardened Jessica Coran, who was making for the door, looked seriously rattled by the scene.

Alex took his boss aside. "Don't you think the crime scene's been trampled over enough today, Captain?"

"Alex, we've got to accommodate Dr. Desinor, plain and simple. What part of that don't you understand?"

Landry ordered everyone except the two detectives, Dr. Desinor, Meade, Coran and himself out.

Alex said through grinding teeth, "If she's on the case, I'm off, Cap."

"You make that move, Alex, and I swear, I'll use the tape those IAD clowns brought to me."

"Not like you to threaten, Carl."

"My options aren't many, Alex. Now if you and deYampert had anything for me, maybe things would be different, but so far all you've managed to do is go around in circles trying to find that transvestite snitch of yours. Meanwhile, you don't have the slightest idea of the hounds on my back or how often I've taken shots for you."

"I'm telling you, Carl, there's something strange about Gilreath's disappearance right after we got the first call, after the Kenny Stimpson killing, and I'd swear it was his disguised voice on that 911. And if he did find Stimpson's body, he either knew him or his killer. And now this victim, Captain, if you haven't heard yet, is a transvestite."

"You really think Gilreath knows something?"

"I do."

"Then find the bastard."

"I've been working on it day and night."

"Obviously not good enough, Alex."

"Ben and I are busting asses on this—" Each man was alerted to a sudden keening cry of anguish and, looking up, they saw Dr. Desinor, her right hand on the body's forehead, her left in the open chest wound, her eyes closed, her cry of pain and terror turning Alex's blood into a thick oatmeal.

"What the hell's she doing?" shouted Sincebaugh. "Get her out of here!"

Landry grabbed Sincebaugh and pushed him against one of the blood-spattered walls. "Shut up, Alex . . . shut up and let her do her thing."

"So"—Sincebaugh was fighting for breath—"to hell with protocol."

"Protocol hasn't gotten us anywhere. You find a door locked, you go round to the back."

"I don't need this shit, Carl."

Ben deYampert was now beside Alex, telling him, "Give it a chance, Alex. If it fails, we've cleared the runway, and if it helps, more power to the lady. Got to admit, she's got guts."

Meade placed a hand over his lips, silently asking for quiet. Frowning, Alex relented.

The three hardened police detectives and the FBI field chief all watched now in silence as the psychic did her work.

"No . . . no . . ." she was moaning. "I never hurt you. . . . Whyyyyy?"

Alex continued to frown at the show of histrionics, but no one else seemed to be bothered by the theatrical demonstration and obvious pretense.

Kim Desinor raised her arms in mock self-defense, and as she went to her knees after a flurry of self-defense moves, her fists clenched and doubled as if wielding a heavy object. She rose and seemed to score a hit with the ghostly weapon in her hand, but suddenly the phantom object was dropped from her grasp, and she stumbled backwards, clutching her chest as if fighting to keep her heart intact while fending off invisible blows.

Sincebaugh almost laughed at the display, but when he saw her falling, he reacted instinctively to catch her in his arms, but not before she grazed her head on the bedpost.

"Get her outside, Alex. Get some water, Ben," the captain was shouting.

Meade reacted nervously. "Good God, is she all right?"

The bruise weltered up in a dark ring over her eye, but this seemed the least of her worries. She'd gone into some sort of seizure, epileptic in nature, and she was shrill and pleading against an invisible attacker.

She lashed out at Alex, who raised an open hand and slapped her hard, bringing a red hue to one side of her face and startling her out of her vision.

Alex felt the reality of her fear, deep and lifting, an ocean of it running current-swift through the woman. Whether she was a fake or not, no one short of Meryl Streep could act this well. Had she locked onto something evil and unimaginable in the room? Alex momentarily and helplessly wondered, feeling the intensity of her struggle in his arms.

He held her against his chest, shouting, "It's all right, Kim . . . you're all right . . . you're among friends."

His words sounded so banal to himself, but he could think of nothing more comforting to say; still, the words seemed to be working as she relaxed under his grip. He held her now with her eyes closed. She had shut down as if a control or safety mechanism had taken over.

Alex tore the looped black rosary beads from her twisted fingers, somehow knowing that only when her touch was severed from the strange crystal cross would she relax. This done, he shouted, "I think we'd better get her over to St. Luke's now!"

"You do that, Alex," said Landry. "Ben and I'll finish up here."

"That's all right, Sincebaugh. I'll take her to the hospital," suggested Lew Meade.

"Right, right," Alex replied sarcastically before carrying her off, down the narrow corridor and steps and outside, where a mist shrouded the waiting crowd. He bolted toward his squad car, passing by other cops and reporters held at the ribbon, all of them very curious about the limp woman in Alex's arms, some of them recognizing her as the psychic called in by the NOPD to work the Hearts case.

"First time on a crime scene," he shouted. "Hey, what can

I tell you. Happens to the best of us.'' It was both a lie and a weak defense, but he bullied past them all.

He put her into the backseat of his squad car and drove the six blocks to St. Luke's Presbyterian Hospital.

In the rear, she was coming around, mumbling to herself, something about a bloody baseball bat. He paid little heed as he turned the car into the E.R. port.

Less than half an hour later, Kim Desinor was lying comfortably in an E.R. bed, her condition considered fair, and she was opening her eyes to find Alex standing over her, the glint of genuine concern steeling his gaze.

"You okay, Doctor . . . Kim?'' he asked.

"Where . . .''

"Hospital. You kinda went berserk back there. Went out. We kinda panicked, so here you are. Doctor says you're okay. He patched your forehead and . . .''

She reached up, touched the wide bandage and said, "Ouch! What happened?''

"Sorry, but you fell against a bedpost. I caught you before you did any more harm to yourself.''

She shook off a cold chill that swept through her. "I saw something, didn't I?''

"Hmmmph, you tell me.''

"I can't . . . remember.''

"Can't remember what? Being in the room, parading around, acting out the part of the victim, or what you saw while in trance?'' How very convenient, he thought. So it was all a show that maybe got out of hand.

She saw the telling look in his eye. "Lieutenant, I'm only human. What I saw, my mind refused to accept. I saw my-self—as someone else—being murdered.''

"You saw yourself.''

"As her, as him . . . as the Dumond woman. His real name . . . I know it, but it's sealed away with everything else I learned. I was her . . . him . . . for the duration.''

"But you can't remember what you saw as Ms. Dumond?''

She detected the ripple of humor in his tone. "Nothing . . . a total blank, a protective measure. My subconscious has the negatives, though, and after hypnosis, I think I could piece together what I saw as Dumond.''

''You'll have to forgive me, Doctor, but I'm just not convinced of any of this. Tell it to Captain Landry.''

''Alex, what occurred was real.''

''I think it's late. I'd like to get out of this hospital and go home. Can I drop you anywhere?'' he asked, ignoring her now.

''God, you're infuriating.''

''Me? What do you think . . .'' He hesitated and lowered his hands. ''Look, how do you think I feel about you?''

''You deny your own psychic abilities, repress them even, and you can't stand the thought of anyone else having any either, it would appear.''

''That's the biggest load I've heard from you yet.''

''You forget, I've seen the tape of you at the coffee shop. I've seen you in action.''

''I claim no second sight.''

''Claim it or not, you've got it.''

''Listen, for the duration of this night, can we talk about anything other than this?''

''I'd be happy to discuss any subject with you, Lieutenant— over dinner perhaps?''

''Dinner?''

''I still haven't eaten.''

''Dinner? Okay, you're on.''

''Good, then perhaps we can have a civil conversation?''

''Perhaps.''

''Have you all my things?''

''Your handbag,'' he said, lifting it from a nearby table.

''Thank you.''

''Shoes,'' he said, handing these to her.

She took them and began placing them on. ''Where's my gun?''

''Right here. I suppose you have a permit for that .38?''

''I do.''

''And what about these?'' he asked, handing the rosary beads to her. ''Got a permit for these?''

She gave him a mock look of disgust. ''Where'd you get this?''

''I've noticed you use 'em whenever you go into trance.

What? Do the beads hold some special power or meaning for you?''

"Haven't you seen these beads, this amulet before?" she asked, puzzled. "I mean, they must look familiar to you."

"No, Doctor, they don't."

"Stephens brought the rosary with him . . . I mean, sent it ahead for me to examine. Said he . . . said it was from one of the victims, Surette."

"Oh, yeah, I recall now. We found it where it'd fallen between his legs."

"I'll tell you what I told Stephens."

"Which is?"

"The rosary beads belonged to the killer, not the victim."

Alex measured this information carefully in his mind, testing it for meaning. "That's a remarkable leap."

"Are you willing to consider the possibility I'm right about the beads?"

"Maybe. Like your gun, I didn't notice them until I picked you up and carried you down to my car. Told the people here you were a fellow cop, flashed my credentials."

"God, you didn't have to lie for me. The gun is registered."

"Guess I don't need to ask you why you carry one."

"Nowadays? With one fourth of the homes in this country touched by crime each year? No, no need to ask."

"I'll just let 'em know you're up and running; meanwhile, if you'd like a mirror and a sink, it's that way."

She thanked him again and went to freshen up, the throbbing pain in her head reminding her to go slow.

In the mirror, she studied her image and tried to recapture what had been so shocking to her system; there'd been something unusual this time, something that didn't fit with the other attempts to see the killer. Something had changed and drastically, but she wasn't sure what it was, not yet, and the more she tried to revive the images, the more her head hurt.

She decided to sleep on it after a decent meal. Maybe it would return to her in time; maybe she'd need the help of a professional hypnotist. She'd never had to use a hypnotist before, but there was plenty of precedent for it in the literature when a vision was blocked by one's own mind, whether it was a simple memory or a psychic insight.

She would just have to be careful to instruct the hypnotist not to lead her in any way, but merely facilitate the process. She wondered if anyone on the case might suggest a competent person for the job, but she knew better than to ask Alex.

She did what she could with her hair and her face, fearing she could not do much. What little makeup she used about the eyes had run, giving her an Alice Cooper look that might easily scare Alex off. She rinsed her face of all makeup, opting for the natural look that shone through. She finished up just as he returned to the room for her.

— 23 —

Those sweetly smiling angels with pensive looks,
innocent faces, and cash-boxes for hearts.

—Balzac

On the drive from the hospital Alex talked about how much he loved and hated New Orleans. "Food and jazz drives the urban soul here," he told her with a short laugh that withheld any true humor. "The chefs here are like gods, feeding the soul-satisfying food of the earth and sea, and the musicians walk on water, and you can go down some streets here in full daylight and you'll find less-than-half-dressed whores in the doorways and windows, waving you up, many of them men. There's no place like New Orleans for a cop, no. All the chefs, the jazz musicians and the whores all have one commonalty: They all whip up their unique brand of appetite-suppressant by using their inbred intuition to improvise. The transvestite community's no different. You'll find more outrageous clothing per capita here than on any block in San Francisco, I assure you."

"I've seen quite enough between my hotel room and your precinct, thank you."

They were traversing the large, long bridge spanning huge Lake Ponchartrain, heading for a favorite restaurant that seemed miles off the tourist routes, a place Alex called Leopold's.

The city of 1.2 million was wide awake, bustling, threatening to never sleep. The city had maintained, after all these years, its heavy European, eighteenth-century air—as if the same air breathed in by the pirate Jean Lafitte were still available for the modern visitor to inhale. It was a place for the rich to party, to bask in their wealth, as it had always been a haven for the sophisticated and worldly; but for the poor, many of whom were black, Spanish, Creole and Cajun, the city's lack of a manufacturing and industrial base extended very little hope of improvement, elevation or advancement over the years. Alex talked of these matters in a grim tone.

She tried to lighten him up a bit by saying, "When a Creole goes to heaven, first thing he asks Saint Peter is, 'Where's the *jambalaya*?' right?"

He laughed at the familiar saying. "Either that or *filé gumbo*." But he lapsed back into his somber concern. "We pay homage to the past here; the past is our bread and butter; it's what brings in the tourists, the Old South in all her radiant splendor. The New Orleans port on the Mississippi was once second only to New York, but now it only supports an interest in the arcane and tourism."

"The past is a double-edged sword here. That's for sure," she agreed.

"Give me that old-time religion and that Old South drowsiness in the shade. Shame that the same mint-julep mentality which gives New Orleans its mystic flavor, old charms and her iron-lace balconies is also the same kind of thinking that has allowed poverty and homelessness to flourish at her core."

"But they got religion and Carnivale!"

"Yeah, Carnival Season . . . begins shortly after Christmas and winds down with Mardi Gras."

"Fat Tuesday, I know, ends on Ash Wednesday."

"Then you haven't forgotten New Orleans altogether since leaving?"

"Not at all. *Laissez les bon temps rouler!*"

He translated for her. "Let the good times roll."

"One hundred and fifty years of tradition . . ."

"Of spontaneous street parades and displays."

They both knew the history well, that in 1857 a group of locals banded together to form the first Carnivale parading organization, the Mystick Krewe of Comus, and that after that other private clubs, picking up the notion, sprouted up, and the elaborateness of the balls which spilled out into the streets and became madcap parades had become a tradition. Kings and queens were still chosen from among the *krewe* membership, and in some Carnivale clubs, the balls still served as "coming out" parties for debutantes. It all culminated in floats, marching bands, enormous balloons, jazz bands and wildly decorated flatbed trucks. Souvenir doubloons, cups, saucers, painted coconuts and beaded necklaces were tossed to onlookers from the parading masses. All this while in the French Quarter there was the annual costume competition for the best-looking transvestites, who so colorfully and spectacularly jammed the corners of Burgandy and St. Ann Streets.

"There's no other place like it on earth," she said.

Alex nodded, checking his rearview as he pulled into a turn lane on the other side of the bridge. "Shame, isn't it, that such a place, known worldwide for its jazz funerals and tunes like "Didn't He Ramble" and "I'll Be Glad When You're Dead, You Rascal," and such legends as Louis Armstrong, Buddy Bolden, Joe 'King' Oliver, Jelly Roll Morton, Kid Ory, and . . . and *gaiety*—in every sense of the word—has such crime problems as well."

She smiled at this, remembering aloud another song title. " 'If You Ain't Gonna Shake It, What Did You Bring It For?' Goes back to what I was saying before about a victim for every four households, I guess."

Alex turned the car into a gravel lot in front of a bright sign announcing "Leopold's on the Wharf." "Shame of it is that in the most technologically advanced nation on earth, in the history of all mankind, almost every single person in America will be the victim of one crime or another in his lifetime."

"Yes," she agreed, "and in spite of strides in forensic investigative techniques, electronic surveillance, colossal and complex fingerprint files and other modern means, the percentage of crimes solved by arrest has remained appreciably unchanged since, what, the early seventies?"

"Hey, compared to other heavily populated areas of the country, the NOPD's doing a hell of a job."

"No need to get defensive, Lieutenant. But the fact remains that New Orleans, like Chicago, L.A., Miami, New York and Atlanta, has actually seen a decrease in arrests made in violent crimes."

"Maybe that's because-just-because, as they say."

"What's that? Southern-style philosophical equivocation and sophistry to avoid the issue?"

"It helps when it helps."

She laughed. "More of the same."

His tone grew serious again. "There's been such an enormous increase in violent crime that it makes me weak to give it too much thought. If that's equivocating, then that's equivocating. I call it gettin' by."

"With drugs, child molestation, rape and murder on the rise, public anxiety about the effectiveness of both local and federal police agencies to serve the public has steadily grown, while manpower and monies haven't kept up," she conceded.

"That's why everyone's so ready to turn to psychics for help, and thanks in large measure to the media saturation of stories dealing with freaks like Jeffrey Dahmer, John Wayne Gacy, and the Queen of Hearts killer. . . . ''

"You like to think you've got a ready answer for everything, Detective Sincebaugh, all life's problems, don't you?"

"It helps, but no . . . not by a long shot do I have all the answers, but I have one for you. People latch onto your kind of magic and voodoo—"

"What I do is not voodoo or magic!" She raised her voice for the first time.

"People need you like they need Dear Abby, to tell them it's okay to believe in something that's not present, to hold onto something that's not there. So society appears to be going to hell. It has always appeared to be going to hell and it always will, but conjuring acts aren't going to change that."

"Most cops are superstitious, but not you, right?"

"That's right."

"You worked Missing Persons for a long time, didn't you, before you got into Homicide?"

"That's right, and I don't appreciate your going through my file."

"So, it was there you used psychics?"

"It was never my idea to use a psychic on any case, no."

"But the Department did?"

"That's right."

"So, you had a bad experience with a psychic, so you now judge all psychics by that one experience, and you say you're not superstitious?"

He fell silent, the verbal jousting taking its toll on him. After a moment, he said, "I thought we agreed to talk about things other than this bloody case."

"Sorry, guess we did, but I'm also talking about stressful situations, a stressful job, like a cop's. It brings out a need to tidy up the world, to seek answers, find control amid the chaos, an explanation for the void. A psychic worth her salt wants the same thing, Alex.''

''If it wasn't for missing-persons cases, your kind would be out of business. You're like bounty hunters, coming in on a case for the money it can afford you.''

''That's bullshit.''

''How much're they paying you? My year's salary? For your consulting fee?''

''I get paid by the day, same as a P.I., and I don't collect the consultation fee if there're no direct results stemming from my participation.''

''Stemming from your participation, sure . . .'' He let it drop, not speaking his mind. She knew what he was thinking, however.

''I'm no fool, Dr. Desinor. I know Stephens and Captain Landry aren't fools either, but we had strict guidelines we followed in Missing Persons when we dealt with psychic detectives called in on cases. From what I've seen and from what I've deduced, it's apparent to me that Meade, or someone, has provided you with far more than the type of crime, the name of the individuals involved, the dates and items lifted from the scene, like those beads. The sensitive, as we called him then, filed a report immediately on the basis of that scant information alone. You, you've been given access to all the police reports, all the coroner's reports, in essence my complete case file on the murders. Then you expect me to be dazzled when you come out with information you couldn't possibly know?''

''The more information I have, the more I can learn from the psychometric evidence.''

''You got that right. Well, you just go right on dazzling deYampert and the others, Doctor. Just don't expect me to fall in line, okay?''

''Tell you what,'' she said, ''you're right.''

''Right?''

''About my coming in with full disclosure. I won't work a case without it and when . . . when Landry called me in on the case . . .''

''Landry called you in on the case?''

''He's in charge of it, isn't he?''

"Yeah, yeah . . . sure he is."

"When he called, I made it clear I wouldn't work blind, that the more I know, the more I can reveal."

"Exactly my point."

"The Harkness boy's case must've hurt you very deeply. I'm sorry for your pain, Alex, and I can easily sympa—"

"That's got nothing to do with it."

"I can sympathize completely. I had my own such heart-wrenching cases, the Hughes case I told you about."

"I remember reading about it," he admitted.

"I wasn't much more than a rookie that year."

"Ever regret giving up being a cop?"

She hesitated before responding. Thus far, she'd not had to lie to him directly, and was able to excuse this necessary lie by omission since she was working for the FBI, for Meade. "Yeah, sure . . . sometimes I miss it, but I've learned I can do far more good as a sensitive."

"Let's eat," he said, and got quickly out of the car.

She waited to see if he'd open her door, and she was pleased when he did.

Over dinner she said, "You hate my being here, don't you?"

"What?"

"And you're uneasy with yourself, your own intuition, if you wish?"

"Whoa, whoa, wait a minute."

She barreled forward. "You're a tough guy, a former Navy SEAL. You don't have a sensitive bone in your body, or so you want the world to think, but—"

"Hey, I don't hafta sit here and take this kinda ridicule and verbal abuse, Doctor, and I don't hate your being here, no."

"I mean in New Orleans, on your case."

He hesitated before answering. "Eat, stay healthy."

"You really do make quite a sparring partner."

"What's that suppose to mean?"

"You're very good at deflecting direct questions, Lieutenant."

"I've had a good trainer."

"Your father." It wasn't posed as a question.

"What a surprising and fortuitous guess. How did you ever

come up with him, of all people?'' Sarcasm had seeped back
into his voice. ''What exactly are those lovely eyeballs made
of anyway? Transylvanian crystal? Or are you just an extremely lucky guesser, huh?''

''All right, okay, so much of what I do is instinctive, but
that doesn't lessen the fact I know what I'm doing. Lieutenant,
I'm the best.''

The restaurant's atmosphere was steeped in a French motif,
a sidewalk cafe on a grander scale in a semi-casual and darkened series of rooms with quaint street-corner lamps posted
every four feet, the windows overlooking the huge lake. It was
in the heart of some smaller town outside the big city, far from
Bourbon Street and the concerns of the French Quarter. It
seemed a place where a different breed of people dined, na-
tives not of New Orleans but elsewhere. Still, on the menu
alongside the traditional French dishes were traditional New
Orleans dishes from jambalaya to such specialties as shrimp
Creole and Cajun gator tail. Alex was eating the gator, while
she'd opted for vegetarian veal *parisien*.

He finally said, ''I have every reason to suspect you're
having us all on, Dr. Desinor.''

''And you resent the implication that others, seeing me
come in on the case, might construe you as a fool?''

''I don't give a damn what others think, but think they do
and the appearance of im-impropriety in a case is as bad as
the real McCoy, Doctor. And we both know that your coming
in on this high-profile case is going to feather your cap no
matter the outcome while making the NOPD look like
it's . . . well, jacking off.''

She bit back a snide smile and shook her head. ''If the hand
fits, Alex.''

''Very clever, Doctor, but nothing's changed.''

''Oh, I think a lot has changed. And it's about time you
called me Kim.''

''Such as what has changed, Kim?''

''How we view one another for one, Alex. I think we can
work together and not at odds, if you will just give me a
chance. Your partner Ben's willing to, Jessica Coran, P.C. Stephens, your own Captain Landry.''

''Yeah, so why do I get the feeling I'm the last holdout in

The Invasion of the Body Snatchers? Ben's got a wife and children to go home to. He can turn the case off when he wants, he's gotten so used to partitioning off the separate lives he leads. Me, I'm on my own, so maybe the case is a little more important to me than—''

''Is it importance or self-importance and a little obsession thrown in for good measure?'' she asked quickly, stopping him.

''I'm no more obsessive about my work than most cops.''

''Bullshit. You're as bad as . . . as . . . as Jessica Coran. You're a workaholic from what I can see.''

''There are worse things in life.''

''Your father's nearby. Why don't you spend more time with your family?''

The muscles of his jaw tightened. ''That's really none of your business, now, is it?'' He wondered from whom she had learned that tidbit of information with which she thought she could astonish him.

''He's a former cop. Someone you could share your thoughts and feelings with on the case.''

''I got Ben for that.''

''And that's enough?''

''It is.''

She nodded. ''Your father hurt you very badly, didn't he.''

''What the hell's with you, lady? I'm not in the market for psychoanalysis, not even your brand, so let it go.''

''My father hurt me very badly too, when I was young. He pretty much destroyed all faith I had in him. Took me a long time to get over it, and I'm still not sure I am. Over it, I mean. He gave me up to the state for safekeeping. How do you like that?''

Alex dropped his gaze and said, ''I'm sorry to hear it.''

''You can rationally rid yourself of a thing like that, but emotionally it's like a growth or a virus that's still very much within, biding its time, waiting for you to slip and when you do, it'll be there to take you into the depths of pain stored up over the years. Out of sight but not out of mind, or is it stored in the human heart?''

''My problem with my father is not the issue here, Kim, nor is it a matter for discussion, do you understand? And while we're on it, my every waking moment isn't predicated on how

I view my relationship with him, understood?''

''Perhaps . . . perhaps I do understand more than you know.''

He stared across at her and felt her eyes probing into and through him. ''You don't understand anything about me.''

''I understand your anger, your frustration and even your fear.''

Now he gritted his teeth and pulled back, as if physically severing the eye contact between them would help his cause, before he said, ''I'm not afraid of a damned thing. Lightning doesn't scare me; dying doesn't scare me. So, what's left? I've faced death in a goddamned jungle a world away from home, and here on the streets as a cop. No, there's nothing I'm afraid of.''

'You're afraid of the small things.''

He shook his head and frowned, pushing away his plate.

''Dark spaces from which you cannot retreat?''

''You're crazy, you really are.''

''Relationships from which you can't hide.''

Shut up—his thought leaped but did not cross the table, yet she caught it as if on some sort of telepathic tractor beam, yanking it into her.

''I'll shut up, Lieutenant, when you accept me for what I am, and while you're at it, accept the fact there are black holes in everyone's mind.''

''Exactly what you count on.''

''Perhaps.''

''Both as a shrink and as a snoop.''

''*Touché*. If we could leave it at that. But the dark little holes into which you tumble and lose your way and all control, these need to be explored, not run from.''

Christ, he thought, she's been talking to Ben deYampert, but then he realized that not even Ben had knowledge of the exact nature or details of his recurring nightmares of recent months. He'd had nightmares for years as a child, and now again, awakened in him by the first Hearts victim, Surette. And here was this all-seeing, all-knowing being staring through him, revealing him to himself here over table scraps.

''Waiter! Clear these dishes away, will you?'' he called out, his thoughts tumbling on. It was as if Kim Desinor had climbed inside his head and had watched a film there, a film about his agony, as if it were being played over and over for her private screening. The feeling was one of invasion which sent a shiver through him, making him add one more item to his fears—fear of her.

The waiter rushed their dishes away, asking about dessert, which both of them declined, Alex calling for the bill. Then he turned to her and said, ''How . . . how the hell could you—''

''You're surrounded by parasites, Alex, on all sides. You even see me as a parasitic creature, someone or some thing that's come to chew away at you and your precious case, someone who will eat you alive if you're not careful. Then, of course, you've got Ben, Frank Wardlaw, Landry and IAD, Meade, every one trying to siphon off a piece of you in order to feed themselves.''

''This is all nonsense. You don't know what the hell you're talking—''

''But I do. Men like you, men who have so much strength bottled within, so powerful . . . people gravitate to your power, your confidence, wanting to touch it, Alex. They want to touch me too, all the time. People like you and me . . . we're appealing on many, many levels. Think of the old saying, Alex, how two separate people with differing worldviews look at a glass of water.'' She placed a forefinger on the glass before him, which was half full.

''People like you and me?'' she said. ''We see it as half full. Others who see it differently are also emptied by their unfulfilled relationships, and when they see people like you and me who are absolutely comfortable in who we are, they come to us for a drink, and they work to fill their empty souls with us. Because they never see our unfulfilled needs, the emptiness within us, because we guard that place like hell.''

''Taking from us?''

''All they can get, sure . . . why not? They must feed; it's their nature to feed, as it is in all living things, Alex. I see people every day siphoning off energy and emotion from me, but I gain from the encounter while most of them do not. It's because I gain in giving.''

''You know, you could be quite scary if I didn't know better.''

''Last thing I want is to scare you, Alex.''

''Really?''

''Really.'' She reached across the table and took his hand in hers. ''Sit quietly for a moment and take from me.''

Alex felt the warmth of her touch and the throbbing life within, heard the heartbeat as it moved along the corridors of her being and into his. The warmth became a radiant heat flowing between them, growing in intensity like the heat from a sun lamp.

"I'm not a psychological vampiress, Alex. I'm not here to take anything from you. If anything, I'm here to give, not take. I'm no leech, no insect, no worm you need to fear."

He involuntarily shook with the thought of the worms in his nightmare. "I'll . . . I'd like to take you home."

"Wish you could, but I've got that early morning appointment."

"Whoa, I didn't mean my home."

"Oh, sorry . . . misunderstood, I guess."

"Well, I mean, I wouldn't mind . . ." He stopped short and looked curiously at her, his eyes narrowing. "What early morning appointment?"

"You know, the—"

"Oh, yeah, the famous or soon-to-be-famous exhumation. Do you really think they'll be going ahead with it, even after what you went through tonight? Isn't there a limit to what you can . . . reasonably expect to . . . to give?"

She liked his choice of words and the level of concern in his voice. "I'm okay, really." She touched a sensitive spot below the bandage to her temple.

"I just hope it doesn't turn into a circus."

"I don't like the idea of exhumation any more than you do, but . . ."

"But you have to establish patterns from out of chaos here, right?"

"Like you, Alex, it's not what I do, it's what I am, and if what I am can indicate a direction, locate a clue, then how can you continue to stand in the way of that? Why won't you let me help you? Is it because I'm a psychic or a woman? Or both?"

"Me? Stand in your way? How am I standing in your way? You and the others are working right around me, for cryyyy-sake! Everybody saw what happened at the crime scene tonight. No . . . wouldn't want to be in the way, would we."

His sarcasm had returned full force, and she gripped the thin edge of the table to remain calm. "Nice try, Alex, but you're hiding again."

"Who's hiding? I'm right here, going nowhere."

"I have come to believe to a great extent that it is our fears and anxieties that make us who and what we are, or will become, Alex."

"Is that supposed to be reassuring, Doctor? Because it isn't."

In a flashing vision, she saw fat, hungry maggots around him, but ignoring the ugly image, she forced her way through the jungle of his tangled emotions. "We defend the weaker portions of our personalities with an array of defenses, either positive or negative, bright or dreary, such as diplomacy, humor—often macabre humor—patience, self-deceit, temper, clowning and stubbornness."

"Ben'll love to hear it. He's the bull-slinging yahoo and I'm the bullheaded mule, right? Nice butter you spread, Doctor."

"I think the butter is all yours, Alex, and you're spreading it on thick to cover your true—"

"That's enough with the psychobabble, Kim. I've heard quite enough, and coming from you, it's doubly rewarding."

She wasn't sure what he meant by this. "I didn't say I was without fear and anxiety. Quite the contrary."

"I'm not going to swap my personality for one you'd like me to try on, Doctor." He stared across at her, stood and said, "Now, it'll be my pleasure to see you home."

He threw out a wad of bills onto the table like an angry man who's too upset to count and said, "Are you coming, or do I call a cab?"

"I'll pay for my own meal, and I'll call my own damned cab, Lieutenant!" she fired back, drawing stares and bawdy laughter from others in the restaurant.

Alex's jaw tightened, his face turning red. "All right, fine . . . suits me." He then stormed out ahead of her, mumbling something under his breath about women in general. She stared after him disbelieving, yet fully understanding. She'd touched a raw nerve that had been successfully protected for a long time.

She found the pay phone and called for a cab. "To hell with him," Kim told the lady at the cash register.

"You just go right on stickin' up for yourself, dearie," suggested the elderly woman behind the counter.

• • •

Alex Sincebaugh was angry with himself. He had never in his life walked out on a woman, leaving her stranded in a public place, and it didn't sit well with him now. He'd gone back to the restaurant to apologize, try to start over with Kim Desinor, but she'd already left. He had thought about locating her at her hotel, but then decided that such a move would only widen the rift between them. He didn't know what to say to her anyway, how to build a bridge between them, how he could comfortably work with her feeling as he did, and the thought of an unnecessary exhumation as a media event continued to gnaw at his gut.

He was a practical man who had come up via a tough life with little love or compassion either received or given, and yet he saw the empathy and heart-wrenching love that the families of victims demonstrated every day, and he respected, even admired people who could convey their emotions so openly and honestly, although he himself could not.

His father had been a policeman with all the military bearing of an army officer in all his dealings, including those that concerned his son. His mother had died when he was eleven years of age, and he recalled her as the only loving influence in his life. It was little wonder that he pushed women away when they got too close, when they began to make plans for him, plans for them, plans that included a home, a family, commitments he felt ill-suited for.

He understood pain and isolation, hard reality, toughness. Toughness saved you from any hurt. It had been with this attitude that he'd left his father's house to go out to San Diego, California, to join the Navy, and having shown so much promise during basic, he was asked to go from there to Coronado, California, to begin a twenty-five-week training session that would culminate in his becoming a Navy SEAL. The course work and field work were grueling, but nothing could have prepared him for week number six, Hell Week, considered a hazing which separated the determined from the doubtful. Sincebaugh's Hell Week had been in January of '67, when he was a boy of nineteen. It took a lot of guys two and even three attempts to pass muster at Hell Week, but Sincebaugh made it through his first time, although it nearly killed him.

Instructors, each one a SEAL himself, worked eight-hour

shifts in teams of six throughout the week, while trainees were given only three hours' sleep. One instructor named Gahan told them that Hell Week was to see how young men operate under extreme stress, and that he'd be providing the stress. Everything they did for the entire six days was a race of one sort or another, and the winning team won rest time while the losers had to repeat the race. For those who succeeded, it was not just a physical feat, for they were also subjected to mental pressures, mind games and mockery. For twenty-four hours, he and the rest of his crew, Class 127, were each given their own personal 250-pound log to toss, catch, hurl, twirl and kick uphill; they had to kick the damned thing up sand dunes. In a nonstop marathon they had to shoulder their log and race to a stack of deflated rubber rafts, inflate the rafts and row out to markers some ten miles distant and back. They swam relays, scaled rough-hewn wooden walls and ropes dangled from a chopper, which went clear around the bay with each man hanging on until they began falling like flies. They raced in deep sand and when nightfall came, they didn't sleep, for there were night maneuvers to complete.

On the second night, Sincebaugh, by now a Navy seaman apprentice, along with the others, was ordered into San Diego Bay. Now recalling the hypothermia he'd suffered that night, he felt a rush of icy panic ripple through him again. For twenty minutes the fully outfitted men were made to swim in the January waters of the bay. He recalled now how the instructor, calling through his bullhorn from atop a warm boat with his Mackinaw on, had shouted the order to remove boots and socks in the water, to stuff socks inside boots and tie them over the shoulders and around the neck.

Alex's hands could hardly function, but he'd made them function. After twenty minutes of mind-numbing cold, they were ordered out to lie on the metal pier, where they were ordered to do one hundred push-ups, "to heat up your sorry-assed bodies," while the instructor called for the hoses and they were blasted with bay water on the pier.

"Keep you all from overheatin' too quick," the instructor called out sarcastically from his vantage point on the now-docked boat.

The man beside Sincebaugh, Slattery, confessed to having

lost his boots to the bay. The instructor replied, "What a shame, boys. Slattery here's lost his goddamned Navy issue. Ordinance don't come cheap. All right, everybody dive!"

"What?"

"Oh, shit!"

"That's an order! Till we solve Slattery's little mystery and locate them damned boots, nobody's dry!"

Slattery was sincerely and universally hated after that night. Everyone returned to the water, bitching under his breath, until Gahan, the drill instructor, ordered silence.

They dived until they found Slattery's fucking boots, which fortunately had remained tied to one another. It was the cold and the darkness out there which had stolen Slattery's foot-wear from him. Frigid temperatures and frozen fingers and darkness had a way of taking things, and by then the SEAL would-bes and wanna-bes had been reduced to children fearful of what their own bodies might do against them. Slattery, had he not been stopped by Sincebaugh, would have taken his own hand off at the wrist with his bayonet.

Slattery didn't last the week. Nor did many others. During Hell Week, the recruits were almost constantly wet and cold. They lost toenails, were rubbed raw in places, losing huge patches of skin. Their joints were swollen like melons. Since-baugh learned early never to remove his boots unless ordered to do so, since getting them back on was hell, and some guys never did get them back on, having to continue barefooted. A constant sight was of exhausted men fainting, vomiting and hallucinating, sometimes all at once.

It was the toughest military training in the United States, and all for the privilege of becoming a sea-air-land commando. Over half of those enrolled failed to complete the week-long intensive training and torture. Sincebaugh only made it by turning a corner in his mind, which left him with a strange aloofness in which he felt he literally sucked up pain, went looking for it, enjoyed it. It was what had gotten him through the ten-times-worse tortures of Vietnam when he became a prisoner of war.

So why was he afraid to sleep now?

Instead, he drove around his city, New Orleans, at night. The place had everything any other large American city had and more, yet it was unique. A blend of Spanish, French, Louisiana, Creole, Cajun and American. Street corners were lined with storefronts, fast-food restaurants, dry cleaners, taverns and hardwares, billboards and free-standing signs; sections of the city were grimy and lousy, rotten little holes into which children were born, areas completely at odds with Bourbon Street and the museums and shopping malls along the rivers and lakes of beautiful downtown Orleans.

He drove down to the district he guessed that Kim Faith Desinor most likely grew up in. He kept driving through it, around it, about it, staring, wondering how she'd gotten so good, so smooth, so well educated, coming from this cesspool. Had she been born with the gift of a great mind, or were drive and determination beaten into her at an early age as he'd had them beaten into him?

Either way, she was intriguing, and he wished that he had met her under different circumstances. He'd pulled over to the curb now, staring out at St. Domitilla's, its small enclosure, church and reformatories for boys and girls looking like a prison yard with ten-foot-high wrought-iron fencing going the length of the concrete grounds. He'd done a little checking of his own, and records showed a Kim Faith Desinor had spent time here, that in fact her father had placed her here after the death of her mother.

It was a far cry from New Orleans' ornate and world-renowned St. Stephen's Cathedral, with its huge pinnacles reaching into the night sky, its lavish spires and colored lights piercing the fog cloud which almost nightly descended over the darkened city this time of year. By comparison, the fog here at the poor parish church lay like a confining canvas over an open grave, reflecting only the neon and orange vapor lights of the street sign and lamp.

"Where are the answers?" he asked the empty interior of his unmarked squad car.

Big Ben was home with his family. Sincebaugh had no one but an uncommunicative, uncaring father, a father whose only response to his having completed the SEAL training course was, "Will that get you more on your paycheck?"

His father didn't know him.

Who really did, for that matter? How could anyone truly

know the heart of another, isolated as each man and woman was from another?

Being a SEAL still meant something to him, but it meant nothing to anyone else. But she knew he was a SEAL, knew all about him, respected him. She'd read his record, thanks to Landry, who'd forked it over without a thought. She knew his history . . . but Kim Desinor knew even more than that. She knew of his fear, and this fact most of all had caused him to run from her.

"Hey, Rockefella man! Lookin' for some action, *mi amigo*? *Compadre comprende?*" It was a pimply-faced Spanish boy barely out of his pre-teens. "I know where you can get your fantasy come true, bro."

Sincebaugh lifted his .38 and jammed it into the kid's face, making the boy shake in the shadow of the cathedral. "Who've you got in mind, son, your sister?"

"Hey, man, I'm gone. I'm outta here, out-cho face gone!"

"Don't move!"

The kid froze. "Whatchu want with me, man? I don't go that way."

"You know the word on the street about the Hearts Killer, though, don't you? Don't you?"

"Christ, you . . . you ain't him, are you?"

"What's being said? Who knows what?"

"Nothing . . . nobody knows nothing . . . I don't hear a word. Everybody's stone cold on it, man."

"Stone cold, huh?" replied Sincebaugh. "Tell you this, man . . . if you don't talk, you're going to be stone cold."

"Whatchu mean, man? I'm tellin' you, there's nothing on it that's goin' round, except now they got a psychic on the case and the guy doing the killing, his time's runnin' out."

"Who knew the victims? Give me a name, kid."

"Philly."

"Philly? A guy from Philadelphia? What's his real name?"

"You the fuzz, aren't you?"

"What's his goddamned real name?"

"Don't know. All I know is he's a transvestite; sings in one of the bars. Calls himself Phyllis and ain't got nothing to do with Philly. Now, that's all I hear or know."

"Phyllis . . . okay, kid, get out of here and get a productive life."

"Sure, sure, dickhead, maybe I'll work on that degree."

The kid disappeared the way he came, like a ghost, materializing and dematerializing amidst the landscape he knew so well.

A powerful wind began to sweep through the area, lifting drooping tree limbs and blasting here and there in drafts. Alex gave another thought to Kim Desinor as a child inside the prison compound of St. Domitilla's with its paper refuse rising in a miniature tornado and flying about the courtyard as bits and shards and fragments of ghosts. The old place had been condemned years before, its doors closed forever, awaiting the wrecking ball.

Alex heard no refrain of long-ago laughter in her walls.

~24~

The light that lies
In woman's eyes,
Has been my heart's undoing.

—Thomas Moore

Kim Desinor had seldom met a man so infuriating as Detective
Lieutenant Alexander Sincebaugh, yet he posed an interesting
challenge for her. What did it take with him? she wondered.
A little more time perhaps? Perhaps not; it was quite possible
that all the time in the world wouldn't change his obdurant,
bullheaded and fearful notions about psychic investigators in
general and her in particular. Still, for a brief while there in
the restaurant, gazing over at him through the candlelight, she
had sensed that deep, abiding need in him to confess and be
consoled, to shout out his needs, his desires, his most intimate
fears and wants. It was then she saw the bevy of human maggots clawing at him, the symbolic representation of an abiding
agony which he'd unwittingly and psychically conveyed to
her.

The symbolism was clear enough, she believed. And although she had wanted to come away a friend, this obviously
wasn't to be, it appeared. He had made that much painfully
clear.

She'd been attracted to him, had let down her own guard,
revealed to him that she too had fears and anxieties and needs
that daily went unfulfilled, the same sort of needs that had
caused her to dig herself into a hole in which she found herself
helplessly mired, thanks in large measure to Chief Paul Zanek.
Though if she were totally honest with herself—one of life's
impossibilities?—she knew that she alone was to blame for
the Zanek affair regardless of Paul's role in it. Maybe it took
coming to New Orleans and running into Alex Sincebaugh to
reveal this much to herself.

She thought about her seemingly endless nightmare of days

and nights and overwhelming loneliness at St. Domitilla's, wondered if she dared go see the damned dungeon sometime before leaving New Orleans, to manfully face down her fears as she always told others to do; wondered momentarily about her father's last days in an emphysema ward in some small town called Corinth in Mississippi, which had sent word to the school, the head nun breaking the news to her, explaining to her what the strange medical term meant, saying, "It's a defect in the lung system."

"Christ," she moaned as she undressed and found her way into the shower, ignoring the phone messages left her by Zanek throughout the evening. "Now there's a *real* and not an imagined parasite," she told herself, wondering what was on his mind.

The hot and pulsating spray of the shower was soothing to her aching muscles. It had been a taxing day in so many ways. If she could relax completely, she knew that her subconscious would play over the events of the day in a mysterious and subtle fashion, refashioning them, cutting and stitching and embroidering them into a whole cloth of meaning.

She let the hot water play over her head, neck and shoulders, turning up the heat in increments until the room was filled with a velvety, warm and enveloping fog. She found herself thinking anew of Sincebaugh, even his name alluring, different, curious. He was a handsome man, filled with kinetic energy of his own, much of it left untapped. She'd felt it pulsating through him when she'd boldly taken his hand in hers, stared into his midnight-blue eyes and aura, which sent showers of silvery sparks out whenever he grew enraged; with no regrets now, she replayed the moment slowly in her head. He had been intrigued, glued to her, at that moment, and he had been frightened at the same time—afraid of what she might reveal about him to others? Or did he fear what she might reveal about him to Alex Sincebaugh? Her psychic eye had pierced him, peered beneath the layers and held for a brief moment his heart in her hands, and that touch had made him draw back even further than before. Had made him doubly, triply suspicious.

Even shaken and distraught, he remained handsome, a firm gentleness always kept at bay, just below the surface, despite his outward rancor. It was something about him being just the opposite of her father, a man who still dominated her own worst nightmares whenever she broke down and allowed nightmares back into her life, that drew her. For years now she'd somehow controlled her own night visions, dreams and excursions into the fears that had haunted her as a child. How she did it, she could not tell, not even to herself; however, at odd times of stress, a huge shadow descended over her like a living liquid cloud of tar, and in it she found her father's eyes, nose, mouth, ears and hands, all crushing her, taking the air from her, torturing her and beating her.

Her father had never once beaten her in the real world, not physically at least. The nightmares were symbolic, like Sincebaugh's, and they told of a more sinister torture that she had participated in with her father, one she had all these years hidden from herself. But more and more now the specter of that terrible and formless horror stalked her.

She might more readily face the old reform school into which he had cast her than face him, to learn exactly what kind of man he was. He'd been a failure in so many ways. That much she knew. He'd been a heavy drinker, and he wasn't a pleasant drunk who curled up on the couch, but one who lashed out at unseen, invisible demons that provoked him into violence. She remained very shady on precisely how her mother had died, but some corner of her brain kept a caged thought that said it was his fault and he knew it. Her mother's death was the beginning of the end for him and them.

She shook loose from the disturbing core of memories she'd so successfully locked away years and years before. She stepped from the hot shower, toweled herself off and pulled on her thick white robe. She found a dry bar and poured herself a glass of wine and nibbled on some crackers, trying desperately to think of anything other than her father when a knock at the door shook her.

Sincebaugh? she wondered, intrigued. *As unable to get me out of his mind as I've been unable to get him from mine?*

It was a delightful thought that drove her to the door, causing some disappointment when she heard Jessica Coran's whiskey voice from the other side. "Open up. We've got to talk."

She pulled the latch and opened the door wide, allowing Jessica in, catching the perfume of alcohol as it wafted past with her. Jessica was filled with a nervous energy and her speech was nonstop. But she was more frightened than drunk.

"He's here . . . he's in New Orleans. Crazy . . . isn't it? I bait him to get him here and now he's here and now I'm a walking mess, but I . . . I didn't expect him so bloody soon, yet somehow he's come and somehow he's following me— no, preceding me—to the damned crime scene on the Hearts case! How? How can he get there ahead of us, paint the wall in blood and disappear before anyone can know? Is he super-human, super-inhuman? No way, the bastard set it up to look like a Hearts killing, but he's really the one. He's here . . . here, Kim . . . here and stalking me, taunting me."

"How do you know that, Jess? How can you possibly know that?"

"I was at the scene, 34 East Canal Street, just like you. You saw the writing on the wall."

"I saw it, yes, but—"

"I freaked . . . left . . . left the crime scene, Kim. Didn't follow proper protocol, just rushed out of there. I was standing on the street when Alex Sincebaugh carried you out of there and rushed you to the hospital. I was so distraught, I couldn't think straight, you know . . . after it dawned on me what I'd done, and I looked for him in the crowd, ready to kill him outright, but he never showed his goddamned face."

"How can you know for certain he's here, Jessica?" Kim didn't know how to console her.

"Oh, God, it's his writing, his printing, identical, and he knew the moment I saw it that I'd know, don't you see? That killing was no Queen of Hearts killing. It was Matisak, pure and simple. Matisak leaves bloody messages on walls, not the Hearts guy."

"There's nothing says Matisak has a corner on it. There've been bloody messages left on walls in many serial killings."

"Damnit, Kim, I've seen enough of Teach Matisak's perverted poetry now to know how he spaces his letters, precisely how large his loops and swirls are. It was in Matisak's hand! I was so rattled, I couldn't do my job."

"Jesus, then *who* carried you out?" Kim asked, thinking of Sincebaugh.

"I ran out."

"Unprotected, believing he'd just left the scene ahead of you?"

Jessica paced the room. "I know it sounds crazy. Maybe I am crazy."

Kim was wondering as much. "So, you tore out into the street without anyone's help, knowing—fearing—that Matisak was nearby?"

"Nobody can help me. Don't you see that? It's between him and me now."

"I'll make us some coffee. Let's talk this out, Jess."

"I'm telling you, it was him. He knows that I'll see through his despicable game, his disgusting message meant for me. God, how many others are going to die because he's after me?" Jessica had grabbed hold of Kim's wrist and now stared deeply into her eyes while Kim held firm to the coffeepot where they stood in the small kitchenette.

"I'm not going crazy, Kim. For the last few days I've felt someone following me, watching me. Even on the way over here—"

"Take it easy, Jess. We'll work this through. Did you bring any of Matisak's things with you?"

"Yes, in my coat pocket."

"Good . . . good girl. Now, let's have that coffee, and we'll take it one step at a time. I take it you've talked with Lew Meade about your . . . suspicions, haven't you?"

"Negative. He'd be more in the way than anything else."

"Oh, come on, Jess, you can't seriously expect to do this alone."

"I don't like Meade, nor do I particularly trust him."

She laughed. "Neither do I, but he could be of help."

"Likely do the same as Paul did; put bodyguards on me and then go back to sleep. Got anything to drink?"

"There's a dry bar here, but I really think we need to stay clear, Jess, and focused."

"You know about my bout with liquor, don't you, Kim? You know everything there is to know, don't you, and I . . . I know the rest, right? What a team."

"Tomorrow we move you, bag and baggage, to here, to stay with me."

"No . . . if you don't mind . . . tonight. Let's do it tonight."

"You have a seance in mind—Matisak items in your possession." Kim knowingly pointed.

Jessica's eyes did her pleading for her.

Sincebaugh went toward the French Quarter in search of a transvestite named Phyllis. By now most revelers and night people had ended their partying in a boozy brown daze-cloud of well-wishing and good nights, some club lights blinking off. Still others ran all night. He was amazed to see by the dash clock that it was nearly one in the morning.

Seeing a patrol car whose call numbers he knew, he pulled in alongside the officers. It was Ray Samson and his partner Calvin Toombs, a paired black team who liked it that way, and they were glad to have the company to break the monotony, but they were also a bit suspicious of Sincebaugh's showing up like this, alone and without his partner.

"What the hell gives, Alex? Thought you went off at midnight, Detective," asked Samson.

"Where's your pal deYampert?" added Toombs.

"Just doing a little moonlighting. Listen, guys, I'm putting out feelers for a transvestite in the area and—"

This made each of the other men break into laughter, Toombs saying, "Better watch how you wordin' that line, Sincy."

Alex mentally flashed back on what he'd said that was so funny, registered this and went on. "Someone calls himself Phyllis. You ever hear?"

Samson pursed his lips and shook his head. "Not really."

"How 'bout you, Calvin?"

"Wish I could help you, but only Phyllis I know is the legitimate item."

"Keep it in mind for me, will you?"

"Sure, sure thing, Lieutenant."

"Important?" asked Samson. "Got to do with your Hearts-Afire case?"

"Maybe . . . maybe nothing. Unreliable source for damned sure. Either of you guys've heard word one about the whereabouts of my usual snitch?''

"Gilreath?"

"Not a word, Lieutenant. Sorry."

"Seems that mother's gone to Alaska where things ain't so hot, maybe."

"Yeah, well, thanks anyway."

The squad car, smelling of greasy Cajun fries and burgers, pulled away and Alex stared after it, wondering what the men in the ranks were saying about him these days.

It'd be sunrise in four or five hours and the exhumation would be well under way against all better judgment. Still, perhaps he ought to be on hand. He'd go to his apartment, freshen up and try to look like he was rested in any case. From there he'd call Landry, learn what was going on.

He drove back across the city, his depression overtaking him, making him wish that he'd played out the scene with Kim Desinor in a far smoother and more heroic manner than he'd opted for. She'd seen right through him, through his bitterness, through his evasiveness, through all his shields. She was scary in her precision, her accuracy and her focus.

Once at home, he was surprised to find Ben deYampert waiting half-asleep in the parking lot. It was just past one A.M. and the exhumation was scheduled for dawn, in order to disturb as few Joe Q. Publics as possible and so that the gravediggers involved couldn't cry overtime.

"There's no reason for you to be at the exhumation, Alex," Ben told him.

"I wanna be there."

"After what went on at 34 East Canal?"

"I'm sorry about having disrupted things, Ben . . . honestly."

"I don't suppose you heard about what happened with Dr. Coran at 34 East Canal?" Ben cautioned.

"No, I didn't. What gives?"

"She just vanished on us. Left her bag there with her work half undone. Had to call Frank in to clean up after her."

"You're kidding. Dr. Coran just up and walked out, just like that?"

" 'Fraid so. Meade's talking about disciplinary measures

Any case, I haven't a clue as to where she is at the moment, and no one else has heard from her. She may be a no-show at the cemetery.''

Alex recalled what Jessica Coran had said to him about her fear that Matisak had done the victim at 34 East Canal Street just to leave her a message on the wall. "Yeah, that's Cemetery Number 27, as I recall.''

"That's the place.''

"Yeah, we were there when they put Surette's body into that city crypt. Gay community is usually more supportive of its own, but he just had a handful turn out for his burial, a bag of losers. I figured at the time it had to do with the AIDS epidemic.''

"How so?" asked Ben.

"Well, not that the burial was well publicized or anything like that, but the grapevine sure had it. I just figured, they'd seen so much death in their ranks by then . . . well, you know our city motto and mentality.''

Ben dryly groaned under the street light. "Life is for the living.''

"Enjoy it all while you may.''

"Here's to the here and now.''

"Don't waste time on bright tomorrows.''

"Credo of the street punk, heh, Alex?''

"Look, Ben . . . I've got a new lead. You want to play it out?''

"I don't know, pal. Where to and for how long? You already look like you've been rode hard and put away wet.''

"Just humor me, will you. Let's go see what's cooking on Bourbon Street.''

Ben nodded. "OK, but you're buying.''

Unable to sleep, Jessica now stacked the few items she'd brought with her onto the coffee table fronting the sofa in Kim's room. These consisted of a shredded patch off the prison shirt last worn by Matisak and left at the bloody dispensary where he'd killed Dr. Gabriel Arnold, some blood still adhering to it; a full set of the man's fingerprints; a strange tube which Jessica explained to Kim was part of the apparatus the monster used to drain his victims of their blood; a child's safety pencil said to have been used by Matisak while he was incarcerated, along with a diary he'd kept.

"Are you getting anything, anything at all?" Jessica asked.

"This may take time," Kim assured her.

The tenor of his diary, a self-absorbed diatribe of madness in the handwriting of a disturbed man found below his mattress in the cell which had been his home for years, was at complete odds with the letters of contrition and self-awareness he'd written for Dr. Arnold's eyes.

Kim spread her fingers just above these few items lying on the coffee table as she sat on the floor in the lotus position. Her hands slowly revolved in an ever-widening circle over the material possessions of the madman.

She tried desperately to get some reading from the scant objects. "You're right, Jessica. He is quite close, very near, definitely here in New Orleans."

"I told you. . . ."

"Quite close. He's an animal, rabid now, with such a single-minded obsession that he must find you. . . ."

"I know all that. Give me something useful, Kim."

"He's biding his time; playing out his hand, so to speak."

"Then it was he who wrote that message across the wall at the murder scene last night. He somehow heard the call on a police band. He's very clever. And he somehow got inside with no one seeing him or noticing him. Or else he actually committed the murder to make it look like just another Hearts killing, knowing that I'd know better."

"I can't say . . . not for certain, but I don't believe so. The evil I felt in that room was different somehow."

"Somehow different . . . different?"

"Matisak's energy is that of a strong, secure type, a man who has accepted his bloody nature; not any doubt in his mind that he's the heir apparent to Satan. The one who killed at 34 East Canal Street, he was not at all sure of his own identity. In fact, he was quite confused, even as to why he killed Dumond."

"What about Matisak?"

"I don't believe he wrote the message on the wall. It . . . tonight's murderer had an insane attraction for the heart muscle. He was no blood drinker."

"What're you saying? That I'm imagining things now? Tha

I imagined it was Matisak's handwriting on the wall?''

"No, I'm just saying that I'm getting a very confused picture . . . very confused. It's highly improbable that Matisak was there, and a handwriting analysis would prove beyond doubt that the message left at 34 East Canal Street is not in Matisak's hand.''

"What about these objects of his? They telling you anything?''

"I'm sorry. It could be me. I'm extremely tired, having not slept.''

"Try harder.''

Kim lifted the diary and held it between both hands, one below, the other above, feeling her body heat circulate through the object.

An impression of pure hatred slammed through her. "God, this man is more monster than human.''

Something else I already know, Jessica thought, becoming further frustrated. "I was being watched on the way here. I know he's out there, Kim . . . out there now. So, you've got to help me hone in on the beast.''

It was a macabre twist on an old theme, Kim thought as she stared across at Jessica: Beauty and the Beast. "I'm trying, but there's too much emotional energy between the two of you, the picture is completely muddled. I see the collapse of a roof, or is it a blanket, maybe a cage—something confining and utterly dangerous coming down over the top of you. You have to be wary. If he catches you up . . . wait . . . yes, a trap. He's laid a trap for you and—''

There was a loud drumming pounding at the door which silenced them both. It was after midnight.

"Who the hell is that?'' asked Jessica, whipping out her gun.

Kim went toward the door to stare out through the peephole. On doing so, she instantly drew back, screaming.

"What is it?'' Jessica pleaded, tearing the door open and staring into the dead eyes of Ed Sand. "Oh, no, noooo! God . . . it's Ed Sand. . . . '' Jessica crumpled under the weight of this sight, the massive image physically knocking her back against the doorjamb, where Kim rushed to her, trying to support her as she slid to the floor. The pilot's head dangled, slightly swaying, at the end of a rope coiled about his blood-smeared sandy hair. Jessica's eyes instinctively sought another direction, any other sight than the one before her, and she saw that the end of the rope was twisted about a light fixture in the ceiling. A mixture of bodily fluids, caught in gravity's pull, dripped from the open neck wound and onto the plush carpeting, dying the mild blue a deep indigo. Blood all around the enormous scar had congealed to a near-black scaly texture, telling her that Sand had been killed some hours earlier.

Not twenty-four hours earlier she and Ed had had a quarrel and he had since sent flowers and a note of apology for being a *complete ass,* as he'd put it, pleading that she might give him another chance, see him again, claiming that he'd gone to great difficulty to arrange to stay on later in New Orleans so that he might see her again, *to patch things up,* as he'd put it. Now things—Ed Sand in particular—would never be patched up again. She had ignored Ed and his Humpty Dumpty plea, knowing that she was not interested, that she wanted to remain faithful to Jim Parry. She had innocently used Ed to get a rise out of Kim that morning on the plane but since then she had ignored Ed . . . until now.

"The bastard killed Ed."

Kim instinctively tugged at Jessica where she had slumped half in and half out the door. "Get back inside here, Jess. Your instincts were right, then. Matisak *is* stalking you." Kim knew enough about the monster to understand the rising fear within her own being was a healthy one, one of self preservation. She slammed the door behind them.

Jessica, however, suddenly did a 180-degree turn, pulling away from Kim, snatching the door wide open and pushing past the decapitated head, her .38 raised and ready, all to a chorus of disagreement from Kim. Searching the hallway for any sign, any movement, she shouted in each direction, "Show yourself, you son of a bitch! Show yourself, Matisak!"

"Jess, there's something here . . . my God . . . in th mouth."

Jessica returned to see that Mad Matthew Matisak had sent her a note. She shakily reached for the paper that'd been plunged into Ed Sand's mouth.

Special delivery . . .

"What is it? What does it say?" asked Kim, still shaking, disturbed to her core that such horror could be so easily and readily visited upon her doorstep. She wished now that she'd fought Zanek and had remained in her lab behind the safe confines of Quantico, but Jessica, she surmised, felt quite differently. Jessica wanted to race out into the street as she'd foolishly, recklessly, bravely done at 34 East Canal Street, find Matisak and do war with the demon.

Jessica peeled apart the paper and read the stained message:

> Come midnight alone
> to join me
> at Metairie Necropolis
> to find eternity and bliss.

"What the hell's he talking about? What's Metairie?" Jessica wanted to know.

"It sounds like he's talking about the Mctairie Cemetery."

"A cemetery?"

"Yeah, aboveground cemetery; a rather large and easy placc to hide, in fact. You can't go there, Jess. He's laying the trap we spoke of."

"But if I don't go . . . what's the result . . . where does it end? Poor Ed. He . . . he didn't deserve to get mixed up in this, and now . . . now he's dead. Everybody around me is in danger, Kim, including you, so long as that fiendish, satanic creature roams free. And I'm the only one who has a shot at stopping his crazed brain from hatching his sick plans, and this is one heart I intend to put an end to."

"It's too dangerous, Jess."

"It's more dangerous going on the way I have. Poor Ed; he must've seen Ed with me. Must've stalked Ed, then killed him, just to hurt me. Damn him . . . damn that evil bastard."

"We've got to call someone," said Kim, going for the phone.

"Didn't matter one damn to Matisak one way or another if Ed was a friend or just my pilot, did it? All that madman knows is that he wants to hurt me any way he can. Hell, he killed four others in Oklahoma for me—to send me a message. Now this . . .''

Jessica kept her gun and her eyes alert to the possibility that Matthew Matisak might materialize at any moment from any direction. Then she closed the door on the horrid sight of Sand's dangling head. She next went to the balcony and searched there for any sign of the killer, despite the fact they were some twelve stories up. She even looked overhead, in case the sky was falling. In the distance she saw lightning flashes and heard the rumble of a storm. The TV newscast had warned of possible high winds due to an approaching hurricane out in the Gulf of Mexico. But Jessica's concern was on another force of nature, Matisak.

Before anyone else arrived, Jessica gripped Kim by the wrist hard and exacted a promise from her. "You're not to tell anyone about the note Matisak left behind, do you understand? Do you? Promise me you won't. Just promise.''

"I can't do that.''

"Damnit, it's got to be kept between us. Damnit, Kim, I need your promise on this. If you say a word to anyone about it, our friendship is over before it's begun.''

Kim bit her lower lip, dropping her gaze and considered this and the state that Jessica Coran was in. "I wasn't aware we had a friendship.''

Jessica was still waving her .38 around. "Please, promise me, Kim . . . promise me.''

"All right . . . all right, Jess.''

"All right, what?''

"All right, I promise.''

Inside fifteen minutes the hallway was cordoned off as a crime scene, uniformed police and detectives everywhere, including Carl Landry and Lew Meade from the FBI. Word was buzzing that Alex Sincebaugh and Ben deYampert could not be located.

Ed Sand's head was bagged as evidence. Kim kept her promise about the note from Matisak. Frank Wardlaw did the forensics honors, and he kindly assured the two women that the perpetrator was nowhere to be found, but neither was the rest of Ed Sand's body.

A distraught Jessica Coran was told a half hour later that

Sand's body was found in his hotel room at the Hilton, a floor up from her own room, blood everywhere from the decapitation. Jess had had no inkling that Sand even had a room at the Hilton. There was also found a briefcase in Sand's possession filled with surveillance devices, wiretaps, bugs. Jessica realized too late that Ed Sand had bugged her room and was shadowing her, and that his interest in her was part of his job as an FBI undercover man. He'd been handpicked by Zanek to protect Jessica.

Jessica and Kim had been followed from her room to Kim's by the stalking Matisak.

Landry confided that Lew Meade had led them to Sand's body, having known all about Sand. "When my men got there, they found a Do Not Disturb sign on Sand's doorknob outside. Inside, they found Sand's torso and limbs stretched across the bloody bedding."

25

An honest heart is hard to find.

—From the Notebooks of Jessica Coran

The morning found all of New Orleans in a silver veil of haze, fog and drizzle, an occasional groundswell of rumbling thunder electrifying the gravestones, reminding everyone of the approaching hurricane and the fragility of life as a handful of ghostly people walked amid the desolation of the city-maintained Cemetery #27 in the Uptown district. They'd gotten a late start due to the murder of Ed Sand, and the disruption it had caused both Dr. Coran and Dr. Desinor, but both women had steeled themselves to continue on with the manhunt for the Hearts killer. Unfortunately, there were people milling about the ancient cemetery and some would definitely notice the unpleasantries. It was nine A.M. and Alex Sincebaugh had long given up on anyone meeting him here, so he'd come and gone and come back again, learning belatedly of the goings-on at Kim's hotel room. He was kicking himself now at not having followed a strong desire to go to her hotel after their fight at the restaurant, but he and his partner had found a trail which smelled keen, so deYampert and he had pursued it hotly the night before. They had gone to a gay nightclub where Alex intended to shake some information from the patrons one way or another. Ben had had several off-color jokes in response to that, but Ben was also uneasy with traipsing through gay bars, and he'd registered his concern plainly enough, along with his concern that maybe the whole direction they were taking, hinging as it did on the words of a creep named Pigsty Gilreath and the Surette killing, might be leading them down the wrong path.

Surette had been one of the better-liked performers in the French Quarter shows; he'd played nightly at the Blue Heron just off Bourbon Street. Sincebaugh had never caught his act, but he'd heard that Surette had been impressive, that Horny Vicki Surette had had them on their knees—both male and female. And it was there that Davey Gilreath, otherwise known as Pigsty, had met Surette. This was old news, all gleaned on the first sweep of interrogations and interviews with suspects in the wake of Surette's death. In the newspapers at the time, Surette had merited a two-inch column and an obit in the crowded pages of the Sunday *Picyune*.

Alex had been frustrated and stymied on the investigation after Gilreath had disappeared without a trace; no one, not even the streetwise, knew of Pigsty's whereabouts. It was as if he'd fallen into the Gulf.

As they pursued leads the night before, Alex had reminded Ben of all that they knew of Davey Gilreath, that he'd been raised on a farm somewhere in northern Louisiana, that he was an addict, a snitch and that he had once been Surette's lover.

"Guys like that come and go with the wind, Alex. He could be in Alaska or Maine or on a merchant marine ship getting it on with all the boys there. I tell you, it's a dead end," Ben assured him. "Besides, we ruled him out as a murderer long time ago."

"I don't suspect him of killing Surette."

"Well, then . . . why're you pursuing it?"

"I'm uneasy with his disappearance. He seemed quite contented here before . . ."

"Before people like him started getting bumped off daily? Hell, I see nothing strange in his getting out of New Orleans," Ben countered, laughing. "What I find strange are the transies we've seen tonight who damned sure ought to've gotten out of this area till we catch this creep."

Ben, always the voice of reason, did make sense. Alex still felt compelled to say, "Yeah, but what if the little bastard knew more than he was telling?"

Ben next breathed in a deep breath of night air and gave his best patience-in-action glare as he said, "Listen, Sincy, let me pose a slim but possible theory here, okay?"

"Shoot! Be my guest."

"Supposing our dim-witted Pigsty—chosen, mind you, as a snitch for his fine propensities in ratting out his friends and selling his mother on the street—just supposing this piece of human filth got some sort of Phantom of the Opera syndrome, and with—''

Alex's laughter cut Ben off. ''Phantom of the Opera syndrome? Is . . . is that something you got from Dr. Longette?''

Ignoring the interruption, Ben continued. ''And with all of New Orleans his stage, Gilreath suddenly lashes out and strikes back at some festering cancer within him and—''

Again came Alex's laughter, turning to tears with a mental image of Pigsty in tights and cape.

It was then that Alex pulled the car to a stop across from the third gay nightclub they'd visited that night, The Warm Fuzzy.

Ben just kept rattling on as they stepped from car to bar. ''Striking out at his own gayness, maybe . . . or the fact he was powerless, always the puny runt, pushed aside by life, people, siblings, always of no consequence, always sucking hind tit.''

''You think he sucked hind tit with Vicki Surette?''

''Last one on, last one in . . . I'd bet my last dollar on it.''

''Maybe you've got something, there, Ben. But I'm having a hard time seeing Gilreath in the role of—''

''Don't you get it? Maybe Gilreath decided to be of consequence for once in his miserable life, to prove a villain since he can't prove a hero, so to speak, another Lee Harvey Oswald, only his anger is directed toward those resembling him.''

''You maybe ought to become a shrink, Ben.'' Alex stepped through the doorway and into The Warm Fuzzy, his eyes instantly alert and searching. He was also instantly made as a cop along with his nervous, fidgeting partner beside him. But Alex also spotted a known male prostitute and sometime snitch known among his street friends as Ricky Aspen for his physical attributes. He was tall, slender and firm, but the aspen in Aspen was a mere willow at the moment. If anyone knew anything about Pigsty's whereabouts, it might be Ricky.

Alex's thoughts were now brought to a jarring halt when finally the officiating grave-keepers started up the noisy backhoe, which began to hungrily, greedily chew at the huge stone over the aboveground city plot paid for and maintained by the taxpayers. Here lay Victor Surette's body as it had rested since the year before.

Jessica Coran, holding together like a person bound in baling wire, no doubt had popped a Valium, Alex decided staring across at her. But she was tough, strong, even in her voice as she spoke to Landry.

"Given the conditions of the cemetery and the fact he was buried by the state in a pine box inside a moldy old aboveground crypt with cracks about the seal," Jessica began, "I wonder at the possible condition of the body."

She had obvious plans to run her own tests and make of this a chance to autopsy the man whom Sincebaugh had become convinced was the first victim of the Queen of Hearts killer.

The umbrellas were of little help, the rain slanting inward as if it consciously knew it must work around the obstacles to get at people. It beat a soft chorus against them. The crypt, thankfully, did not have to be pried from the earth as might be expected in most any other place, because in New Orleans the eternal rest for all souls was aboveground, due mainly to the fact that the water level was so close to the surface and the city itself was below sea level. Cremation was often the first choice in cases involving unclaimed bodies such as Surette's; however, for some unaccountable reason, the authorities had chosen burial instead in this case. When Jessica asked about this, no one seemed to know the reason why, until Alex Sincebaugh reminded them that Dr. Frank Wardlaw had suggested the arrangement in the unlikely event that an exhumation might become necessary should someone claim the body at a later date, or if further forensic review of the body became necessary—as coincidentally it had.

The crypt opening was, however, taking undue time, the graveyard attendants noticeably delaying. During this delay, Jessica Coran asked about the seal, which looked to have been broken before they had arrived.

"We knew you were coming," replied the chief caretaker, a wizened little man named Oliver Gwinn whose liking for the bottle was well illustrated in his complexion and nose. "So we started early."

When finally Captain Landry blared a few obscenities into

the man's ear, the lid was further pried loose by the backhoe, and a second cemetery caretaker signaled the man in the machine to shut it down. The two attendants worked with thick gloves, crowbars and a butane torch, which burned off the final remnants of the seal. Inside they found what the city of New Orleans called a coffin, a simple unfinished white pine box discolored by a grimy, green mildew on all sides, microscopic life having taken up residence on the wood long before it was sealed and now growing in complete darkness.

"Pop the lid?" asked one of the attendants.

"No, we'll take it to Morrison's nearby," said Landry to the men. "Just load it in the van, okay?"

The two attendants, with Gwinn backing off and looking on, lowered thick, coiled ropes through metal brackets on each side of the coffin and worked the ropes below it with some difficulty. The problem was the lack of space between coffin and crypt sides. Soon, however, the box and body were up and straddling the crypt, and in the next few minutes loaded on the waiting van.

Alex's mind wandered again to the previous night. Could Ben have been right about Gilreath? Pigsty was the product of a dysfunctional home, his father ever ready with a belt and a backhand. Maybe something inside the weasel did snap. But Alex had pursued Aspen, who'd attempted to leave via a back door down a passageway. Alex caught the boot-licking, freckled creep just as he was about to exit, and he got rough with him, shoving him against a bathroom door and then into the room itself.

"Whataya want from me? I ain't done nothing."

"Shut up and listen! I want you to tell me how to get in touch with Pigsty."

"Pigsty, hell, man, Sincebaugh! I ain't seen that mother and he owes me a hundred and—"

Alex lost his cool at that point, bodily picking Ricky up and ramming him into the wall, making him cry like a little girl. Ricky also lost it in his pants, and Alex was disgusted at the same time that he was taken aback. He let the other man ease down the wall, but he kept the pressure on by pulling out his .38 and shoving it into Ricky's cheek.

"Don't hurt me, please, man! Don't hurt me," Ricky

pleaded, his face a mask of fear now, wet all over.

"Then tell me what I want to hear."

"I don't know where that fag is, man! I swear it on my mother's grave, God! God, I hate you! God, I swear, I don't know!" he pathetically blubbered.

Alex felt a moment's weakness and was about to relent, but instead screamed, "Then who the hell does know?"

"I don't know!"

"Give me a name now, Ricky, or I do your pretty face. You'll be marred for life."

"You . . . you can't threaten me like this. It's not right. I know my rights."

"In here you don't have any fucking rights, Ricky! They're all flushed down the toilet! Now give it up!"

"Sue Socks, man . . . go see Sue."

"Where?"

"She . . . she works at the Pink Anvil."

"Who is she to Gilreath?"

"I   don't   know.   They're . . . they're   family   or something . . . cousins, I think. Now, let me outta here."

Alex let go of the man, who stank now of urine. Ricky wiped at his tears with his sleeves, speaking like a woman, saying, "I just hate you. I hate you."

"Here, take this for your troubles," Alex replied, pushing a pair of twenty-dollar bills at him.

"I don't want your fucking money."

Alex tossed the bills at him and watched them feather-fly toward the urinals. When he looked back, Ricky was snatching the bills from the floor.

Alex found Ben outside, waiting in the car, talking to his wife on the radio, something about bringing home some groceries and a lottery ticket. Alex told Ben that he had a line on Gilreath, explained how Ricky Aspen had given up a cousin who worked at the Pink Anvil.

"Let's go see this guy, then," replied Ben.

Alex didn't correct Ben, but rather stared into his tired St. Bernard's face and saw the depth of the other man's fatigue like a mirror of his own. "Tell you what, partner. Tonight we go home, get some rest. We'll pursue this tomorrow."

"Yeah, but who's the guy?"

"Tomorrow. Tonight, we get our minds off it."

"But Alex, you were so gung ho before and now—"

"You were right, partner. It's most likely a blind alley anyway, and it's late, damned late, and you've got a family waiting on you. Go home, Ben."

Now the rain-soaked, green and mildewed pine box was being carefully hoisted and loaded into the van here at Cemetery #27, and so much that had happened the previous night seemed a confused jumble. While Alex was pursuing a lead which likely would take him into another black hole to nowhere, he might've been with Kim in her time of need, and for this reason he'd been unable to speak to her or to meet her gaze today.

But now he did so, and his stare went across a wide gulf as though the moments they'd shared earlier meant nothing. Was it his imagination, or was she simply preoccupied with the business at hand? What did she think of him? Why was it so important to him? When did he fall in love with her? All questions he could not answer.

Jessica Coran waited for the others to look away while she examined the striations on the top edge of the crypt where the lid had been pried open and forced across it, initiated by machine and completed by hand. She also closely examined the area where the butane torch had burned away the last remnants of the seal. Something seemed awry and odd, but she couldn't quite put her finger on it just yet, and having had no sleep, she couldn't focus her attention on exactly what it was that bothered her about the damned seal. But there seemed an excessive number of striation marks, more than might have been caused here this morning, and this made her wonder about the type of stone used in the area as it seemed unduly brittle; she also wondered, perhaps foolishly, just how old the crypt was, and if it had had previous inhabitants in years past, and if the premium on graveyard space was so great here that a new form of body-snatching in the 1990s was carried on. She caught Kim Desinor's gaze and the two of them, still sharing the secret of Matisak's note, now shared a questioning look.

Alex's eyes went from Jessica to Kim again, making Jessica wonder what secrets the two of them harbored. Had Kim told

Alex about the note, about her intention to go to Metairie Cemetery tonight? Or were the two of them simply feeling queasy and uneasy about this exhumation? Or was it simpler yet? Were the two of them sharing strong feelings for one another and struggling with those feelings? It was impossible for Jessica to know, but she had exacted another promise from Kim to stand back and stay out of the Matisak affair.

Alex Sincebaugh called to Kim and Jessica to join him in his car or be left stranded.

From Alex's perspective, Jessica surmised that it must seem that the two women had suddenly grown closer. Of course, shared trauma, such as their predawn experience with the death of Ed Sand and the hideous way in which Sand's killer had chosen to alert Jessica Coran to his presence, certainly was enough to bring the two women around to an emotional understanding of the need for one another—comrades in arms, woman to woman. Hell, the damnable monster now knew where Kim was staying; had followed Jessica to Kim's doorstep obviously; had stood inches away from Kim just outside Kim's door. It was enough to drive the two women apart if Kim Desinor were a weak person, or bring them into extremely close unity as it seemed to have done. It also had the NOPD rethinking the blood message left on the wall at 34 East Canal, but a handwriting expert with Meade's FBI unit had gotten samples of Matisak's handwriting and a comparison showed, no contest, that it was not Matisak's script.

Jessica and Kim joined Alex, who appeared to want to take them under his wing—quite a stark comparison to the first time they'd met. Now the procession out of the cemetery with Surette's body was filing through the gate and away to Morrison's, a nearby mortuary where they could work under lights in sanitary conditions.

Ben deYampert had remained uncharacteristically silent throughout the exhumation, this ghoulish business having an obvious and profound effect on him. Sincebaugh drove with Ben beside him. Kim and Alex sat silently in the backseat, like mourners off to a funeral but going the wrong way. Jessica realized that Kim was staring back over her shoulder in the direction of the open crypt, making Jessica also turn to see that the shabbily dressed cemetery caretaker, standing quite alone, was anxiously staring after the parade of officials. The man looked like a large, thin and hungry vulture at standstill, his wings shrouding him. Jessica thought she saw a worry shadow pass like a dark angel across Kim's brow. "Something about that man Gwinn I don't like," Kim muttered.

Their eyes met. Their secret was intact.

The slab room at Morrison's Funerary Services was commandeered for the occasion, much to the delight of old Enoch Samuel Morrison, who'd been wanting more police and city business for years. He made everything available to Dr. Coran, asking out of the side of his tobacco-stained mouth about the whereabouts of Dr. Wardlaw.

Jessica and the others now looked down upon the desiccated body of a young male, and she had started to cut away the clothing when suddenly Kim Desinor said, "This . . . this isn't Surette."

"What?" asked Landry. "That's nonsense."

Ben deYampert quickly agreed. "That's right, Dr. Desinor. Alex and me, we were here a year ago when they put Surette into that very crypt."

"Yeah, we were near about the sum total of his mourners. Wondered then where his gay buddies were, and Ben's right, it was the same crypt."

"Perhaps you're being too hasty, Dr. Desinor. Give it time," suggested Landry.

"I think she's right," Jessica defended.

"What do you mean?"

"Did Surette have red hair?"

"Strawberry-blond, he liked to say," Alex corrected, "but that's pretty close to red, and it has been a year without a perm." Ben chuckled alone at this.

"It's got to be Surette. One way to be certain," Jessica replied. "We'll see about matching the fingerprints, the hair, the DNA, but I gotta tell you, I think we're dealing with a not uncommon problem here with grave sites for the indigent."

"I get a sensation that this man's body has been . . . plundered, but this man was not . . . murdered," added Kim. "Death by injury, accidental . . . automobile . . ."

"Maybe the good doctor's having second thoughts about

laying on of hands on a dead guy,'' suggested Ben deYampert in Alex's ear, shrugging.

Alex nodded heartily to this, thinking that Ben had finally come to see the light as he had. "Hell, his chest is splayed open and caved in, and I'd be willing to bet that below those sutures his heart's gone. Go ahead, Dr. Coran, cut those sutures and check for a heart.''

Jessica nodded, agreeing this would be a simple test of whether they were indeed looking down at the remains of the first Queen of Hearts victim or not. She expertly slipped her scalpel below each suture, commenting that they were not at all tough or dried up but surprisingly supple.

She followed the familiar Y section of the autopsy's viscera cut. "He's obviously had an autopsy,'' she commented. In a moment, her rubbered hands pulled back the dried thin shield of the chest and stomach, sending the flaps across each shoulder, and probing with forceps, she located the various organs, but found the heart missing.

"I guess that little suspicion is cleared up,'' said Landry. "Now, can we carry on with the physical autopsy, and once that is done and he's patched again, Dr. Desinor, you can carry on with your psychic autopsy.''

Alex momentarily wondered where P.C. Stephens and Lew Meade were; he'd imagined that both men wouldn't want to miss the show. He wondered why there weren't any camera crews to film it.

Dr. Desinor stuck to her guns. "I tell you this is not him.''

"I'm inclined to agree.'' Jessica said, shocking the men.

"Based on what?'' Landry was unable to believe what he was hearing. "The man's heart is gone, for God's sake!''

"Based on the age of those sutures, based on the surgical neatness with which the heart muscle was removed, and based on my faith in Dr. Desinor. And if you want further proof, I'd be happy to compare DNA samples. Those of Surette are on file, I presume, at the lab.''

"Who'd go to such lengths for such a hoax, Dr. Coran?'' asked Ben. "That'd entail paying off a lot of people, and who is this guy if he's not Surette?'' DeYampert waved his hands as he questioned her.

"And who cut out this guy's heart to make him look like

Surette? And who switched the bodies and why?'' pressed Landry.

"Gwinn! We better go have a talk with the caretaker," Alex said to Landry.

"You're buying into this, Alex?" asked a skeptical de-Yampert, confused at Alex's sudden turnabout. "Since when?"

Landry looked from the two women to his two detectives. "Go ask the man the hard questions. If the SOB's lying, you'll know it, and if so, haul his ass downtown and let's dig for the rest. Meanwhile, Doctors . . . you'd better be right about all this."

"All right, Captain, we'll go talk to the caretaker and his guys, but if you want my advice, you don't want this one getting around the stationhouse," cautioned deYampert.

Alex agreed. "Yeah, Big's right about that, Carl."

Big Ben looked apologetically down at his captain and rushed to keep pace with Alex.

"What the hell goes on in your frigging cemetery at night when nobody's around! Where're your records on this crypt? Goddamnit, man, what kind of business are you running? Tulane University pay you for cadavers, what?" DeYampert's voice reverberated around the interrogation room. If he couldn't frighten a man with his NFL-lineman features, no one could.

"I ain't done nothing like that, ever . . . ever, Detective. I'm telling you the truth. I wasn't nowhere near the place last night. I don't go out there much after dark. Gives me the willies . . ."

"Just great," wisecracked Alex Sincebaugh, coming off the wall where he'd been leaning. "A cemetery man who's afraid of the dark, and you got a guy taking up space in a plot, but he's in the wrong apartment, but you don't know jack-shit about how he got in there or what happened to the other guy before him. Now an expert's telling us that Victor Surette's body was removed and replaced, Mr. Gwinn . . . says she can prove it by the way the seal on the crypt was cut not once but twice in the last twenty-four hours. Now do you want to come clean?"

"Do you really think you know more than the doctors do?" pressed Big.

"We got your attendants next door, and they're going to give you up, Mr. Gwinn. So, maybe you'd best tell the truth," added Alex.

"Don't know nothing . . . saw nothing . . . can't help you with nothing . . ."

"We're going to walk out of here, Mr. Gwinn . . . going to have a break, maybe a sandwich, some coffee, make a few phone calls. You want anything, Mr. Gwinn?"

"I want to call my wife."

"Sure . . . we'll get a phone in here when we come back."

"Thank you."

"And maybe some Nautilus, a whirlpool, a juice bar," added Alex.

Outside the interrogation room, Ben once more objected to what they were doing, reminding Alex that they still had to follow proper procedure, that Gwinn had asked for his phone call and earlier he'd asked about a lawyer, but that Alex had convinced him he didn't need a lawyer. "It doesn't do any good if we nail this guy for whatever the fuck he's done with that body, if it gets thrown out on one of those damned technicalities, pal, and you know it. Besides, at the moment, we got no definite proof that a crime's been committed by Gwinn, or anyone else for that matter. Whole thing could just be a foul-up. I mean, hell, they sure all seem adamant, Alex."

"Hey, man, I'm just following orders. This Gwinn character was shaking in his boots when we returned for him. He's hiding something. We both know that."

"Yeah, maybe he's renting out space for friends, but I don't think he's intentionally hiding Victor Surette's body from us. Come on, what motive would he have?"

"You remember that rumor that always circulated about Surette, I mean before he was killed?"

"Rumor . . . what rumor?"

"That he came from a wealthy family, possibly an old-money New Orleans family?"

"Okay, maybe I heard something about that, so?"

"Money can buy anything or anybody, Ben. We've both seen it a thousand times in this life. And suppose money bought silence on Surette's killing.''

"You mean from the beginning?''

"From day one.''

DeYampert thought long and hard about this, going to the coffee urn, pouring himself a cup and then returning to Alex. "Whataya saying, Alex?''

"I'm saying I think my instincts about Frank Wardlaw were right on from day one. No wonder he didn't put Surette's death down as a Queen of Hearts killing. He was gotten to.''

"By whom, Alex?''

"The family . . . the freaking family. They didn't necessarily want Victor's body back, but they damned sure wanted to keep the family name unblemished, so—''

"Whoa, wait up, hoss . . . unblemished? This day and age, who gives a shit if you're nephew's a homo or if your niece's a lesbo? Get real, Alex.''

"Surette was a 'showgirl,' remember? He was a headliner in the Quarter. He was no quiet, closet homosexual who picked his lovers out of magazines that came in a brown paper wrapper.''

"So?''

"So, they take the body a year after the fact because they hear of the amazing talents of a psychic detective named Desinor who could well blow the lid off their dirty little family secret.''

"And future victims of the Queen of Hearts killer be damned in the bargain?''

"Don't know about you, but the rich, the filthy rich I've had occasion to deal with, they don't care about our problems, Big.''

"Christ, Alex, that's one hell of a leap from where we're at.''

"Maybe . . . maybe not. Keep pressing Gwinn in there, and I'll see what I can shake loose from his employees.''

"If we accept what Coran and Desinor are telling us about the body being snatched, Sincy . . . well then, somebody's been a busy boy.''

"Someone with a lot of clout and influence had two bodies moved recently on the q.t. One from a recent fatal accident, likely a John Doe whose heart was used to save someone else.

The other a year-old corpse. Now tell me, Big, who do you know who has that kind of clout?''

"You really think Frank Wardlaw is that bitter?''

"Frank may be just the tip of the iceberg. Hell, whoever's behind this, Ben, our Mr. Gwinn in there is scared silly of. Don't need a psychic to tell me that much.''

"But when and why and who, goddamnit, and what would it take to make such a move? That section of the cemetery is city property, filled mostly with John and Jane Does. At least with Surette, he had a name and records, so what gives? His own family consigns him to a John Doe's grave while some fresh new John Doe takes his place?''

"Only after Frank Wardlaw makes the final cut, taking the heart. Did he really think he could get that past Dr. Coran? Wonder where Frank is now?''

"If what you're saying is true, he might well be out of the country.''

"I'll ask Malloy to run him down, see if Frank'd be willing to come in for questioning.''

"Sure, do that, Alex. I'd better get back to our friend inside.''

"See you later then, Ben.''

"Guess that Kim Desinor really is psychic, huh, Sincy?''

"Yeah, better watch out for her, pal. Can't hide much from that one.''

Ben's nervous laughter went with him back into the interrogation room, and Alex made a detour for the squad room. As he went, he thought of how great a partnership he and Big had. They seemed to complement one another perfectly, and Ben kept him on target, humble and laughing. They'd been through a lot together, but this body-snatching thing was something new, and it obviously gave Ben the jitters. They both sensed behind the snatching one big mother of a hand.

Alex looked around the squad room and found Grant Malloy, and asked him if he and his partner would do him a favor.

"Sure, Alex. What's up?''

"Seems Frank Wardlaw has disappeared. Can't locate him in or around his lab, the courthouse. Could you guys locate him and bring him to us?''

"Wardlaw?''

"It's in connection with a sensitive matter."

Malloy smiled appreciatively. "Ahhhh, and how're you and the sensitive Dr. Desinor getting along, Alex? Heard you got your hands on her last night."

"She's light as a feather, Grant, and we're doing pretty well, thanks. How 'bout finding Frank for us?"

"Sure thing."

When Alex returned to Interrogation, he found that Police Commissioner Stephens along with FBI Chief Lew Meade and Captain Carl Landry were on the inside with Gwinn and deYampert. When Ben saw Alex coming through the door, he pushed his partner back into the hallway, and the two of them were followed out by Landry, who informed Alex loudly, "Meade was notified about the situation by Dr. Coran and he's tearing to get at these boys. Says he'd like to scare shit out of 'em by placing them in FBI custody. Tampering with graves is a federal offense, he's telling them."

"What're you saying, Carl? That we just turn these yo-yos over to Meade after all the time we've already invested on this?"

Ben explained that the caretaker's assistants, like Gwinn, weren't giving anything up, at least not yet; it seemed that they were more concerned about what might happen to them if they talked than if they remained silent. "This'll give us a chance to pore over the caretaker's records. Somebody's got to do it. Besides, these guys are asking for lawyers now. Not any more we can get from them."

Alex stared for a moment at Ben, wondering if his big partner had figured out all the angles, and maybe he had. He thought of the boxes of cemetery ledgers, bills, balance sheets and registers they'd only skimmed so far, not having had time to thoroughly digest them as yet. They'd confiscated all the paper along with the men, but so far nothing out of the ordinary had jumped out at them. Still, Alex reasoned aloud, "Who puts this kind of 'transaction' into billable hours, Ben?"

"You kidding, partner? That guy Gwinn and his yak-yaks are certifiable idiots. Crime makes you stupid, remember?"

Alex had earlier paused over the so-called record of internment on one Victor Surette, and he had noted the number on the crypt matching the time and date of internment as well as the location of the crypt on a cemetery map. It all fit. The grave they'd opened was, at least at one time, home to Victor Surette's remains.

"Besides," added Landry, "Coran's preliminary report shows no match on fingerprints or hair, and so she fully expects that DNA'll show the same when those results are in."

"Whataya saying, Cap, that just because you die your fingerprints don't change?" Alex's misplaced sarcasm made Landry heave a sigh. Alex continued in the same vein. "So, we get the records, the Feds get the caretakers? And what about Meade? Doesn't he want the goddamned records too? What's to say he won't yank them out of our hands too, Captain?"

"Ever heard of judicial delay? There's been a court order delaying anyone from looking into those records, including us, but it's going to take us some time to turn those records over to Harry Livingston."

"Harry who?"

"Attorney for the caretaker, Gwinn. He moved on this thing very quickly. Now, if you want time with those records, I suggest you two get to work. Leave the interrogation to Meade for now."

"Ben, you feel the same way?" asked Alex.

"I think . . . I think maybe we ought not to waste more valuable time on those yo-yos than necessary. Let Meade have the headache. It'll keep him busy while we work on the real case at hand. You remember, the Queen of Hearts killer? The SOB is still out there."

The unspoken element in Ben's speech beat a laser-like path through Alex's brain: *Let's do so while there's still time before we're taken off the case completely.*

He stared through the one-way window to see Lew Meade throwing his weight around inside, shouting at the cemetery caretaker while he pounded Dr. Coran's reports on the table-top. Alex switched on the intercom, and Meade's voice came through from inside. "Confound it, man! You're responsible for what goes on out there. You've got to know something. Now, you may's well save all of us a lot of time and start talking; it'll go easier on you if you cooperate.''

"You got something to charge me with, then do it,'' said the grimy man named Gwinn. "Otherwise, I know my rights, and you can't hold me without you got a charge.''

"Now, Mr. Gwinn, you're interfering with an ongoing investigation, and the more you fuck with me, the better your chances you won't ever screw with anyone else ever again! You got that?''

"Told you, I want my lawyer.''

Alex turned to Ben and Landry and asked, "How does this yo-yo afford a guy like Livingston?''

"He must have a bankroll someplace,'' Ben dryly replied.

"The detectives did read you your rights, didn't they?'' asked Meade now.

"Rights? What rights? I ain't so sure I remember any rights being read to me, no.''

"Well, let me read them to you, now that you're going to be in FBI custody.'' Meade began to read the man his Miranda rights.

Looking on at the one-way window, Alex said, "The little weasel is telling the chief of the FBI that we failed to Mirandize him. You did Mirandize the creep, didn't you, Ben.''

"Well . . . perfectly honest with you, Alex . . . no.''

"What? You dumb ox! How could you miss a simple thing like that?''

"We just brought him in for questioning. We didn't at that time arrest him, if you recall. We didn't have anything but the word of that psychic.''

"Whom I thought you believed in at one time.''

"You convinced me otherwise, pal, remember?''

"Shit . . . shit . . .''

Landry grimaced at the two detectives and grunted, "You fools. Do you know what a lawyer can do with that?''

Landry stepped back into the interrogation room to stand and stare at the guilty man. From inside the interrogation room, Meade's raspy voice came over the intercom where the detectives stood watching. "You want to save yourself a lot of time and grief, Gwinn, give it up now. How did the body placed in that crypt a year ago get up and leave from that crypt?''

"And no records kept," Landry said, pressing the sallow-faced, skinny little caretaker.

"Maybe the family showed up; maybe they just wanted to take him to another place."

"What family? According to record, no one claimed the body, ever," said Landry.

"Right move, Captain," said Alex to himself. "Let the ferret sweat, knowing we're climbing all over those records."

"Let's get to it then, Sincy," suggested Ben.

"Right . . . right you are, Big. Let's get to it."

"Kinda too bad about the autopsy being broken up."

"Why's zat?"

"Might've cleared up a lot; might've led us in the right direction."

"What's zat? I thought I just heard you say, Ben, that you don't believe in that woman's witchcraft anymore."

"Well, I don't, not completely . . . but I wish it was so, and I wish we'd have found a new direction on this thing."

"You and all of New Orleans, I guess. I'm still having trouble understanding why Landry asked Dr. Desinor in on the case to begin with."

Ben stopped him cold and angrily said, "Look, Alex, they were going to go ahead with Dr. Desinor's reading of one of the bodies anyway. Captain Landry, he pushed for going back as far as Surette, which, if you recall, was your idea, remember? So don't get down on Carl."

With that Ben left Alex standing in the corridor. Ben had seemed not himself, as if something was eating at him, and maybe this was it. Maybe Ben was tired of bailing Alex out of one scrape with a higher official after another. He'd helped in the IAD matter, providing character props for Alex; he'd always backed Alex against Lew Meade's underhandedness, like the time Meade tried to exact information about Alex's so-called involvement with an underworld informant to the mob, inferring that Alex was on the take. Ben had always been a stand-up guy against such ridiculous allegations, and had in fact warned Alex about Meade early on.

Now the big guy was standing up for Carl Landry. All in a day's work for the veteran, older officer deYampert, the heart and soul of the NOPD detective bureau.

26

> Pure instinct is as rare as musical genius,
> medical miracles, white tigers, an Einstein
> or a pure heart.
>
> —From the Notebooks of Jessica Coran

With the exhumation now a bust, the investigation went grinding slowly forward at the precinct, deYampert and Sincebaugh meticulously going through the caretaker's damnably frustrating records for anything whatsoever that might explain the disappearance of the Surette body. But nothing was surfacing from the moldy, crumbling records, which in effect were eight-by-five cards in shoe boxes. The city sure knew where to spend its money; the computer age hadn't caught on in the cemetery game, at least not in the city cemeteries.

Sincebaugh's telephone rang amid the clutter, and he dove for it, delighted over the disturbance. Ben almost caught the call, but as always Alex was quicker on the draw. "Yeah, Detective Sincebaugh."

"I know you're not Dr. Desinor's greatest fan, Alex, but—"

"Whataya talking about, Captain?" he said.

Landry started again. "I know you don't like Dr. Desinor or what she stands for, Alex, but you also, apparently, don't like to be left out of the loop."

"What's going on now, Captain?"

"Why don't you meet me at Dr. Longette's office this afternoon at two, and don't be late."

"I've got these records to comb through, Captain, and last bloody thing I need right now is a shrink in my face."

"Not past noon, you don't."

"Come again?"

"The records, they're all gone bye-bye by then. The lawyer Livingston'll be here by then."

"So much for that avenue; hell, it's eleven thirty-five now. When the hell do we get to do our jobs, Captain?"

"We don't have any choice, Alex. So, just be *chill-civil,* okay?"

Alex smiled at this Landryism. Carl had a way with words. "I'll be my chillin'-civil best, Carl. Now, what's this about Dr. Longette's office? What the hell's deYampert been telling you? Christ, Captain, I really don't have the friggin' time for a shrink, and I sure as hell don't need a shrink, and—"

"Longette's not going to be looking at you. The shrink's for her!"

"Her?"

"Dr. L for Dr. Desinor, yes."

"Whataya mean?" Alex was confused. "He's going to examine Kim?"

"As an aside, without her knowledge, yes, but the main event which she's agreed to—"

"You've asked her to submit to what, a psychological evaluation? How'd you get her to submit to ''

"No, no! Will you just listen? She called me, asked if I could suggest a good hypnotist. She wants to be put under."

"Under hypnosis . . ." He recalled her having said something about being hypnotized in order to recall what her own visions had been during her last trance, but he'd assumed she was just talking to hear herself or to impress him. She was full of surprises.

Landry continued to explain. "So she can reveal all that she saw last night at the Marie Dumond murder scene."

"Are we still jacketing this guy as Marie Dumond?"

"It's all the name we have so far, unless you prefer John or Jane Doe. Take your pick."

"So Dr. Longette's going to be operating when?"

"Operating," Landry repeated with a laugh. "It's called regression therapy. Anyway, Dr. Longette's going to perform the . . . the surgery at two. Now, do you or don't you want to be on hand?"

He hesitated. Longette was good. Did Kim Desinor know what she was letting herself in for? If anyone could damage her credibility, it was Longette. Maybe now Alex would have an ally for his case against using psychics in police detection, particularly this psychic on this, his case, but at the same time, on an emotional level, he truly didn't want to see Kim hurt. Still, if she were a fraud . . .

"Okay, I'll be there. I'll bring Ben, if he wants to be on hand."

"Fine . . . should prove interesting."

"Yeah, maybe . . ."

"Alex, none of this psychic business was my idea, but I have to admit, the woman puts up one hell of a front. If you recall, it was she who first called into question the identity of the Surette body this morning at Number 27."

"So she did and so she does . . . put up one hell of a front, I mean. But she told me you called her in on the case."

"Not hardly; I argued against it. Stephens found her somewhere, rammed her down my throat. 'Fraid I wasn't much more polite with her than you at first. Well, see you at two, Alex." Landry hung up, and Alex stared across the room while Ben stared back at him with a *what-in-hell* look on his horse face.

"She's going to go under regression therapy with Dr. Longette."

"Really? The psychoanalysts' answer to Michael Jordan? Talk about hang time . . ."

Alex only shrugged, knowing Ben was right. Dr. James Aubrey Longette wouldn't be so easily taken in by the cunning and chicanery of a phony psychic.

"A strange sensation . . ."

"What kind of sensation, Kim?"

". . . has overtaken my mind . . ."

"Yes?"

". . . know I'm going to die . . . that I'm about to be killed . . . fear . . . the fear is like an enormous, pounding muscle inside me, exploding up through me."

"Fear." Dr. Longette's whisper was a penetrating knife that dug into Kim Desinor's unconscious mind.

"Not fear of dying . . . fear of being forgotten . . . wrong to die here, like this . . . as . . . as Marie Dumond. My family so far away . . . they don't know about Marie. . . . "

Kim Desinor was perspiring profusely as she spoke in a

hypnotically induced trance produced by Dr. James Aubrey Longette; her beautiful features distorted by some pain from deep within, she seemed to speak to the rhythmical hum of Longette's tape recorder alongside the couch where she lay. Longette worked out of two offices, practicing psychiatric medicine for St. Christopher's Episcopal Hospital in the heart of the city and here at NOPD headquarters, moonlighting as a police shrink, doing an in-depth study of police under stress which he hoped to see published in *Scientific American* or *Psychology Today* by the end of the year under the title "No More RoboCops." Beyond his manuscript, he had definite plans for the Oprah TV show and the Montel Williams program, hosted by a person he much admired. From there, he decided, the sky was the limit. But the police work which he'd taken on with a mild interest had become a passion, and he wasn't sure he'd ever be able to completely walk away from it; not that it was glamorous—far from it. But it was gamesmanship, involving every level of the psyche and the emotions; it was Clue, only for real, three-dimensional Clue.

Longette was trained in hypnotism and regression therapy. He moved about the room as he spoke to and responded to Kim Desinor, ever aware that they were being watched by Captain Landry, Alex Sincebaugh and Ben deYampert through a one-way mirror he'd had installed on his arrival here. Longette was something of a showman himself, and for cases involving criminals, or for something like this, he wasn't about to pull the curtain over the portal. Longette was a tall, imposing man—living up to his name. Elegant in his mannerisms, and as handsome as he was black, he brought to mind a darker version of the singer/actor Harry Belafonte. Impeccably dressed, he looked as much a lawyer as a shrink, and his baritone voice filled a room.

Sincebaugh had had to deal with him on a few cases, but usually their contact was indirect, and while Sincebaugh found him to be quite capable and found his reports done with extreme care, the man made Alex nervous only to a small degree less than did Kim Desinor.

"Can't die as Marie . . . can't!" she was saying now.

"Can you see your attacker's face, Marie?" asked Longette.

"No, not Marie . . . Thomas . . . my name is Thomas."

"Thomas? Really?" Longette sounded dubious, suspicious. Sincebaugh, watching, wondered exactly whom he was suspicious of, Marie Dumond or Dr. Desinor? Sincebaugh knew which one he was more suspicious of, but for test accuracy, Dr. Longette had been told nothing of the pending case.

"Thom . . . Thommie . . ."

"Thommie who?" pressed Longette.

"Way . . . lon . . . Wal . . . ley . . ."

"Really?"

"No . . . Whiley, yes, Whiley."

Longette's voice was like the voice of God, or maybe James Earl Jones.

Outside, Landry told Ben deYampert, "Run a check on the name Thomas Whiley. See if we got anything on him."

Ben deYampert's eyebrows arched in a V, and he stared for only a moment at his boss, glanced at Alex, raised his wide shoulders and said, "Alex, you know, I seem to recall we talked to a guy named Thommie Whiley after the Surette body was discovered."

"Yeah, I remember . . . one of the last guys to see Surette alive. He was a boyfriend for a time. Had a rap sheet for male prostitution, right?"

"The guy hung out on Royal in the Quarter at the time. You don't suppose he and this Marie Dumond are one and the same, do you?"

"That's what she's saying. She had to've read about Thommie on the police reports we filed. So she lifts his name. I'm telling you, the woman's dangerous. You know what they say, Captain . . . a little bit of knowledge is a dangerous thing."

"So I've heard. So let's find out more about this Thommie Whiley just the same, Ben. Find out if it's the same guy as in the morgue, okay? Call it in; have 'em go to priority one on it," Landry ordered.

Ben nodded and left.

On the other side of the glass, Dr. Longette continued in his mellow and soothing tones. "All right, Thomas . . ."

"Thommie . . . I prefer Thommie . . . with a T-H . . ."

"All right, Thommie . . . can you see your attacker's face?"

"It's not his face anymore. Changed . . . distorted . . . was lovely but now filled with . . . rage, venom."

"Who, Thommie? Who killed you?"

Behind the mirrored wall, Sincebaugh dropped his gaze and muttered, "This is bullshit, Captain."

Landry waved him off, listening for Dr. Desinor's answer.

"I thought it was E. You know . . . said he liked me. Said he liked vulnerable things. But it wasn't E that killed me . . . what killed me was unusual, queer, demonic, insane. It wasn't E anymore . . . any more than I'm really me here now."

"What do you mean by that, Thommie?"

"I know I'm being channeled through someone here now. . . ."

"What does E look like, Thommie, and what does E stand for?" Longette came closer now, leaning in over her unconscious form. "How tall is E?"

"He's beautiful, really; can't recall real name . . . full name, but I liked calling him Easy or E. He didn't seem to mind, and he was easy . . . too easy as it happens . . . Lied to me . . . probably lied to me about his relationship with Vic . . ."

Outside Alex shook his head and repeated the name Vic, telling Landry, "This is just too pat to be real."

Inside she continued. "What's it they say? If it looks too good to be true, it is! But fine-looking . . . in heels . . ."

"Heels?" Dr. Longette repeated, looking through the glass and shaking his head at this.

There'd been a puncture in the dead boy's forehead at the temple that might match up to a spiked heel, according to Frank Wardlaw's report on 34 East Canal Street.

"Tall, five-eleven to maybe six-one . . . two maybe," continued Dr. Desinor as Thommie Whiley.

"Weight, Thommie?"

"Slim, well proportioned, thin but muscular and firm at the same time. A beautiful man, really. Always careful to keep his weight below one-forty, or so he told me on the way. . . . "

"Color of eyes, Thommie?"

"Usually blue, but green now . . . definitely green."

"Green or blue, Thommie?" Eyes don't change color, Longette was thinking.

"Not a pretty green, a snake-scale green . . . when he killed me."

Dr. Longette looked dubious. "Green eyes or blue, Thommie?" *Eyes don't change but contacts do.* Longette was thinking more and more like the policemen he worked alongside these days.

"Green . . . green, insane eyes, but they'd changed."

"Any distinguishing marks, birthmarks, scars on E's body? Thommie? Thommie?"

"E's makeup accentuated a . . . a strawberry red mark on her left cheek . . . but it *changed* too . . ."

"Changed? Changed how?"

"Disappeared. It wasn't there when she killed me."

Makeup, Longette thought, could cover a strawberry mark, but a transvestite would want to make the most of such a mark. "How did he—she—kill you, Thommie?"

"Butcher's knife . . . ran it to the hilt here . . ." She pointed to her sternum. "Blade was deflected to right of my sternum, sank deep as it would go; put all her weight against it; punctured my right lung and came out the back."

"Jot that down," said the captain into Sincebaugh's ear. "We'll check it against Dr. Coran's report later."

Sincebaugh reluctantly did as told.

"Why did E murder you, Thommie? Can you tell me that? Why did he"—Longette paused to mutter a curse to himself—"she, why did she take your heart? What does she do with the hearts?" Longette's voice was melodious, soothing, at odds with his words, and his professional bearing was curtailed for the moment by his curiosity, a curiosity he shared with the entire population of New Orleans.

Desinor took a long time in answering.

"E did it. She . . . she wanted my heart, even said so. Said she wanted to keep my heart close to her forever. Knife was in me; my eyes fixed on it; ears ringing, fever rising, but I heard her say, 'I just want your heart, hon . . . you . . . you can keep the rest.' "

Kim was writhing on the leather couch, the pain clearly etched in her features. It was hell having to relive Thommie's painful and bloody death all over again, but a small corner of Kim Desinor's mind remained hers, and this part of her looked on and listened as if from a corner of the room above, near the ceiling where her astral self stared down on her form, Dr.

Longette and their ghoulish dialogue.

She knew that Dr. Longette was dubious, but she also knew that she'd shown herself to be a person of strong determination, moral fiber and old-fashioned grit, which nobody, not even Sincebaugh behind the glass, could deny.

"Thommie," she said now in the third person, "Thommie didn't know until the last moment that he was being killed."

"Is that you, Dr. Desinor?"

She didn't directly reply. "He believed that E was on something when he was first knocked to the floor beside the bed; Thommie's head struck the bedpost, but he was in such shock . . . didn't feel this blow. Instead, he managed to grab onto the baseball bat."

"The bat was discovered below the bed, fresh blood on it," Landry whispered into Alex's ear as if afraid Kim could hear through walls. "We'd assumed it was the victim's blood, but now, maybe not."

Alex recalled Kim's having mentioned a ball bat the night before. Had she seen it below the bed when she'd fallen? Not likely, since she'd been out cold before she hit the ground.

Kim continued speaking as Thomas Whiley. "Been beaten by my father most my life . . ." A distinct bayou dialect was beginning to filter into her voice. "Wasn't going to take no beatin' from nobody no more, ever . . . and when she come at me, I grabbed up that bat. Hit him good once't, but he was insane strong, didn't even feel it; jus' grabbed the bat from me. I tripped up and 'fore I hit the floor, she come down on me with a spiked heel to my head. Don't 'member him puttin' me 'cross the bed. Woke up with the knife in me . . ."

"He, she, him, her, what's his real sex, Thommie?" pressed Dr. Longette.

"Louisville slugger . . ."

"What?"

"The bat . . . it was my Louisville slugger. Didn't slow him up a hog's breath, though."

There was a moment of silence as Dr. Longette turned to face the glass and raise his shoulders. *Is she under? Yes. Is she faking this? Maybe, but to do so, she'd have to have one hell of a mind,* he thought.

"Thomas is my real name. Thomas Peterson Whiley the

Second. But now I'm a woman. I'm Marie . . . Marie Dumond. Died a woman and will be one in eternity. Please bury me as a woman."

"We'll . . . we'll do what we can to respect your wishes, Thommie."

"Marie . . . please, Marie."

"Yes, of course."

"No one'll claim my body anyways, like what come of poor Vic's body . . . I watched from my car. Guess I'll be buried by the state, another nobody."

"We're looking into your true identity, Thomas," Dr. Longette assured the disembodied spirit. "We'll find your family. Your passing will not go unnoticed."

"Name on my driver's license purchased from a paper mill on Quincey."

Sincebaugh had seen the beautiful job that someone had done on Marie Dumond's driver's license. He knew that for the right amount of cash, anything could be had on Quincey Street in New Orleans. Of course, Dr. Desinor would know that too, having grown up in the city.

"I'll be dead . . . Marie'll be dead, and nobody'll know who she is, and nobody'll care. . . . "

Sincebaugh, from behind the glass, muttered in Landry's ear, "Got that right . . ."

"We care," said Dr. Longette. "We really do."

"What about Marie? Do you care about Marie?"

"Is there anything more, anything at all, that you want to tell us, Marie?" he asked, deflecting the question.

"E . . . he . . . he really didn't mean it. He . . . E just wasn' himself."

"Wasn't himself how?"

"Crazed . . . beside himself . . . I think in his right mind, he couldn't've done it. It was when he became she."

"E then is a cross-dresser too, you mean?"

Captain Landry turned to Sincebaugh. "I want a line on this E guy, where he hangs, what he does, where he goes, who he goes with, all of it."

"I've never heard of anyone on the street goes by that o Easy, but we'll certainly follow up."

"Looks like your instincts were good all along, Alex. The

killings are not aimed at the gay community from outside forces, but rather from within the gay community itself; one of them is killing his own, and the key has to be this guy, E or Easy. Doesn't ring any bells, huh?''

"You know how many of these guys are transient. They come and go like the pigeons. Still, thought I knew all the street names, but no . . . no, sir, it doesn't. We can run 'im through the computer, see what kicks out."

"Either way, Alex, you nailed it, gay community."

"Transvestite community, French Quarter."

"What's the difference?"

"Big difference in their ranks. Not all transvestites are gay, not all gay men are cross-dressers."

"As in not all bats live in caves? Give me a break, Alex."

"As in not all gays are HIV positive, Captain. Look, I'll be at my phone, see what I can dig up on our man E. I've seen enough of this hocus-pocus."

"You've seen enough, but you're willing to investigate this E character based solely on a psychic's recall under hypnosis? I'll tell you what, Alex, if this E guy turns out to be our man, this *hocus-pocus* will have been worth every dime, my friend."

"And if it doesn't pan out? You gonna give her the heave-ho? You gonna bring the tent down on this . . . circus?"

"I'll certainly try, Alex, but as you know, it's rather out of my hands. . . . ''

"Do Stephens and Meade know about this session with Dr. Longette?"

"No, thought we'd keep this among us for now, and Dr. Desinor was obliging."

"And Dr. Coran?"

"No FBI for now."

With that news, Sincebaugh felt a bit relieved. Good move, Captain, he wanted to shout. Anything to ax Lew Meade from the new deal. "I'll go find Big, and we'll see what we can scrounge up on this *Easy* guy." Alex knew that he'd combine the search for E with the search for Susie Socks, the alleged cousin to Davey "Pigsty" Gilreath.

— 27 —

May the light fade from your eyes, so you never see
what you love. May your own blood rise against you,
and the sweetest drink you take be the bitterest cup
of sorrow. May you die without benefit of clergy;
may there be none to shed a tear at your grave, and
may the hearthstones of hell be your best bed forever.

—Traditional Wexford Curse

Matthew Matisak pretended an aimless, wandering gait along
the streets of New Orleans, a free man, his attention on the
final steps that would bring him to the coming, decisive duel
with her, Jessica Coran. He fully expected to take his due from
her, after wrapping up a few loose ends, and this time he
would be completely in control, all arrangements having been
made— *All systems a go and me aglow,* he wickedly thought.
This time her own blood would rise against her to become his
absolutely and forever.

He had thoughtfully mapped out how they would meet, how
he would lead her into his snare, what his final meal would
be like, for it would be supplied by her and it would be his
last. She would so fulfill him that he would have nowhere
afterward to turn. He would have reached his personal zenith.
So he would destroy himself while her blood was coursing
through him, taking a part of her into eternity with him.

The means was at hand. He had already prepared and tested
the equipment on a young girl he'd found wandering about
the Greyhound bus station the night before. All was operational at the location he had paid well for.

He had paid top dollar for the portable dialysis machine
which would remove Jessica's lifeblood in a controlled fashion
and filter it into him in just as controlled a fashion. He planned
to O.D. on her blood, to burst his own blood vessels with an
overabundance of the good stuff.

''What a way to go,'' he told himself.

Not riddled with bullets, not electrocuted or gassed, not plummeting to his death during an escape or progressively rotting away in a cell, but to die in a fashion befitting such a demonic force as himself, in a manner which he would have chosen, master of his own fate. He intended to be literally imploded from within by her blood—at least all his arteries and veins would detonate, so full would they become with their commingling of blood.

It was so rare and evil an idea that it could not have been born overnight, but rather had crept up in inchworm fashion over his mind, coming on at first softly to tickle his psyche, a playful half-formed, seeking-cohesion, heat-seeking idea of a lifetime. At first slow to form and coalesce and live fully, the idea had in the past few months—since killing Dr. Gabriel Arnold with his own dialysis machine—begun to chase through Matisak's consciousness like a steam engine bound nonstop for Hades, and now . . . finally . . . years in the making . . . it was here in New Orleans that the complete beauty of this perfect notion had come to pure fruition like the blossom on a passionate flower.

She must come to him now . . . come for him, unable to help herself any longer.

She would do so alone.

He knew that she would abandon all her training, that she knew, like him, that eternity was waiting for them to step into its waiting void together.

She would come for the same reason that he must beckon her: They were locked into meeting their death angels at the same instant in time. For all eternity hereafter they must grapple with one another. Besides, she was noble and nobles like her couldn't help themselves, not really, not after all the numbers who'd died in her place because she was so noble. She must feel great remorse for the others; it was not in her makeup to feel otherwise, especially with the last person to take her sacrificial place—this special agent named Sand whose cover as a pilot might have fooled Jessica but had not fooled him. The fool had led him directly to her.

He had learned of her relocation to New Orleans on temporary assignment through a series of phone calls, pretending an urgent message from her last tour of duty office in Honolulu. He had even learned the name of the Hawaii bureau chief, a man named James Parry, and he had used this name to get information about her whereabouts and current operation, tracking down this Queen of Hearts pervert. Think of it, he told himself now, some sick bastard's going around ripping out the hearts, likely cannibalizing them. "And they call me sick," he said aloud to the wind, a nearby doorman in a phony general's uniform giving him a dubious look, having overheard him.

Matisak moved on down the street. He wasn't surprised to learn that his Jessica had tackled the gruesome case that had all of New Orleans in turmoil. He'd been reading about the case, which had been making national headlines, and there had been talk of FBI involvement, and the moment he'd read of it, he'd somehow known that Jessica would come here. This hunch, and a little fast talk with some lab technician he'd managed to reach inside Quantico after several other people had disconnected, had been enough to seal Jessica's fate. She'd come from hot, humid D.C. to the even steamier jazz capital of the world to party with a monster, do a little Mardi Gras of her own. But *he* was the monster that was going to get her, not this heart-eating bastard who went for gays and cross-dressers.

He needed now only to bide his time. Killing Special Agent Sand was his first calling card. Maybe now he'd take out another of her bodyguards, the guy who was in the car across the street from her hotel for the past two nights, the guy whom Ed Sand had shared a great deal of time with, another of Jessica's bodyguards.

Jessica must know by now that she was being watched by others ordered by the Bureau to protect her. She'd no doubt found a way out of the hotel and was on her way to Metairie Cemetery by now, but in the meantime, Matisak wanted to make her feel safe from all these prying eyes.

He moved toward the car and stepped behind and around it, to knock at the passenger-side window. The man inside rolled the window down, expecting his replacement perhaps.

"Who the hell're you?"

Matisak's tongue pushed forth a miniature blowgun and he

puffed once hard, sending the thin, deadly shard of a needle into the FBI agent's throat along with some spittle. The tiny dart brought on an instant seizure of the heart, respiratory paralysis, vomiting for a few agonizing moments, then full paralysis and death. It was a fine drug, this Jericho rose, and he'd read with amusement that if bees pollinated their honey with it, they would create poisonous honey. Nature's a wonderful thing, he thought.

Matisak got in beside the man and pulled forth a thick loop of wire attached to two small handles that fit nicely into his large hands. The wire, which he placed around the dying man's head, he began to twist, using the handles around one another in tourniquet fashion. Pressure against the throat was instantaneous, the blood careening forth from veins and arteries along the throat, all this before the man's bulging eyes popped completely.

Matisak now viciously twisted the wire until the man's head slumped forward, having nothing but the top of the spinal column to hold it on. A good pull, and the head came off in its entirety to land bowling-ball-fashion in Matisak's bloodied hands.

Lapping at the blood from time to time, much of it washing the dash and interior window, he was tempted to drink heavily from this fount, but he mustn't. The little darts with the concentrated poison had worked extremely well and effectively, so he knew that he mustn't consume very much of the man's blood. The fast-acting toxin would have worked its way through the man's system even as he'd severed the arteries.

He was pleased with his simple and crude decapitator. It was an effective way to deal with those who stood between him and her, and there were few killings more disturbing than decapitation murders, so he'd have the police looking for a serial killer whose patterns resembled anything but those of Matthew Matisak, while at the same time he'd be telling Jessica Coran exactly what he needed to tell her.

He was saving himself up for her like a virgin groom. He meant to feed on her alone now.

Having removed the head completely now, he balanced it back atop the agent's bloodied throat just long enough to snatch out the folded leather pouch he carried with him. He opened the small leather bag and now removed the man's head for a second time, placing it, dripping and spoiled with perspiration and blood, into the bag.

Checking his watch, he knew he had to hurry out to Metairie. He wanted to be there far in advance of the moon and long before his sweet Jessica might arrive. There were, after all, provisions to be made.

He placed the head-filled bag in the rear of the vehicle with a slight tossing movement. It hit the seat, bounced readily and came to rest on the floorboard, all quite neat, no blood rivulets and stringy matter clinging to the cushions. He next got out of the car and manfully dragged what was left of Fouintenac—whose cover likely disguised his true name—over to the passenger side of the black sedan. He then quickly got behind the wheel and turned on the ignition, and in a moment Matthew Matisak moved the death car into traffic, following the highway signs for Metairie.

Stepping from out of a black entryway at Orleans and Esplanade Avenues, a lifelong resident of New Orleans, Chester Lewis, wiped his forehead of sweat. He'd lived a long life at seventy-two years of age, and before tonight, before moments ago, he'd believed that he'd seen all things human and awful, but tonight he had witnessed the worst brutality in his experience.

He took several more pulls on his Red Label, gulping the liquid down as if life depended on it, wondering if he ought to tell somebody what he'd seen, wondering if his son would listen to him, or maybe Maybelle Saunders, his landlady and girlfriend. What should he do? He wondered if he'd just become the only witness to a Queen of Hearts murder, or more likely a murder by some new monster. Maybe he'd just tell his son and Maybelle . . . maybe . . .

"Jesus, tell me, what is dis world coming to anyhow?" he asked the dark street and the handful of transients and passersby, who just stared at him as if he were a freak. "What is yo world coming to, Jesus?" he drunkenly repeated.

He could be a good Boy Scout, play by the rules, but what could he tell anybody? He was near blind, and even nearer drunk when he saw what he saw, and who was going to listen to an old retired nigger bus driver anyhow? The governor? Sure. The mayor maybe, or perhaps the police commissioner? He laughed at the idea, but his nerves, his eyes and his conscience were already preying on him. Just a few years ago the city had finally begun to hire black cabdrivers in what was once an all-white profession. He had to do his duty. Maybe if somebody had just come forward and done their duty before now, lives would have been saved.

"Christ-on-my-knee, what chance anybody gonna wanna hear what I gots to say," he told himself aloud.

Still, he did know the license plate on the car. He'd been frozen in place by what he had witnessed from the doorway where he'd been resting and drinking; he'd been there long enough to memorize the license plate as he'd had a clear view of it, just as he'd had a clear view of the attack. He'd seen the man inside slouch over like he was shot by some silent bullet. He had seen the man's head cut clean away. Seen it all through the back window from where he sat, his feet against one doorjamb, his back to the other.

"God, that killer-man waza mostest brazen human bein' I ever seen in all my days. Damned if he didn't move like the Devil hisself," he quietly warned himself, ambling toward home, still debating with himself as to what he should do, still wondering why the hunched-over, bloated guy who did the killing had taken off the man's head to place it in a tote bag, wondering what the devil intended doing with the head.

He cautioned himself a last time to not get involved. "Nobody gonna b'lieve an ol' fool nigger anyway," he rationalized aloud. "Leastways, not a liquored-up one."

Just the same, he had to tell somebody. He'd tell his boy, if he could find him home. If not, he'd confide in Maybelle. Maybe she'd know what to do.

In the dark confines of the yellow cab Jessica Coran felt completely alone—as she should be, she told herself. No one else would come between Matisak and her, no one in harm's way. It was nearing midnight and the monster awaited.

She recalled her most important confidence to Kim, the one she'd wanted everyone to know: She didn't want to be responsible for another soul to pass from this world because of Matisak's sick obsession with her, and one way or another it had to end tonight.

And if Kim were like Ed Sand, here as one of Paul Zanek's carefully placed bodyguards, then Jessica would know that too before the night was over. But nothing must happen to Kim, she firmly told herself. No one could ever again fall victim to Matisak.

Jessica had earlier found a back way out of the hotel, and using a London Fog coat, a pair of dark glasses and a service elevator, she had quickly located the tunnels below street level. A few blocks from the hotel, she'd located a cab, which now bumped the curb and came to a sudden halt before an old stone and metal sign that read: "Metairie Cemetery."

The cabdriver had been dubious, but after she'd slipped him a few bills he'd kept his concerns to himself. Now he said nothing, even as he stared out at the desolate location and the high gates to the cemetery. The place was closed and locked against the public this time of night.

This wasn't exactly the time and place she'd have chosen for an end to her life, and it wasn't that she particularly wanted to die here tonight, or that she felt suicidal, but she was determined that no one else on the periphery of the combat would die because of the indiscriminate, all-encompassing conflict that had become like some cosmic battle between her and Matisak.

"You wan' I should wait, lady?" the Spanish driver finally asked, having no idea of the danger he was already in.

"No, no, thanks . . . I'm . . . well, I'm expecting someone."

"I hope it ain't Dracula, lady," joked the cabbie, unaware that he was so close to the truth.

"Thanks for your concern, Mr. . . . ahhh . . ." She scanned for his name on the dash I.D., but he supplied it with a flurry of his hand before she could eyeball it.

"Santiago, Andreas Santiago . . . Andy for short. You sure you don' wan' me to wait round, lady?"

"No, please . . . I'll be all right."

"Okay den, dat'll be fifteen-fifty for de trip, miss."

She quickly paid the fare, thinking simultaneously of the job that lay ahead of her and of the neon lights of a Lil' Champ all-night convenience store a block and a half back. If she needed assistance, she could go there, she reasoned, find a phone—if she should survive this encounter.

Stepping out of the cab, she felt a blanket of damp fog engulf her spirit. As the cab drove away, an eerie glow below the few street lamps in an area dominated by the cemetery made the darkness so much darker. Peering in through the gates, she saw a necropolis in the truest sense of the term. Staring back at her was an underworld turned inside out, an aboveground cemetery of bleak tombs and grim memorials. And somewhere crouching behind one of these burial stones, waiting for her to enter his chosen field of battle, was Mad Matthew Matisak.

He wasn't likely to be stepping out into the open or coming from behind those black wrought-iron gates, she told herself, a damp chill penetrating her bones, tickling like fingers across a piano up and down her spine. A disturbing uneasiness, creeping up from deep within, filled her every fiber, pore and cell all the way to the surface, the epidermal layer, with dread. Core fear, rising . . . climbing . . . mounting like mercury in a thermometer. Rising from inside her. Fear from the center of being . . . interrupted only by ugly, jolting flashes of the last time she was under "Teach" Matisak's control.

She stepped away from the gates, fully realizing that he was in there peering out at her from the fog-laden world of the dead. She could feel his eyes on her. She walked beside the high stone walls at a quick step, taking herself out of his view, seeking the comfort of stone walls thrown up between them, and seeking another way in, which appeared most likely to mean climbing over the walls.

This did little to reinforce the courage she'd started out with. She felt as if the eyes of the monster could easily see through the stone wall she now moved along. He could see through stone and straight into her private hell to her frightened heart, which was beating like a wounded bird's. How often had he read her mind; he certainly must know her thoughts now that she meant to destroy him at all costs.

She felt a sudden shameful yet overwhelming weakness take control of her limbs, fear robbing her of strength and resolve. Her lungs were hot lead in her chest, two pistons rising and falling with the falsetto voice of her startled heart. She was out of step, not herself, unsure, her hands trembling.

"Damn him," she cursed aloud, "damn him to hell and me with him if necessary." She had to get a grip on herself and now.

A shaky, shady-looking character in rags came stumbling from nowhere and was coming directly toward Jessica, an outstretched hand running along the cemetery wall for balance. His face was shrouded in shadow as was his physique, but he appeared to favor his left-hand side as Matisak had always done, and there was a familiarity to this lumbering shadow's gait and that hunchbacked appearance. She flashed on the memory of how easily the fiend slipped into disguise. It was him. He had come out of the cemetery at some point up ahead of her and was coming straight for her.

She raised her weapon, about to fire when the ragman's face was suddenly tinted with a flood of light from a black wrought-iron New Orleans lamppost, revealing a wide-eyed wino with a toothless mouth the size of the Grand Canyon.

"You . . . you Dr. Coran?" asked the strange, ugly man under the light.

"Yes, I am."

"You're to go alone to Gatorland Storage, the old Jacobi warehouse district. That's alls I know." He'd gone wide-eyed on seeing her .38 leveled at his brain. Now he turned and stumbled away.

"God, Jess," she cursed herself. "Get hold."

She'd imagined this moment for a long time now, and she had wondered how she would find the strength, the courage and the will to carry out her own deadly plan against the madman. Now that she was here, however, she only felt alone and weak and fearful and stupid; she'd almost gunned down an innocent, harmless man who had no notion he acted as Satan's messenger this night.

How was she going to cope with facing Matisak outside his cage if she couldn't make the simplest judgments with some accuracy? She began to question herself. Was she being foolish? Was she being suicidal, courting death coming here this way? What might happen if he were to survive their encounter but she were to die? Who would stop him after she was gone?

She heard every sound now as if it were in Dolby stereo, the creaking of a branch in the chill wind, the rustle of leaves as they skittered across graves on the other side of the wall, the humming of electricity through the veins of the city, a cat on paws sliding across a trash can and onto the stone fence overhead, its bulging green eyes glaring at her. A night bird keeping a wary eye on the cat while spying on Jessica. All accoutrements for the Halloween setting of this place.

She knew that he waited patiently within. Just like the old Buddy Holly song title, "True Love Waits."

She could feel his eyes on her, the staring, unblinking, uncompromising sonofabitch. She was his easy prey now.

Matisak had every advantage. He knew where she was. He merely had to wait for her to step closer, to commit totally to his trap.

Woman is like your shadow; follow her,
she flies; fly from her, she follows.

—Sebastian R.N. Chamfort

Alex Sincebaugh had spent the entire evening in desperate pursuit of a line on a guy named Easy or Big Easy or any variant, such as E-Z. But none of those he came up with who used any of those aliases seemed a likely suspect. So Ben and he had spent a frustrating night—that is, until Alex talked Ben back into pursuing the Davey Gilreath angle. He wanted to put the touch on Gilreath's relative, this Susie Socks.

Ben didn't share Alex's single-minded determination, and they had some words when, after long hours, Ben began to moan, too fatigued, he said. Still, they drove for the Pink Anvil only five blocks riverside from the Blue Heron. At the club, Susie Socks—no doubt her name was an alias—wasn't on duty, but on her night off people were more inclined to talk about her. When Alex learned that she was in fact Gilreath's sister, he became doubly excited. She had been living and working in the area for a little over a year, having come on the scene at about the time of Victor Surette's death—also an interesting wrinkle, thought Detective Sincebaugh.

He and Ben got an address on Susie, Ben admitting that maybe something just might shake out when he said, "Geez, I never knew the weasel had a sister."

"You learn something new every day," Alex replied as they made their way back to the car. From there they started for Susie's place, but there was no rush. When they arrived, they found she was not home. Alex wanted to stake out the place for a while, but Ben argued for letting it go for another day, that they'd find her at the nightclub the next day. Ben followed this with wide, long yawns, stretching and talk of a soft bed and a softer Fiona waiting for him at home.

"Look, Ben, on the surface, it always appeared that Victor Surette fell from the sky without a background, without people or connections, and I think that was by design. He had no photos when we searched his place, remember? No albums, postcards, not so much as a phone number. It was unnatural then, and it stinks now, that his place was so goddamned clean of information. You remember that?"

"Sure, but we chalked it up to a spartan life, a guy who didn't want ties or anyone from his past to know his whereabouts."

"No high school yearbooks, nothing," Alex continued. "Unless all such materials were cleaned out before we got to the apartment. Remember the delay between finding and identifying the body?"

"Yeah, but I don't think there's some conspiracy going on here, Alex."

"Well if there's no conspiracy to hide Surette's true identity, then why the hocus-pocus attempt out at the cemetery? And who clse'd make off with the man's photos and correspondence and papers? His killer?"

"None of the other victims had their places cleaned out, Alex. It was just how Surette lived."

"Maybe . . . maybe not . . ."

"What's that suppose to mean?"

"What if someone didn't want Surette to have a past?"

"What if that someone was Surette himself?" Ben countered.

They were getting on each other's nerves, so Alex left the car for the building, to wait on the steps. They had a fair description of Susie, and he believed he'd know her if she showed up. As for the mystery of Surette's past, everyone questioned claimed no knowledge whatever of his childhood or parentage. Perhaps Victor had cut himself off completely from all connections with his childhood.

"Maybe Davey Gilreath killed Victor Surette in a lovers' quarrel," said Ben, who'd wandered over to sit alongside his partner. "Outta jealousy, rage. You know how it goes. Love kills. . . ."

"But that doesn't explain the others."

"Yeah, it could . . . it could," countered Ben. "They're all the same; they're all interchangeable; he kills them all because they're all extensions of Vicki, get it?"

"Could be . . ." Alex gave Ben a nod. They had found threads of information linking the victims: They all belonged to the cross-dressing gay crowd, they frequented the same nightclubs and gay bars, they lived within a twenty-seven-block radius of one another and mutual friends knew more than one of the victims by more than just reputation. Maybe Ben was onto something.

Alex half expected to find that Sue Socks was in fact Pigsty, dressed in women's clothing and acting out the life he'd always wanted, the life of a woman. But the woman who climbed from a cab, draped in the arms of another woman, the two kissing one another passionately here on the street, was not Pigsty.

Alex flashed his badge at the lesbian couple. The painted peroxide-blonde almost spat at them. But beneath her bravado, Alex sensed a deep-seated fear.

"Susie Socks? We need a word with you."

She took a moment to plead with her lover to stay, to not leave her alone with the "pigs." But her lover was equally nervous given the situation, so she begged off, going back to the cab.

"All right . . . come on up," Susie told them, her alcohol breath parting the detectives.

It was a sordid little apartment just off Bourbon Street in the French Quarter. The walk up was straight and narrow. Once inside, Alex and Ben posed questions amid a bare room without adornment or pictures. They questioned a bare woman adorned in phony makeup and clothes that hearkened back to the flower children of the late sixties.

"It's a lie," she told them. "I ain't no relation to that bastard and prick David Gilreath."

He took note of the fact she called him David.

Susie Socks was a gaunt, rangy lesbian who turned tricks with men for money when she wasn't waitressing at the Pink Anvil, or so their information had told them, and it would appear that their sources were correct. Alex and Ben knew what prostitutes hated more than anything, so they went to work, squeezing her for information, threatening her with daily harassment and arrests if she were not cooperative.

"What the hell you want from me?"

"Just a line on Gilreath's whereabouts . . ."

"Or it's a trip to night court," Ben added.

"He's afraid, and he won't come out of hiding. He doesn't know anything." Her voice was deep, resonant and thick, like a man's.

"Then what's he afraid of?"

"Power."

"Oh, really? I would've thought your answer different, that he's afraid of the Queen of Hearts killer."

"That is power, sugar . . . power in its rawest form."

"Power, huh?" replied Ben, tired of the games. "Then try this on for power. We bust your ass tonight, sweetie, for prostitution and anything else we find in your place that isn't legal—say, crack. Then we exercise our power to do so again tomorrow and the next night and the next."

"Why don't you make this easy on yourself, Susie Q," suggested Alex, a half smile playing on his face. "We just want to question him. That's all, Miss Gilreath."

"S-Socks, Susie Socks," she corrected him. "He's no longer in the city."

"Where is he then?"

"I don't know!"

"All right," bellowed Big, "guess we do this the hard way. Want to get a coat, make a better impression on the judge, sweetie?"

Alex escorted her toward the back of the house, both cop and civilian knowing the rules of discovery should he see something illegal in her back room.

"All right . . . all right . . . he's back home, out at the farm."

"Where's the farm, honey?"

"Up-country . . ."

"Where exactly up-country!"

"Palladium . . . my daddy owns a place up there. Davey went home to hide out. He was afraid when Surette was killed. Something . . . something about it all scared the hell out of him, and now I know why."

"Oh, and why's that, sugar?" pressed Ben.

"Hell, all of the victims were men of my brother's . . . persuasion, and he knew most of 'em, and he was close, real close to Surette. He knew whoever was doing the killing would get round to him if he didn't run, so he ran, and so you fools . . . you think he's the killer because he disappeared from sight, but you don't know jack-shit. It's about power, is what it's about . . . power."

"Are you going to tell me what you mean by that, Jodi?" Alex pressed now, using her real name just to annoy her.

She lit up a cigarette. "You didn't hear nothing from me, you understand?"

"Sure, nothing."

"Not a word of it," added deYampert.

"Half the police force in this damned city's been paid to look the other way, and my baby brother was paid to leave town. Money . . . money is power."

"Paid by whom?"

"People high up, that's all I know. Hell, if I knew any more, I'd have got my fair cunt outta here too, but Davey wouldn't tell me nothing, the little bastard . . . wanted it all to himself— the money, that is. Had some fool notion he could buy Daddy's love with it. Stupid shit . . . said it was for my own good that we never speak on it, not ever. Said it could cost me my life, which I didn't at first believe, but then the killings kept on happening, and then I decided maybe he wasn't lying after all."

Alex was skeptical, and deYampert laughed aloud, saying, "So, you want us to believe there's been some big conspiracy here, that people in high places don't want the Queen of Hearts killer's identity known? Baby-cakes, that kind of bullshit will get you nowhere with us, you understand that? Nowhere. Right, Alex?"

"Two fuckin' dumb cops who can't find the most vicious freakin' killer this city's ever known, and why? Because you can't see past your slimy noses. Why do you think they called in a psychic? They want to manipulate this whole case."

"Who are they?" pressed Alex, snatching the cigarette from her mouth and tossing it into the sink.

"Why do you think the fucking governor and the mayor

and all those muckety-mucks are interested in the case? For tourism's sake? For God's sake, open your eyes. The killer is one of their own, and—''

''What the hell're you talking about, snatch?'' shouted Ben, approaching her like a stampeding rhino until Alex held up a hand to him.

''I'm talking about the country-club set. I'm talking about people with enough money and power to bury all three of us in this room tonight, if they wanted.''

''You're talking about some sort of cover-up surrounding Surette?'' asked Alex, wondering again about the complete lack of paper in Surette's apartment on the night they had searched it.

Jodi-alias-Susie sniffed back a tear of concern. ''They're covering it up by paying off people like Davey to get the hell out of town.''

''Craziest wad of crap I ever heard,'' said de Yampert, dismissing the entire notion. ''Come on, Alex. Let's see about reality. Let's go, Miss Susie.''

She only frowned at the big cop, but her eyes went pleadingly to Sincebaugh. ''Look, what reason do I have to lie? I'm just telling you what little I know. Davey wouldn't say much, but he was paid plenty to leave town.''

''Who paid him to leave? Who?''

''He wouldn't tell me.''

Alex nodded and forced a fifty into her hand.

She pushed the cash back at him. ''My life's worth more to me than fifty bucks, pal.''

''All right, sure.'' Alex retrieved the money. ''We'll be in touch.''

''Not if I can help it.''

Alex then followed his partner down to the waiting unmarked squad car. Ben got on the radio, struggling with a pack of gum at the same time.

''Put out a warrant on Gilreath,'' Alex said.

''We tried that once before, remember?''

''This time extend it to Palladium. Have the cops up there pick him up for us.''

''*If* he's there.''

''You have to be so skeptical all the time?''

"Hey, skeptical's part of what we do, or have you forgotten that, Alex?"

"Something eating you, Big?"

"Shit, Alex, think about it. You're taking advice from a lesbian prostitute on how to conduct an investigation? When before you refused any help whatsoever from Dr. Desinor? Give me a break, Sincy."

"So who are you calling?"

"I'm making a phone call home to Fiona and the kids. I know, I know, the brass don't want us patching through and tying up the lines, but do you see a working pay phone within a mile of here?"

"That's okay, Ben."

"Damn right it's okay. It's okay to check in to home once in a while. Maybe if you had a home . . . oh, for Chrissake, Alex, we're chasing phantoms here."

"Hey, we've chased phantoms before. New Orleans is full of phantoms. Home of Anne Rice and the Vampire Lestat, remember? So what's got you so steamed and on edge?" Alex could feel there was a problem.

"Ahh, nothing that can't be fixed with another one of those home equity loans. Sorry, partner. I'll make that bulletin call."

"Never mind. Drive! I'll call in the warrant."

"Drive where?"

"Let's have another look-see at Surette's old place."

"Are you kidding? The tape came down on that freakin' place a year ago; no idea who's living there now; you go in there poking around and the landlord loses a tenant when the new people decide the friggin' place is haunted or something; then we get another citizen's complaint, and Landry'll have our—"

"Hey, it's not like Surette met his violent end there. He's not likely to be there in spirit."

"Then what in hell do you expect to find there after all this time?"

"I'm not sure. I just want to nose around."

"But Alex, we did that when the body was still warm, remember? And we found nothing useful. Like you said, not so much as a photograph, not even of himself in drag."

"And didn't that strike you as strange?"

"Strange? What's strange among all these weirdos, Alex? Give it a break . . . strange . . . where the hell've you been?"

"Dammit, it was like someone had gotten there ahead of us and cleaned the place out. No paper, no bills, no laundry lists, no goddamned letters, nothing."

"Even if that was true, going back now . . . I mean it's not like we overlooked *anything,* partner."

"But we did. We overlooked the emptiness of the damned place."

"Did you look around Sue Socks' place, Alex? Listen to yourself. These people got no family albums, pal."

Alex turned back to that moment in time when Surette's apartment would have been vulnerable to someone scavenging it. He'd remained a long time with the body out in the woods because Frank Wardlaw was dragging his butt. By the time Wardlaw had officially I.D.'d the body and it had gotten out over the wires, Ben had gone to Surette's place ahead of Alex, and when Alex arrived, Ben had told him how pathetically empty the place was, showing him the barren fridge and vacant bookshelves. The only thing remaining of Surette was his elaborate wardrobe, a collection of pumps and other shoes, handbags and the like—and except for cosmetics, even these were empty.

Alex wanted to return to the Surette apartment tonight, perhaps foolishly, just to snoop around for anything that might have fallen through the cracks, particularly anything in the realm of paper. Paper couldn't be gotten with a search warrant, however; there was no probable cause to serve the new tenant or tenants with one. Still, he couldn't convince Ben that it was necessary that they go back to Surette's place tonight, and Ben won the argument.

Later, near midnight, sleep was finally shutting down the feverish activity of puzzle pieces which only gave the illusion of fitting into place, and Alex's body screamed for an end to the internal war. He gave in, and was sleeping deeply when he was rudely startled awake by the ringing, insistent telephone, which he knocked to the floor. Picking up the receiver, he heard an excited female voice.

"Alex, Alex . . . it's me . . . it's me, Kim, Kim Desinor."

"Oh, yeah, Doctor . . . what the hell time is it?" He yawned unceremoniously. "What can I do you for?"

"I need your help."

"You need my help?" Alex was sounding flip, but he was mostly curious. Why in God's name was she telephoning him at this hour? Insomnia, inability to sleep knowing someone on the NOPD hadn't fallen for her psychic scam maybe?

"It's . . . well, it's . . . Dr. Coran." The hesitancy in her voice made Alex sit up in bed.

"Exactly what's the problem, Dr. Desinor?"

"She's . . . Jessica's gone from her hotel room."

"Well, she is a big girl, and I'm sure Meade's got someone watching her night and day, so . . ."

"You don't understand. She's gone out to one of the cemeteries tonight, and . . . and . . ."

"What, another exhumation?"

"No, no . . . nothing of the sort."

He was getting impatient now. "What then?"

"I promised her I would tell no one, but I'm terribly worried about her safety, and—"

"Tell no one what?" He yawned again.

"That she's meeting with that madman Matisak at the cemetery, to . . . to have it out with him . . . alone . . . do you understand, Alex?"

He went silent, piecing all of it together. The pilot's headless body, the gruesome head dangling at Kim Desinor's hotel room door, the whole, bloody incident hushed up, kept off the police band, the press kept out of it entirely. The murdered pilot turning out to be FBI, a bodyguard assigned to Dr. Coran in the event she fell into peril. Lot of good that had done. He also recalled the strange, thin, tubular little shard of glass which Dr. Coran had plucked from Ed Sand's cheek. Coran had said that she'd have the lab test it for poisonous substances, believing that Sand had been too easily and quickly overpowered for his size and build.

"Did Matisak contact her directly?" he asked now. "How does she know where to meet him?"

"I . . . I can't say. She didn't tell me," Kim lied badly.

"Where are you? Are you calling from your hotel room?"

"Yes. I tried to talk her out of going out there alone, but she's . . . she's . . ."

"Stubborn, bullheaded?" He sounded as if he were speaking of all women.

"Determined."

"Determined to get herself killed?"

"Determined that no one else should suffer at this fiend's hand so long as she lives. She's begun to blame herself whenever he kills, and he kills often."

"Which cemetery is it? I'm on my way there," he said, getting to his feet.

"Swing by here and pick me up first. I want to be with you."

"If there's a chance this bastard shows up, Doctor, I can't put you in jeopardy."

"You pick me up, or I don't tell you where she's gone, Lieutenant. Swing by and I'll be waiting out front."

"There's no time to argue, Doctor."

"Then don't waste time doing so!" She hung up and hung onto the information he so needed.

A half hour later, with Alex still replaying their one-sided last conversation in his head, he and Kim were racing toward Metairie Cemetery, Alex's dome light flashing. Kim was clearly upset and agitated, obviously torn between what was right and what was necessary. She'd made a promise and had had to renege on it, her conscience not allowing anything else.

"God," she moaned, "I should've called you earlier."

"What made you change your mind?"

"No psychic visions or anything of that sort, I can assure you. Just old-fashioned remorse and fear. If anything's happened to her . . ."

"We'll get there in time."

"Is that a good ol' New Orleans gaar-ron-tee?" she asked in a moment of jest.

He put the accelerator to the floor.

"Are you going to level with me now, Doctor?" he suddenly asked.

A car pulled from the curb ahead and was planning to turn onto an adjacent, facing street. Alex laid on the horn and swerved in one fluid motion, the other driver stomping his brakes and Alex weaving around to miss the other car by mere inches on the passenger side where *she* sat. Kim could feel the metal on her side suck in its breath and arch inward to avoid the impact; it was that close.

"Stupid moron!" Alex uselessly shouted to the other driver, who, in the rearview mirror some fifty yards back now, sat frozen, likely in a state of shock.

Kim mentally agreed with Alex's assessment of the man who'd failed to signal, but she also thought Alex had only made the situation worse, that there was a streak of reckless- ness in him. They could hardly afford a collision at the mo- ment.

But as Alex ignored the near-fatal lesson, they continued to soar along at sixty and seventy down the quiet backstreets he'd selected to reach the cemetery grounds, the strobe light atop the vehicle pulsating like a living heart, telling everyone to get out of the way.

Kim stared at Alex's determined profile. Obviously, to him, a guarantee was a guarantee.

"Are you going to tell me the truth about what's going on here between Jessica Coran and this madman Matisak?"

"The bastard's become obsessed with wanting to kill her and kill her slowly, by draining her of her blood."

"Damnit, I know all that. I want to know how Matisak contacted her, and what the hell's going on in her head that she'd be so goddamned foolish as to come out here alone Now, how did he contact her?"

"By phone, I think . . . she wouldn't tell me."

"For a psychic, you sure have a problem telling lies, Dr. Desinor."

She looked curiously over at him as the speed of the car rocked it against the impact of old brick streets in this district. "Am I to take that as a compliment? Coming from you, I would judge yes."

"Well, what you did with our police shrink, that was really something. My partner ran the names and numbers and you were right on about Thommie Marie Dumond Whiley."

"I'm only glad that I can be of help here, Alex, but you've got to know that by now. I never wanted to oust anyone from the investigation, and I hope you no longer feel threatened by my—''

"Threatened? I never felt threatened by you, Doctor."

"Ahh, well . . . good then . . . good."

"And it's time we stopped feuding."

"Agreed."

"Or withholding information from one another."

She nodded and replied, "How much further to the cemetery?"

"Five, ten minutes tops."

"You mean if we don't run over somebody or into something?"

"You let me worry about the driving."

"Always . . ." She hesitated saying more.

He glanced over, catching a glint of amusement in her eye. "What's that suppose to mean?"

"Oh, nothing . . . just that you always seem to be in need of the wheel. A control freak."

"No, that isn't so. I just have to first trust in a guy or a lady who's at the wheel before I'll put my life in his or her hands. Is that asking so much?"

A stock cop answer, she thought, but she only replied, "No . . . no, I don't think so."

Then they were at the cemetery, and Alex plowed through the gate, sending it in two directions, his headlights careening off the pale, staring tombstones and crypt walls, the strobe sending crazy shadows in all directions.

Alex ordered her to stay with the car as he leapt from the seat and tore out his .38 police special. He rushed to the trunk and located a twelve-gauge shotgun, and then he headed out into the darkness beyond the headlights of the car—as if he were going down to the river to fish for bass, she thought.

She quickly exited the car and fell in behind him.

"Damnit, do you ever do as told, Kim?"

"I got lonely back there."

"I don't see or hear a thing," he admitted.

"Me neither."

"What does your . . . intuition tell you?"

"It's not good."

"What?"

"She's not here."

"Let's do a sweep. Call out to her, just in case."

But there was no answer to Kim's repeated calls.

They wandered through the densely populated necropolis, the city of dead giving up nothing now but silence, and yet Kim felt a thousand eyes upon them.

Many of the tombs appeared expensive, and Kim knew that the cemetery was filled with famous politicians and prominent businessmen dating back to the late nineteenth and early twentieth centuries. She saw elaborate and grotesque architectural styles of all sorts here, from Egyptian to rococo, including medieval period pieces complete with monstrous, bug-eyed gargoyles on haunches with batlike wings and human features sewn together by demonic hands. Some of the statuary and bizarre examples of funerary art were on a monumental scale, further giving the impression of a skylined city of the dead within the city of frivolity, beer and jazz.

She searched the fog, searched the stones, cautious at every alleyway, byway and intersection, noting the well-kept, manicured grounds, so totally at odds with the city-owned paupers' cemetery where Surette's body had lain until they'd gone in search of it.

She felt like they were the only life on the planet when suddenly they came upon a sign which read: *Free tape-recorded tour of the cemetery available at the Lake Lawn Metairie Funeral Home, 5100 Ponchartrain Blvd., or call 555-6331*. Tacked to the sign were several notices which blew in the wind. A distant rumble of thunder threatened more storms from the lingering hurricane activity in the Gulf of Mexico.

Kim was wondering how Matisak had made off with Jessica. How had he chosen to materialize here? From the shroud of fog, from a tomb he'd broken into? What sort of a stand had he made? Had he taken her by complete surprise? Did he have her now in his power? Were they too late to save her? What sign could she hope for?

She looked down along alleyway after alleyway of the necropolis peering into the black rows of funerary tombs, when suddenly she stopped cold. There was a howling of dogs in the distance and a light, misty rain came up from nowhere, as if it blanketed only the Metairie Cemetery. Without a moon or light, she could make out no definable shapes amid the purple and burnt sienna and umber-colored kaleidoscope of leaves flurrying in the night sky where an ancient oak resided.

"I don't believe this, the balls of this guy Matisak. Look at this," said Alex, drawing her attention to the sign and a message tacked to it bulletin-board fashion. "It's a message to us from *him*."

Matisak figured Jessica would call in help; he figured there'd be backup, and so he'd come and gone before they arrived, Kim realized as she read the note Alex handed over to her. It merely read: "You're getting closer."

"How're we going to find her?" asked Alex.

"Shhhhhh . . ." She tried desperately to get something out of the note, something extrasensory. "Do you know of a nearby warehouse, anything used for storage? A large industrial area?"

"There are several within an hour's drive."

"Then let's get going."

"Come on."

They made their way back to the car and the strobing lights in the distance. The rain was pelting down around them now, soaking them.

Kim stopped, seeing a spiritual entity flit across her line of vision. She instinctively shouted, "Jessica! Jess! Damn her . . . damn her for taking so much on herself! Matisak's not just her problem; he's my problem, your problem, Alex, every decent policeman's problem!"

But Jessica was gone, skirting about the tombstones, a mere phantom, not wanting to be found. It was an illusion, and Kim knew it.

Alex took Kim into his outstretched arms to reassure her, but he was wondering just how long the two women had known each other. It was his understanding they'd only met since taking on the Queen of Hearts case, and since one was a scientist and the other a psychic empath, it made quite an impression on him when Kim had called claiming that Jessica Coran had confided her plans to her; it made another strong impression on him now to feel this woman's heart-wrenching sobs, to realize she was so openly weeping over Jessica's disappearance, and that she still called herself a cop.

Sincebaugh's natural curiosity had been aroused by their confidences, and Kim's recent remark, including herself in as a cop, but now wasn't the time to press for information.

Kim looked again off into the distant grounds of the sprawling cemetery, and there saw the rows upon rows of crosses, which in the fog and flashing lightning strikes and the whirling strobe light atop Alex's car looked aflame; in fact, the crosses seemed to rise and fall as if breathing, and they appeared to be moving in tandem to the strobe lights.

Little wonder she was having trouble pinpointing the Queen of Hearts killer; her psychic impressions had been distorted by the enormous duel between Matthew Matisak and Jessica Coran. She'd all along been picking up signals which belonged to the other case, and those symbols of crosses afire, marching like trees—Macbeth's enemies in disguise—began to bleed when pierced with arrows of light. All of it had come from Jessica's psyche. Jessica was a Macbeth now, an obsessed, tragic figure, and her only way out was to fell the one tree that marched at her.

"Alex, I have a confession to make."

Sincebaugh looked into her eyes, his hands firmly pressing into her flesh. "Really, and you want me to act as father confessor?"

"These images." She pointed at the shadow and light display across the tombs and crosses.

"Yeah, kinda eerie, but what about them?"

"They're the rosary images I've been getting right along, but they've got nothing whatever to do with the Queen of Hearts killer after all."

"Then what are they? What do they mean?"

"They mean I've been a fool, and Jess is in danger because of me."

He shook his head and tugged at her to go with him to the car, get out of the rain. "It's not your fault she's come out here on this vendetta alone. You can't blame yourself, Kim."

"We've got to help her. We've got to find her."

"We will . . . we will," he firmly lied, as unsure as he was wet.

"Something to do with green . . . a large green beast . . ."

"Come   on . . . back   to   the   car . . . We'll   locate   her somehow."

They returned to the dryness of the car, and once inside, the scavenger hunt was initiated when Alex got on the radio and put out an all-points bulletin to locate Dr. Coran.

"How? How're we going to find her?" Kim pleaded.

"Use some of that psychic power of yours. Meanwhile, I'm going to locate a phone book."

29

Jessica had brought two guns, one in a shoulder holster, a Browning automatic, and a .38 police special strapped to her ankle. She tried to bolster her courage, lifting the automatic once again from its home, gritting her teeth and voicing a curse. "Come on, you bastard, just dare to show yourself . . . come on . . . come on . . ."

She'd located the dilapidated old warehouse teetering along a stretch of the wharf buffeted by the Mississippi River. The wind had blown up into a fury in the past few hours as if in collaboration with Matisak, but she knew better: The car radio in the cab had been blaring out warnings to residents all along the coast, warnings about a tropical disturbance that had become a hurricane; crossing the midsection of Florida, Hurricane Lois had recoiled for a second go at the U.S. mainland, experts predicting that it would likely hit in the vicinity of New Orleans.

All available personnel were on alert and people were boarding up windows and stocking supplies. Landfall could be as early as dawn tomorrow if Lois so deemed it. But gale-force winds had already arrived ahead of her, some gusting up to sixty and seventy miles per hour, and some taking out telephone and electrical lines to parts of the city, including this area.

The warehouse was nothing more than a large Quonset hut—of World War II vintage, she guessed. The place was surrounded by black, sooty red-brick buildings, also warehouses, all of which appeared a century old, and any one of which might fill in for a bleak Dickens backdrop or one of Hawthorne's ominous customs houses. The place was as dank, dismal and dark as the cemetery from which she'd just come.

An excellent shot on the firing range and proven in the field, Jessica only worried about the dense fog permeating the entire area and impairing her vision. If her theory regarding exactly how Ed Sand had met his end had any validity, the instant Matisak showed himself she must react, for he'd be sending a shardlike dart at her to immobilize her. He wouldn't use any fast-acting poison, just something with a paralyzing effect, to gain complete control. He didn't want her to die easily or quickly, so she must be vigilant and prepared to react instantaneously to the slightest sound or sight of him.

She recalled Kim's warning about an attack coming from up overhead. She readied her gun and moved ever closer toward the large overhanging sign with the tattered, faded shape of an enormous alligator staring back at her through the mist and fog.

She was soon standing at a side door left standing open, an invitation to enter a gaping, black maw. She reached into her purse for the flashlight she'd brought along with her and, taking a deep breath, entered. The place inside was strung with ropes and pulleys overhead, with a myriad of mechanical devices at every turn. Matisak liked to use ropes, chains, cords to tie his victims up and dangle them upside down, to bring all the blood rushing to the head, where he then released the pressure by relieving his victim of that blood.

She must be careful. She must give Matisak the false sense of security that would give her an edge, give him the impression he had the upper hand, as if she were walking into his trap. But at the same time, she must also be prepared for anything.

She'd purposely not wanted to use the flashlight, only if absolutely necessary, as the beam would signal her exact location. But there was no help for it. The place was pitch black. The beam picked up an occasional shape, creating greater and bigger shadows that danced at every turn.

She then realized that the warehouse was enormous. Stretching into what seemed infinity were rows and rows of paraphernalia from the fourteen or so parades and the Mardi Gras presented each year for the sake of a good time in the Big Easy. It was by far one of the largest such storage houses for the dolls and balloons and life-size figures, a veritable garden for Alice to fall into Wonderland.

''Appropriate to Matisak's witticisms,'' she said aloud to the caricatures staring back at her. They ranged from Bugs Bunny and the Road Runner to enormous, complex dragons amid castles and costumes of knights, knaves, jesters, beggarmen, princes and princesses. She found staring back at her Indians in buckskin, aliens in metal, monstrous creations from *Star Wars* figures to *Babylon 5* creatures with two and three heads. All of the costumes, porcelain figures and wire-mesh animals and papier-mâché creations—any one of which might be Matisak—hung suspended in air overhead, while beautiful and elaborate floats littered the enormous corners of the hut, each float filled with its own assortment of gaily colored figures, both human and animal as well as fantastic. What's more, all their marble eyes, onyx and amber and blue, seemed to be watching her every move.

There were literally thousands of disguises the madman might take here, so caution had been thrown to the howling winds just outside the Quonset hut the very moment she'd entered this bizarre still life which had become Matisak's lair and her lure.

She uselessly pulled down on the huge arm that would trip on the light switch, but she found what she'd expected—the power had been conveniently denied her. Only her flashlight beam could pick along from one gargoyle's menacing eyes to the eerie grin of a clown to the sinister talons of a bird of prey, until the colorful phantasmagoria of this silent and individual screening of the Mardi Gras all became as one.

She could see no additional electrical box, and was unable to bring up the lights. Through the thick, enveloping darkness she moved, ever cautious of her prey. Instinctively, she kept her weapon raised and ready to fire; at the same time, she tried to recall what the psychic sleuth, Dr. Desinor, had told her to watch for, a falling sky. She might well have meant Hurricane Lois on its approach, making mincemeat of the sky and the world.

Still, she superstitiously clung to the notion that Kim Desinor might well have seen something other than a hurricane force wind blowing about in her vision, and for this reason

Jessica kept her eyes on the overhead struts and beams and an artificial sky filled with ornamentals and caricatures and likenesses. A hundred clown faces stared back out of the darkness, faces meant to amuse and create laughter and lightheartedness during the debacle of Mardi Gras, but here, like this, they only engendered a sense of cold terror, their smiles turned to grimaces, their eyes as large and watchful as moons.

Amid them, Matisak lurked.

"Show yourself, you cowardly demon! I've done as you asked! I'm here, now, alone . . . so come ahead." *Fuck with me*, she silently seethed, her Scorpio ire up. She thought of her next birthday, November 17, 1996, a time when she was to revisit Hawaii and Jim Parry, a time when the whales came into the big harbor on Maui to breed there. She wondered if she'd ever see the spectacle.

Again her eyes scanned innumerable dummies and displays, costumes and Mardi Gras figures and figurines, most of which were dangling from the ceiling. Her flash lit on figure after figure, all of which grinned evilly back but all of which were lifeless, the eyes without depth or meaning. All except one, which she recognized as a mother recognizes her child in a crowd, knowing that this single body was real.

All in an instant her mind took in the simple and strange facts: The dangling man wore expensive Italian shoes—out of place here like something in a Dali painting—slick, pinstriped Brooks Brothers three-piece suit, the yuppie-thick suspenders, a Rolex on the arm. The light beam next revealed a thin-legged torso with deathly pale white hands. The beam could not find the face as it seemed buried in the darkness overhead.

Was it just as a prop to seduce her attention, to decoy her here to the very spot where he wanted her to stand? At the same time, her instincts screamed, "It's him," and this made her fire, pumping several slugs into the body dangling overhead, her mind spinning with Kim's warning that the sky would fall in on her, and it did.

When her gunshots rang out, an ear-wrenching cacophony of sound screeched through the warehouse as the mechanical pulley device holding all the Mardi Gras figures and the dead man overhead began to carousel around the room. The moment it started up, the lifeless body gave up its head, the ugly, dismembered thing nearly hitting Jessica as it tumbled to the concrete floor with the sound of a ripe melon.

She instantly recognized the grimacing face as that of Deputy Mayor Fouintenac, killed in exactly the same manner as Ed Sand.

Jessica gasped and twirled away, the array of color and netting and fabric swishing by her eyes in dizzying succession. Matisak might have taken her at any given point, but he was showing extreme patience—toying with her—or was it out of caution that he'd not shown himself?

She instantly wheeled, her body, arm, hand and gun doing a 360-degree turn. Only after she was satisfied that he was not near did Jessica move the flashlight beam to the deadman's chest, seeing the sparkle of a half-hidden badge against the lifeless body, rising and dipping, as it came around on the carousel again. She instantly realized that Matisak had killed her last bodyguard, this one no doubt also taking orders from Meade.

Her flash next caught sight of a large upside-down garlanded banner of silver and blue, with words she made out as "HEAVEN'S DELIGHT" printed across it, obviously a sponsor for one of the floats, perhaps a local restaurant or nightclub or ice cream parlor. And as she neared the banner, she saw the cause of the words: a swirling of moons, stars, planets all caught up in a huge bayou netting to create the illusion, once righted, of heavenly orbs floating above a nightscape of New Orleans.

Before she heard the clap of the metallic release that sent the float's netting hurling toward her, Jessica dove as far to her right as possible, catapulting herself into a row of standing dummies, sending them cascading in domino fashion as the heavens overhead came crashing down within inches of her, the netting dragging along her ankles, clawing at her. She'd avoided the heavy net filled with stars which was released to trap her. But outside, the wind was ripping over the warehouse so powerfully that she imagined the roof being taken apart piece by piece. She could hear both the howling and the tearing sounds as the vicious winds slammed into the enormous Quonset hut.

She'd lost her flashlight, and seeing that it lay under the

netting, in Matisak's trap, she took perverse pleasure in waiting now for him to step out of the darkness to claim his prize.
He might well think that she, along with the light, was beneath
the net he had released over her.

She had slithered animal-like into a dark corner between a
stack of colored doors leaning one against another and a pyr-
amid of fallen mannequins. Now grateful for the cover of darkness, she waited to spring her own trap. A single indication
of him, and she meant to fire.

But suppose someone else, hearing the clatter, stepped from
the shadows? She silently cautioned herself, recalling how earlier she'd almost killed the hobo and how she had placed three
slugs into Leon Fouintenac's lifeless corpse.

In the middle of her recall, all hell broke loose. Another
enormous grating noise like an elephant suddenly gone on a
rampage was followed by more sinister, lurching figures overhead on yet a second metal track. The ghostly, suspended
Mardi Gras people began their dead and levitated parade, the
lifeless forms of animals both imaginary and real in concep-
tion, of clowns and nebbishes, gnomes and giants, began, all
to the sound of carousel music, to fly peacefully by, all suspended on great wires, hooks and pulleys, alternately bobbing
upward and downward. It was an enormous contraption, this
second and larger, circular-shaped pulley device, reminding
her of the sort of mechanical arm used in a Laundromat to
locate the proper ticketed clothing item.

Obviously Matisak was enjoying his new role as puppet-
master, and clearly he thoroughly knew the building, its infra-
structure and its inner workings, all to her disadvantage. He
was manning the controls, and now the Mardi Gras was spinning slowly overhead, in a controlled maneuver designed to
unnerve her, and it was working . . . had the desired effect . . . created a nightmare of images passing by what little
light came in from the street lamps at the windows, some
twelve feet overhead.

Matisak churned up the speed, and so too the atrocious
racket accompanying it. Images passed by her in a blur of
blinding color and tawdry tassels, a Grateful Dead circus of
clowns awakened from long sleep.

She watched carefully from her crouched position, her gun pointed and ready, the madness of the moment creeping slowly into her brain, dripping an acidic, bitter hatred for her prey.

She was sick to death of his endless mind games.

She could stand the noise and the chaos no longer.

She began to fire indiscriminately at the now-ugly, satanic figures which flirted past her, in and out of the light. She fired nonstop, emptying the clip to her Browning automatic, which she'd felt would be more easily controlled and deadlier than her .38, still in place at her ankle.

She now reached for a new clip, and as she did so, the mannequins continued their wild dance along the struts and metal hooks which held them, an occasional large hook, empty of any contents, flashing its metal smile and claw as it whizzed by. The pace of the march of this madman's Mardi Gras had increased in steady increments, so Matisak obviously had the controls near at hand—or was it on some sort of automatic timer?

If she could only find the control box, then she would find him, she reasoned.

As she fought to place in the second clip, however, the wind from outside shattered several of the huge windows above, sending down a rain of glass, tiles and spray. She instinctively reacted, covering herself with a tarp, listening to the raining shards of glass thud against the protecting envelope she'd created for herself, knowing that she would otherwise have been struck and badly injured.

When it was over, she slowly extricated herself from the tarp and heavy debris, rain still pattering down on the canvas.

When she clawed her way out, she stood stark still; she saw an eye was trained on her, that he was looking directly at her. She could see the single eye even if he, in the shadows, thought she could not. It was a silver-blue iris, only half open, as if meaning to wink closed at any moment. She wanted to close her own eyes, wish it away, afraid to accept it as his human eye. *Must be one of the dummies* . . . But staring into it, she realized that this eye in the dark beamed a cold, alien intelligence back at her, mirroring her own dark iris now filling with the tears of vengeance and malice she'd carried for so long with her.

She moved in slow motion to position the gun to fire into the eye of evil across from her. She fired, shattering only a mirror, and he suddenly swept at her on an overhanging cable. He was so suddenly upon her, blocking out what little light the fallen flashlight had afforded her, that he became her sky and his powerful legs kicked her square in the midsection, knocking the air from her and sending her cascading into some cardboard boxes. As her body arched over the pile of boxes, she lost control of the clip, her gun useless without it—and he, the Devil, was hovering and coming nearer.

She was dazed by the blow, unable to think clearly, unable to make her hands work to locate the remaining gun strapped to her ankle, hidden below her pants leg. She struggled for the strength and clarity of thought required.

He came ever closer while her eyes struggled to adjust to the darkness in which he stood. He was wearing a costume that had successfully camouflaged him here, looking like he was stepping from a Shakespearean ball in Venice, his smile curling like a snake along each cheek.

"So, my sweet, my precious, my dear Jessica . . . at last . . . together again at long last . . . As they say, the play's the thing, and it's time for our eternal play to begin. Oh, precious one, how now does my cup runneth over. . . . ''

She was trapped with no way out, her back to the wall, and if she made a move for the gun too soon, he'd discover it, overpower her and render her powerless. She stuttered even as she formed the words to reply to him. "This time, Teach, you're going to die before we part."

"As I am prepared to do. The question is, dear one, are you?"

Concentrate . . . concentrate. Kim repeated the mantra where she stood beside Alex's car, trying desperately to calm herself for Jessica's sake. She clutched a scarf belonging to Jessica tightly in her hand. Jess had left the scarf in Kim's room the night before.

Alex had left her in the car while he fought a battle with a phone book locked into a metal straitjacket below a phone outside a convenience store. Finally, he'd given up and gone inside, flashed his badge and ordered up the store's book, following the clerk to the rear office.

Kim took in a deep breath, the electric hum of the New Orleans night and a gale-force wind vying for her attention. The wind was ripping now in powerful gusts as the hurricane all of New Orleans was talking about neared, a beast on drunken paws. New Orleans herself could be the point of landfall for the killing might. And somewhere out there, alone, Jess stood against a power more sinister and evil than anything in nature.

Kim closed her mind to the store, its light flooding her, to the storm threatening her as more rain began to patter over her; she closed her sense of smell, touch, sound, taste and sight down, allowing her own inner power to surface.

She found herself in a cold, unfamiliar fog, knowing that she was searching and lost. She wandered a water-stained, water-soaked boardwalk, fearing she might any moment slip over the side and be lost forever. She heard the soft tinkle of lilting ropes against mastiffs become insistent, blaring as if an orchestra were prepared now to render an opera that would blast away the audience in an orgy of sound. It was the storm smashing against boats moored at a wharf somewhere nearby.

She sensed the odor of ancient, rotting wood and the remains of dead fish that littered this place. All was wet now, dank, eerily so, like the bottom of a casket. The salt air brought in by the storm mingled with the ancient odors of the river wharf. Yes, she told herself, this place was somewhere along the Mississippi.

Parting the wall of mists, searching the effluvium, Kim was suddenly startled by two huge, penetrating green eyes—something ugly and grotesque waiting just beyond reach, something larger than life with the ridiculous features found on a horror-novel cover. She wanted to back away from the image, but she couldn't. She must reach out toward the monster eyes, to understand their intent, to decipher their symbolic meaning, if they possessed any.

She found herself adrift in the haze and fog, however, blown by the winds threatening to take her over the side of this bizarre world created from the ether. Still, with one hand and foot firmly in the world where Alex raced through the Yellow Pages, and where her body was supported by the tangible metal of Alex's car, Kim's mind struggled to relocate the fore-boding, giant's eyes—the ones which had been watching her progress through the dense nebula surrounding her in the place where she believed Jessica had gone.

A rendition of carousel music began to play somewhere in the back of her consciousness, an unrestrained, unpracticed, shabby and tinny sound, woodenlike, mechanical.

Suddenly she was shaken, the whole world around her collapsing, replaced with the blinding lights of the convenience store and Alex asking her if she were crazy. She was soaked from a pelting, stinging rain which she hadn't felt until now.

"I know where she is!" she announced over the roar of the storm.

"Whataya talking about?" he shouted a confused reply, flapping a page of the Yellow Pages in his hand.

"A place with an alligator, a giant alligator sign over the top, a place called Gatorland Storage."

"I'll be damned," Alex replied, crumpling the page of warehouses and shoving it into his pocket. "I know where it is. Come on . . . into the car!"

They raced toward the Mississippi.

30

I saw eternity the other night
Like a great ring of pure and endless light.
All calm, as it was bright;
And round beneath it, Time in hours, days, years,
Driv'n by the spheres
Like a vast shadow moved; in which the world
And all her train were hurled.

—Henry Vaughan

Jessica's terror froze her in place while Matisak calmly took her in with that mad glint she'd come to recognize. As he towered over her where she lay, her face dirty with sawdust and grease, his laughter was cut short by his cruel words. "We're going to die here together, Jessica, with you sacrificing your blood to me and me sacrificing my life in order to go into eternity with you."

The mad metallic, ricocheting racket of the warehouse continued as stiff mannequins marched like wooden soldiers in their suspended poses—like so many marching crosses, she thought, recalling what Kim Desinor had said about burning crosses.

Every so often, instead of a clown or masked marionette, a nasty-looking hook scurried by, winking at Jessica.

Jessica fought to regain her footing, climbing to her knees, careful to tuck her right leg behind her, careful not to alert him to the fact she still carried a gun strapped to her. She easily played the part of one completely cowed and fearful, for she was, and this only helped in her charade, allowing the madman every confidence that he had at last won.

But somehow he knew; he saw some sliver of disdain and hope left in her eyes, and so he quickly backhanded her across the face and tore at her pants leg, having seen the bulge there, and as he tore away the weapon, she tore from him, running her life depending upon the distance she put between them. But in the dark, she ran into the fallen netting, causing her to tumble and become entangled amid the counterfeit stars and imitation planets and moons. Her heels were lost to the net.

He laughed and pounced tigerlike on her, wrenching her wrists and arms in his powerful grip, his acrid breath burning her eyes. "I've got something I want to show you, Jessica, dear." His voice was the sepulchral sound of Hades torn open.

He forced her forward through the dark interior of the warehouse until they came to a corner where he switched on a tensor lamp, which revealed a surgical table complete with four straps, one for each of her limbs. Beside the steel table, which looked like something he'd gotten from the back room of a mortuary, stood a squat little machine with light-emitting diode numbers on a screen, its electrical humming a mewing, mild chant within the deafening sounds of the large warehouse. He'd rigged the machine and the tensor lamp to a generator, not leaving anything to chance, or perhaps because he'd cut the power to all sources but the ones he wished to use, for apparently, he also controlled the whirling parade of Mardi Gras creatures that remained spinning over his shoulder about the center of the warehouse.

"Here is where we die together, sweet Jessica," he whispered in her ear like a demented lover, holding her tightly against his chest, speaking directly into her ear with his putrid, hot breath. "You first, and I to follow."

"How do . . . how do I know you'll go through with it . . . that you'll follow?" She led him on, trying desperately to stall for time, but also anxious to know that he did indeed intend suicide after dispatching her. She would at least have that much, she told herself.

"It's a dialysis machine, like the one I used on Dr. Arnold back in Philly, you remember?"

Now she realized what the small, portable machine was capable of, drawing blood and drawing it quickly and efficiently, Matisak's favorite hobby.

"Only this time," he continued, "it's going to pump me so full of your blood that I'm going to implode with you inside me and take us both into eternity's light together, dear one." He laughed lightly at the thought which would soon be reality.

"Think of it," he continued as he guided her unwilling form to the table. "You and I for all time, locked in a blood embrace, filled to the brim with one another like the lovers we are, off to explosive heights, not with *my* blood, not with *your* blood, but with *our* life's blood, Jessica, so that we'll always be locked together throughout the rest of eternity . . . like I always promised."

"Extracorporeally transplanting my blood into you, all at once, using the dialysis machine," she said to him. "That's no fun, taking it intravenously; it will burst your veins and you'll bleed to death internally."

"That's the beauty of it."

"But where's the kick in that? How're you going to enjoy my suffering when I won't suffer at all? It'll be over in seconds." She couldn't believe herself, arguing for him to make her suffering last. But the moment he placed those straps on her and started mechanically inducing her blood from her body, she knew her chances for survival were nil.

"I can't do it any other way. Drinking it all at once is impossible. You know that."

"Blood is a mucolytic, an expectorant. You'd be vomiting your guts out. Yeah, I know." She tried to keep him talking, to sound as if she were on his side now, trying to help him think through the puzzle, but he was possessed, and he forced her onto the table and brought up a syringe before her eyes.

"This will help you accept me and my plans for you, Jessica. No sense fighting what fate there is which has brought us together, Jessica. We were meant to become one, you and I, all along. Now we finish what we'd begun so many years before."

"But I'm scared, Matthew," she pleaded.

"Fear becomes you." He tested the syringe, removing any air left in the miniature world of the vial.

She tore at the restricting strap dangling just below her right hand as he did so, and she viciously brought it up in a burst of anger and desperation, the strap buckle hitting him squarely in the hand, so painfully and shockingly that the syringe soared over the table and onto the floor. At the same instant, she brought up a naked foot, having lost her heels in the mesh netting earlier, and she kicked him squarely in the jaw, so hard that she hurt the ball of her foot in the effort.

Matisak staggered back just long enough for her to regain her feet and ram the table into his midsection, doubling him over. She grabbed onto the polyethylene tubing and yanked with all her might, pulling it from the dialysis machine, sending it rolling off and out of the circle of light Matisak had created as his artificial bonfire.

She then ran, but she felt him directly behind her. He grabbed onto her shoulder, but she struggled free from her long coat, leaving him with only the cloth and cursing. He pursued demonically, as if he might sprout wings.

She wheeled and barged into a large, freestanding tank, larger than a diving tank. Unsure what was inside the unmarked metal receptacle, she nonetheless grabbed firmly the nozzle and flint attachment. She quickly snatched up the hose handle and turned the gas on—propane, she guessed. Striking the flint, she sent out a spewing gasp of fire into Matisak's eyes, suddenly blinding him, singing his bushy eyebrows and burning his left cheek. He let out a scream of pain and backed away, but she took the fire to the length of its tether, backing him further from her.

"Bloody bitch!" he screamed.

As he continued to back away from the fire, fending it off with his arms now while still holding firmly to his recovered syringe, Jessica saw her chance to put an end to him.

She tugged on the nozzle hose, keeping the fire at his face, dragging the now-toppled, rolling tank with each step she took, keeping him at bay.

Matisak might have turned and run, but he instead jousted with the fire, trying to rush into and through it to overpower her, but the heat was too intense.

"Burn, you sonofabitch! Burn!" Jessica shouted.

Matisak continued to back away. She continued to pursue, hoping the propane would last even though a blinking yellow light on the gauge indicated that it was low.

At the same moment that Matisak backed into the array of mannequins and papier-mâché animals that were careening by, one of the needle-pointed, razor-sharp hooks mechanically anticipated him, and the ugly hook caught him at the base of the skull, viciously slicing into him, its upward-thrusting tip meeting the brain stem. But death was not instantaneous by any means. The robotic hook arm, feeling weight on its end, now lifted the man from the sawdust and raised him several feet into the air. One leg was caught in a pair of gripping stirruplike arms, but the other flailed wildly with his human arms, and Matisak's entire body quivered and showered blood as away he flew with the rest of the floating carnival all around her.

Jessica dropped to her knees and released the jet flow of the propane torch, the light gone with the flame. Her face now was streaked with tears as well as dirt and grime.

Overhead, a portion of the ceiling creaked, moaned and collapsed in on itself, revealing a black, roiling sky beyond, a kind of black hole that had opened up perhaps to suck in Matisak's soul, which she imagined would rise only so far as Hell.

Once again the whirling, spinning track overhead brought Matisak into her line of vision. She saw that he was still somehow alive, responding spasmodically to the pain and torture dealt him. She searched the dirty floor for one of the two guns she'd brought to kill Matisak with, but was unable to locate either without light to see by.

Finally, she pulled her flashlight from below the netting that Matisak had hoped to trap her beneath, and with the beam she found her .38 police special. She raised it now, awaiting Matisak's return trip.

He looked to be still now as he moved closer toward her, the terror of his pain clearly etched on his unremittingly grimacing face, yet the spasms had ceased. He appeared dead. He was finally dead.

But then his head fell forward and his open eyes stared down at her and he grinned.

She prepared to fire, aiming for the forehead. She squeezed the trigger inward, inward . . . about to put him out of his misery . . . but then decided otherwise.

She thought of the suffering he'd brought into this world. He had created chaos and horror, not only for all his victims, but for her as well. She was his victim.

She lowered her gun, located her coat and watched the dying man's parade of horror continue on and on and on with the tumult of metal wheels rolling about steel grooves. She then went for the exit, leaving Matisak to his death, his last scream diminished by the rattling mechanical pulleys, chains and tracks and the pounding winds further rattling the warehouse walls and exterior.

Jessica stepped out into God's breath, the storm winds now at gale force, having found landfall somewhere along the Louisiana coastline. For all she knew she was stepping into the eye of Hurricane Lois. But it didn't matter. Matisak was dead, and she was free of the ugliest human force she'd ever encountered.

She saw a light sluicing back and forth along the wharf ahead of her, and she heard the insistent shouting which came from Kim Desinor. Kim and Alex Sincebaugh parted the mists around them, racing toward her, Alex throwing a dry blanket over her shoulders. For the first time, Jessica allowed herself a moment's attention, realizing she was ill-equipped to deal with the raging wind which buffeted her about like a crumpled paper boat on the waves of a great ocean. Missing her shoes, her blouse ripped, a cut above her left eye, she still managed a broad smile, for seeing the others was like looking again on life and light. She crumpled into Kim's arms, tears coming freely.

Hurricane Lois was still in the Gulf, lingering there as if to tease, as the three of them stood on the wharf below the eyes of the tattered alligator in the backdraft of a roiling air pocket.

Alex ushered the women toward his car, asking about Matisak. Jessica simply said, "You'll find him inside. It's finally over."

A great cloud of closure had enveloped her, a sense of completion and wholeness and strength which even Kim with her amazing sensibilities could not begin to fathom. Kim placed a protective arm over Jessica's shoulder and guided her through the stormy night, down the length of the pier and toward Alex's waiting car, where the strobing light seemed the only beacon left in the world. Overhead, the satanic wind threatened to destroy everything in its path.

Even as she climbed into Alex's car, feeling the machine rocking left to right under the pressure of the storm wind, Jessica only felt relief, for at last she'd managed to do what she'd only dreamed of doing for so long: from the day that she had examined his first victim so many years before in that black little cabin in Wekosha, Wisconsin, from the moment he'd maimed her, from the second he'd killed Otto Boutine, and since the day of his arrest. Real revenge was rare and so long in coming in this life. . . .

"How . . . how are you, Jess?" Kim asked.

She looked up into her friend's eyes as the storm whipped Kim's hair wildly about her head. "It's over at last . . . no more struggling with the devil of devils . . . I can dream again . . . can believe in a safer, better world . . . hurricanes, earthquakes, and killer storms notwithstanding . . . and it's already a better world without him in it."

After a look inside the warehouse, where he'd located the power switch which illuminated the place, Alex returned to the car, a stricken look on his face, and called it in. Within minutes squad cars jammed the entryway to the wharf and warehouse area, everyone working a beat interested and curious about the latest twisting development in the Mad Matthew Matisak affair, as many as possible turning out for a look at the monster Coran had brought down, anxious to lay eyes on the sight of him dangling at the end of a meat hook.

Fouintenac was indeed one of Lew Meade's operatives; his real name Leon Stedman, and he'd had a wife and several children. He'd taken on the character of real-life Deputy Mayor Fouintenac merely to remain close to Jessica Coran, to act, as Sand had acted, in the capacity of bodyguard. Apparently, he'd let his guard down. Stedman, alias Fouintenac, had to be bagged, as did Matisak's remains, and Lew Meade was flying in a pathologist from nearby Mississippi to do the honors. Meade, Police Commissioner Stephens and Carl Landry put in appearances.

Meanwhile, Alex saw to it that both Kim and Jessica Coran were ushered off to a safe location where they might gather perspective and breathe a little easier.

He later returned to make sure that evidence techs did their jobs to the fullest, and he even helped by bagging a shardlike piece of glass, thin and beveled to a point—a high-tech blow dart likely dipped in poison, which had miraculously remained in Fouintenac's neck despite the rough treatment Jessica Coran's .38 had given the dead man's torso. If Jessica's story could be believed, and he had no reason to doubt her, she'd fired three times into Fouintenac's lifeless body when she'd mistaken it for Matisak.

Alex also helped in the triangulation of both Matisak's body and Fouintenac's body, but this was a useless gesture since both bodies had carouseled about the huge warehouse repeatedly.

Lew Meade was understandably upset at the loss of his agent, and he remained uncharacteristically charitable, allowing Alex to do his job, not fighting for territorial or jurisdictional rights or flashing his FBI badge about the place. He muttered something about Stedman's having been a good man in such a way as to make Alex wonder if he meant that Stedman was too good a man to have wasted on Jessica Coran's safety.

Even Meade's calling in the pathologist from the Mississippi FBI field office did not get in the way of the data and evidence collection. This surprised Alex. Since Dr. Jessica Coran was both FBI and the principal in the incident, Alex half expected everyone other than FBI would be given the heave-ho, but this didn't happen.

When Matisak was being pulled from the hook which had entered the base of his brain via the neck from behind, it took several men and a number of sweaty tugs to unhook him. The man had a noticeable hunchback and thick, even bloated skin with splotches of discoloration, as if he had suffered from some unusual disease. Located in the warehouse, not far from the body were a definitely out-of-place surgical table and dialysis machine, which the warehouse owners claimed to know absolutely nothing about.

Reporters from the *Times-Picayune* did their best to get past barricades and get a photo of the dead Matisak. A picture of the vampire killer beside the sad-faced clowns amid the ruined menagerie in the Mardi Gras warehouse would go for big bucks, and Yancy Rosswell, the police photographer, got what he termed some great surreal shots of the hapless victim.

When two body bags came out of the warehouse, news photographers went to work.

•   •   •

New Orleans was spared the brunt of Hurricane Lois as she made landfall between Biloxi and Gulfport instead; still, the city was ravaged by a primal wind and storm surge that destroyed whole sectors, putting many sections under water, the death toll mounting into the thirties, even as the newscasters spoke, since bodies were being discovered beneath flying debris and rubble. But due to the National Weather Service warnings, the time given to prepare and the fact that the center of the storm had bypassed the heart of the city, opting for the east, and because most people were either in their homes or evacuated northward, many lives were spared.

Back at the precinct house, the day was filled with paperwork involving the Matisak case. Both Kim Desinor and Jessica Coran were brought in to give statements. The day wasted away beneath a gunmetal-gray sky. At one point Alex and the others learned that a black man named Lewis was telling a story about having witnessed a beheading inside the confines of an automobile matching the one Stedman had been driving, one found abandoned not far from Gatorland Storage. Lewis's unobstructed view of the beheading had occurred just outside the hotel where Jessica Coran was staying.

"The bastard was stalking Coran all along, no doubt about it," Alex told Ben as they drove for Surette's former apartment. Tonight, Alex meant to do what he could to get some sort of lead on Easy that might lead to the Hearts Killer. It was time New Orleans was rid of such filth and garbage along with Matisak.

Darkness had descended over the city again. It was half past eight when Alex pulled within sight of Surette's place. Beside him, Ben yawned and guzzled the final drop of a soda he'd been drinking.

"This is crazy, Sincy," Ben complained again. "I mean, we looked that place over from top to bottom the first time, and it was clean as a baby's behind after a bath. I remember saying how great it'd be to be able to live like these damned transients, you know? 'Member that? No paper, no bills, no bull, I said. Never seen such a clean place in my life. Always thought these types were messy, but not this guy."

Alex kept his own counsel. He just wanted to get back inside Surette's place.

"Transients live empty fucking lives," Ben said now. "Wish I had a little less paper on me. You know I'm still paying on that freakin' van I bought four years ago?"

Alex replied, "He wasn't transient, though. He worked seven blocks down the street at the Blue Heron, remember? And not so much as a paycheck stub lying around that apartment."

The silence built between them like a wall until Alex finally broke it anew. "I . . . I just can't help feeling we overlooked something. Will you just bear with me? Hell, you can warm your seat here while I go up, if you like . . . have a doughnut, but I'm going to pay a visit."

"I don't know, Alex . . . this time o' night, dem dare French Quarter folks asleep with der derringers unner der pillows, mon."

"We'll pol-lite-ly knock and ask."

"Suppose Gilreath's sister is covering for him, Alex."

"You really think Gilreath's been lurking around New Orleans all this time, sleeping in some hole by day and coming out nights to overpower larger men and rip their hearts out with a butcher knife?"

"Just 'cause Surette was bigger than Davey, you don't think so, Alex? Come on, we both know that men can find superhuman strength while under duress. There was a struggle with Thommie Whiley, right? And Thommie was bigger than Davey Gilreath too, but that don't prove nothing, partner."

"I don't know . . . doesn't figure, Big."

"What doesn't figure?"

The old sounding-board game between them was back, and it felt good, Alex thought. "Pigsty Gilreath struck me as one of the few cross-dressing cretins around here who actually had his feet on the ground."

"That fairy? I never saw anything particularly stable about him. I wouldn't rule him out, Alex, certainly not on the say-so of that whore Susie Socks. Our little Davey, in an attempt to make up for a variety of shortcomings of one sort or another, and taking into account an upbringing that involved a beating every other day . . . well . . ."

"Well, be that as it may, I just can't buy him as a mutilation murderer, Ben. He wasn't above getting his hands dirty in the small-change department, but murder, getting blood on his hands . . . I just don't see it with Pigsty, no. Of all the street transies in the area, he was at least concerned about good hygiene."

"Including oral?" Ben's joke fell flat.

"And AIDS and other diseases, and yeah, that's what I mean. Hell, man, he couldn't stand to see blood or roadkill, much less kill someone. It just doesn't wash, him as the Queen of Hearts killer."

"Guess we'll know more after we bring him in for questioning," Ben said, letting it drop.

Alex gave Gilreath another thought. Perhaps he *had* gone off the deep end, perhaps he'd become a Mr. Hyde, roaming the street by night, picking his prey—gay men known to him—choosing his moment and attacking them, cannibalizing them for some bizarre religious-fantasy experience understood only in the heart and the mind of the madman.

But somehow Alex doubted it.

➤ 31 ➤

May I meet him with one tooth and it aching, and
one eye to be seeing seven and seventy divils
in the twists of the road, and one old timber
leg on him to limp into the grave. There he
is now crossing the strands, and that the Lord
God would send a high wave to wash him from the world.

—John Millington Synge

Once at the apartment which had previously been Victor Surette's, the two detectives first learned from the superintendent who was the current occupant. It was a young man named Michael Dominique, and they were greeted with a smile from a tall, sallow-faced youth whose eye shadow was half on, half off, his eyelashes startlingly long and lovely, though the rouge and lipstick were a bit overdone. His eyes were extremely feminine, piercing and hypnotic, and as green and hard as jade as he peeked from behind the door chain.

"I'm Detective Sincebaugh and this is Detective de-Yampert, ma'am, ahh, sir . . . Mister . . . ahh . . ."

"Dominique, Michael Emanuel Dominique, and don't mention being sorry around me, sweet cakes. So, you're two big strong strapping cops here just to see me? Really now . . ." He opened the door wide to reveal that he was in a tie-dyed, rainbow-colored terry robe, his hair in a towel as if just washed.

"Freshly dyed," he said, pointing to the towel atop his head, his eyes following Alex's. "Must keep up appearances, you know."

"We're here . . . well, we've been investigating the Queen of Hearts killings from the beginning, and—"

"Oh, dear, how tragic . . . how terribly, horribly tragic it all is, but what has it to do with me?" Mr. Dominique looked truly perplexed.

373

"Well, we'd like to ask you a few questions about the apartment."

"The apartment?" He was now clearly confused, turning to stare inward at the place. It wasn't a bad place. Lots of room and closet space as Alex had recalled, the bedroom, living area and kitchen three separate rooms, a full bath rounding it off. Most of the older apartments in the area, you had to share a bath at the end of the hall. The furnishings were Surette's or belonged to the super, exactly as they'd last seen the place, a hodgepodge of styles from a steel-and-glass Scandinavian coffee table to an Early American couch with flowers and turkeys as a pattern.

"Yes, well, one of the victims once lived here," Alex said. "His name was Victor, Victor Surette."

The young man turned away and stepped to the couch, asking them to come in before he sat, crossing his cleanly shaved legs, displaying his manicured nails, the fingers long and delicate, his feet covered in bunny-eared slippers. "I wouldn't know. No one's ever told me about that."

Alex thought him extremely composed at learning such information. For all this guy knew, Surette's body might have been found right here in this room, on the very couch where Dominique now sat.

"Well, it has been a long time," Alex volunteered, "but my partner and I would like to ask you if at any time during your stay here . . ."

"Yes?"

"If you've gotten mail for Surette, or a phone call asking about him, or just anything about the previous tenant. Or if you'd found anything lying about that might've belonged to Mr. Surette."

"Well, no . . . I'm sorry, but I haven't."

"You didn't know him?"

"Well, no . . . I didn't."

"But you knew of him?"

"Of him?" He shook his head.

"Well, he had something of a reputation. He was an entertainer, a cross-dressing entertainer, so I assumed you might have met others in the area who knew of him." Alex had calculated the number of potential victims for the maniac who preferred cross-dressing gays, and realized that he could well be speaking to a future victim of the killer at this moment.

"Well, if there's nothing else, gentlemen," said the young man whom Sincebaugh placed at around twenty-three or twenty-four, a couple of years older than Surette would have been. Looking around and seeing no photos or loose papers lying around, no books or magazines or even a newspaper, made Alex flash again on the sameness of the room. Mr. Dominique or whatever his name was had not put any individual stamp on the place, at least not on this room.

"Yeah, Sincy, we'd best be on our way," said deYampert, regaining his feet.

"Would you mind terribly if we looked around, Mr. Dominique?"

"For what?" he asked, surprised by the question.

"Well, for any loose boards or bricks, anything below or behind which Mr. Surette may have placed papers."

"What precisely are you looking for?"

"Frankly, we don't know."

"You don't know?"

"We won't know until we see it."

"I see . . . I think. Well . . . feel free in here, but as I've said, I have an engagement and must finish dressing. I'll do so in the other room."

"Very nice of you to allow us to search," said Ben, who began to do so in haste—anxious to leave, it appeared.

"We'd like to search all the rooms, if that's okay with you, Mr. Dominique," said Alex. "Your cooperation in this matter would be most appreciated."

Dominique frowned and made a feeble joke. "Guess I'll have to check with my lawyer first." Then, laughing, he said, "Sure, why not. But, if you should find something useful, and it actually leads you to this maniac, maybe I'll see some—you know . . ." He seductively blinked his fake lashes at Alex. "Some sort of . . . reward?"

Ben stifled a laugh.

Alex simply replied, "Your reward might just be in saving your own life in the bargain, Mr. Dominique."

"Please, call me Dom or Dommie for short. Everyone does."

"All right, Dom."

Dom then twittered and started on his way into the next room. But he stopped at the door to add, "Just as soon as I'm dressed, you two boys can sniff around my bedroom all you like for all you want." Now the coyness and the flirtation were overt, challenging.

Alex and Ben exchanged a putrid look as Dominique left the room. When he'd shut the door behind him, the two detectives fell out laughing, each shushing the other. In a moment, they returned to the business at hand, searching every corner of the room, Ben still filled with a disgruntled disbelief that they were even here and a powerful, preconceived notion that they'd find absolutely nothing as before.

"We're drawing at straws here, pard," Ben was saying when his eyes fell upon something. His sudden silence made Alex wheel and look down at the hardwood floor below the couch where a strange-looking, white-laced doily with a queen of hearts playing card stitched into it lay half in, half out of the darkness. Dominique had first been sitting and then standing there, possibly trying to conceal the thing earlier. At the same instant, the door to the bedroom burst open and Dominique, in full feminine dress, attacked Ben, who was closest to the door, the huge blade plunging into the big man's chest even as he fended him off.

Alex snatched out his gun, but Ben's enormous form was between them, and with successive strikes of the knife, the big man fell into Alex, knocking him to the floor, Alex's head striking hard against the edge of a bureau.

His vision blurred, with no idea how long he'd been out, Alex's eyes opened on the horrid sight of Dominique in women's clothing, forcing his hand into the cavernous wound he'd opened up in deYampert's chest. Alex saw him come away with his best friend's heart and he cried out, his hands frantically searching for his weapon, which had skittered across the room.

But he was trapped under Ben's dead weight, and now *he* as *she* was coming for Alex, prepared to open him up with an enormous, serrated knife that looked like something out of an operating room.

When the killer leaned in over Alex, he saw clearly that

Dominique's dress had been ripped and the carefully created breasts were *real*. The madman had all along been a madwoman.

The knife loomed larger and larger as she approached with Ben's blood-soaked heart in her left hand.

Alex fought a useless battle to struggle free of his best friend's dead weight, but being pinned beneath Ben deYampert was little different from being pinned below a dead horse. Only Alex's arms had worked free, but they were no match against the cutting machine she would become once she began wielding the knife. He had a second gun strapped to his ankle, but there was no way to get at it.

She enjoyed his complete helplessness.

"You loved Vicki, too, didn't you? Everybody loved sweet, little Vicki," she said in a cooing voice. "Ring around the rosy, pocket full of hearts, not posies . . . a heart is a terrible thing to waste, isn't it? Well, isn't it!"

"What have you done with the hearts?"

"Same as I'll do with yours and your friend's. You all have a place waiting at Raveneaux, just like little Vicki."

He expected her at any moment to bite into the heart which had beat in Ben deYampert's chest only moments before, to cannibalize the organ, but she instead caressed the still-pumping muscle, and reverently placed it onto the glass tabletop, which had miraculously escaped the kicking and fighting that'd been the death dance between Ben and Dominique.

The heart flapped like a fish there on the glass-topped table, and Alex's heart sank to see the awful sight, his grief for Ben almost overpowering the evil image of his own dislodged heart lying alongside Ben's.

She came closer with the knife, an elongated ratchet-toothed thing which could cut bone, shining swordlike in its sharp thin lines. Enjoying herself immensely, her tongue flicking about her lips, her animal appetite whetted, she plunged it at his exposed throat and upper torso, but he grabbed her wrist at the last moment, battling her for control. She placed both hands over the knife, shoving her whole weight against it, powerful with the strength given the mad.

Suddenly someone was pounding on the door, shouting from outside for the occupant to open up.

It was garbled, but it sounded like backup or at least the landlord. Someone had heard the disturbance and had called for help.

She glared at Alex and back at the door, which was now being pounded with great force, readying to buckle under the combined weight of at least two men on the outside who continued to shout and storm. She snatched up Ben's heart and rushed into the back room, slamming the door behind her.

Alex shouted for help as two uniformed policemen came crashing through the door, followed by the IAD detectives who'd been hounding Alex's heels since the incident at the cafe. "Get him off meeeee! Get me up!"

"What in the name of Holy God!"

"Jesus have mercy," said one of the uniformed cops, his gun trained on Alex's forehead.

"We're both detectives. His killer's in the next room, damn you! Tell them, Hirschenfeldt! Get me the hell up and use extreme caution over there!" he shouted to the second uniformed cop, who was trying to get into the other room, having heard noises coming from that quarter. "Damnit, man, it's the Queen of Hearts killer! She's locked herself inside there! Help me to my feet!"

She'd jammed a chair beneath the knob of the inner door, and it took them several minutes before they could break through, but she was gone through an open window where the sash flapped madly as if shouting her direction. Through the window a wild wind howled in on them like a ghostly warning not to follow, but Alex heeded only his rage and instinct, hurling himself toward the window. Half in and half out the window, he realized only now that a sudden storm had blotted out the sky with ominous and inky clouds, ready to burst forth with a heavy rain, the sweet, metallic smell of it insinuating as much, while all around him the wind swept in angry eddies, rattling the fire escape, a backlash of the hurricane.

The woman calling herself Michael Dominique had vanished with little trace of ever having been here, but she'd mercifully dropped or had decided to leave Ben's now-still heart on the wrought-iron fire escape two flights below, where it hadn't met with a gentle landing. Having obviously decided to race on without the organ she'd killed for, she had instead bounded acrobatically up or down the fire escape, and now like a vicious killer out of an Edgar Allan Poe story, the monster had been swallowed up in the stormy New Orleans night.

"What in the name of God happened here, Detective?" asked Hanson, Hirschenfeldt's partner, in an accusatory tone, grabbing hold of Alex at the windowsill.

"Never mind that! Beat hell back to your unit. Tell 'em what we have here. I want men scouring the area, including the roof and adjacent buildings. It's the Hearts killer, damn you, and he's a she . . . a she pretending to be a he, pretending to be a she."

All the other policemen stared at him, wondering what he was babbling. "The killer's a woman pretending to be a transvestite," he said, attempting to clarify, "and she gets them that way. Lulls them into a false sense of security and then lets fly with that damned knife of hers."

He started out the window after the killer.

"Where're you going?" asked the older of the two uniforms, his partner on the way to the unit, the two IAD guys useless, wide-eyed and gaping.

"After her." Alex yanked free of Hanson's grasp and climbed out onto the fire escape, trying to find any clue as to which direction she'd taken, up or down. From the look of the undisturbed dust below him, he opted for going straight up.

"I think she's on the roof. Send backup as soon as you can!"

Alex raced for the roof, taking the steps two at a time until a powerful gust of wind threatened to lift him over the side. He held on more firmly, and once he'd made it to the top of the roof, he stared across at the expanse, having trouble standing, the powerful wind threatening to send him back over the side without aid of the fire escape. He hunkered down low to the black-tar roof, scanning in a 360-degree turn for every possible avenue of escape. There were hiding places everywhere, and the roof was closely aligned with another.

Something told him it was useless, that she was gone, and only then did he realize just how much blood covered his shirt. Both of his forearms were crisscrossed with knife wounds where he'd fended off the bitch's blows. His shirt and coat were caked with his and Big's blood. He felt a sudden lightheadedness, an inability to focus, and not even the wind could calm the stench of blood now in his nostrils. He felt an over-whelming sense of loss engulf him, realizing that when he went back down off this roof, he'd never again speak to Ben or be yelled at by the big goon.

A cold, bitter rain began to fall over Alex, drenching his hair, melting his tears and washing his wounds. It was the last thing he felt or remembered before blacking out.

32

Envy's a coal comes hissing hot from hell.

—Phillip James Bailey

Alex, still wracked with pain from his own wounds, had cornered the sadistic Hearts killer, and he had destroyed the monster, at least in his fevered mind where he slept in hospital.

After the storm had subsided, after his wounds had stopped palpitating, he found himself chasing Thommie Whiley's E, alias Dominique, out that window in Surette's apartment. E leaped manfully from building to building, as if capable of flight, but Alex was also up to the challenge, despite the profuse bleeding from his wounds—stitches already in place and torn now. Regardless, his dream ego kept on the killer's heels, shadowing every move, every dodge.

The killer made one leap too many for a wall too far, landing on the other side and barely holding on with those ugly clawlike fingernails Alex so vividly recalled now. The bastard was a guy wearing fake nails and even a set of false breasts which dangled below his shirt.

"Help! Help me!" screamed the bloody killer who had just brutalized Ben.

Alex backed up and made a prodigious leap across the crevasse between them, miraculously landing on the black-topped roof. He then crawled on his belly to where the SOB clung to his/her petty life there at the ledge.

The killer's pleading eyes were framed in fear, a cowardly creature with heavy makeup, rouge at the cheeks and thick, red lipstick, a kind of crazed clown.

"Pull me up, damn you! Pull me up, now!" she/he cried in a falsetto voice.

Alex grabbed hold of the killer's flesh and found it soft to the touch, feminine and warm. This startled him, and he looked again into Dominique's eyes. He was a she, she was a he . . . and then back again. There was no earthly way to tell, save for the ferocity of his/her strength as she/he clung now to Alex, ripping into Alex's skin with those bird-of-prey claws of his/hers.

"Let her fly, Sincy," said Ben deYampert, standing alongside, having materialized from the cloud of dream. "Let's see how well the bitch flies."

"Save me, you must . . . you must save me!" came the killer's plea, piercing and painful to his ear.

"Kill it, Alex . . . whatever it is . . . kill it!" demanded Ben's vengeful spirit. "You owe me that much!"

Alex couldn't easily let go even though he wished to fulfill Big's last request. His struggle with himself was nothing compared to the struggle against her clawing, bloodletting grip; in fact the connection between them, killer and hunter, became so slick with blood that it was the red milk of life which soon and ironically made it impossible for the monster to hold onto Alex any longer.

She/he slid in minute increments, one lurch at a time, from Alex's grip. He was unsure whether he wanted the fiend to die so easily or not. He wanted to see the thing suffer as he had suffered the loss of his friend, and as he had seen Surette and Thommie Whiley and other victims of the Queen of Hearts killer suffer. He wanted to rip the bastard's heart out, make it a clean, even, full-circled kind of revenge, but too, amid all the rage and chaos of the moment, Alex also pleaded to have his curiosity quenched.

"Tell me where the hearts are kept and what you do with them, and I'll save you!" he lied.

But the blood slick created from the gushing wounds and a handful of bloody human hearts the maniac clung to was too much, and the moment the monster sailed away into the oblivion of the pit below Alex's dream self, he awakened with one resolve.

Sweating, his wrists in pain from the imaginary rents and tears inflicted on him, Alex had recalled the one word the ugly demon had whispered to him when he'd asked where she kept the hearts: Raveneaux.

He opened his eyes to find that he was not at home but in a hospital room surrounded by Captain Landry, Kim Desinor and Dr. James Aubrey Longette, the hypnotist and shrink.

"The regression therapy worked, Alex. You've told us everything that happened in that room," Kim assured him.

Landry was staring out the hospital window, quietly cursing to himself and repeating the name Raveneaux.

Even Dr. Longette knew what the name stood for in New Orleans and Louisiana.

"Just who or what is this Raveneaux?" asked Jessica, who looked on behind a concerned Kim Desinor.

"Big plantation home north of the city," replied Landry.

"Home to Senator Raveneaux, retired General George Maurice Raveneaux," added Dr. Longette with some bemused delight. "How could that old upstanding white cracker man know anything about these horrible killings? How could the killer be connected to one of the most powerful men in the state?" The doctor was awestruck, yet jaded enough to accept the possibility. "You know, to this day some people believe that Jack the Ripper was born of royal blood and lived in Windsor Castle."

"Unless the killer was having us on," replied Landry. "Listen, doctors," he said solemnly to Kim, Jessica and Dr. Longette, "I don't want a word of it, not a single word, going beyond this room. Do you understand? An accusation like this . . . well, it must be handled with all due caution and by the book."

"Yes, indeed, an important man like Raveneaux, a member of the white elite, a member of the old family guard. Be a different story if the man were black, though, wouldn't it, Captain Landry?" said the shrink and hypnotist, his eyes bulging with rage.

"I'm surprised at you, Dr. Longette," countered Kim in her most facetious voice. "Do you mean to say there's different laws for Cajun, Creole and black folks than there are for whites in New Orleans?"

Landry just gritted his teeth and pretended he'd heard no objections. "Alex and I'll have to pursue this by the book, and that will mean somehow, some way we're going to have to convince a judge in this town to give up a warrant on former Senator Raveneaux. You know what that's going to entail?"

Alex attempted a laugh, which only hurt his bruised insides, and then he said, "Maybe by the time you get that warrant, I'll be ready to walk out of here, go up-country with you, Carl. Just be sure it covers *all* the Senator's dwellings and vehicles."

Landry's usually deep worry lines had just sunk deeper into the folds of his skin. "Christ . . . it would have to be Rave-neaux. . . ."

Kim was worried about Alex, the wounds he'd suffered, and she was also worried about her associate and friend, Jessica Coran. Jessica had been subdued, like an exhausted swimmer just finished with the English Channel. She'd been on the phone all morning in an attempt to locate James Parry, wishing to send him news, but she'd been unable to reach him. Meanwhile, she'd refused to check in with Paul Zanek, who had become irrational about the whole matter, blaming Lew Meade for having bungled the whole operation.

Zanek had called Kim, shouting at her, but she hadn't taken any crap from Zanek either, telling him, "What operation's that, Paul? The bag-Matisak operation? Well, you can stop worrying about Matisak. Jessica bagged him just fine. Meade's got a report on the Matisak matter coming over your fax as we speak, and I'm sure you'll like the results." She'd then briefly explained what had been found at the Gatorland Storage facility.

Paul had punctuated all she said by remarks such as, "Are you sure? Are you putting me on? Is that exactly how it went down? But that's damned good news, damned great!"

"Yeah, sure it's great, but at what expense to Jessica, Paul? Have you given her any thought at all?"

"What're you, crazy? She's all I've thought about. Damned straight I have. I put round-the-clock surveillance on her, despite the fact she didn't want it! I arranged everything through Lew Meade with clearance from Santiva."

"Well, congratulations, Paul. Hoist a glass for Jessica. In the meantime, she's surviving quite nicely."

She'd hung up on Zanek, and turned and looked across the room at Jessica, who'd chosen to hide out at her place. Kim had realized that Jessica simply needed some time and emotional distance. She'd been consoling Jessica when she learned of Alex's brush with death and how poor Ben deYampert had met his end.

At that point, Kim had dropped everything and rushed to the hospital, Jessica chasing after. Moments after her arrival, Kim had learned of Landry's request that Alex undergo hypnosis so they could learn all they could about what had happened in the apartment where Ben deYampert was killed.

Alex was now insisting on getting up and going straight for this place called Raveneaux without a warrant, on probable cause alone, and he meant to do it with or without anyone's help, and he meant to do it this moment, disregarding his doctor's advice, disregarding his captain and Jessica's objections or Kim's concern for him. His attempt to get up, however, caused a flurry of dizziness and a tongue-biting pain searing up from his midsection where damaged, bruised ribs were still sending out shards of gnawing distress. His arms were both in bandages, but his hands were free.

An orderly was called in by Landry and the hospital machine was put into motion, and in a few minutes Alex was being pumped with a sleep-inducing medication that calmed him into a stark white doze.

Just as Alex was going under, he mumbled to Landry, "I'm going . . . with you . . . to this place . . . Raveneaux."

"For now, you get some rest, Alex," Landry said. But now he was speaking to an unconscious man.

Jessica took Landry aside and said, "Me too, Captain. I want to be with you when you go out to this Raveneaux place."

"Listen here, I want you to get some rest yourself, young lady. You've gone through a terrible trauma with that fiend Matisak, and both of you"—he included Kim with a gesture—"you've been up all night on this vigil over Alex, and I appreciate your concern for him, but you're not going to be any good to anyone if you collapse."

"I'll get some rest now, knowing he's okay," Kim countered.

"It's going to be a while before I get that warrant—if I can get it at all. As to probable cause, that's a long shot and not a very good long shot at that."

"I'll see what I can do about a federal warrant," suggested Jessica.

"That would be great."

"But don't count on it," cautioned Jessica. "Meade doesn't like the idea."

"I'll be in touch, and truth be known, there's some things we picked up at the scene which I'd like you to touch over, Dr. Desinor. See what comes of 'em. Would you mind terribly?" asked Landry.

She shook her head. "No, of course not. That's what I'm here for. Anything I can do to help, which so far hasn't been much."

"You don't go second-guessing yourself now, Doctor. You've done far more than we could've expected here."

Dr. Longette shook Landry's hand. "I want to see you raid that old plantation out there. Wish I could be with you, in fact, but . . . anyway, that's going to be a sight for the six o'clock news."

"Hold on now, Dr. Longette, you promise me you won't go calling Channel 2 or anybody. Say it . . . say it."

Longette took a deep breath and finally nodded. "All right, Captain. If that's how you want it."

"Say it."

"I promise you, Carl."

Now Landry breathed out of relief. Longette then left, a light chuckle on his lips.

"You'd best get that rest yourself now, Dr. Desinor, Dr. Coran," suggested Landry.

"I will," replied Kim, "but for now, I think I'll just stay a while with Alex, so he doesn't wake up alone."

He wakes up alone every morning, Landry thought, but did not say. "He'll be out for hours, maybe till tomorrow. Go home . . . get some rest, both of you."

"You go on back to the hotel, Jess. I'll just stay a little longer," Kim lied, and sent Landry and Jessica on their way.

When Alex's eyes opened and cleared after the dreamless white-cloud sleep which only sedation could bring, he found Kim Desinor sitting alongside him, holding his hand in hers, her eyes red and moist from her having had no sleep and from weeping.

"Hey, what gives? What're the tears for? You okay?" He tried to clear a dry, cracked throat. "Somepin happen while I was out?"

"Everything's such a mess. Ben's gone, you've been hurt so badly, Jessica's so depressed, and I . . . I haven't been of any use to any of you. If I'd only heeded my own best voice. I knew I was getting crazy, mixed messages from the killer about identity, so why couldn't I have—"

"You're talkin' nonsense, Kim. That's crazy talk, and I don't want to hear you blaming yourself over Ben's death. God, if anyone's to blame, hell, the big lug wanted to go home to his wife, and I insisted we make one more stop."

She leaned in over him and found herself hugging him. With bandaged forearms and wrists, he returned the hug as best he could, and they were both surprised at how casually he found her lips, his own passion rising to the surface of its own volition. "It's all right," he reassured her. "I'm going to be okay."

Behind them someone had stepped into the hospital room. It was Carl Landry, accompanied by Jessica Coran, who was polite enough to noisily clear her throat, a smile coloring her features, obviously happy to see that Kim and Alex at long last were getting along so well.

Landry cleared his throat almost in echo of Jessica and said, "Glad that I've found you here, Dr. Desinor. Alex, how're you feeling?"

"Some better."

"Doctors are saying bruised ribs, nothing broken," Kim began, pushing away from Alex, standing now, a bright and energetic glow about her. "And the forearm gashes should heal in a few weeks like new."

Landry nodded knowingly and muttered, "Battle scars." Then his tone changed to one of accusation. "You never left this room, did you, Dr. Desinor?"

"I've been in and out . . . for coffee and whatnot."

"Oh, leave her alone, Carl," said Jessica, playfully shoving Landry. "Can't you see she's worried about Alex? Nothing wrong in that."

Landry, a bit uncomfortable with the joviality, spoke directly to Alex. "Alex, I talked with Ben's wife while you were out . . . tough, tough business. Meanwhile, I've been busy. Got something here I pulled from Surette's apartment. I'm sure it belonged to the killer we're after, and he or she, as you suspect, would've worn it close to his . . . ahh, her body. Look familiar?''

"She, Captain," Alex said, sure of himself. "He—our killer—is a she. It's the same she that killed Thommie Whiley. Calls herself Michael Emanuel Dominique, Thommie's E for Easy . . . pretends to be a man who likes to dress as a woman, but those breasts of hers were real enough.''

"Any rate, he or she likely wore these beads close to the skin, and in the scuffle with Ben, they were torn off." Landry held a set of dark rosary beads up to Kim's eyes. "Look familiar?'' This time there was a red-eyed gargoyle on the amulet along with a skull and crossbones, but the gargoyle had not been as cleanly fused to the rosary as the earlier crystal amulet had been. "This too." He pulled forth a pair of lacy, round cards with the image of a queen of hearts on them, along with two brushes and eyeliners, a comb and a handheld mirror.

"There weren't any convenient photos lying around with her picture on them by any chance?" asked Jessica.

"We . . . I retrieved the damned cards, incidental items; nothing as useful as a photograph was in the place. It was as if it were being used as a dressing room only; nothing but water, Diet Pepsi, cheese and bread in the fridge.''

"No, not a thing in the way of paper in that place," Alex said, "I'd just been remarking about that to Ben when he saw the card below the couch, and that's when all hell broke loose. That's why it was so eerie, because the place was cleaned out after Surette was killed long before we got there that first time almost a year ago, and the place had remained almost exactly the same since. I should've known then how dangerous this wacko-creep was . . . I should've known; should've felt it and gone with my instincts, but not me . . . not this time . . . Still she didn't look strong enough to hurt a fly, much less Big Damn me . . . damn me, anyway . . .''

"Beating up on yourself's not going to accomplish anything, Alex." Kim said, returning to him, her hands going to his shoulder in a consoling squeeze.

Landry cleared his throat and added, "The bad news is I'm

still working on a court order for a search and seizure out at Raveneaux, but—''

''Whataya mean? What's the flaming holdup, Captain?'' asked Alex, his agitation showing clearly on his brow.

''Even in the best of circumstances, Alex, you know how these things can take time, and this is hardly the best of circumstances. We don't have a whole hell of a lot to go on. We have the word of a cop who thinks he heard the killer shout the name Raveneaux as the place where he or she plants the victims' hearts, and we only have that through hypnosis, which doesn't always fly with the justices, as you also know. Now—''

''Gotta be somebody over in the courthouse who'll listen to you, Carl.''

''I'm working on it. Now let's do what we can to improve our chances. For that, we need your help, Dr. Desinor.''

Landry went to the blinds and drew them against the afternoon sun, darkening the room, knowing now how Kim preferred to work. Everyone became silent while she ran her fingertips gently over the items which Carl had brought her. She got nothing at first, the items cold and useless. The first card she held in her hand, like the rosary, yielded little, something about black birds, possibly crows or ravens filling in a night sky, yet fixed there as in a still life; they were large birds with evil eyes and worse intentions, but that was all she was getting. She picked up the second card, and got a disturbing wave of information.

''The killer has no sense of compunction. He . . . *she* hates her victims with great intensity. They have all taken something precious from her and like a child, she is confused about her own identity. . . . ''

The two NOPD policemen and Jessica Coran listened for Kim's every word now.

''She strikes out with the venom of a child that has been wronged.''

''How can she be taking back what is hers by tearing out the hearts of others?'' Jessica asked, puzzled.

''If I were a clinical psychologist, I wouldn't have any problem with that, but I couldn't tell you for sure.''

''Kim, is the killer . . . is she . . . are you saying that the killer is at this place called Raveneaux?'' asked Jessica.

She was no fool. If she said yes, then Landry could take this information back to the right judge, the one who believed in the power of psychics and thereby assure his warrant.

If she said no, and she was by no means certain of it, they might not get the warrant which Alex was so certain would net them their strongest lead yet on the Hearts killer.

''Yes or no, Doctor?'' pressed Jessica.

''Yes,'' she lied.

''All right, that tears it,'' Landry gruffly replied.

''You think you'll have any luck getting a judge to sign on this, Carl?'' asked Alex, pulling up to his elbows.

''I'm down to the bottom of the barrel, but yes, I believe so.''

''So, you're taking it to Judge Flint then?''

'' 'Bout the size of it. Nobody but nobody wants to touch this with a ten-foot flagpole, pal.''

Alex didn't particularly care about how they got the warrant to search, so long as they got it, but Flint's reputation being what it was, he worried nonetheless about what might happen on the other side of it when, after they apprehended the Queen of Hearts killer, the legal loopholes started to work in favor of the fiend.

''I see. A black judge to issue a warrant against a plantation home. Make good copy for the *National Enquirer*. Very good, Cap'n, but you know that going through so many judges and their clerks, you've tipped the entire legal community to unfolding events. Someone's sure to call out there.''

''One stroke of fortune. The power lines up that way got hit by eighty-five-mile-an-hour winds. No phone calls going in or out thataway, and we get ourselves a legit warrant in the meantime.''

Alex laughed harshly. ''Even if it's from a boozy old derelict who's up on child abuse charges—pending, of course.''

Jessica began pacing the room. ''How soon do you think we can get the warrant?'' she asked. ''Every moment we lose, the killer gains.''

''How about right this moment?''

''What?''

Landry made the warrant materialize before them in magician fashion.

"But . . . how'd you do that? I thought you needed Kim's added info about the items here," Jessica said as Kim blinked.

"I told Flint it'd already been done, and I told him the results. It's on file. I felt a need for speed too."

"Great. Then we'd best go now." Alex got up from his hospital bed without any pain this time—or without enough to matter. He located his clothes, and was soon dressed and prepared to walk out with them. In ten minutes they were outside in Landry's squad car, headed across town for Raveneaux's Georgetown home, the warrant actually covering all properties belonging to the distinguished former general and senator.

The servants, who hadn't seen the master in several months, were astonished and put out by the gestapo-like intrusion into their world, but a search revealed nothing save a framed photograph of a pair of children, a boy and a girl, the boy barely five or six, the girl a head taller, her arm draped protectively around him. When pressed for who the children were, the servants could only say that they were the senator's two children, Victor and Dominique.

Soon after, the squad car was turning off Interstate 10, darting through the countryside where Raveneaux stretched on for miles in the darkness beyond the windshield. Jessica and the others had seen the first sign on the first gate leading onto the property six or seven minutes before when the headlight beams had picked it up. Now they'd passed no less than six additional gates. Out on the meadows beyond the gates, cows lulled in the night. There were horses and sheep and pigs out there as well, and field upon field of sugarcane.

They were less than twenty miles northwest of the New Orleans city limits, on a rural road in Ascension Parish now, just down from Interstate 10. The countryside here was flat for the most part, but it had become so solidly pitch-black out here, where the insects now reigned and rang with noise, that little of the land could be seen.

Raveneaux played home to a large stable of racehorses, some first-class winners, but most of the old man's money and wealth had been achieved through a clever mix of sugarcane and politics. In daylight the lush black earth and green fields seemed a far removed world from that of New Orleans' teeming French Quarter; even at night it seemed a world without malice or hatred, envy or greed, bitterness or remorse, deceit or wounds either healed or weeping. So Captain Landry, sitting in the driver's seat beside Alex, looked as skeptical as Jessica, whose frown he had caught in his rearview.

Beside Jessica in the backseat, Kim kept her own silent counsel.

Jessica thought about the road which had led them here. Raveneaux was the one clue left Alex Sincebaugh by the murdering Michael Emanuel "E" Dominique, quite likely the same E as in Kim's uncanny vision after Thommie Whiley's death. Alex had admitted, with some conviction, to having been impressed by Dr. Desinor's near-magical abilities; he'd even admitted a possible connection between her mysterious E and the murdering Dominique, who'd readily used the middle name of Emanuel. Alex had admitted that Dr. Desinor had miraculously unveiled the killer to some degree; unfortunately it hadn't been enough to save Ben, perhaps in large measure due to Alex's own stubborn blindness. What was it about hindsight and 20/20 vision? And what had Kierkegaard said? *Life can only be understood backwards, but it must be lived forwards.*

As they drove on, Carl Landry told Alex how he'd had to break the news of Ben's death to Ben's wife, Fiona. Alex fought to control himself. Ben's family, his children, were like Alex's own.

"Anyway, Fiona told me some disturbing news about Ben, Alex," Landry said by way of preparation. "You may's well hear it now and from me."

"What're you talking about, Captain?"

Jessica and Kim, sitting behind them, were also curious.

"Fiona told me that deYampert was upset and worried . . . that he had . . . well, taken some money . . ."

"That's bullshit. Ben wasn't on anyone's take!"

"Said that Ben had been paid off to keep quiet about the case involving Victor Surette, and . . ."

"What?"

"And to doctor some items in the reports."

"Christ, that's . . . that's crazy, Captain, just crazy. Nobody approached me to doctor any damned records, and . . .''

"Said he was most upset not about the money so much as having lied to you, Alex, to steer you away from any serious investigation into Surette's past. And obviously it was working, up until your nightmares began and you began to put two and two together.''

"Money? Who, Carl? *Who* offered him money to stomp all over the case?'' Alex was still disbelieving, but at the same time his mind raced over moments when Ben had wanted to go in another direction, as when they'd gone looking for Gilreath, and later when they'd returned to Surette's apartment.

"You gotta understand,'' Landry said. "He never felt Surette was connected—you know, to the string of murders— least not at first. He was like me, hell . . . like everyone else . . .''

"Who offered deYampert the bribe?''

"She didn't want to tell me, but I made her.''

"Who?''

"It came through Dr. Wardlaw, Frank Wardlaw.''

"That sonofabitch. I knew it . . . knew all along that he was covering something. Christ, can't believe Ben'd turn over like that. And why?''

"Ben was hurting financially. Made him an easy target. Anyway, Ben rationalized it all out for himself and was living with it just fine, but for the lies he told you. According to Fiona, Ben just thought he and Frank were protecting someone high up from any public embarrassment—about Surette, I mean.''

"One of Surette's regulars in high office, you mean?''

"Actually, no . . . not exactly.''

"What then?''

Kim Desinor and Jessica Coran listened intently as the drama of truth unfolded.

"Seems Victor Surette was related to someone high up, and they—the family—didn't want it dragged out, you know, public embarrassment, ridicule, all that.''

"Christ, so the guy was a transsexual, AC/DC . . . big deal. My God, only in the South today would anyone bat an eye,'' moaned Alex. "All right, did Ben ever tell Fiona who it might be?''

"I had to shake it out of her, but yeah, he did. It goes very high up."

Alex released his white-knuckled grip on the dash.

"Fiona asked that I take the money, all of it, back," Landry went on. "Said it was set up in a trust fund for their boys, but that it only got Ben killed. Something about how God punishes the wicked."

"You reckon Ben earned every cent?"

"I do, and it'll stay with their boys."

"So who was making payoffs to Wardlaw and Ben?"

"She didn't know just how high up it went, but the payoffs to him and Wardlaw came from Richard Stephens."

"Stephens? Commissioner Stephens?"

"Wardlaw threatened once to expose him in Ben's presence, but the P.C. was being pushed from someone above too. I suspect the Raveneaux estate."

"Jesus, then this thing has come full circle," said Jessica from the rear seat.

Alex allowed this news to sink in before he asked another question. "So what're your plans for our pal Frank Wardlaw, Captain?"

"He's out. Went down to see Frank at the lab. He honestly thought he'd be protected."

"Protected by the P.C.?"

"He claimed Stephens and Lew Meade set up the whole deal; said they said it was for the good of the city to keep such filth from staining the Raveneaux name. He truly thought he'd still have a job when this was over."

"Damned fool," muttered Jessica, "tampering with evidence, the chain of evidence and the integrity of that evidence in a murder investigation. Damned fool."

Landry continued. "I gave him a choice to either step down or face charges."

"Either way now he's ruined," Jessica suggested. "I mean, when we expose the bastards behind the cover-up of Surette's link with the Queen of Hearts killings and the subsequent body-snatching, none of the old boys who'd put him up to it will be standing with him."

Kim nodded. "They're likely all scrambling at the moment to save their own butts."

"Name of the ancient game," added Alex dryly, concealing the wellspring of emotions surrounding Ben's involvement as best he could.

"But are you sure Meade and Stephens were involved in this sordid body-snatching effort?" asked Kim. "I mean, the P.C. and the head of the New Orleans branch of the FBI? Literally robbing us of evidence and planting a false confirmation of our suspicions?"

"You know anyone else who enjoys playing God behind the scenes more than Meade?" Alex asked.

"That's one hell of an accusation, Alex," Jessica cautioned, not wanting to believe the New Orleans FBI Bureau Chief had manipulated evidence.

"If it wasn't them, who else, Dr. Coran?" asked Alex. "Who else in this city wields such authority and omnipotence?"

Carl Landry put up his large right hand for silence. He then said, "I asked myself that same question, Alex. I also asked myself who could buy a cop like Ben, an M.E. like Wardlaw, a way *around* the investigation, and why?"

"So, how did you make Wardlaw come up with Stephens and Meade?" asked Alex.

"I put the fear of death into Wardlaw," Landry began. "He was in his office when I burst in knocking files and pencils and cups over and shouting threats. Wardlaw lunged for the phone, but I'm afraid I sent it flying through a pane of glass."

"God, wish I coulda been there," Alex interjected.

"It was Wardlaw who had done the crime-scene lab work-up at the Surette murder investigation. He also did the apartment where Ben died since Jessica was in no condition for it. He was already unnerved and shaken by deYampert's death, and I blamed him for it. Told him he'd gotten Ben deYampert killed before Ben ever set foot in that apartment in the Quarter.

" 'To hell with you,' " he told me. Then he attempted to throw me out of his office, which resulted in him getting his lip cut. I then grabbed the good doctor and pushed him against his door, the glass partition shattering against the man's back. Raised my fist then and threatened him. 'Talk, you SOB, or your face is going to look like yesterday's pizza,' I assured him.''

"Let me guess," said Alex. "He only did what he was told, and even then the bastards tried to send him packing."

"I damn sure did a double take when he finally came clean." Landry recalled how at first he'd been unable to decipher the words which accused Stephens and Meade.

"How did they ever expect to get away with it?" Kim asked. "And then to bring in Jessica Coran and me. It seems crazy."

"They truly believed at the time of Surette's death that his murder was a one-time occurrence. Even after the other Hearts killings, even when they brought you on board, Dr. Desinor, they still believed there was no connection. Wardlaw was to cover up the Surette killing as much as possible, to shield it as much as possible from the public. Frank never knew why; he never wanted to know why. That's how it started, and that was supposed to be how it ended. Then Sincebaugh wouldn't let it go, coming back again and again to Surette even though Frank gave Alex nothing whatever to link that first killing with those that followed."

"Must be some psychic talent at work in you, Alex," Kim commented.

Landry continued. "Everyone by then was of a mind that since there were so many other killings, we didn't all need to keep pecking over Surette's carcass to locate the killer, and when I suggested the psychic exhumation and autopsy, they almost lost everything in their pants right then and there. I recall how nervous they all got, including Frank."

"What the hell was Frank Wardlaw thinking from the beginning? Just following orders?" asked Jessica, disgusted with Wardlaw.

"Meade had something on him, holding it over his head."
"Blackmail?"
"You never heard of a G-man who'd stoop to blackmail?"
"Blackmail for what?" Jessica asked.
"Frank had a wife and kids at the time of Surette's death; they've since left him, of course."
"I hadn't heard."
"Meade had him on a couple of things . . . gambling, skirt-

chasing . . . I never knew Meade could be so vicious, but for reasons of their own, he and Stephens wanted the Surette kid's death kept as John Doe as possible, you understand?''

"Hell, was Meade sleeping with the guy?'' Alex sneered.

Landry smirked, and then laughed full-blown, which eased the electrified air inside the car. ''Both the P.C. and Meade have powerful connections. That's all Frank needed to know. He wasn't going to trust his fate to a grand jury investigation into his alleged wrongdoings. Now, he'll be facing one anyway.''

Alex nodded grimly. ''So you've deduced from the amount of pressure put on Frank that whoever Stephens and Meade were out to protect, these people have position and wealth and power—like Susie Socks tried to tell Ben and me, Ben already knowing. People with old-money connections in the highest circles, the mayor's office, the governor's office.''

"And we get squeezed by the mayor's office and the state to close out the Queen of Hearts killings so that Surette—with the same first name as Raveneaux's son—can be quietly forgotten as having had no relation to the crimes,'' Carl concluded.

Kim sat shaking her head in disbelief, fearful of the truth. "All nice and tidy for the people who took Surette's body, people who obviously don't give a damn about the whereabouts of either Surette's heart or his killer, or whom the butcher might choose next.''

"Hey, wealth and position can do that to a person, you know that, Kim,'' replied Alex with a warm look over his shoulder for her.

"I guess we take this case to a higher level of inquiry then; we raise it out of the gutter and the gay ghetto of the French Quarter to here—a place the size of the governor's mansion?'' Jessica said.

"The home of retired general and senator George Maurice Raveneaux, a friend of the governor's,'' Landry declared.

"Now you tell me, Kim,'' Alex said. ''Are the missing hearts really at Raveneaux?''

"I can't honestly say. . . . ''

Landry pushed on, saying, ''I checked the senator out thoroughly. His wife's maiden name is Surette.''

"Damn, and we put out a request for information if you recall," Alex noted, "a televised plea for anyone who might know Surette to come forward, claim the body. All we got were a handful of his friends from the Quarter, all of whom have either disappeared or have themselves been killed by the Queen of Hearts killer. Some coincidences you can shirk off, but some cling to you like burrs on Velcro." Alex's anger could not be checked.

Now they were pulling into the blacktopped drive at Raveneaux, and none of them knew whom they could trust any longer. The thought seemed to coalesce into a palpitating question that hung in the cab where they sat. Backup squad cars came careening along and pulling in behind them.

"I guess all that we can trust is one another," Alex said, voicing his thoughts. "Can we trust you, Dr. Coran?"

"What?"

"Well, you were called in by Stephens, right? And you do work under Lew Meade's direction."

"That's not entirely fair," Kim declared. "I mean, just because she's FBI doesn't mean she agrees with or goes along with everything Lew Meade has to say, Alex."

"I'm glad to hear that, because a showdown with Meade and Stephens is inevitable. You up for it, Dr. Coran?"

Jessica produced a document. "If I were in Meade's pocket, would I have served the sheriff of Ascension Parish with a federal warrant to back you guys up? I have a few connections of my own."

33

Steady of heart, and steady of hand.

—Sir Walter Scott

The police party had arrived here at the plantation home of one of Louisiana's most honored and decorated citizens, having exhausted all other avenues, having moved the venue of their search from the squalor of the French Quarter's back-alley flophouses to this place of opulence and wealth; it seemed a contradiction, and nothing here spoke of murder or mayhem. The night air was fresh with the scent of blooming jasmine and old hickory trees that fluttered high above them in the wind, rows of them on either side of the long, expansive driveway ahead, just the other side of the huge, black gates.

Landry had halted the car at the gatekeeper's little watch booth, the gatekeeper long since replaced by electronic surveillance cameras and intercoms. Landry announced them, explaining their business and telling some butler or other servant at the other end to leave the gate open long enough for three trailing police units to follow him through.

"We'll see you up at the house," Landry finally said to the disembodied voice at the other end. "Now buzz us through."

"But this is so . . . highly irregular, sir. I must confer with the general, sir."

"The hell you do, hoss! All you have to do is press a god-damned button or be charged with obstruction of justice, you got that? Now which is it to be? You can confer with your boss afterwards."

Landry held his badge up to the camera again.

"How do I know you're really the police. Police never come out here. All the general's business is done in the city, and—"

"Goddamnit, man! If you don't open that gate in the next five seconds, we're going to blow a hole through the locking

399

mechanism and you're the first SOB we're going to handcuff when we get up there to the house! You got that?''

The buzz came, and the gates rattled apart and opened wide for them to pass. Along the top of the gates, a series of ornate black ravens all in a row began to ''dance'' before their eyes, all the ravens' eyes like enormous stone receptacles, filled with secrets forever locked inside their wrought-iron hearts. The ravens adorned the black iron gates at intervals of two feet, large birds of prey with eyes that pierced the night.

Kim instantly recognized the ravens as those in her vision, and she imagined each taking flight after dark when no one was looking; they did seem to be *flying* now as the gates opened wide. A child might easily be frightened of the images. Kim had spoken of great black ravens in the air surrounding the killer, but here they were at Raveneaux, the only two-thousand-acre Southern plantation which had survived both the Civil War and Reconstruction, the possession of one of Louisiana's most honored and oldest of families. The Raveneaux family was at the top of the social register. Every major charitable organization across the state and many across the nation owed some allegiance to George Maurice Raveneaux.

Having two search warrants, one a federal document, the party entered the gate, closely followed by a trio of cars filled with sheriff's deputies, familiarized earlier with the FBI search warrant. All of the green-suited officers were filled to the brim of their Smokey-the-Bear hats with loathing and serious doubt directed at the NOPD cops who'd crashed their jurisdiction with a warrant to disturb the general and his family. They were also filled with a certainty that nothing untoward would come of the visit, that all Landry and Alex Sincebaugh would accomplish with their damned warrant was a loss of income and profession. At this point the deputies were more in Raveneaux's camp than that of the city cops. Still, somehow Captain Landry had in fact gotten on a first-name basis with two of the deputies, who were worried sick about ''making a 'raid' on the ol' gen'ral's home.''

General George Maurice Raveneaux had served his country with distinction during the Korean conflict, and had for the last three decades been a pillar of society and commerce in the region. In fact, a newspaper article of a few years past had credited him as being the single most powerful influence in rejuvenating the entire New Orleans region, thanks to his influence in Washington and the years he'd served there as a distinguished senator.

Little wonder when they'd arrived at the sheriff's office with a request for assistance that the sheriff himself had laughed in their faces.

The deputies were understandably nervous about their mission, and Landry was not at all sure if they would carry out his orders. The sheriff himself had left ahead of them, presumably to warn the old general of their coming.

It was also little wonder that a court-ordered search warrant had been a damnably hard document to secure. George Maurice Raveneaux, a man whose money had secured the local economy during the oil debacle of the seventies, and more recently had secured the government jobs that would be coming into the region, was no paper tiger.

As they passed now along the black river of freshly coated road which formed a long, twisting drive up to the mansion, they were not surprised to see several vehicles ahead and men standing beside Raveneaux outside. He had been well warned of their arrival by the sheriff and others, it appeared.

They came up the circle drive to a building that might otherwise be a museum. Landry, Alex, Kim and Jessica were taken a little aback by the faces they saw on the expansive wraparound portico to the mansion, for beside the aged general, standing as erect as the Grecian pillars, were Chief Lew Meade and P.C. Richard Stephens, each man no doubt having learned of the proposed search from the buzz-eaters back at the courthouse in New Orleans. They were here, no doubt, to assure the prosperous, aging millionaire who'd built his kingdom on sugarcane that there was an obvious and idiotic blunder of monumental proportions being made, and that they at least would stand by him in any event.

"They all look guilty as hell of something," Jessica commented.

In the backdrop stood Mrs. Raveneaux, looking ashen, pale and drawn, her gaunt figure hardly more than a stick. Kim believed she looked like she had been through an emotionally draining day. It was past dusk now, and the matriarch of this place watched as her plantation was being overrun with police vehicles. Jessica, Kim, Alex and Landry got out of the lead car and walked toward the waiting aggregate of power standing above them on the pure-white porch, the lights emanating from the house brilliantly bathing the mansion, spreading attenuated shadows out from each of the huge Grecian columns on either side.

"Mr. Raveneaux," said Landry, taking the initiative, "I'm Captain Carl Landry of the—"

"I know very well who you are, and I'll thank you all to leave my property at once. This entire proceeding is without foundation, based on the word of some lunatic killer who has nothing whatever to do with Raveneaux."

"Sir, isn't it true," Jessica began, "that Victor Surette's stolen body was exhumed by your order and buried in your family plot here at Raveneaux?" She was bluffing, a thing she did well. "We have forensic evidence to prove as much. We don't need the testimony of the caretaker or his men. Now I asked myself, what interest would you have in Victor Surette's body, and naturally—"

"All right, Victor was my son, goddamn you—Victor Raveneaux, and as soon as we learned of his horrible death, we . . . we brought him home. Is there any crime in that?"

"Well, there could be, sir, yes," Jessica said.

"You've got no evidence any crime has been committed by this man," countered Lew Meade, standing as stiff and erect as his paunch would allow, carrying out his own bluff. Had he arranged for Jessica's earlier findings to somehow be lost or skewed? she wondered.

"Dr. Coran's findings tell us differently," Alex countered.

"That's right," Landry agreed.

"It's clear that the grave-robbing took place only in recent days," Jessica added, "and that you let Victor's body stay in that paupers' cemetery all these months, Senator, until there was the threat of an exhumation."

"That's a lie." The general's voice was firm, steady, the voice of a man always in control.

His wife whispered some disturbing words to him, making the general turn and scowl at her, ordering her indoors.

"You know how microscopes have a way of pointing to

the truth, General," Jessica continued. "Microscopes don't lie about fresh striations against stone, sutures and that sort of thing, so I'd say you aren't being entirely forthcoming with us."

"We only learned recently that Victor Surette—the deceased going by that name—was our son," the senator replied. "We moved the body on learning this. It's been quite enough strain on Mother . . . on us all, and in the meantime, you people've done nothing whatever to apprehend this fiend who viciously killed Victor and has wantonly destroyed others for . . . for their hearts."

"We're going to look around, General Raveneaux—just to be thorough, you understand," Landry said, playing the diplomat.

"The very idea that you men have come on such a preposterous mission, Captain Landry, jeopardizes your jobs. I hope you know that," replied Stephens firmly, his eyes like dark, seething coals, the threat taking on a venomously slithering nature.

"Is that a threat, Richard?" asked Landry. "Or would you place that kind of talk under job harassment or maybe even blackmail, sir?"

Kim Desinor could see that Captain Landry was now too angry to suppress his emotions; not this time, she thought.

"It may interest you to know that we know you blackmailed Frank Wardlaw into this game, and you paid off Ben de Yampert," he went on.

Meade erupted now. "Goddamn it, man, it was the general here who called in the FBI and financed Dr. Desinor's coming here! He wants New Orleans safe for everyone, you fool! And now you turn the investigation against him and his family?"

"This is absolute madness, Landry, and tomorrow morning you can damned well clean out your office." Stephens's teeth were gnashing. "That goes for you too, Sincebaugh."

"You can pick your friends, General," Alex called out, his bandaged arms white against the night, "but you're stuck with your kin and their sins, right? Victor, your son, is somehow at the heart of all these nasty deaths."

"Do you know of a man or a woman named Michael Emanuel Dominique?" Kim asked the general.

"You're not obligated to answer any of these questions, General Raveneaux," cautioned a gray-haired, three-piece suit, likely a lawyer.

"Be that as it may, we have a court order here saying we can search the premises and all outbuildings and mobile units." Landry informed the man, depositing the papers in his hands as he ascended the porch stairs.

Alex added, "And we're here to exercise that right tonight, before things go cold on us and people wash out their unmentionables."

Raveneaux looked to his powerful friends for support. Meade took the court order from the lawyer, scanned it as the lawyer had and said, "Ridiculous . . . Judge Flint . . . that natty-haired neegra booze-hound's got some nerve. He won't be able to sit on a park bench after this."

"Let me have that," added Stephens, tearing it from Meade, ripping it to shreds and throwing it at Landry's feet like a gauntlet. "That's what I think of a warrant from Judge Homer Flint."

Landry stared in disbelief at Stephens. "What the hell're you men covering up here?"

"Stand down, Carl."

"No, Richard, I won't."

"You men," shouted Stephens to the uniformed cops who'd come in behind the detectives. "Arrest Captain Landry and Detective Sincebaugh. They're trespassing here."

Landry and Sincebaugh snatched out their weapons almost in unison, backing to each side, Alex tugging at Kim to stay close to him, Jessica siding with them, her own .38 raised and poised. The uniformed deputies, confounded, not knowing what to do, looked to their sheriff, a man named Hodges, for a sign.

Hodges calmly presented Meade and Stephens with the federal warrant given him by Jessica then he just as calmly stepped off the porch and told his men, "Boys, we're here to uphold the law as I see it, and these fellas might be pricks and assholes with nothing worth a lick of sulfur to base their allegations on, but . . . they got a federal warrant, so they got a right to serve that warrant. We back 'em."

Alex felt a sense of relief fill his chest, and Landry put his weapon away in a show of good faith, saying, "Thanks, Sheriff Hodges." Jessica Coran was the last to holster her weapon.

Hodges looked up at the general and apologetically appealed to the others with a shrug. "Let's just get this damned search over, boys, so's these folks can go back to the peaceful business of their lives. Whataya say, Commissioner, Chief Meade?"

"I'm giving the orders here," countered Meade. "This is an official FBI matter now, so you men will do as I say!" Meade's eyes were surveying the situation, and as he spoke, he reached for his weapon.

Kim shouted, "Don't do it, Meade! You'll be dead before you hit the stairs." She had a gun trained on him.

"This is rank insubordination, Agent Desinor. I'll have you up on charges."

Alex stared at her, his mouth open wide, finally repeating the word, "Agent?"

"FBI," she admitted, her mind's eye filling with an image of a raging Paul Zanek storming about his office, wanting to know why she'd drawn her weapon against the New Orleans bureau chief. "Are we going to get on with this search, General Ravencaux? Or will you be responsible for bloodshed on your lawn?"

"Davis, Scully," Captain Landry said to the two uniforms he'd gotten to know a bit. "Take Chief Meade's weapon and any that Commissioner Stephens is packing."

The officers hesitated, staring at one another for the courage to take the first step.

"Just do it!" shouted Hodges, startling his men into action to defuse the explosive standoff.

Now Jessica had joined Kim, the two of them holding guns on three of the most prominent citizens in New Orleans. "I sure hope we know what the hell we're doing, Kim," Jessica whispered.

"All right, do your blasted search," the general announced. "Search all you want, but you won't find a thing, not a damned thing other than our son's body out there in the tomb where it belongs, and there's no law against that."

"There are laws against body-snatching even today, sir," Jessica said, "and when you failed to come forward to announce the true identity of a murder victim, you were with-holding vital information in a murder investigation. And that doesn't sit well with the courts, because you inadvertently contributed to the deaths of other victims of the Hearts killer, sir, and most judges don't take kindly to that sort of behavior, no matter who you are.''

"Get on with it," snarled Stephens.

"We . . . we'll cooperate in any way we can," squeaked Mrs. Raveneaux, who'd silently floated back out onto the porch, hoping to fend off trouble, though no one knew how. "Won't we, Maurice?"

"Yes, I suppose we haven't a choice . . . not at gunpoint at any rate. Barney," he spoke directly to his lawyer, "are you getting all this? We're going to have grounds for a hell of a suit against these hooligans."

"We quite understand your concerns, gentlemen. Please, do what you have come for," the frail Mrs. Raveneaux cooed forth in the best tinkling tones of Southern hospitality, as if they'd come for tea or mint juleps.

Jessica sensed a childishness in the woman, perhaps a feeblemindedness, the sort that comes with having to bury one's only son. There was a warm exchange of looks between the old general and his wife. Jessica unaccountably made her own exchange of glances with Kim, Kim somehow telling her that she'd just had the same emotional response to Mrs. Raveneaux.

"Then be done with it!" the general shouted. "And then you people, you included, Meade—Stephens, take your entire fucking circus and get the hell off my place!"

"Why, Maurice, is that any way to speak to visitors!" Mrs. Raveneaux said, bringing him up soundly.

"Get inside, Coretta. Get to your sitting room, dear. Go now, dear . . . go."

She timidly did as told, leaving them all to stare after her.

"Alzheimer's . . . can be so awful," the general said "yet I must admit her lack of understanding has saved her from any disgrace in this sordid matter."

Jessica wondered which matter he referred to, the search, the body-snatching, or the fact their son was gay and had lived under an assumed name. In a window overhead, Jessica thought she saw a sash move against the pane.

"I think there's someone inside the house," she muttered under her breath to Kim.

"Could be servants; they've got to have a houseful to maintain a place of this size."

"In that case, maybe we should've come with a larger army."

"You kidding? All we need is one good psychic to point the way."

Jessica, Landry, Alex and Kim went inside the enormous mansion, finding it lit with expensive Waterford crystal chandeliers in almost every room on the main floor. It was three stories high with sixty-four rooms, large enough for any suspect to hide in for days, if he or she so wished.

"I want you to ring for all your servants, General," Alex said. "We have a few questions for anyone in your employ."

"This is preposterous."

"Just do it now!"

The general nodded to a frail, thin man now standing beside him, the butler. "Right away, sir," the butler said.

"Tell me, General, did your son, Victor, spend much time in the servants' quarters?" Kim asked. "Did he play as a child with any of the servants' children?"

A slight hesitation preceded the general's response, "No . . . it was not permitted."

"Well, then, did he have any brothers or sisters to play with?"

"You will not be questioning my entire household or family about these horrid matters," he insisted.

"We can do this here, sir, or at the precinct in downtown New Orleans," Landry stated.

"Then Victor did have a sister, didn't he? Is she the girl in this photograph?" Kim asked, handing the framed photo to Raveneaux. When Landry had pulled his car inside the gates of Raveneaux, Kim had had a dreamlike vision of children playing on the lawn here at the plantation, and there were more than several children in the vision. It was a peaceful spectral image, until one of the children began badly bleeding from a cut. It had occurred so quickly, even in the vision, that there was no telling where the cut had come from, but it had to do with one of the children.

"Where did you get this picture?" Raveneaux demanded.

The general's wife had reappeared, and she went to the photograph as if drawn by a powerful magnet.

"Why, it's little Victor and Dommie," she said.

"Then Victor did have a sister. Dominique?" Kim pressed.

Jessica exchanged a knowing look with Kim, and an anxious Alex Sincebaugh was perched and ready to bound up the stairs, to tear open doors to locate Dominique, his heart still harboring a fiery desire to avenge Ben.

"And is Dominique here now?" Jessica asked.

The general shushed his wife and answered, saying, "No, no, she's not at present, and even if she were . . . you see, we've shielded her all her life from any harshness. Even if she were here, gentlemen, she would be of no help to your search."

"Shielded her?" asked Kim.

"That's right. She doesn't even know about her brother's death. Of . . . of course she knows of his absence, but we've . . . I've told her nothing of the nature of . . . just how Victor died. You see, she's a delicate creature, actually, quite easily disturbed."

"Are you telling us that your daughter is retarded?" asked Landry.

Alex stepped before Raveneaux. "Oh, no, General! No way's she getting off. She knows more than all of us put together. No way is she going to cop a . . ."

Kim pushed between Alex and the general. "What precisely do you mean, sir? With regard to your daughter?"

"I beg of you, she's . . . she would be of no help whatever to your investigation, please." The general took Captain Landry aside, whispering, "The girl has never been quite . . . well . . . quite right."

Landry's piercing look needed no words.

"She's been in and out of hospitals, has been seen by the best men in medicine. I wish you would not upset her with questions about her brother's death. We've not told her that Victor is dead. It . . . it could crush her. She loved . . . continues to love him so. We're . . . I, rather, I have been waiting for just the right time, but so far . . . things being so delicate with her condition . . ."

"What is your daughter's age, sir?" asked Jessica, while Meade menacingly eyed her and Stephens swelled with zealous gasps.

Alex pressed in. "Do you have a current photo of her nearby?"

"She's twenty-four, and of course we do," replied the general's wife, going for the white baby grand piano on top of which perched a bevy of photos of Victor, the general and his wife, along with several of Dominique herself. Returning with one of the photos, she remarked, "Isn't she a lovely child?"

The girl in the photo had close-cropped hair, her appearance quite close to her brother's, save for the piercing, faraway, yet stern and angry serpent's look in her eyes.

"Where is Dominique now?" Jessica pressed.

"She's traveling," the general said with a restraining hand on his wife's forearm, his body language giving his lie away to the trained detectives. "I couldn't quite say precisely where she is at the moment, since she's doing the Continent . . . in the company of a guardian, of course."

"Europe, you mean?" asked Landry.

"Then you won't mind if we take a look at your daughter's room?" Jessica asked.

"I see absolutely no reason why you should be the least inter—"

"Oh, but we're very interested, General," corrected Alex.

"Why, it's a lovely room, Maurice. Let them see how we've decorated Dommie's room. Come . . ." Mrs. Raveneaux obviously enjoyed playing the hostess.

By now the servants had assembled, some six on duty tonight, along with the butler, so Landry said, "I'll talk to these folks, Alex, while you look around." Landry also asked the deputies to fan out.

"And look for what?" asked Hodges.

"Anything out of the ordinary, anything unusual."

Alex, Jessica and Kim followed behind Mrs. Raveneaux, taking the spiraling staircase for the next floor, the old woman twittering on like a social bird now, talking about Dommie's coming-out party, little Vic's first communion, the time when . . .

As they approached Dommie's room, the old woman pointed it out as the last at the end of a long corridor, but just before they got to it, Alex and the two FBI agents heard a strange whine. It sounded like a poorly oiled machine of some sort, like grinding gears or Jacob Marley's ethereal but clamoring chains.

"—I try to tell the children they mustn't play rough, that their little heads crack easily . . . but children are full of the devil and they will be—"

Alex jumped in and cut her off. "Pardon, Mrs. Raveneaux, but what is that noise?"

"Noise? Noise?"

"That mechanical grating sound."

"*Irrrrrk, irrrrrrk, irrrrrrk,*" it sounded again.

"That noise," Kim said.

The old woman was truly befuddled or deaf. "I don't hear any noise."

"Seems to be coming from behind Dom's door." Alex imagined the bestial blond woman slicing up hearts in super-thin sheaths behind the pearly white door, using a butcher's electric cleaver.

Kim felt her own fear rising. "Why don't you step over here with me, Mrs. Raveneaux," Kim suggested, seeing that Jessica and Alex were about to burst through the door.

"It's the dumbwaiter," Mrs. Raveneaux announced, as though on a TV game show. "Of course, it is."

After a perfunctory knock, Alex barged through the door, followed immediately by Jessica, their guns drawn. Inside, they found a child's room, filled with frilly lace, white all around, with marching blue-and-red-suited soldiers on the wall, dressed in British colonial uniforms, beating out a cadence in the pattern with big, wide drums, each displaying a cross-like pattern about the chest where each wide white cross-belt met. Kim had seen the marching crossbelts in her visions.

The marching wood. The drummer boys were not real in appearance, but rather intentionally drawn by the artist as so many Pinocchio lookalikes.

"Marching crosses, marching woods afire," said Jessica, recalling Kim's prediction.

"I don't see any fire," replied Alex.

"You'd have to be Dominique to see the fire," answered Kim from the doorway, her arms protectively enfolding Mrs. Raveneaux.

The drone of the dumbwaiter continued, alerting them to the adjoining room, where Alex easily located a small elevator meant to bring trays to and from the room, obviously connected to the kitchen below. The dumbwaiter was large enough for a person of Dominique's size to squeeze into.

"Yeah, right, traveling the Continent," muttered Jessica.

"She's in the kitchen!" cried Alex.

"Oh, Dommie loves the kitchen. She loves to cook," replied Mrs. Raveneaux, her hands and arms waving. "Cooks for Daddy and me all the time; makes her own recipes, and she's got the best red bisque you'll ever want to taste, my dear." She was speaking almost exclusively to Kim now, feeling uneasy with Jessica, who began wildly digging about the closets for anything incriminating, such as a heart in a jar atop a closet shelf, the weapon Dominique used in her attacks, anything. But nothing was forthcoming, not here.

"What's the quickest way to the kitchen, Mrs. Raveneaux?" Alex pleaded.

"Little Dommie used to take that dumbwaiter up and down when she was a child. Still is a child in my eyes . . . always will be . . ."

"Stay here with her, Kim, Jessica," ordered Alex. "I'm going to check out the kitchen."

"Not on your life," replied Jessica over her shoulder. "I'm in this to the finish."

"Then find me some damned useful physical evidence here! Keep looking!"

Kim was speaking to Mrs. Raveneaux at the same time, asking, "Then Dommie uses the kitchen often?"

"Why, yes . . . yes . . ."

"But how does that make your cook feel? Isn't she underfoot, a nuisance?"

"Oh, we fired the cook some time ago, after Dommie returned home from her . . . her travels.''

"Really?''

"Dommie just insists on preparing our meals. We tried to tell her how unseemly it was, but she'd taken courses, you know, with the best European chefs, and she simply insisted until Daddy just had to give in!''

Jessica went tearing through shoe boxes and hat boxes found in the closet, and when she turned to face Kim and Mrs. Raveneaux, she frowned her annoyance and called after Alex to wait up for her, but he was gone down a back stairwell, descending quickly for the kitchen, where he hoped to find Ben's killer waiting for him.

"Jess, slow down,'' pleaded Kim when Jessica rushed for the hallway. "Landry and the others are downstairs. Let Alex handle it from here.''

"He may need backup.''

"Back stairs'll take you down if you want to find Dommie,'' said Mrs. Raveneaux. "Come along . . . I'll show you the way.''

Captain Carl Landry's questioning of the servants in the presence of General Raveneaux, P.C. Stephens and Lew Meade had also revealed the fact that Victor's sister, Dommie, had in effect become the chief cook in the house. Like Alex, Carl had put two and two together and gone to search the kitchen. He'd actually gotten to the kitchen a few minutes ahead of Alex, and had snatched open the walk-in freezer door, fully expecting to be greeted with what he now looked at—full slabs of meat, sides of beef and venison dangling from a series of hooks—when from somewhere behind him he heard or felt someone there. Half turning, he saw the glint of a huge carving knife as it dove into his upper left quadrant to the hilt, barely missing his heart, hitting the bone at the shoulder. Like a man watching a film from some distance away, he saw himself fall backward from the impact, the freezer door slamming and locking on cue in front of him.

Inside the chilled room, he staggered about, unsure of the wound's depth or the extent of blood loss. Since it was so cold in here and his body temperature was rapidly decreasing, the blood was quickly coagulating. In fact, the freezer temperature might save his life, up to a point.

He fought to regain his feet and his vision. Then he fought with the door, but there was no escape from this side. He began to scrape away at the frost covering the small window, and through the trails left by his broken fingernails he saw *her*, recognizing her from her picture and Alex's description. She was lying in wait, a cornered animal with a maniacal leer and a huge carving knife still painted with Landry's blood held against her ear. She seemed to be slobbering on the knife, talking to it, listening to its whisper. She was anxious for her next victim to step into her high-tech lair.

The kitchen had every modern convenience and was as large as many of the other rooms. She'd been hiding in one of the cupboards below the six-foot preparation table at the center of the room when Landry had poked his nose into the freezer.

Now she moved toward the front of the kitchen, having heard someone approaching from that direction. Landry had to do something and fast.

He tore out his gun, but his hands were already freezing and the heavy object slipped easily from his grasp. He went to his knees with much pain and trembling. Others were counting on him and this thought made him grasp the gun and hold firmly to it, despite the cramping in his hand and body. With his left hand, he pulled himself back up, using a shelf for counterweight, but suddenly the shelf gave way and objects began raining down on him, frozen food as heavy as bricks.

He opened his eyes where he lay propped against the wall now, and he saw several bulging, red eyes poking through the cakes of ice lying at his feet. From their fist-sized shape and hue, Landry knew he was looking at the evidence which would put Dominique Raveneaux into the gas chamber or an insanity ward for the rest of her life.

The hearts of her victims continued to wink up at him through the ice that covered them.

He snatched up his weapon again and from his prone position, began firing at the glass in the door.

34

All lovers live by longing, and endure:
Summon a vision and declare it pure.

—Theodore Roethke

Alex crashed through the door on hearing shots fired from a direction he could not determine. He went directly for the stone tile floor, skidding across it and coming up on his knees, his own weapon extended and ready, when, from behind a metallic cupboard door, she suddenly appeared. He saw her too late.

Her knife embedded in him, caught up in the metallic web of the bullet proof Kevlar vest which Landry had insisted they all wear under their jackets emblazoned with the word POLICE. The vest allowed for little penetration. Still, the impact and shock from the sheer force his attacker put into it jolted Alex over and onto his back.

At the same instant, madly determined to finish what she'd started, she'd snatched the knife back, and it came flashing down at Alex again.

Alex's gun had fallen, and he was dazed when the knife entered his body a second time in his upper left quadrant, just shy of his heart, but the Kevlar vest again proved its worth.

Alex grabbed onto the knife hand and felt the enormity of Dominique's power as Emanuel. She was reaching for some other weapon even as she fought him, tearing at something above Alex on the oven. Her hands extended like the claws of a bird of prey, she only half-grasped the boiling pot above her, and it came crashing down around them, burning Alex's unprotected arm and sending spikes of hot liquid toward his eyes, but he instinctually arched away, the fiery brew bringing welts to his neck and chin instead.

Stewed tomatoes and mixed vegetables in a thick gumbo sauce had made the tiles beneath the killer slick, so now she was having trouble keeping a firm footing and a hold on him, but once again she was reaching upward for some hidden weapon atop the chopping block. The stench of the stew, which Mother Raveneaux had called bisque, filled Alex's nostrils, and he wondered if he'd die here with the unhealthy odor in his brain.

Now, suddenly, she had a huge meat cleaver in her left hand. Even as she held firm to the knife they continued to fight for control over, Dominique—having some demonic strength he had never known before—brought the shimmering cleaver blade at his face like a pendulum, missing him by inches when he jerked to one side.

Alex could hear help on the way, Stephens and Meade, having heard the shots and the commotion, but the witch atop him wasn't waiting. Again the cleaver was over her head and about to descend when a single gunshot rang out and Dominique came crashing down over Alex's body, her dead weight slamming into him with a great thud.

From over the dead killer's shoulder, Alex saw Jessica Coran, her gun still raised, and beside her stood Kim and Mrs. Raveneaux, who was caught up in Kim's arms when she fell away in a faint.

Alex fought to extricate himself from the killer's dead weight while the others ran into the kitchen. Alex shouted for Stephens and Meade to help Landry who'd shouted from the freezer while he went to Jessica Coran, meeting her gaze. "Thanks . . . you saved my life just then."

"Is she dead?"

"The way you shoot, you needn't ask."

Jessica now sat on the stairs with Kim beside her, Kim holding onto the old woman. Kim squeezed Jessica's hand and said, "You did what you had to do."

"It's not as if I've never killed anyone before."

"But it is the first time you've shot and killed a woman." Kim managed to place her free arm around Jessica.

"All in the line of duty," Jessica mused, "for the FBI . . ."

"No, you did it for Alex."

General Raveneaux, who had rushed in behind Stephens and Meade, went to his knees over his maniacal daughter, softly blubbering, his anguish deep-felt and eternal.

"First my son . . . and now Dommie . . . oh, poor long-suffering, afflicted, imperfect child . . . Dommie . . ."

Mrs. Raveneaux had come to, and was now staring at the pitiful sight of her dead daughter and distraught husband. From her half-prone position on the stairwell, she spoke to her husband in a harsh whisper, saying, "I told you, Maurice . . . I told you it would come to this . . . told you we should've never let her come back from Europe, Maurice. I told you she wasn't ready . . . I told you so. . . . "

"But she was . . . acting so . . . normal . . ."

"How . . . how long've you known, really known, about my connection with the FBI?" Kim asked Alex.

"I didn't know for sure until tonight, when Meade gave you away, but I'd wondered about it last time I saw you and Dr. Coran together. Something about your relationship. The way the two of you worked together; maybe 'cause you were working too hard to appear to dislike one another. I don't know."

"She was cured, you know," Mrs. Raveneaux said, "by her doctors in Stockholm. She even lived in Europe with one of her doctors, a man she claimed to love, and they were happy for a time . . . just before she showed up on our doorstep again."

"When was that, Mrs. Raveneaux?" asked Alex.

"Ohh . . . ohhh . . . maybe a little over a year ago And you know Victor had been gone by then, and we . . . the general and I didn't have anyone else, you know, not really . . . not family, that is . . . and we did love her so. We loved both our children very, very much, but neither of them were ever completely . . . all right, you realize? Victor always seemed the feminine one and dear Dominique was so dastardly toward him, so mannish. We tried to break her of it, especially after the . . . the incident . . ."

"When Dominique hurt Victor that first time, you mean?"

"Sweet Victor, such a sweet-hearted boy, really . . . did the authorities ever find him? Completely disappeared. Isn't that right, Maurice?"

The general let go of his dead daughter, laying her gently down amid the spoiled bisque she'd earlier prepared, reaching up now for his infirm wife instead. The two older people held fast to one another.

"She was doing so well," he muttered into her ear before he continued sobbing.

Jessica surveyed the complete mess that had been made of the once-spotless kitchen. Landry was being helped from the freezer, but the frozen-handed cop wouldn't let go of something he had carried out with him. Jessica and Alex joined the captain and together they stared down at a solidly frozen human heart.

"Thommie Whiley?" asked Kim from across the room, voicing all their thoughts.

A shivering Landry replied, "C-c-could be, but there're're two o-o-others inside." His teeth still chattered on after his words were finished.

Jessica stared at the frozen heart, and then past it into the freezer. "Forensics'll have to match each one through DNA tests."

"What the hell was she doing with the hearts? Why keep 'em in the freezer?" Stephens's astounded question came out in tentative fashion.

"Keepin' 'em on ice, obviously," Jessica said, Meade staring now over her shoulder into the fog of the freezer.

"But for what?" Meade asked.

"Her secret ingredient in the gumbo bisque stew, would be my guess," replied Jessica, who now turned and lifted a pointed stiletto kitchen knife, then bent and jabbed one of the chunks of meat from the stew which had discolored the tiles when Dominique had pulled the boiling liquid over onto herself and Alex during their struggle.

"What is that?" asked Stephens, squinting.

Meade turned his attention to the red chunk of flesh as well.

Jessica simply replied, "It's nothing I've ever eaten."

The general's eyes had widened on seeing the frozen heart come from his freezer, and now his eyes widened further. He softly pushed away from his wife, telling her to go upstairs now. "You don't want to hear any more of this, Coretta . . . Coretta dear, just go on ahead."

She did as instructed, the docile puppy once again, glancing back only once at her dead child on the kitchen floor. When she was out of earshot, the general said, "She couldn't've been using the hearts of dead men in her cooking. She just couldn't've been."

"Well, our lab people will determine that soon enough, Maurice," said Richard Stephens, who placed a shaky and awkward hand on the old man's shoulders.

"Determine what, that my insane child killed her brother, cut out his heart and fed it to me! God damn you all for imagining such a thing! No, she loved us, Coretta and me . . . she loved us, despite any sickness she endured over the years, and she loved her brother with a pure love like nothing I have witnessed in all my years."

The general's lawyer tried to pull him away, but the old man snatched free and shouted, "She had a bad heart as a child, a deficiency, but she was never evil toward anyone except, at times, her brother. Yes, I admit she was at one time extremely envious of her brother, but with therapy she had worked through all that and had in fact learned to love Victor and us very, very much. She spoke of him fondly always, and she treated Mother and me with great respect and admiration, always . . . always. She loved us. She wouldn't've harmed Victor. I knew that from the beginning, and that was how I knew she couldn't've done the terrible things attributed to the Queen of Hearts killer. You'll never . . . ever convince me otherwise."

"Alex was right all along. She killed her brother for a reason," Jessica shouted. "Don't you see? All of you men who've been in one way or another shielding the truth? She took that first heart for a reason, General!"

Stephens tried to motion her into silence; Meade shushed her, so Kim continued on Jessica's behalf. "A reason, General, you know full well. She wanted to *be* Victor; she wanted to possess his heart—the heart you and her mother most loved. She wanted to be the kind of son you never had, so she became a man for you and Mrs. Raveneaux, and in her deranged state, that meant she had to be 'of good heart,' and how better to be of good heart than to consume the one heart you and your wife doted most over."

"That's enough of your psychoanalysis, Doctor," Meade said to Kim, the order to stand down clearly unmasked now.

"You men brought Dr. Desinor here for the truth," Jessica countered, defending her friend. "It's time these people in their ivory-tower mansion, so far removed from the deaths in New Orleans, yet so close to them, hear the truth for once."

"The truth won't accomplish anything here, not now," shouted Stephens.

"Neither of you ever for a moment thought this case had anything to do with New Orleans gentility, did you, Meade?" asked Alex, his wrath growing steadily.

Jessica continued, saying, "No, to you men it was about gays living in a gay ghetto in New Orleans, and you all wanted it confined there. You never expected Surette's death, the subsequent cover-up to keep the family name untarnished and the payoffs ever to surface again, did you?"

Kim added, "You ruined Frank Wardlaw's career, you dirtied Ben deYampert, and then when calling in Coran and me backfired on you, and it looked as if not only would the general be exposed, but your little parts in the sordid game also might surface, you forced Wardlaw into body-snatching."

"You don't have any basis in fact to back that claim up in the least," Meade declared.

"The general and his wife were just glad to get the body back—or at least the general was—but it was minus one heart," added Jessica. "Little did the general know that the heart had come home a lot sooner, and had most likely been consumed by three remaining Raveneauxs with wine in bisque gumbo. And since then, there've no doubt been many unusual dishes served up by your Dominique."

"Get out of my house!" shouted the general. "I want you all out of my house!" He was on the verge of tears and collapse.

"I'm afraid we can't do that, at least not until there's a complete evidence-gathering taken here, General. That will mean some time," Alex explained.

Stephens exchanged stares with Alex and nodded to his political friend, resigned to what Alex Sincebaugh had said.

"I'm going to have your heads for this, Meade, Stephens!" The old man stormed from the room, likely in search of his wife and some respite from the horror of the moment.

Landry suddenly collapsed from his wound. Alex and Jessica rushed to him, Alex shouting for someone to get to one of the units outside and call for medical assistance, while Jessica did what she could to staunch his wound.

Landry's color had bleached from his face, crystallized shards still hanging in his hair. His wound was now openly bleeding. Jessica worked to stop the bleeding, tying off the shoulder. As she did so, Landry, seeing the bloodstains and the fiery welts about Sincebaugh, asked, "You okay, Sincy?"

"No serious damage."

"Two real tough guys, huh?" Jessica muttered at them.

Landry managed to say to Alex, "Why don't you get on the radio; see what you can do about getting Dr. Coran all the help and equipment she'll require here."

"You got it, Captain." With that Alex went for Landry's car and the radio, pushing past Hodges and his men, who'd been staring in on the scene, their mouths hanging open.

"You up for this, Jessica? This could be an all-nighter," said Kim, who came close to her friend.

"Actually, no . . . I'd just about made up my mind to get on a plane for Hawaii, chuck it all."

"I can well understand how you feel after seeing what went on at that warehouse and now this. You've gone through hell."

"As have we all. What about you? You gonna be okay?"

Kim managed a wane smile and a nod. "Yeah, matter of fact. Think I found out what I'm made of, in great part thanks to you. But I tell you honestly, I'm not so sure I don't prefer the safety of a laboratory to all this." She indicated the body of Dominique Emanuel Raveneaux and the scattered remains of life that were pieces of people about the floor.

"You have any doubt whatsoever that we have the Queen of Hearts killer here, Dr. Coran?" asked Landry in a near-whisper.

"No . . . no doubt, sir."

"Dr. Desinor?" asked Landry.

"None whatever, and I sense something else."

"Oh? What's that?"

"This is the only peace Dominique has ever had in her unhappy life."

"Maybe that'll put your General Raveneaux at peace with himself, Commissioner, Chief Meade," said Jessica. "Maybe death holds more meaning for his daughter than life ever did."

EPILOGUE

Unto the pure all things are pure.

—The Epistle of Paul to Titus, 1:15

A sordid picture of old family money and madness began to come together once the Raveneaux family was examined more closely.

Dominique had attempted to murder her brother at the age of seven. She'd been secreted away to doctors for several years and on return, she'd again showed tendencies of hatred toward her little brother. When the barrier between anger and murder burst again, the general had had her locked up in a pretty cell he'd created for her in the basement while he searched the world for doctors who might possibly *fix* her.

At times she'd spent long months and even years of her childhood in such places as New York's prestigious Psychiatric Center for the Mentally Disturbed, Menninger's Clinic in Stockholm and a special hospital in Brussels.

She was declared mentally competent and had the papers to prove it, so when she returned home under her own steam in July of the previous year, no one had ever connected her with the strange mutilation death of a young man she'd lived with for a time in Brussels. The man's heart had been carved from his chest. He'd been an intern at the hospital in Brussels, and had been instrumental in Dominique's recovery. Interpol had been interested in locating the former patient, but had lost contact with her. She'd been placed in the institution under a false name, and records were intentionally sketchy.

Dominique had learned of her brother's whereabouts from her father, the general, who had told her that her brother's once-pure and innocent heart had become—in her absence—demoralized, depraved and tainted. He'd explained her brother's absence away in this manner, by blaming it on his life-style.

She'd been a model daughter at the time, at least by day, discharging all the kitchen staff and insisting on providing her parents with only the healthiest and freshest of meals, a talent she had learned while in Europe. She'd talked of starting her own catering business, saying that if she couldn't cook for someone, she'd become so bored to distraction that she'd be quite depressed. The general and his wife had acquiesced, allowing their daughter to indulge herself, despite the unseemly appearance of having her running the kitchen and preparing food.

By night, she would become a Hyde creature, anxious and bloodthirsty in her relentless search for her brother. She began frequenting the bars and clubs in and around Bourbon Street until she found Victor. When she and Victor clashed, it was for control of that innocent, so-well-loved heart now gone from her parents' life, the same heart she detested, her brother's heart. Victor never saw it coming, didn't know what hit him. And as for Dominique, who'd become Emanuel when she went on her quest, that single heart did not fulfill her needs entirely, and so, when that first taste of murder and heart-taking wore thin, she went after the hearts of others, repeating the process in an endless need to feed on the very thing she could not have, a pure heart.

Among the many skills she'd learned during her long years of "captivity" were sewing, darning and embroidery, and she never forgot the pure-white doilies her mother made and spread about her basement cell room—and her upstairs room, where she was allowed only if she were good.

The general's little princess, Dommie also formed a passion for the image of queens, thinking herself quite the little princess all her life, believing that she would one day grow into the role of a queen. She'd learned lace embroidery with colored silk string first from her mother, and had improved her talents with the help of a kindly nurse in Stockholm, and she never forgot her lessons.

A more thorough search of Dommie's current living quarters at Raveneaux—which turned out to have originally been Victor's room, not the child's room Jessica and the others were escorted to—unearthed all the materials Emanuel had used in creating her calling cards.

As authorities and an army of lawyers took over the case, to put to rest the Queen of Hearts killer and all the destruction left in her wake, each day more details of the bizarre story exploded onto the pages of the *Times-Picayune*. Every awful thought anyone had ever had about inbreeding and family secrets in the Deep South was brought to life in the Raveneaux story, and each day became a painful reminder of how madness and insanity and dysfunctional elements visited all families at one time or another, in one generation or another.

And finally, Victor Surette might at last stop walking across Alex Sincebaugh's dreamscape.

Kim Desinor revisited the remnants of her past and found that St. Domitilla's was a sad, much smaller place now, a shell of its former self. And she cried long and hard, but she forgave as well, and in the forgiving, she found release, freedom, sanctuary and peace; while Meade, Stephens and Wardlaw faced charges of misconduct.

Jessica looked out over the runway at the New Orleans Lakefront Airport, and in the dusk she saw Kim and Alex Sincebaugh's embracing bodies silhouetted against the terminal glass where they were saying their final good-byes. Kim would be last to board the plane returning Jessica and her to their Virginia headquarters and home. In the terminal, Jessica had said her good-byes with a firm handshake and a smile for Carl Landry and Alex, but Kim was having a heart-wrenching time. She and Alex continued to exchange long, sensual kisses, their pending separation painful and prolonged, a heady reminder to Jessica of the bond she and James Parry had shared in Hawaii the year before.

She had contacted James from Kim's hotel room to inform him of her success in routing the awful soul of Mad Matthew Matisak to the grave and to the bottom rung in the seven circles of Hades. James had been sick with worry, and had been trying desperately to get in touch with her when he'd learned that she was in New Orleans and possibly facing Matisak there. He'd gotten word through the FBI grapevine, and had been poised to get on a plane to locate her there, to do whatever was in his power to help and to protect her.

He'd next spoken of pending cases on Oahu and a visit from

his sister, and had wanted to know if Jessica was coming in November when the whales returned to spawn, so that they might together return to Maui.

Jessica had said yes over and over to his invitation, spending two hours long-distance with him on the phone. They'd talked of diving the Maui reefs and the underwater volcano, of revisiting old haunts, and Jim had made it sound as if her returning to Hawaii was the most important thing in his life, something to look forward to. And listening to his melodic and resonant voice had made her realize just how fortunate she was, because now life once more seemed full and rich and pure, and it was so because his love for her was pure.